INTERNATIONAL ACCLAIM FOR
THE CAMP OF THE SAINTS
THE CONTROVERSIAL NOVEL ABOUT
THE END OF WESTERN CIVILIZATION

"Its scale is apocalyptic and its implications awesome ... a global Golgotha ... This is a story to read, mark, learn and inwardly digest, especially by those under 40."
—John Barkham Reviews

"It is possible that the new, sensational novel *The Camp of the Saints* projects the most savage view of the human race since the 4th voyage of Lemuel Gulliver.... M. Raspail's satire is harsh... He views everyone through a fisheye lens, scathing all classes and a variety of cant... has moments of appalling power and occasionally a terrible beauty... It confronts the white West with dreads from its deep unconscious. It leaves a reader to ponder a haunting, 'What if?' "
—Edmund Fuller, *Wall Street Journal*

"Shocking and controversial... A macabre thriller... no reader will remain unaffected by the questions it raises about the future of the world."
—Linell Smith, *Baltimore Sun*

"Audacious and imaginative fiction... it suggests, if comparisons are made, Camus' *The Plague*.
—William Hogan, *San Francisco Chronicle*

"Reading it is a memorable experience... Raspail's macabre vision of the world 20 years away is not science fiction. His society is the end product of current conflicts carried to their extremes."
—Carol J. Felsenthal, *Chicago Sun-Times Showcase*

"[The novel] shrewdly exploits a dilemma that the world may well face: the moment when the burgeoning Third World rises from misery and forces the West to share more of its resources."
—*Time*

"*The Camp of the Saints* is...the work of a writer whose power is unquestionable. It will attract thoughtful readers.... It am still haunted by the drama and suspense and horror of that armada!"
—Germaine Bree

"A haunting book of irresistible force and calm logic.... The suspense is total.... A thriller to make Hollywood pale by comparison."
—Jean Anouilh

ABOUT THE COVER PHOTO

Jean Raspail's novel portrays a flotilla of natives from the Indian subcontinent washing ashore. Some years ago an event which provoked images of his story took place in real life.

On Sunday, June 6, 1993 at 2 a.m. the freighter *Golden Venture* ran aground off Rockaway peninsula beach in New York City. The ship held a cargo of over 300 illegal aliens from the Chinese province of Fiujian. Most were young men; about 20 were women.

The ship had been at sea for three months, sailing by way of the Cape of Good Hope, when it finally hit a sandbar some 200 yards off the seaside park.

At the time of the incident, the *Golden Venture* was the 24th ship carrying Chinese illegals known to have reached the United States over a two year period. Federal authorities admitted that they may intercept only five percent of the Chinese illegals smuggled into the United States by ship every year.

The passengers mortgage their futures by promising to pay $20,000 to $35,000 apiece to the professional smugglers employed by Asian organized crime syndicates, based in Hong Kong and Taiwan, who were in charge of the expedition. They work off their debts with years of indentured servitude. The average wage for unskilled labor in New York City's Chinatown is substantially lower than in other parts of the city.

Chinese television viewers are bombarded with images of affluent Americans living in luxury. The apprehended aliens said they came seeking work. Instead of being deported, most immediately requested political asylum. None have been sent home.

It is noteworthy that critics who called for stiffer enforcement of U.S. immigration law were accused of displaying a "*Camp of the Saints* mentality."

THE CAMP OF THE SAINTS

THE CAMP OF THE SAINTS

Jean Raspail

Translated from the French
by Norman Shapiro

THE SOCIAL CONTRACT PRESS
Petoskey, Michigan

THE CAMP OF THE SAINTS

Originally published in French as LE CAMP DES SAINTS
©Editions Robert Laffont, S.A., 1973

First American Edition, 1975
©Charles Scribner's Sons

Second American Edition, 1977
Ace Books/Grosset & Dunlap

Third American Edition, 1982
Institute for Western Values

Fourth American Edition, 1987
Immigration Control Foundation

This Social Contract Press edition is reprinted
by special arrangement with Editions Robert Laffont-Fixot
24 Avenue Marceau, 75381 Paris, Cedex 08, 1995;
English language version reprinted by permission
of Scribner, an imprint of Simon & Schuster.

Eighth Social Contract Press Printing, 2015

THE SOCIAL CONTRACT PRESS
445 East Mitchell Street
Petoskey, Michigan 49770
Phone: 231.347.1171
FAX: 231.347.1185
www.thesocialcontract.com

ISBN: 978-1-881780-07-6

TABLE OF CONTENTS

A Note from the Publisher

We have been honored to bring back into print Jean Raspail's *The Camp of the Saints* and to do so just as the immigration policy debate has risen to new heights in the United States—indeed across the world. We began negotiating for the rights to publish this edition long before two seminal events helped focus attention on the wider issues involved.

The first was the passage in California of Proposition 187, a citizen's initiative calling for an end to most social services and welfare benefits, including schooling, for illegal aliens. Fought out in the context of a California gubernatorial race, this was the first time in recent decades that immigration policy played a role in actually electing or defeating candidates for public office.

Then there was remarkable use of *The Camp of the Saints* in the cover article of the December 1994 issue of *The Atlantic Monthly*, "Must It Be the Rest Against the West?" by Matthew Connelly and Paul Kennedy. *The Atlantic Monthly* has the record of the longest continuous publication of any magazine in the United States and is arguably one of the most prestigious. Their article did much to renew interest in Raspail's book and legitimize reconsideration of its thesis.

The Camp of the Saints has been a controversial book in the United States since its first release in 1975 by the respected publishing house of Charles Scribner's Sons as translated from the French by Norman Shapiro. The novel alternately has been praised as a clear minded view of the future or, contrarily, vilified as "racist." Individuals have been attacked for merely being familiar with it.

A word is warranted about the role of a novel in the immigration debate. We humans do not seem to like our truths unvarnished. Rather then "just the facts," we commonly prefer to have them dressed up in the memorable form of plays, poems, allegories, metaphors, fables, parables, tragedies or satires. The poet, the playwright, the novelist, the filmmaker can present truths and open our eyes in ways that demographic analyses, comparative income studies, or social welfare statistics never can. The storytellers can advance notions prohibited to others.

Over the years the American public has absorbed a great number of books, articles, poems and films which exalt the immigrant experience. It is easy for the feelings evoked by Ellis Island and the Statue of Liberty to obscure the fact that we are currently receiving too many immigrants (and receiving them too fast) for the health of our environment and of our common culture. Raspail evokes different feelings that may help to pave the way for policy changes. *The Camp of the Saints* has taken the immigration debate in a new direction. Indeed, it may become the *1984* of the twenty-first century.

To this Fifth Printing of the novel we have added several articles of interest at the back of the book including an interview with the author, Raspail's comments to the French newspaper *Le Figaro* near the 25th anniversary of publication, and a collection of reviews of the book, both when it was first published, as well as more recent comments.

We are indebted to Jean Raspail for his insights into the human condition, and for being so many years ahead of his time. History will judge him more kindly than have some of his contemporaries.

—THE SOCIAL CONTRACT PRESS

Jean Raspail and His Work

It is always the soul that wins the decisive battles.

"In 1951, during a trip to Tierra del Fuego, in crossing the Strait of Magellan, I found, in the space of an hour, under the snow, in the wind, one of the last boats of the Alakalufs. I will never forget it."

This vision — these survivors of a people forgotten by God in an inhuman climate — would never leave Jean Raspail. His books are haunted by it, and it is at the heart of the Patagonian myth created by Raspail, made so real that it almost lives. It also sparked his romantic imaginings.

He was 25 then, living the adventure of his first book of travels: *Tierra del Fuego to Alaska*. In it he explores the two poles of the American continent — seeing and experiencing the greatness between them.

Jean Raspail favors naked, rocky, limitless landscapes. These are the writer's landscapes, populated and animated by the imagination's whim which brings meaning to the unfolding story. They are internal landscapes, seen only by the author and the characters he projects onto these empty spaces.

For always — or almost always — the characters in Jean Raspail's novels disappear. If they don't disappear, they dream, which is the same thing. Whether they flee (voluntarily), are chased and pursued, or are given an order or mission, they leave. And space opens up in front of them, absorbs them, like the time of which they lose track. They are not hopeless — or perhaps they are beyond hopelessness ... so much so that they no longer hope for anything. It may come to pass, that at the end of a long voyage, a door will open, the characters pass through it, exhausted but serene, having accomplished their mission and met their destiny. It is a matter between them and God, whether or not they are believers. The essential matter is to venture forth, to undertake the search. And what is one looking for?

One gets the impression that the characters are not alone and abandoned during their protracted wanderings. One would say that someone watches over them as they discover trails and road signs. They are not easy to interpret, just small pebbles which permit progress bit by bit. Someone has certainly laid them on their path, someone never named but always present, though sometimes inattentive. Then one realizes that their march is a conquest, and the men are actually knights.

There is something of a medieval verse chronicled in this work. Better yet: an echo of the legend of King Arthur.

The *Seven Horsemen* — after *The King's Game*, after *Septentrion*, after *Who Remembers Man* — appeared suddenly, in this light, as the richest expression to date of Jean Raspail's work.

They are seven — imagine! — that leave the city at dusk, facing the setting sun, through the Western Gate which is no longer guarded. The only men still able to carry arms in a kingdom devastated by the worst imaginable calamities. They have received an order from their sovereign, the hereditary margrave, to go see what remains of life in these domains which flourished not long ago. "They didn't flee, and betrayed nothing, hoped for less still, and did not allow themselves to dream." They obey; they are soldiers.

They are young. Colonel-Major Count Silve de Pikkendorf, who commands them, is 35 years old; so is Osmond Van Beck, the coadjutor-bishop (there must be a man of God in the troop); the three other petty officers are between 16 and 20 years of age; only Vassili the corporal and Abai the stable-keeper are older. (They're young as the heros of Jean Raspail's novels often are: the little boy in *The King's Game*, the boy and girl in *The Blue Island* and in *Sire*). With these seven horsemen he represents that which anyone steeped in history and tradition would consider the ideal society, according to the three orders: the nobility, the clergy and the third estate. But, as in all harmonious societies, they are fundamentally equal.

This aristocratic view of the world is the signature of the works of Raspail — it is readily evident in *Sire*. It is the sought-after dream of a society of upright citizens driven by noble sentiments: honor, and loyalty to the chosen cause — with the opposite as well: arrogance, pride, contempt. These are contrasted further with the virtues of self-respect, gallantry and courage. Thus Jean Raspail makes it understood that he does not share the "values" of the modern world. He finds refuge in his imaginary worlds, in his timeless stories which, however — because nothing is simple — speak of today. "Never," he said, "will I write a historical novel about the Templars of the 12th century; but about the Templars of today, yes." And so it is that the conjured-up calamities that led the kingdom of the *Seven Horsemen* to ruin is a transposition of actual evils: epidemics, violence, drugs. In addition to these evils are "the others," the Chechens that prowl about at the borders and infiltrate — reminiscent of *Camp of the Saints*, and the infernal vision portrayed in the last pages of that book.

A stack of books does not necessarily constitute a great work. The ten books that Jean Raspail created from 20 years of writing, these constitute a great work: because an ambition and great expectation live within them, and because they were born of great spirit and vision.

—From an Editions Laffont flier about Jean Raspail
Translated from the French by Laura Tanton

About the Translator
of *The Camp of the Saints*

Norman R. Shapiro, professor of Romance Languages and Literatures at Wesleyan University, Middletown, Connecticut, is a leading translator of French theater, poetry, and fiction. Among his verse translations, medieval to modern, are *The Comedy of Eros: Medieval French Guides to the Art of Love*, *Negritude: Black Poetry from Africa and the Caribbean*, *Fables from Old French*, and *Fifty Fables of La Fontaine*. Most recently he is the author *A Flea in Her Rear, and Other Vintage French Farces*, *The Fabulists French: Verse Fables of Nine Centuries* (chosen by the American Literary Translators Association for its Outstanding Translation Award of 1992), and *La Fontaine's Bawdy: Of Libertines, Louts, and Lechers* (nominated for the PEN-Book-of-the-Month-Club translation prize). Among his previous theater translations are *Four Farces by Georges Feydeau* (National Book Award nominee), *Feydeau, First to Last: Eight One-Act Comedies*, and a series of comedies published by Applause Theater Books: Meilhac and Halévy, *The Brazilian*, Labiche, *A Slap in the Farce* and *A Matter of Wife and Death*, and Feydeau, *The Pregnant Pause, or Love's Labor Lost*. His translations are widely performed throughout the United States and other English-speaking countries.

Author's Introduction to the 1985 French Edition

Published for the first time in 1973, *Camp of the Saints* is a novel that anticipates a situation which seems plausible today and foresees a threat that no longer seems unbelievable to anyone: it describes the peaceful invasion of France, and then of the West, by a third world burgeoned into multitudes. At all levels — global consciousness, governments, societies, and especially every person within himself — the question is asked belatedly: what's to be done?

What's to be done, since no one would wish to renounce his own human dignity by acquiescing to racism? What's to be done since, simultaneously, all persons and all nations have the sacred right to preserve their differences and identities, in the name of their own future and their own past?

Our world was shaped within an extraordinary variety of cultures and races, that could only develop to their ultimate and singular perfection through a necessary segregation. The confrontations that flow (and have always flowed) from this, are not racist, nor even racial. They are simply part of the permanent flow of opposing forces that shape the history of the world. The weak fade and disappear, the strong multiply and triumph.

For example, since the time of the Crusades and the great land and sea discoveries, and up to the colonial period and its last-ditch battles, Western expansionism responded to diverse motivations — ethical, political, or economic — but racism had no part and played no role in it, except perhaps in the soul of evil people. The relative strength of forces was in our favor, that's all. That these were applied most often at the expense of other races — though some were thereby saved from their state of mortal torpor — was merely a consequence of our appetite for conquest and was not driven by or a cover for ideology. Now that the relationship between the forces has been diametrically reversed, and our ancient West — tragically now in a minority status on this earth — retreats behind its dismantled fortifications while it already loses the battles on its own soil, it begins to behold, in astonishment, the dull roar of the huge tide that threatens to engulf it. One must remember the saying on ancient solar calendars: "It is later than you think..." The above reference did not come from my pen. It was written by Thierry Maulnier, in connection with *Camp of the Saints*, as it happens. Forgive me for citing yet another, by Professor Jeffrey Hart of Dartmouth, a literary historian and a famous American columnist: "Raspail is not writing about race, he is writing about civilization..."

After all, *Camp of the Saints* is a symbolic book, a sort of prophecy, dramatized rather brutally by means of shipboards, at the rhythm of inspiration. For if any book came to me through inspiration, I confess that it was precisely this one. Where the devil would I otherwise have drawn the courage to write it? I came out of these eighteen months of work unrecognizable, judging by the photograph on the back of the jacket of the first edition in 1973: my face exhausted, older by ten years than my age today, and with the look of someone tormented by too many visions. And yet, my true character came through in this book, precisely in the coarse humor found in it, derisory humor, the comical under the tragic, a certain amount of clowning as an antidote to the apocalypse. I have always maintained that in spite of its subject matter *Camp of the Saints* is not a sad book and I am grateful to some, notably to Jean Dutour, who have understood that exactly: "That West of ours having become a buffoon, its final tragedy could well be a joke. That is why this terrible book is basically so funny..."

But, to go back to the action in *Camp of the Saints* — if it is a symbol, it doesn't arise from any utopia; it *no longer* arises from any utopia. If it is a prophecy, we live its beginnings today. Simply, in *Camp of the Saints*, it is treated as a classic tragedy, according to the literary principles of unity of time, place and action: everything takes place within three days along the shores of Southern France, and it is there that the destiny of white people is sealed. Though the action was then already well developed along the lines described in *Camp of the Saints* (boat people, the radicalization of the North African community and of other foreign groups in France, the strong psychological impact of human rights organizations, the inflamed evangelism of the religious leadership, a hypocritical purity of consciences, refusal to look the truth in the face, etc.) in actuality the unraveling will not take place in three days but, almost certainly, after many convulsions, during the first decades of the third millennium, barely the time of one or two generations. When one knows what constitutes a generation in our old European lands — a rump-generation in the image of a rump-family and a rump-nation — the heart constricts in anticipation, and is overwhelmed by discouragement. It's enough to go back to the scary demographic predictions for the next thirty years, and those I will cite are the most favorable ones: encircled by seven billion people, only seven hundred million of them white, hardly a third of them in our little Europe, and those no longer in bloom but quite old. They face a vanguard of four hundred million North Africans and Muslims, fifty percent of them less than twenty years old, those on the opposite shores of the Mediterranean arriving ahead of the rest of the world! Can one imagine for a second, in the name of whatever ostrich-like blindness, that such a disequilibrium can endure?

At this juncture, the moment has arrived to explain why, in *Camp of the Saints*, it is human masses coming from the far-away Ganges rather than the shores of the Mediterranean that overwhelm the South of France. There are several reasons for this. One pertains to prudence on my part, and especially to my refusal to enter the false debate about racism and anti-racism in French daily life, as well as my revulsion at describing the racial tensions already discernible (but for the moment not fit for discussion) for fear of exacerbating them. To be sure, a mighty vanguard is already here, and expresses its intention to stay even as it refuses to assimilate; in twenty years they will make up thirty percent, strongly motivated foreigners, in the bosom of a people that once was French. It's a sign, but it is only one sign. One could stop there. One could even engage in some skirmishes, all the while ignoring, or pretending to ignore that the real danger is not only here, that it is elsewhere, that it is yet to come, and that by its very size it will be of a different order. For I am convinced that at the global level things will unleash as at a billiard game, where the balls start moving one after the other following an initial shove, which can start up in this or that immense reservoir of misery and multitudes, such as the one over there, alongside the Ganges. It will probably not happen as I have described it, for the *Camp of the Saints* is only a parable, but in the end the result will not be any different, though perhaps in a form more diffused and therefore *seemingly* more tolerable. The Roman empire did not die any differently, though, it's true, more slowly, whereas this time we can expect a more sudden conflagration. It is said that history does not repeat itself. That's very foolish. The history of our planet is made up of successive voids and of the ruins that others have strewn about as they each had their turn, and that some have at times regenerated.

For the West is empty, even if it has not yet become really aware of it. An extraordinarily inventive civilization, surely the only one capable of meeting the challenges of the third millennium, the West has no soul left. At every level — nations, races, cultures, as well as individuals — it is always the soul that wins the decisive battles. It is only the soul that forms the weave of gold and brass from which the shields that save the strong are fashioned. I can hardly discern any soul in us. Looking, for example, at my own country, France, I often get the impression, as in a bad dream dreamt wide-awake, that many Frenchmen of true lineage are no longer anything but hermit-clams that live in shells abandoned by the representatives of a species, now disappeared, that was known as "French" and which did not forecast, through some unknown genetic mystery, the one that at century's end has wrapped itself in this name. They are content to just endure. Mechanically, they ensure their survival from week to week, ever more feebly. Under the flag of an illusory internal solidarity and security, they are no longer in solidarity with anything, or even cognizant of anything that would constitute the essential commonalities of a people. In the area of the practical and materialistic, which alone can still light a spark of interest in their eyes, they form a nation of petty bourgeois which, in the name of the riches it inherited and is less and less deserving of, rewards itself — and continues to reward itself in the middle of crisis — with millions of domestic servants: immigrants. Ah! How they will shudder! The domestics have innumerable relatives on this side and beyond the seas, a single starving family that populates all the earth. A global Spartacus... To cite but one example from hundreds, the population of Nigeria, in Africa, has close to seventy million inhabitants which it is incapable of feeding even while it spends more than fifty percent of its oil income to buy food. At the dawn of the third millennium, there will be a hundred million Nigerians and the oil will be gone.

But the petty bourgeois, deaf and blind, continues to play the buffoon without knowing it. Still miraculously comfortable in his lush fields, he cries out while glancing toward his nearest neighbor: "Make the rich pay!" Does he know, does he finally know that it is he who is the rich guy, and that the cry for justice, that cry of all revolutions, projected by millions of voices, is rising soon against him, and only against him. That's the whole theme of *Camp of the Saints*.

So, what to do?

I am a novelist. I have no theory, no system nor ideology to propose or defend. It just seems to me that we are facing a unique alternative: either learn the resigned courage of being poor or find again the inflexible courage to be rich. In both cases, so-called Christian charity will prove itself powerless. The times will be cruel.

— J. R.

— Translated from the French by Gerda Bikales

And when the thousand years are ended, Satan will be released from his prison, and will go forth and deceive the nations which are in the four corners of the earth, Gog and Magog, and will gather them together for the battle; the number of whom is as the sand of the sea. And they went up over the breadth of the earth and encompassed the camp of the saints, and the beloved city.

APOCALYPSE 20

My spirit turns more and more toward the West, toward the old heritage. There are, perhaps, some treasures to retrieve among its ruins . . . I don't know.

LAWRENCE DURRELL

As seen from the outside, the massive upheaval in Western society is approaching the limit beyond which it will become "meta-stable" and must collapse.

SOLZHENITSYN

I HAD WANTED TO WRITE a lengthy preface to explain my position and show that this is no wild-eyed dream; that even if the specific action, symbolic as it is, may seem farfetched, the fact remains that we are inevitably heading for something of the sort. We need only glance at the awesome population figures predicted for the year 2000, i.e., twenty-eight years from now: seven billion people, only nine hundred million of whom will be white.

But what good would it do?

I should at least point out, though, that many of the texts I have put into my characters' mouths or pens—editorials, speeches, pastoral letters, laws, news stories, statements of every description—are, in fact, authentic. Perhaps the reader will spot them as they go by. In terms of the fictional situation I have presented, they become all the more revealing.

J. R.

One

The old professor had a rather simple thought. Given the wholly abnormal conditions, he had read, and reasoned, and even written too much—versed as he was in the workings of the mind—to dare propose anything, even to himself, but the most banal of reflections, worthy of a schoolboy's theme. It was a lovely day, warm but not hot, with a cool spring breeze rolling gently and noiselessly over the covered terrace outside the house. His was one of the last houses up toward the crest of the hill, perched on the rocky slope like an outpost guarding the old brown-hued village that stood out above the landscape, towering over it all, as far as the tourist resort down below; as far as the sumptuous boulevard along the water, with its green palms, tips barely visible, and its fine white homes; as far as the sea itself, calm and blue, the rich man's sea, now suddenly stripped of all the opulent veneer that usually overspread its surface—the chrome-covered yachts, the muscle-bulging skiers, the gold-skinned girls, the fat bellies lining the decks of sailboats, large but discreet— and now, stretching over that empty sea, aground some fifty yards out, the incredible fleet from the other side of the globe, the rusty, creaking fleet that the old professor had been eyeing since morning. The stench had faded away at last, the terrible stench of latrines, that had heralded the fleet's arrival, like thunder before a storm. The old man took his eye from the spyglass, moved back from the tripod. The amazing invasion had loomed up so close that it already seemed to be swarming over the hill and into his house. He rubbed his weary eye, looked toward the door. It was a door of solid oak, like some deathless mass, jointed with fortress hinges. The ancestral name was carved in somber wood, and the year that one of the old man's forebears, in uninterrupted line, had completed the house: 1673. The door opened out on the terrace from the large main room that served as his library, parlor, and study, all in one. There was no other door in the house. The terrace, in fact, ran right to the road, down five little steps, with nothing like a gate to close them off, open to any and every passerby who felt like walking up and saying hello, the way they did so often in the village. Each day, from dawn to dusk, that door stood open. And on this particular evening, as the sun was beginning to sink down to its daily demise, it was open as well—a fact that seemed to strike the old man for the very first time. It was then that he had this fleeting thought, whose utter banality brought a kind of rapturous smile to his lips: "I wonder," he said to himself, "if, under the circumstances, the proverb is right, and if a door really has to be open or shut . . ."

Then he took up his watch again, eye to glass, to make the most of the sun's last, low-skimming rays, as they lit the unlikely sight one more time before dark. How many of them were there, out on those grounded wrecks? If the figures could be believed—the horrendous figures that each terse news bulletin had announced through the day, one after another—then the decks and holds must be piled high with layer on layer of human bodies, clustered in heaps around smoke-stacks and gangways, with the dead underneath supporting the living, like one of those columns of ants on the march, teeming with life on top, exposed to view, and below, a kind of ant-paved path, with millions of trampled cadavers. The old professor—Calguès by name—aimed his glass at one of the ships still lit by the sun, then patiently focused the lens until the image was as sharp as he could make it, like a scientist over his microscope, peering in to find his culture swarming with the microbes that he knew all the time must be there. The ship was a steamer, a good sixty years old. Her five stacks, straight up, like pipes, showed how very old she was. Four of them were lopped off at different levels, by time, by rust, by lack of care, by chance—in short, by gradual decay. She had run aground just off the beach, and lay there, listing at some ten degrees. Like all the ships in this phantom fleet, there wasn't a light to be seen on her once it was dark, not even a glimmer. Everything must have gone dead—boilers, generators, everything, all at once—as she ran to meet her self-imposed disaster. Perhaps there had been just fuel enough for this one and only voyage. Or perhaps there was no one on board anymore who felt the need to take care of such things—or of anything else—now that the exodus had finally led to the gates of the newfound paradise. Old Monsieur Calguès took careful note of all he saw, of each and every detail, unaware of the slightest emotion within him. Except, that is, for his interest; a prodigious interest in this vanguard of an antiworld bent on coming in the flesh to knock, at long last, at the gates of abundance. He pressed his eye to the glass, and the first things he saw were arms. As best he could tell, his range of vision described a circle on deck ten yards or so in diameter. Then he started to count. Calm and unhurried. But it was like trying to count all the trees in the forest, those arms raised high in the air, waving and shaking together, all outstretched toward the nearby shore. Scraggy branches, brown and black, quickened by a breath of hope. All bare, those fleshless Gandhi-arms. And they rose up out of scraps of cloth, white cloth that must have been tunics once, and togas, and pilgrims' saris. The professor reached two hundred, then stopped. He had counted as far as he could within the bounds of the circle. Then he did some rapid calculation. Given the length and breadth of the deck, it was likely that more than thirty such circles could be laid out side by side, and that between every pair of tangent circumferences there would be two spaces, more or less triangular in shape, opposite one another, vertex to vertex, each with an area roughly equal to one-third of a circle, which would give a total of $30 + 10 = 40$ circles, 40×200 arms $= 8,000$ arms. Or four thousand bodies! On this one deck alone! Now, assuming that they might be several layers thick, or at least no less thick on each of the decks—and between decks and belowdecks too—then the figure, astounding enough as it was, would have to be multiplied by eight. Or thirty thousand creatures on a single ship! Not to mention the dead, floating here and there around the hull, trailing their white rags over the water, corpses that the living had been throwing overboard since morning. A curious act, all in all, and one not inspired by reasons of hygiene, to be sure. Otherwise, why wait for the end of the voyage? But Monsieur Calguès felt certain he had hit on the one explanation. He believed in God. He believed in all the rest: eternal life, redemption, heavenly mercy, hope and faith. He believed as well, with firm conviction, that the corpses thrown out on the shores of France had reached their paradise too, to waft their way through it, unconstrained, forevermore. Even more blessed than the living themselves, who, throwing them into the sea, had offered their dead, then and there, the gift of salvation, joy, and all eternity. Such an act was called love. At least that was how the old professor understood it.

And so night settled in, but not until daylight had glimmered its last red rays once more on the grounded fleet. There were better than a hundred ships in all, each one caked with rust, unfit for the sea, and each one proof of the miracle that had somehow guided them, safe and sound, from the other side of the earth. All but one, that is, wrecked off the coast of Ceylon. They had lined up in almost mannerly fashion, one after the other, stuck in the sand or in among the rocks, bows upraised in one final yearning thrust toward shore. And all around, thousands of floating, white-clad corpses, that daylight's last waves were beginning to wash aground, laying them gently down on the beach, then rolling back to sea to look for more. A hundred ships! The old professor felt a shudder well up within him, that quiver of exaltation and humility combined, the feeling we sometimes get when we turn our minds, hard as we can, to notions of the infinite and the eternal. On this Easter Sunday evening, eight hundred thousand living beings, and thousands of dead ones, were making their peaceful assault on the Western World. Tomorrow it would all be over. And now, rising up from the coast to the hills, to the village, to the house and its terrace, a gentle chanting, yet so very strong for all its gentleness, like a kind of singsong, droned by a chorus of eight hundred thousand voices. Long, long ago, the Crusaders had sung as they circled Jerusalem, on the eve of their last attack. And Jericho's walls had crumbled without a fight when the trumpets sounded for the seventh time. Perhaps when all was silent, when the chanting was finally stilled, the chosen people too would feel the force of divine displeasure. . . . There were other sounds as well. The roar of hundreds of trucks. Since morning, the army had taken up positions on the Mediterranean beaches. But there in the darkness there was nothing beyond the terrace but sky and stars.

It was cool in the house when the professor went inside, but he left the door open all the same. Can a door protect a world that has lived too long? Even a marvel of workmanship, three hundred years old, and one carved out of such utterly respectable Western oak? . . . There was no electricity. Obviously, the technicians from the power plants along the coast had fled north too, with all the others, the petrified mob, turning tail and running off without a word, so as not to have to look, not see a thing, which meant they wouldn't have to understand, or even try. The professor lit the oil lamps that he always kept on hand in case the lights went out. He threw one of the matches into the fireplace. The kindling, carefully arranged, flashed up with a roar, crackled, and spread its light and warmth over the room. Then he turned on his transistor, tuned all day long to the national chain. Gone now the pop and the jazz, the crooning ladies and the vapid babblers, the black saxophonists, the gurus, the smug stars of stage and screen, the experts on health and love and sex. All gone from the airwaves, all suddenly judged indecent, as if the threatened West were concerned with the last acoustic image it presented of itself. Nothing but Mozart, the same on every station.

Eine kleine Nachtmusik, no less. And the old professor had a kindly thought for the program director, there in his studio in Paris. He couldn't possibly see or know, and yet he had understood. For those eight hundred thousand singsong voices that he couldn't even hear, he had found, instinctively, the most fitting reply. What was there in the world more Western than Mozart, more civilized, more perfect? No eight hundred thousand voices could drone their chant to Mozart's notes. Mozart had never written to stir the masses, but to touch the heart of each single human being, in his private self. What a lovely symbol, really! The Western World summed up in its ultimate truth . . . An announcer's voice roused the old professor from his musings:

"The President of the Republic has been meeting all day at the Élysée Palace with government leaders. Also present, in view of the gravity of the situation, are the chiefs of staff of the three branches of the armed forces, as well as the heads of the local and state police, the prefects of the departments of Var and Alpes-Maritimes, and, in a strictly advisory capacity, His Eminence the Cardinal Archbishop of Paris, the papal nuncio, and most of the Western ambassadors currently stationed in the capital. At present the meeting is still in progress. A government spokesman, however, has just announced that this evening, at about midnight, the President of the Republic will go on the air with an address of utmost importance to the nation. According to reports reaching us from the south, all still seems quiet on board the ships of the refugee fleet. A communiqué from army headquarters confirms that two divisions have been deployed along the coast in the face . . . in the face of . . ." (The announcer hesitated. And who could blame him? Just what should one call that numberless, miserable mass? The enemy? The horde? The invasion? The Third World on the march?) ". . . in the face of this unprecedented incursion . . ." (There! Not too bad at all!) ". . . and that three divisions of reinforcements are heading south at this moment, despite considerable difficulty of movement. In another communiqué, issued not more than five minutes ago, army chief of staff Colonel Dragasès has reported that troops under his command have begun setting fire to some twenty immense wooden piles along the shore, in order to . . ." (Another hesitation. The announcer seemed to gasp. The old professor even thought he heard him mutter "My God!") ". . . in order to burn the thousands of dead bodies thrown overboard from all the ships . . ."

And that was all. A moment later, with hardly a break, Mozart

was back, replacing those three divisions hurtling southward, and
the score of funeral pyres that must have begun to crackle by
now in the crisp air down by the coast. The West doesn't like to
burn its dead. It tucks away its cremation urns, hides them out in
the hinterlands of its cemeteries. The Seine, the Rhine, the Loire,
the Rhône, the Thames are no Ganges or Indus. Not even the
Guadalquivir and the Tiber. Their shores never stank with the
stench of roasting corpses. Yes, they have flowed with blood, their
waters have run red, and many a peasant has crossed himself as
he used his pitchfork to push aside the human carcasses floating
downstream. But in Western times, on their bridges and banks,
people danced and drank their wine and beer, men tickled the
fresh, young laughing lasses, and everyone laughed at the wretch
on the rack, laughed in his face, and the wretch on the gallows,
tongue dangling, and the wretch on the block, neck severed—because, indeed, the Western World, staid as it was, knew how to
laugh as well as cry—and then, as their belfreys called them to
prayer, they would all go partake of their fleshly god, secure in
the knowledge that their dead were there, protecting them, safe
as could be, laid out in rows beneath their timeless slabs and
crosses, in graveyards nestled against the hills, since burning, after
all, was only for devilish fiends, or wizards, or poor souls with the
plague. . . . The professor stepped out on the terrace. Down below, the shoreline was lit with a score of reddish glows, ringed
round with billows of smoke. He opened his binoculars and
trained them on the highest of the piles, flaming neatly along like
a wooden tower, loaded with corpses from bottom to top. The soldiers had stacked it with care, first a layer of wood, then a layer
of flesh, and so on all the way up. At least some trace of respect
for death seemed to show in its tidy construction. Then all at
once, down it crashed, still burning, nothing now but a loathsome
mass, like a heap of smoking rubble along the public way. And no
one troubled to build the nice neat tower again. Bulldozers rolled
up, driven by men in diving suits, then other machines fitted with
great jointed claws and shovels, pushing the bodies together into
soft, slimy mounds, scooping a load in the air and pouring it onto
the fire, as arms and legs and heads, and even whole cadavers
overflowed around them and fell to the ground. It was then that
the professor saw the first soldier turn and run, calling to mind
yet another cliché, arms and legs flapping like a puppet on a
string, in perfect pantomime of unbridled panic. The young man

had dropped the corpse he was dragging. He had wildly thrown down his helmet and mask, ripped off his safety gloves. Then, hands clutched to temples, he dashed off, zigzag, like a terrified jackrabbit, into the ring of darkness beyond the burning pile. Five minutes more, and ten other soldiers had done the same. The professor closed his binoculars. He understood. That scorn of a people for other races, the knowledge that one's own is best, the triumphant joy at feeling oneself to be part of humanity's finest—none of that had ever filled these youngsters' addled brains, or at least so little that the monstrous cancer implanted in the Western conscience had quashed it in no time at all. In their case it wasn't a matter of tender heart, but a morbid, contagious excess of sentiment, most interesting to find in the flesh and observe, at last, in action. The real men of heart would be toiling that night, and nobody else. Just a moment before, as the nice young man was running away, old Calguès had turned his glasses briefly on a figure that looked like some uniformed giant, standing at the foot of the burning pile, legs spread, and hurling up each corpse passed over to him, one by one, with a powerful, rhythmic fling, like a stoker of yesteryear deep belowdecks, feeding his boiler with shovelfuls of coal. Perhaps he too was pained at the sight, but if so, his pain didn't leave much room for pity. In fact, he probably didn't think of it at all, convinced that now, finally, the human race no longer formed one great fraternal whole—as the popes, philosophers, intellects, politicos, and priests of the West had been claiming for much too long. Unless, that is, the old professor, watching "the stoker" and his calm resolve— the one he called "the stoker" was really Colonel Dragasès, the chief of staff, up front to set his men an example—was simply ascribing to him his own ideas. . . . That night, love too was not of one mind. Man never has really loved humanity all of a piece—all its races, its peoples, its religions—but only those creatures he feels are his kin, a part of his clan, no matter how vast. As far as the rest are concerned, he forces himself, and lets the world force him. And then, when he does, when the damage is done, he himself falls apart. In this curious war taking shape, those who loved themselves best were the ones who would triumph. How many would they be, next morning, still joyously standing their ground on the beach, as the hideous army slipped down by the thousands, down into the water, for the onslaught by the living, in the wake of their dead? Joyously! That was what mattered the most.

A moment before, as he watched "the stoker," the professor had thought he could see him move his lips, wide open, as if he were singing. Yes, by God, singing! If even just the two of them could stand there and sing, perhaps they could wake up the rest from their deathly sleep. . . . But no other sound came rising from the shore, no sound but the soft, foreboding chant welling up out of eight hundred thousand throats.

"Pretty cool, man, huh!" exclaimed a voice in the shadows.

Two

Noiselessly, the young man had come up the five little steps from the road and onto the terrace. Feet bare, hair long and dirty, flowered tunic, Hindu collar, Afghan vest . . .

"I've just been down there," he said. "Fantastic! I've been waiting five years for something like this!"

"Are you alone?"

"So far. Except for the ones who were already here. But there's lots more on the way. They're all coming down. And walking, too. All the pigs are pulling out and heading north! I didn't see a single car in this direction! Man, they're going to be bushed, but this is too good to miss. Going to smoke, and shoot dope, and walk all the way. Make it down here on their feet, not on their butts."

"Did you get a close look down there?"

"Real close. Only not for long. I got smashed a couple of times. Some soldier, with his gun. Like I was trash. But I saw a bunch of other soldiers crying. It's great! I'm telling you, tomorrow this country's going to be something else. You won't know it. It's going to be born all over."

"Did you see the people on the boats?"

"You bet I did!"

"And you think you're anything like them? Look, your skin is white. You're a Christian, I imagine. You speak our language, you have our accent. You probably even have family hereabouts, don't you?"

"So what! My real family's all the people coming off those boats. Here I am with a million of my brothers, and sisters, and fathers, and mothers. And wives if I want them. I'll sleep with the first one that lets me, and I'll give her a baby. A nice dark baby. And after a while I'll melt into the crowd."

"Yes, you'll disappear. You'll be lost in that mass. They won't even know you exist."

"Good! That's just what I'm after. I'm sick of being a tool of the middle class, and I'm sick of making tools of people just like me, if that's what you mean by existing. My parents took off this morning. And my two sisters with them. Afraid of getting raped, all of a sud-

9

den. They went and dressed up like everyone else. These real square
clothes, I mean. Things they haven't put on in years, like neat little
skirts, and blouses with buttons. So scared, you wouldn't know them.
Well, they won't get away. Nobody's going to get away. Let them try
to save their ass. They're finished, all of them. Man, you should have
seen it! My father, with his arms full of shoes from his store, piling
them into his nice little truck. And my mother, bawling her head off,
figuring out which ones to take, picking out the expensive ones and
leaving the rest. And my sisters, already up front, huddling together
and staring at me, scared to death, like maybe I was the first one in
line to rape them. And meanwhile I'm laughing and having myself
a ball, like when my old man pulls down the grille in front of the store
and sticks the key in his pocket. 'Listen,' I told him, 'a lot of good
that's going to do! I can open your door myself without a key. And
I will, tomorrow. And you know what they'll do with your goddamn
shoes? They'll probably use them to piss in. Or maybe they'll eat
them. Because they all go barefoot!' Then he gave me a look, and he
spit on me. So I spit back and got him in the eye with a big one. And
that's how we said good-bye."

"And what brings you here? Why this village? Why my house?"

"I'm looting, that's why. I sponged off society while it was alive, so
now that it's dead, I'm going to pick its bones. It's a change. I like it.
Because everything's dead. Except for the army, and you, and a few
of my friends, there's no one around for miles. So I'm looting, man.
But don't worry, I'm not hungry. I've already stuffed myself. And
anyway, I don't need much. Besides, everything's mine now. And
tomorrow I'm going to stand here and let them have it all. I'm like
a king, man, and I'm going to give away my kingdom. Today's Easter,
right? Well, this is the last time your Christ's going to rise. And it
won't do you any good this time, either, just like all the rest."

"I'm afraid I don't follow . . ."

"There's a million Christs on those boats out there. And first thing
in the morning they're all going to rise. The million of them. So your
Christ, all by himself . . . Well, he's had it, see?"

"Do you believe in God?"

"Of course not!"

"And those million Christs? Is that your own idea?"

"No, but I thought it was kind of cool. For padre talk, I mean. I got
it from this priest. One of those worker types from the wrong side
of town. I ran into him an hour ago. I was on my way up here, and
he was running like crazy down the hill. Not in rags or anything, but

kind of weird. He kept stopping and lifting his arms in the air, like the ones down there, and he'd yell out: 'Thank you, God! Thank you!' And then he'd take off again, down to the beach. They say there's more on the way."

"More what?"

"More priests, just like him . . . Say listen, man, I'm getting tired of you. I didn't come here to talk. Besides, you're just a ghost. How come you're still around?"

"I want to hear what you have to say."

"You mean my bullshit interests you?"

"Immensely."

"Then I'll tell you something: you're through. Dried up. You keep thinking and talking, but there's no more time for that. It's over. So beat it!"

"Oh? I daresay . . ."

"Listen. You and this house, you're both the same. You look like you've both been around here for a thousand years."

"Since 1673, to be exact," the old gentleman answered, smiling for the first time.

"Three centuries, father to son. And always so sure of yourselves, so damn sure of everything. Man, that's sick!"

"Quite true. But I find your concern a trifle surprising. Perhaps you're still one of us after all. Perhaps just a little?"

"Shut up before you make me puke! Maybe you've got a pretty house. So what? And maybe you're not a bad old guy. Smart, and refined, and everything just right. But smug, man, so sure of your place. So sure that you fit right in. With everything around you. Like this village of yours, with its twenty generations of ancestors just like you. Twenty generations without a conscience, without a heart. What a family tree! And now here you are, the last, perfect branch. Because you are, you're perfect. And that's why I hate you. That's why I'm going to bring them here, tomorrow. The grubbiest ones in the bunch. Here, to your house. You're nothing to them, you and all you stand for. Your world doesn't mean a thing. They won't even try to understand it. They'll be tired, man. Tired and cold. And they'll build a fire with your big wooden door. And they'll crap all over your terrace, and wipe their hands on your shelves full of books. And they'll spit out your wine, and eat with their fingers from all that nice pewter hanging inside on your wall. Then they'll squat on their heels and watch your easy chairs go up in smoke. And they'll use your fancy bedsheets to pretty themselves up in. All your things will lose their meaning. Your meaning, man. What's beautiful won't be, what's useful they'll laugh at, what's useless they won't even bother with. Nothing's going to be worth a thing. Except maybe a piece of string on the floor. And they'll fight over it, and tear the whole damn place apart. . . . Yes, it's going to be tremendous! So go on, beat it. Fuck off!"

"One moment, if I may. You told me there was no more time for thinking and talking, yet you seem to be doing a good deal of both."

"I'm not thinking, man. I'm just telling you where I stand on things I thought of long ago. I'm through thinking. So fuck off, you hear me?"

"One last question. When they go smashing everything to bits, they won't know any better. But why you?"

"Why? Because I've learned to hate all this. Because the conscience of the world makes me hate all this, that's why. Now fuck off! You're beginning to get on my ass!"

"If you insist. There's really no point in staying. You're not making very much sense. I'm sure you have an excellent brain, but I do think it's been a trifle muddled. Someone has done a fine job. Well now, I'll be on my way. Just let me get my hat."

The old gentleman stepped inside. He came out a moment later with a shotgun.

"What's that for?" the young man asked.

"Why, I'm going to kill you, of course! My world won't live past morning, more than likely, and I fully intend to enjoy its final moments. And enjoy them I shall, more than you can possibly imagine! I'm going to live myself a second life. Tonight, right here. And I think it should be even better than the first. Of course, since all of my kind have left, I intend to live it alone."

"And me?"

"You? Why, you're not my kind. We couldn't be more unlike. Surely I don't want to ruin this one last night, this quintessential night, with someone like you. Oh no, I'm going to kill you."

"You can't. You won't know how. I bet you've never killed anyone."

"Precisely. I've always led a rather quiet life. A professor of literature who loved his work, that's all. No war ever called me to serve, and, frankly, the spectacle of pointless butchery makes me ill. I wouldn't have made a very good soldier, I'm afraid. Still, had I been with Actius, once upon a time, I think I would have reveled in killing my share of Hun. And with the likes of Charles Martel, and Godfrey of Bouillon, and Baldwin the Leper, I'm sure I would have shown a certain zeal in poking my blade through Arab flesh. I might have fallen before Byzantium, fighting by Constantine Dragasès's side. But God, what a horde of Turks I would have cut down before I gasped my last! Besides, when a man is convinced of his cause, he doesn't die quite so easily! See, there I am, springing back to life in the ranks of the Teutons, hacking the Slav to shreds. And there, leaving Rhodes with Villiers de l'Isle-Adam and his peerless little band, my white cloak blazoned with the cross, my sword dripping blood. Then sailing with Don Juan of Austria, off to even the score at Lepanto. Ah, what a splendid slaughter! . . . But soon there's nothing left for me to do. A few trifling skirmishes now and again, none of them too well thought of these days. Like the War Between the States, when my side is defeated and I join the Ku Klux Klan to murder myself some blacks. A nasty business, I admit. Not quite so bad with Kitchener, though, skewering the Mahdi's Moslem fanatics, spilling their guts. . . . But the rest is all current events, a sad little joke. Most of it has already slipped my mind. Perhaps I've done my bit, killing a pinch of Oriental at the Berlin gates. A dash of Vietcong here, of Mau Mau there. A touch of Algerian rebel to boot. At worst, some leftist or other, finished off in a police van, or some vicious Black Panther. Yes, it's all become so terribly ugly. No fanfares anymore, no flags, no hosannas . . . Oh well, you'll have to excuse an old professor's pedantic prattle. But you see, I too have stopped thinking and just want to tell you where I stand. You're right, I've never killed a soul. Much less any of the types I've just conjured up, all of them standing here before me, at last, in your flesh, all rolled into one. But now I'm going to live those battles over, all at once, those battles that I feel so much a part of, deep in my soul, and I'm going to act them out, right here, all by myself, with one single shot. Like this!"

The young man collapsed in a graceful glide along the railing where he had been leaning, and wound up in a squat, arms hanging by his sides, in a position that seemed quite natural for him. The red spot over his left breast spread out a little, but the blood stopped quickly. It was a nice, tidy death. As his eyes closed beneath the professor's gentle thumb and finger, they didn't even look surprised. No flags, no fanfares. Just a victory Western style, as complete as it was absurd and useless. And, utterly at peace with himself—more exquisitely at peace than he remembered ever being—old Monsieur Calguès turned his back on the corpse and went inside.

Three

Now, all at once, with his mind at ease, the professor's stomach began to feel great pangs of hunger. And suddenly he remembered other ravenous flashes, especially those colossal appetites that man falls prey to after nights of well-requited love. Those distant passions were nothing but vague sensations now, recalled without regret. But the meals that had followed in their wake—improvised meals for two, consumed on this very spot—still stood out in his memory, sharp and clear. Great, flat slices of country bread, dark-smoked ham from up the mountain, dried goat cheese from the village, olives from the terraced groves, apricots from the garden, steeped in sunlight, and that wine from the rocky slopes, just a little too tart. It was all still there in the house, all right within reach: the bread, in the cupboard with the cross carved into its lid; the olives, in a stoneware pot; the ham, hanging from the beams in the kitchen; the wine and cheese, outside, under the stairs, like rows of books lined up on dimly lit shelves . . . In no time at all it was set out, spread over the massive table. For a moment the cork in the bottle held fast. When it finally let go, with a sharp little pop, the familiar sound filled the room with a kind of sensual joy. And it occurred to the old professor that once again, tonight, he was celebrating an act of love.

He poured himself some wine, one hearty glass for his thirst, then one for his pleasure, smacking his lips with a touch of ostentation at the obvious excess. He cut up the ham into fine, thin slices, arranged them neatly on a pewter plate, put out a few olives, laid the cheese on a bed of grape leaves and the fruit on a large, flat basket. Then he sat down before his supper and smiled a contented smile. He was in love. And like any successful suitor, he found himself face to face now with the one he loved, alone. Yet tonight that one was no woman, no living creature at all, but a myriad kindred images formed into a kind of projection of his own inner being. Like that silver fork, for example, with the well-worn prongs, and some maternal ancestor's initials, now rubbed almost smooth. A curious object, really, when you think that the Western World invented it for propriety's sake, though a third of the human race still grubs up its food with its fingers. And the crystal, always set out in a row of four, so

utterly useless. Well, why not? Why do without glasses, like boors?
Why stop setting them out, simply because the Brazilian backwoods
was dying of thirst, or because India was gulping down typhus with
every swallow of muck from its dried-up wells? Let the cuckolds
come pound at the door with their threats of revenge. There's no
sharing in love. The rest of the world can go hang. They don't even
exist. So what if those thousands were all on the march, cuckolded
out of the pleasures of life? All the better! . . . And so, the professor
set out the four glasses, lined them up in a row. Then he moved the
lamp a little to give more light, and they sparkled like stars. Further
over, a rustic chest, huge and immovable. Three centuries, father to
son, as the young man said, and so sure of it all. And in that chest such
an endless store of tablecloths and napkins, of pillow slips and sheets,
of dustcloths and fine linen, product of another age, linen that would
last forever, in great thick piles, so tightly packed on the outside
alone that he never had to use the other household treasures hidden
behind them, all lavender-scented, that his mother, or hers, had
stacked away so very long ago, never parting with a stitch for their
poor until it was worn out and decently patched, but with lots of good
use in it yet, convinced—dear, prudent souls that they were—that
unbridled charity is, after all, a sin against oneself. Then, after a
while, there were too many poor. Altogether too many. Folk you
didn't even know. Not even from here. Just nameless people. Swarming all over. And so terribly clever! Spreading through cities, and
houses, and homes. Worming their way by the thousands, in thousands of foolproof ways. Through the slits in your mailboxes, begging
for help, with their frightful pictures bursting from envelopes day
after day, claiming their due in the name of some organization or
other. Slithering in. Through newspapers, radio, churches, through
this faction or that, until they were all around you, wherever you
looked. Whole countries full, bristling with poignant appeals, pleas
that seemed more like threats, and not begging now for linen, but
for checks to their account. And in time it got worse. Soon you saw
them on television, hordes of them, churning up, dying by the thousands, and nameless butchery became a feature, a continuous show,
with its masters of ceremonies and its full-time hucksters. The poor
had overrun the earth. Self-reproach was the order of the day; happiness, a sign of decadence. And pleasure? Beneath discussion. Even
in Monsieur Calguès's own village, if you did try to give some good
linen away, they would just think you were being condescending. No,
charity couldn't allay your guilt. It could only make you feel meaner

and more ashamed. And so, on that day he remembered so well, the professor had shut up his cupboards and chests, his cellar and larder, closed them once and for all to the outside world. The very same day that the last pope had sold out the Vatican. Treasures, library, paintings, frescoes, tiara, furniture, statues—yes, the pontiff had sold it all, as Christendom cheered, and the most high-strung among them, caught up in the contagion, had wondered if they shouldn't go do likewise, and turn into paupers as well. Useless heroics in the eternal scheme of things. He had thrown it all into a bottomless pit: it didn't take care of so much as the rural budget of Pakistan for a single year! Morally, he had only proved how rich he really was, like some maharaja dispossessed by official decree. The Third World was quick to throw it up to him, and in no time at all he had fallen from grace. From that moment on, His Holiness had rattled around in a shabby, deserted palace, stripped to the walls by his own design. And he died, at length, in his empty chambers, in a plain iron bed, between a kitchen table and three wicker chairs, like any simple priest from the outskirts of town. Too bad, no crucifixion on demand before an assembled throng. The new pope had been elected at about the time Monsieur Calguès retired. One man, wistfully taking his place on the Vatican's throne of straw. The other one, back in his village to stay, with only one thought: to enjoy to the fullest his earthly possessions, here in the setting that suited him best . . . So thank God for the tender ham, and the fragrant bread, and the lightly chilled wine! And let's drink to the bygone world, and to those who can still feel at home in it all!

While the old man sat there, eating and drinking, savoring swallow after swallow, he set his eyes wandering over the spacious room. A time-consuming task, since his glance stopped to linger on everything it touched, and since every confrontation was a new act of love. Now and then his eyes would fill with tears, but they were tears of joy. Each object in this house proclaimed the dignity of those who had lived here—their discretion, their propriety, their reserve, their taste for those solid traditions that one generation can pass on to the next, so long as it still takes pride in itself. And the old man's soul was in everything, too. In the fine old bindings, the rustic benches, the Virgin carved in wood, the big cane chairs, the hexagonal tiles, the beams in the ceiling, the ivory crucifix with its sprig of dried boxwood, and a hundred other things as well . . . It's man's things that really define him, far more than the play of ideas; which is why the Western World had come to lose its self-respect, and why it was clogging the highways at that very moment, fleeing north in droves, no doubt vaguely aware that it was already doomed, done in by its over-secretion, as it were, of ugly monstrosities no longer worth defending. Could that, perhaps, have been one explanation? . . .

At eleven o'clock that night an announcer on the national chain read a new communiqué:

"Government sources note with some dismay the mass exodus of population currently under way throughout the south. While they view this movement with concern, they do not feel justified in advising against it, given the unprecedented nature of the situation. Army and police have been put on maximum alert to help maintain order, and to see to it that the migration does not interfere with the flow of essential military matériel en route from the north. A state of emergency has been declared in the four departments bordering the coast, under the command of the undersecretary, Monsieur Jean Perret, personal representative of the President of the Republic. The army will make every effort to protect all property left behind, insofar as its other duties permit. Government sources confirm that the President of the Republic will address the nation at midnight, tonight, with a message of grave concern . . ."

And again, that was all. In a world long exposed to verbal frenzy, such terseness was most impressive. "Do windbags always die without a word?" the professor mused. Then he picked out a book, poured himself a drink, lit up his pipe, and waited for midnight . . .

Four

It was a curious night for New York, more calm and peaceful than the city had been in well over thirty years. Central Park stood deserted, drained of its thousands of Cains on the prowl. Little girls could have gone there to play, pert towheads, soft and pink in tiny skirts, delighted that, finally, they could romp through its grass. The black and Puerto Rican ghettos were quiet as churches . . .

Dr. Norman Haller had opened his windows. He was listening to the city, but there wasn't a sound. It was that time of night when he would always hear the dreadful notes of what he called the "infernal symphony" rising up from the street below: the cries for help; the click-clack of running heels; the frantic screams; the gunshots, one by one, or in bursts; the wail of police cars; the savage, less-than-human howls; the whimpering children; the vicious laughter; the shatter of glass; the horns of distress as some Cadillac, sleek and air-conditioned, would stop for a light and find itself buried in a sea of black silhouettes, brandishing picks; and then the shouts of no! no! no!, those desperate shouts shrieked into the darkness and suddenly stilled, snuffed out by a knife, a razor, a chain, by a club full of spikes, by a pounding fist, or fingers, or phallus . . .

It had been that way for thirty years. Statistics in sound, and each year louder than the one before. That is, until those last few days, when the graph had taken a sudden plunge, down to an unheard-of zero on the night in question. Thirty years for Dr. Norman Haller! Frustrating years, through no fault of his own. As consulting sociologist to the city of New York, he had seen it coming, predicted it to the letter. The proof was there, in his lucid reports, ignored one and all. There was really no solution. Black would be black, and white would be white. There was no changing either, except by a total mix, a blend into tan. They were enemies on sight, and their hatred and scorn only grew as they came to know each other better. Now they both felt the same utter loathing. . . . And so the consulting sociologist would give his opinion and pocket his money. The city had paid him a handsome price for his monumental study of social upheaval, with its forecast of ultimate doom. "No hope, Doctor Haller?" "No hope, Mr. Mayor. Unless you kill them all, that is, because you'll never

18

change them. How about that?" "Good God, man, hardly! Let's just wait and see what happens, and try to do the best we can . . ."

Plush as could be, that suite of Dr. Norman Haller's, on the twenty-sixth floor of Central Park's most elegant apartment building. Protected from the jungle, cut off from the outside world, with its dozen armed guards in the lobby, electronic sensors in every corner, invisible rays, and alarms, and attack dogs. And the garage, like a kind of hermetic chamber. Drawbridge between life and death, between love and hate. Ivory tower, moon base, bunker de luxe. At quite a price. Thousands and thousands of dollars for a few hundred pages, written for the city of New York by the pen of America's most eminent consulting sociologist. Dr. Norman Haller had built himself a perfect world in the eye of the cyclone, and through that eye he could watch the storm that would sweep it all away. . ... Whiskey, crushed ice, soft music . . . "Go on, darling, go put on that nice expensive little thing you call a dress . . ." A telephone call. The mayor of New York.

"Don't tell me, Jack, let me guess. You're sitting there, all dressed up. You in your tux, Betty in a gown. Almost takes your breath away, she looks so good. Never better . . . On your third drink, I'd say . . . Fancy glasses . . . Just the two of you, nice and cozy . . . No special reason . . . Spur of the moment . . . Right?"

"Exactly! But how on earth . . ."

"Look. The old familiar jungle shuts up tight. The white man gets scared. What else can he do? One last fling for his white prestige. One final tribute to his useless millions, to his precious position above it all! So here's to you, Jack! Hear the tinkle? Hear the ice in my glass? My most expensive crystal. Scotch at a hundred bucks a throw! And my wife's eyes . . . Never been greener! . . . So green, I'm going to jump in and drown . . ."

"Listen, Norman. It's all up to the French now, right? Do you really think they can kill off a million poor, defenseless bastards, just like that? I don't. And frankly, I hope they can't. . . . I'll tell you something else. The ghettos here in the city don't think so either. Or in L.A., or Chicago . . . They may be caged like wildcats, but believe me, they're quiet as lambs. Calm as can be. They just sit at their radios and listen to the news. That is, when they're not in their churches, singing up a storm and praying like crazy for those goddamn ships . . . Ever been swept off your feet by a herd of stampeding lambs? No, I tell you, Norman, the Third World's turned into a bunch of lambs, that's all."

"And the wolf is tired of being a wolf, is that what you're saying? Well, do like me, Jack. Have yourself another drink, and run your fingers up and down your wife's white skin, nice and slow, like something very precious. And wait . . ."

Five

If any logic at all can be found in the way a popular myth gets its start, then we have to go back to Calcutta, to the Consulate General of Belgium, to look for the beginnings of the one we can call, for the moment, "the myth of the newfound paradise." A shabby little consulate, set up in an old colonial villa on the edge of the diplomatic quarter, waking one morning to find a silent throng milling around outside its doors. At daybreak the Sikh guard had chained the front gate shut. From time to time he would point the barrel of his antique rifle between the bars, to urge back the ones who had pushed their way up front. But since he was a decent sort, and since there was really no threat to himself or the gate he was guarding, he would tell them now and again, nicely as he could:

"Look, maybe in a little while you can have some rice. But then you'll have to go. It's no use standing around. See the announcement? It's signed by the Consul himself."

"What does it say?" the crowd would yell, since none of them could read. "Tell us . . . Read it out loud . . ."

As a matter of fact, it was hard to make out much of anything now on the notice posted on the gate, smudged as it was with the prints of the thousand hands that had pawed it over, never quite believing the bad news it proclaimed. But the guard knew the text by heart. He had had to recite it now for a week, day in day out, and he droned it through, word for word, from beginning to end:

"Pursuant to the royal decree of such-and-such date, the government of Belgium has decided to terminate until further notice all adoption procedures presently under way. Henceforth no new requests for adoption will be accepted. Similarly, no Belgian entry visas will be granted for those children currently being processed for departure, even in those cases where a legal adoption antedates the present decree."

A long moan ran through the crowd. Judging by its length and volume, and by the fact that it welled up out of the silence each time it seemed about to die, the Sikh guard—a master at gauging mass distress—guessed that their number had doubled, at least, since the day before.

"Come on, now. Move back!" he shouted, shaking his gun. "Let's all quiet down! You'll get your rice, then you'll have to go back where you came from. And you'd better stay there from now on, too. You heard the announcement."

Up front, a woman stepped out of the crowd and started to speak. All the rest stopped to listen, as if she were speaking for each and every one. She was holding a child in her outstretched arms, a little boy, maybe two years old, thrusting his face so close to the gate that it made him cross his big, gaping eyes.

"Look at my son," she cried. "Isn't he pretty? Isn't he solid and strong for his age, with his plump little thighs, and his arms, and his nice straight legs? . . . See? Look at his mouth. See how white and even his teeth are? . . . And his face. Not a scab, not a fly. And his eyes, never any pus, wide open all the time . . . And his hair. You could grab it and pull it, and he wouldn't lose a one. . . . Look between his legs, see how clean it all is? Even his little bottom . . . And his belly, nice and flat, not swollen like some babies his age . . . I could show you what comes out when he goes, and you wouldn't see a worm, not even a speck of blood. No, he's a good, healthy child. Like the papers said he had to be. Because we fed him the best, we fattened him up just for that. From the day he was born. We saw how pretty he was, and we made up our minds we would send him. So he could grow up there, and be rich, and happy . . . And we fed him more and more, just like the clinic told us. . . . Then his sisters died. The two of them. They were older than he was, but such sickly little things, and he was so hungry, and prettier every day. He could eat enough for three, God bless him! . . . And now you're trying to tell me that we fattened him up for nothing, that his poor father slaved in the ricefields and worked himself to death, all for nothing, and that I'm going to have him on my hands for good, and keep him, and feed him? . . . No, it's my turn to eat! And I'm hungry, you hear? Yes, it's my turn now, because he's big and strong. . . . And besides, he's not mine now, he's not even mine. He's got a new family, halfway around the world, and they're waiting to take him and give him their name. See? It says so on this medal they sent us. The one around his neck. See? I'm not lying! He's theirs now. Take him, he's theirs. I'm through. They promised. I did what they told me, and now . . . No, now I'm too tired . . ."

A hundred women pushed forward, each one with a child in her outstretched arms. And they cried out things like: "He's theirs now, he's theirs!," or "They promised to take him . . ." Pretty babies, mostly, all looking as if they had fed themselves plump on the flesh of their mothers. Poor haggard souls, those mothers, drained dry, as if the umbilical cords were still intact. And the crowd howled, "Take them, take them! They're theirs now! Take them!," while hundreds of others pressed forward behind the ones up front, with armfuls of babes by the hundreds, and hundreds of bigger ones too, all ripe for adoption, pushing them up to the brink, to take the giant leap to paradise. The Belgian decree, far from stemming the human flood, had increased it tenfold. When man has nothing left, he looks askance at certainty. Experience has taught that it's not meant for him. As likelihood fades, myth looms up in its place. The dimmer the chance, the brighter the hope. And so, there they were, thousands of wretched creatures, hoping, crowding against the consulate gates, like the piles of fruit a crafty merchant heaps on his stand, afraid it might spoil: the best ones up front, all shiny and tempting; the next best right behind, still in plain sight, and not too bad if you don't look too close; then the ones barely visible, the damaged ones, starting to rot, all wormy inside, or turned so you can't see the mold. . . . Milling about, way back in the crowd, the women with the monsters, the horrors that no one would take off their hands. And they moaned and groaned louder than all the rest, since their hope knew no bounds. Turned back, pushed aside, driven off day after day, they had come to believe that a paradise so well protected was worth besieging for the rest of their lives, if need be. Before, when the gate was open and the beautiful children had gone streaming through, occasionally one of these mothers would manage to slip her monster in line. Which was something, at least. A step toward salvation. Even though the Sikh would always hold up his rifle and bar the Consul's door. They had come close, and that was enough to nurture their hope, enough to make it spring to life with extravagant visions of milk and honey flowing untapped into rivers thick with fish, whose waters washed fields fairly bursting with crops, far as the eye could see, growing wild for the taking, where little monster children could roll about to their hearts' content. . . . The simpler the folk, the stronger the myth. Soon everyone heard their babble, believed their fantasies, and dreamed the same wild dreams of life in the West. The problem is that, in famine-racked Calcutta, "everyone" means quite a few. Could that be one explanation? . . .

Way back, behind the backmost women in the crowd, a giant of a man stood stripped to the waist, holding something over his head and waving it like a flag. Untouchable pariah, this dealer in droppings, dung roller by trade, molder of manure briquettes, turd eater in time of famine, and holding high in his stinking hands a mass of human flesh. At the bottom, two stumps; then an enormous trunk, all hunched and twisted and bent out of shape; no neck, but a kind of extra stump, a third one in place of a head, and a bald little skull, with two holes for eyes and a hole for a mouth, but a mouth that was no mouth at all—no throat, no teeth—just a flap of skin over his gullet. The monster's eyes were alive, and they stared straight ahead, high over the crowd, frozen forward in a relentless gaze—except, that is, when his pariah father would wave him bodily back and forth. It was just that lidless gaze that flashed through the bars of the gate and caught the eye of the Consul himself, staring in spellbound horror. He had stepped outside for a look at the crowd, to see what was going on. But it wasn't the crowd he saw. And all at once he closed his eyes and began to shout:

"No rice! No visas! No anything! You won't get another thing, do you hear? Now get out! Get out! Every one of you! Out!"

As he turned to rush off, a sharp little stone hit him square on the forehead and left a gash. The monster's eyes lit up. The quiver that ran through his frame was his way of thanking his father. And that was all. No other act of violence. Yet suddenly the keeper of the milk and honey, stumbling back to his consulate, head in hands, struck the crowd as a rather weak defender of the sacred portals of the Western World. So weak, in fact, that if only they could wait, sooner or later he was bound to drop the keys. Could that be one explanation? . . .

The Sikh took aim. The hint was enough. They all squatted down on their haunches, hushed and still, like waters ebbing before the flood.

Six

"You and your pity!" the Consul shouted. "Your damned, obnoxious, detestable pity! Call it what you please: world brotherhood, charity, conscience... I take one look at you, each and every one of you, and all I see is contempt for yourselves and all you stand for. Do you know what it means? Can't you see where it's leading? You've got to be crazy. Crazy or desperate. You've got to be out of your minds just to sit back and let it all happen, little by little. All because of your pity. Your insipid, insufferable pity!"

The Consul was sitting behind his desk, a bandage on his forehead. Across from him, some ten or so figures sat rooted to wooden chairs, like apostles carved in stone on a church façade. Each of the statues had the same white skin, the same gaunt face, the same simple dress —long duck pants or shorts, half-sleeve khaki shirt, open sandals— and most of all the same deep, unsettling gaze that shines in the eyes of prophets, philanthropists, seers, fanatics, criminal geniuses, martyrs—weird and wondrous folk of every stripe—those split-personality creatures who feel out of place in the flesh they were born with. One was a bishop, but unless you already knew, it was quite impossible to tell him apart from the missionary doctor or the starry-eyed layman by his side. Just as impossible to single out the atheist philosopher and the renegade Catholic writer, convert to Buddhism, both spiritual leaders of the little band... They all just sat there without a word.

"The trouble is," the Consul continued, "you've gone too far! And on purpose! Because you're so convinced it's the right thing to do. Have you any idea how many children from the Ganges here have been shipped off to Belgium? Not to mention the rest of Europe, and those other sane countries that closed their borders off before we did! Forty thousand, that's how many! Forty thousand in five years! And all of you, so sure you could count on our people. Playing on their sentiments, their sympathy. Perverting their minds with vague feelings of self-reproach, to twist their Christian charity to your own bizarre ends. Weighing our good, solid burghers down with a sense of shame and guilt.... Forty thousand! Why, there weren't even that many French in Canada back in the seventeen-hundreds.... And in

25

two-faced times like these, you can bet the government won't admit what's really behind that racist decree. . . . Yes, racist, that's what I called it. You loathe the word, don't you? You've gone and worked up a race problem out of whole cloth, right in the heart of the white world, just to destroy it. That's what you're after. You want to destroy our world, our whole way of life. There's not one of you proud of his skin, and all that it stands for . . ."

"Not proud, or aware of it, either," one of the statues corrected. "That's the price we have to pay for the brotherhood of man. We're happy to pay it."

"Yes, well, we've gone beyond that now," said the Consul. "Adoption isn't the issue anymore, discontinued or otherwise. I've been on the phone with my colleagues in all the Western consulates. They tell me it's just the same. Great crowds outside, milling around, quiet, as if they're waiting for something to happen. And mind you, none of the others have decrees on their gates. Besides, look at the English. Their visas were like hens' teeth, but that hasn't kept ten thousand people from squatting in the gardens outside their consulate. It's the same all over the city. Wherever a Western flag is flying, there's a crowd out there, waiting. Just waiting. And that's not all. I've just heard that back in the hinterlands whole villages are swarming out onto the roads to Calcutta."

"Very true," said another of the statues, his face trimmed with long blond whiskers. "They're the villages we've been working with, mainly."

"Well, if you know them, what on earth do they want? What are they waiting for?"

"Frankly, we're not quite sure."

"Do you have an idea?"

"Perhaps."

The bearded statue's lips broke out in a curious smile. Was it the bishop? The renegade writer?

"You mean you had the nerve . . ." the Consul began, leaving his question and thought in the air. "No! I don't believe it! You wouldn't go that far!"

"Quite so," said a third statue—the bishop this time, in the flesh— "I wouldn't have gone that far myself . . ."

"Are you saying you've lost control?"

"I'm afraid we have. But it doesn't matter. Most of us are glad to go along. You're right. There is something brewing, and it's going to be tremendous. The crowds can feel it, even if they have no notion what it's all about. Myself, I have one explanation. Instead of the piecemeal adoptions that these poor folk have hoped for and lived for, perhaps now they're hoping and living for something much bigger, something wild and impossible, like a kind of adoption en masse. In a country like this that's all it would take to push a movement beyond the point of no return."

"Nice work, Your Grace," the Consul retorted, simply. "A lovely job for a bishop of the Roman Catholic Church! Mercenary, hireling to the pagans, all of a sudden! What is this, the Crusades in reverse? Judas leaping up on Peter the Hermit's nag, and crying, 'Down with Jerusalem!'? . . . Well, you chose a good time. There's no shortage of poor. There are millions and millions! The year isn't three months old, and already half of this province alone is starving. And the government won't do a thing. They've had it. Whatever happens now, they're going to wash their hands. That's what every consul in the city heard this morning. And what have you all been doing in the meantime? You've been 'bearing witness.' Isn't that what you call it? . . . Bearing witness to what? To your faith? Your religion? To your Christian civilization? Oh no, none of that! Bearing witness against yourselves, like the anti-Western cynics you've all become. Do you think the poor devils that flock to your side aren't any the wiser? Nonsense! They see right through you. For them, white skin means weak convictions. They know how weak yours are, they know you've given in. You can thank yourselves for that. The one thing your struggle for their souls has left them is the knowledge that the West —your West—is rich. To them, you're the symbols of abundance. By your presence alone, they see that it does exist somewhere, and they see that your conscience hurts you for keeping it all to yourselves. You can dress up in rags and pretend to be poor, eat handfuls of curry to your hearts' content. You can spread your acolytes far and wide, let them live like the peasants and dispense their wise advice. . . . It's no use, they'll always envy you, no matter how you try. You know I'm right. After all your help—all the seeds, and drugs, and technology —they found it so much simpler just to say, 'Here's my son, here's my daughter. Take them. Take me. Take us all to your country.' And the idea caught on. You thought it was fine. You encouraged it, organized it. But now it's too big, now it's out of your hands. It's a flood. A deluge. And it's out of control. . . . Well, thank God we still have an ocean between us!"

"Yes, an ocean. We do have an ocean," a fourth statue observed, lost in reflection at the obvious thought.

"You know," the Consul went on, "there's a very old word that describes the kind of men you are. It's 'traitor.' That's all, you're nothing new. There have been all kinds. We've had bishop traitors, knight traitors, general traitors, statesman traitors, scholar traitors, and just plain traitors. It's a species the West abounds in, and it seems to get richer and richer the smaller it grows. Funny, you would think it should be the other way around. But the mind decays, the spirit warps. And the traitors keep coming. Since that day in 1522, the twelfth of October, when that noble knight Andréa d'Amaral, your patron saint, threw open the gates of Rhodes to the Turks . . . Well, that's how it is, and no one can change it. I can't, I'm sure. But I can tell you this: I may be wrong about your results, but I find your actions beneath contempt. Gentlemen, your passports will not be renewed. That's the one official way I can still show you how I feel. And my Western colleagues are doing the same with any of their nationals involved."

One of the statues stood up. The one who had mused about the ocean. He was, in fact, the atheist philosopher, known in the West by the name of Ballan.

"Passports, countries, religions, ideals, races, borders, oceans . . ." Ballan shouted. "What bloody rubbish!"

And he left the room without another word.

"At any rate," the Consul said, "I suppose I should thank you for hearing me out. I imagine I've seen the last of you all. That's probably why you've been so patient. I'm nothing now as far as you're concerned. Just a relic, a dying breed . . ."

"Not quite," replied the bishop. "We'll both be relics together, only on different sides, that's all. You see, I'll never leave India."

Outside the consulate gates, Ballan elbowed his way through the crowd, through the crush of monster children—the most monstrous of the lot—clinging to his legs, drooling on his trousers. Ballan held a strange fascination for the monsters, the same fascination they held for him. He reached into his pockets, always filled with sticky sweets, and stuffed their shapeless mouths. Then he noticed the giant, the turd eater, standing there still topped with his hideous totem. And Ballan called out:

"What are you doing here, dung man? What do you want?"

"Please, take us with you. Please . . ."

"Today's the day, my friend. We'll both be in paradise, you and I."

"Today?" the poor man repeated, bewildered.

And Ballan smiled a compassionate smile.

Could that be one explanation? . . .

Seven

"... in the four departments bordering the coast, under the command of the undersecretary, Monsieur Jean Perret, personal representative of the President of the Republic. The army will make every effort to protect all property left behind, insofar as its other duties permit. Government sources confirm that the President of the Republic will address the nation at midnight, tonight, with a message of grave concern ..."

The ones who knew French turned down their radios and translated the announcement for the horde of compatriots piled on all sides. The cellar had never seemed nearly so full as it did that night. It housed the black rubbish men of the northern wards of Paris. With all of them crammed in together, eight to a double-deck bed, legs dangling over the edges, there was a feeling of solidity and strength that even they themselves had never noticed. Oddly enough for such talkative types, no one dared risk a word, not even the handful of whites that were part of the vast mass of black, among them one of those ragtag priests and a militant tough at war with the social order. Everyone was thinking, straining his mind to the utmost. It's not easy to conceive the dizzying dimensions of something so unbelievable when you live in a strange city, down some godforsaken cellar, and the only time you get out is first thing every dismal morning, to pick up the rubbish along nameless streets.

"And if they manage to land in one piece, what then?" asked one of them, the one they called "the Chief," since he had lived in France for quite some time. "What if they land, will all of you climb up out of your rat holes too?"

The only reply was a long, meaningless murmur. None of those underfed brains worked fast enough to picture the possible chain of events. But something was building up inside, something slow to take shape, but powerful and solemn all the same. Then, from the dark recesses of one of the bunks, a voice boomed out:

"All depends. Will there be enough rats?"

"By daylight," the ragtag priest replied, "they'll be thick as the trees in a giant forest, sprung up overnight in the darkness."

That much they understood, and the murmur rippled with approval. Then they sat back, ready to wait ...

There were others waiting too that night: the swill men, sewer men, sweepers from all the dumps the length and breadth of Paris; the peons and bedpan pushers from all the hospitals; the dishwashers from the shabby cafés; the laborers from Billancourt and Javel, from Saint-Denis and beyond; the swivel-hipped menials digging their pits around gas pipes and cables; the fodder for industry's lethal chores; the machinery feeders, the Métro troglodytes, black crabs with ticket-punching claws; the stinking drudges who mucked around in filth; and the myriad more, embodiments all of the hundreds of essential jobs that the French had let slip through their delicate fingers; plus the ones who were coughing their lungs out in clinics, and the ones with a healthy dose in the syphilis wards. All in all, a few hundred thousand Arabs and blacks, invisible somehow to the ostrich Parisians, and far more numerous than anyone would think, since the powers that be had doctored the statistics, afraid of jolting the sleep-walking city too violently out of its untroubled trance. Paris was no New York. They waited now the same meek way they lived, over-looked and unknown, in virtual terror, whole tribes of fellow suffer-ers hiding away in the depths of their cellars or huddling together up under the eaves, happy to shut themselves off in infested streets, where grimy façades hid unsuspected ghettos as wholly unknown to the people of Paris as Ravensbruck and Dachau, once upon a time, had been to the Germans.

It was only among the Arabs that the thought of the unlikely confrontation brewing off the southern coast of France would occa-sionally take a vengeful turn. Nothing too concrete yet, only shadowy yearnings and suppressed desires, like the wish to see a French-woman smile, rather than dreaming of having to rape her; or being able to get yourself a pretty whore, instead of hearing her tell you, "I don't go to bed with dirty Arabs"; or just being able to take a carefree walk through the park, and not suddenly see all the terrified females cluster around to protect their young, like mother hens ready to pounce. That evening, only the most fanatic envisioned a new kind of holy war, and one that wasn't even theirs to wage. Still, in no time at all, the Algerian quarters all through Paris and the suburbs had been zoned off again into sectors. A certain Mohammed, the one called "Cadi One-Eye," appeared to be in supreme com-mand. By eleven that night he had managed to pass his first orders down the line to all the sector chiefs:

"The time for violence is over. Have them put away their razors, have them break their knives in two. The first one I hear of who spills any blood, I'll see that he's castrated."

He was an Arab, and he knew how to talk to Arabs. And so they all obeyed him. Except, that is, for his schoolteacher wife, who was white and French. Indeed, his own razor was quick to disappear. It was hidden inside her right stocking, flat against the thigh. Élise had known what contempt was like. For all ten years of her married life, not one of its subtle barbs had escaped her. She cherished a dream of redemption by blood, and she wasn't alone. Of all the French wives of ghetto Arabs—a scant thousand, perhaps—not a few had felt that burden of contempt. Among the Arabs, unlike the blacks, they were the only Western intruders. The clan loathed the stranger more as friend than foe; and if it accepted these Christian wives at all, it was only because it had swallowed them up, only because they belonged to it utterly, sex and soul, even more than Frenchwomen do to their Frenchmen . . .

There were some, though, who had a clear notion of just what a crucial struggle the next day would bring. They had closed their shutters, barred their doors, drawn the drapes in their rooms and offices, and sat clustered in silence around their radios, eager for news, waiting like everyone else for the promised address by the President of the Republic. They were the Third World diplomats and students—Africans, Arabs, Asians. On the verge of panic, with nowhere to turn, they had even stopped calling back and forth between their embassies, between their homes, so suddenly crushed by the turn of events, that they—the rich, the select, the leaders, the militant elite—no longer even bothered to keep abreast of each other. Which was all the stranger since, during the fifty days of the fleet's dramatic odyssey over two oceans, they had been consumed in a frenzy of thoughtful reflection, issuing endless communiqués, holding press conferences, interviews, meetings, debates, one after the other, while the fleet pressed on and on, a mixture of fact and myth, a phenomenon so untoward that people would have to see it before they believed it. Then Gibraltar, finally, and see it they did! And suddenly all those eager devotees stopped wagging their tongues, their zeal turned to panic, and some—if the dark truth be known—had to hold back a flood of hate at the brink.

Closed, now, the West Indian bars, the Chinese restaurants, the African dance halls, the Arab cafés. In the light of other reports—from embassy guards, from worker and student informers—these signs all tended to kill any lingering doubts the police might have that the situation in Paris, eight hundred kilometers from the refugee fleet, was as grave as it was along the southern coast. Yes, a state of emergency should be declared here too, with the whole array of preventive measures, while they still had time. . . . The prefect of police called the Élysée Palace. He tried to get through to the Minister of the Interior. But all he was told was that the meeting was still in progress. . . . Three-quarters of an hour to go before the address, and the government still hadn't made up its mind! The prefect, too, assumed that all he could do now was wait.

Could that be one explanation? . . .

Eight

Ballan's smile had worked a miracle. Often a man needs nothing
more to help him discover himself, praise the Lord! And Ballan,
indeed, proceeded to praise Him. Though with jibe and jest, which
was his particular way of being an atheist. "I tell you, God," he said
to himself, "if you've had to listen to that dung man's harangue the
way I have for the last three days, you must be kicking yourself for
letting one smile from me turn him into such a talker! Just listen to
that shit roller carry on, will you! A thousand years of poverty and
degradation! All for what? To produce the most prodigious dema-
gogue this country has ever seen rise up from the masses. I don't
know if you're pleased with your miracle, God. All I can say is, it was
bound to happen. Can a man spend his whole life grubbing for turds
in all the slop pots along the Ganges, shaping them, rolling them
between his fingers, day after day, and not know something about the
true nature of man? He knew all there was to know. He just never
knew that he knew, that's all. Now he knows. And you and I know
where he's leading us, don't we! . . . Seriously, God, is all this your
idea? Well, even if it is, I'm still going to wait and see how it ends
before you convince me. But I will say this much: it would certainly
be your first clear-headed, clear-cut proof that you really exist . . ."
Down under the pier, the river was teeming with corpses, floating
among the wooden pilings, and their saris, flowing free, spread the
black waters with a carpet of light. A few were still struggling, but
most of them had already drowned, quite dead, some since that
morning, some since the night before, or the morning before, drop-
ping like so much excess fruit from some prolific tree. . . . All at once
a young girl fell. A dark-skinned goddess. She fell without a murmur,
feet first, her bare arms, ringed with gold, straight by her sides, and
the Ganges' gelatinous waters opened without a sound to let her
through. A moment later an old man fell, naked, all bones, and he
sank to the bottom; then a baby, wriggling and squirming like an
animal that knows it's about to die; then a pair of children, clasped
in tight embrace. Up above, no one bent down or held out a hand.
Why bother? The ones who were pushed to the edge knew only too
well that their turn would come, that they too would fall, pressed on

by the huge throngs swarming through the port, on every dock; and their plunge to the watery deep held no meaning of death, but rather of life, as they felt themselves drawn on, at last, by a resistless force that nothing could possibly stop. On the pier, the turd eater, perched on a low, flat cart, was speaking his piece, with the monster totem still on his shoulders, stiff as a pike. But, believe it or not, the monster's eyes had begun to shine! And his gaze grew so intense as this latter-day Christopher spoke, that no one in the crowd looked at anything else. They all stood there, drinking it in. And every soul, in the light of that gaze, was filled with sacred fire at the awesome account:

"Buddha and Allah . . ." They groaned. ". . . and Siva, Vishnu, Garuda, Ganesha, Krishna, Parvati, Indra, Durga, Surya, Bhairava, Ravana, Kali . . ." The whole Hindu pantheon passed in review, and each droned name drew wails of ecstasy. ". . . all met together, once upon a time, and went to visit the nice little god of the Christians. They pulled out the nails, took him down from his cross. They mopped his brow, soothed him with their holy balms. And when he was healed, they sat him in their midst, gave a little nod, and said, 'You owe us your life. Now what are you going to give us in return?' "

"Even the pope isn't that ecumenical!" Ballan observed, as he listened, enthralled. "This shit picker beats the Christians at their own game. Ecumenism, all right, but planet-wide!"

"And so," the turd eater continued, "the nice little god, off his cross, rubbed the feeling back into his arms and legs, shook them, twisted his neck a few times in every direction, and said, 'That's true. I owe you my life, and I'm going to give you my kingdom in return. Now the thousand years are ended. The nations are rising from the four corners of the earth, and their number is like the sand of the sea. They will march up over the broad earth and surround the camp of the saints and the beloved city . . .' "

There was a pause. The monster's eyes grew dim. The turd eater suddenly seemed disturbed. He began to jerk and twitch. "Incredible!" Ballan thought. "Who would believe it? Apocalypse, chapter twenty, seven through nine. A few changes here and there, but plain enough . . . Now he's all shaken up, poor bastard! The rest just won't come. Or maybe he's trying to fight it back. . . . Yes, that's it. Good for him!"

The monster's eyes lit up like a beacon, a sign that the pause was over. "That's what the nice little god of the Christians told them . . ."

"Whew!" Ballan exclaimed. "That was close! Do you know how the rest of it goes, God? Do you? . . . Well, let me remind you: 'And fire from God came down out of heaven and devoured them. And the devil who deceived them was cast into the pool of fire and brimstone, where are also the beast and the false prophet . . .' Of course you know how it goes. You knew it all the time, but you kept it to yourself. Right, God? Disgusting! You just don't have the old faith anymore . . ."

There, on the docks by the Ganges, in a silence that defied belief —when you consider that five hundred thousand souls were already massed by the water's edge, and that every road to the port was submerged beneath a human flood—the turd eater took up his inspired narration:

"Yes, that's what he told them. Then Allah and Buddha, and Siva, Kali, Vishnu, Krishna . . . pulled him into a circle around the empty cross. And everyone went to work. With the pieces of the cross, they built themselves a boat, a big one. One that could sail the seas and cross the great oceans. A boat as big as the *India Star*. Then they gathered together their necklaces and diadems, their bracelets and rings, and they said to the captain, 'It's only right that we should pay you. Here, take all this. You've traveled the world up and down. Come, show us the way to paradise . . .' And so the boat put out to sea, with thousands more behind it. But the nice little god of the Christians was left on shore, running back and forth on his clumsy white legs, crying: 'And me? And me? Why have you forsaken me?' And Buddha and Allah called back to him through their megaphones, and the wind brought him their reply: 'You gave us your kingdom. Now the time is past when you can give with one hand and take back with the other. But if you really are the son of God, then come, walk on the water and join us.' The nice little god walked into the water, brave as could be. When the waves came up to his mouth and his eyes, he drowned. And no one heard tell of him much anymore, except in a holy book that no one paid any attention to after that. . . . And so the trip went on. It was long and filled with danger. Everyone on board was hungry. Even Allah and Buddha, and Siva, Kali, Vishnu . . . and all the folk who had joined them. Many, many died along the way, and others were born to take their place. . . . But in time the sun stopped burning hot, the air grew mild and gentle, and the Western paradise appeared, spread out before them with its streams of milk and honey, its rivers thick with fish, its fields fairly bursting with crops, far as the eye could see, growing wild for the taking. And not a soul was there, not a living soul. Which really wasn't surprising, after all, since the nice little god of the Christians was dead. . . . And so the monster children began to dance on the deck of the *India Star*, and the people sang and sang, all through the night. We were finally there! . . ."

A shout burst out that sounded like a cry of victory. Ballan looked up. On the totem's utterly motionless face, he glimpsed that flap of flesh that passed for a mouth, as it opened and shut. At that providential sign, the crowd began to stir. Could that be one explanation? . . .

And that was how the first of the ships, the *India Star*, came to be boarded.

Nine

The *India Star*, moored at her berth for over a year, was a sixty-year-old steamer, veteran of the India mail run back under the British. Old as she was, she had stood up fairly well to the early rigors of independence. But all too soon she had found herself consigned to hauling human wrecks displaced by the partition; and later, worst of all, wretched pilgrims on their way to Mecca. Of her five stacks, straight up, like pipes, four were lopped off at different levels, by time, by rust, by lack of care, by chance. . . . In such a state she hardly seemed fit for anything but one final act of heroic desperation. Perhaps that was what the captain had in mind when he ordered his tattered crew to put the rotting gangplanks down again, the same ones he had had them pull in just three days before, when the crowd seemed about to swell to precarious size.

Actually, the captain's action would be quite hard to fathom, were it not for the strong likelihood that someone had put the idea in his head. As a matter of fact, Ballan had managed to steal on board the night before, with no particular end in mind, but just for a first-hand look at the strangely fortuitous conditions and the chain of inexorable events that seemed to be forming. And he wasn't alone. Several others had had the same idea: to wit, a group of nameless Indians, whites, and a Chinaman, experts one and all in mob psychology. They were the movers, the undercover force. Acting on pure intuition, they knew precisely what to do. One of them stationed himself on the bridge, persuasive grenade in hand, while the others proceeded to question the captain. Just how much would it take—coal, water, supplies, the barest essentials—to make the trip to Europe?

"And back?" the captain had asked. "That is, if she'll make it . . ."

"We won't be coming back," the one with the grenade had replied.

It was then that Ballan had arrived on the scene. And although he was a stranger to their persons and their plans, they all understood one another at once, like a chosen few admitted to the mysteries. But what mysteries were they, and how had they been chosen? . . .

Spontaneous though they may seem, mass movements seldom occur without a certain degree of manipulation. That being the case, one is quick to picture a kind of almighty conductor, a great manipulator in chief, pulling thousands of strings the world over, and aided here and there by gifted soloists. Nothing could be further from the truth. What happens is that, in this world of warped senses, certain creatures of outstanding mind—for good or ill—begin to stir, to look for a way to fight off uncertainty, a way to escape from a human condition whose age-old persistence they refuse to accept. Unsure of what lies beyond, they plunge headlong all the same, in a wild flight into the future, burning their bridges of sober reflection behind them. Each one pulls the strings to the lobes of his brain. But here, precisely, is today's great mystery: all of those strings, independent of each other, are nonetheless bound up together, and stem from one selfsame current of thought. The world is controlled, so it seems, not by a single specific conductor, but by a new apocalyptic beast, a kind of anonymous, omnipresent monster, and one that, in some primordial time, must have vowed to destroy the Western World. The beast has no set plan. It seizes whatever occasions arise. The crowd massed along the Ganges was merely the latest, and doubtless the one with the richest potential. Divine in origin, this beast? Or infernal, more likely? Be that as it may, the phenomenon, hard to believe, is a good two centuries old. Dostoevski analyzed it once upon a time. And Péguy too, though in different form, when he railed against the "intellectual clique." And even one of our former popes, Paul VI, toward the end of his reign, as he opened his eyes and discerned, at long last, the work of the Devil . . . Nothing can stop the beast. That much we all know. Which is probably why the chosen few have such faith that their ideas will triumph, and why the ones who persist in the struggle know only too well how futile it is . . .

Fallen archangel that he was, Ballan knew the lackeys of the beast on sight, and put himself at their disposal. That too is an explanation. And he offered the dung man and his hideous son to their cause. In three days their power over the hordes had reached such heights that the vertical pair, together, had become the crusade's unchallenged leader. Ballan was quite content just to follow along and listen, whispering a practical thought in the turd eater's ear from time to time, between two volleys, and hearing him work them into the epic account with incredible speed and skill . . .

"They'll take over the *India Star* first thing tomorrow," the Chinaman had said. "They're ready, but they don't see it yet. All we need is to find the right idea to open their eyes . . ."

"We'll have to pay for the coal and provisions," the Indians had added. "But our women still have a few jewels, even the poorest. And even our lowliest brothers have a rupee or two put aside for the gods. A pittance, to be sure. But multiply a pittance by a thousand times a thousand, and you have enough coal, and rice, and water to take you to Europe. They're ready, but we have to find the right idea . . ."

"Leave the idea to me," Ballan had answered.

Later, he couldn't remember if he really had put the idea in his head, or if the turd eater had read his mind. An illiterate Hindu pariah who can quote from Apocalypse, transform the Gospels, fabricate legend to inspire an event, could probably read the mind of the likes of Ballan too. . . . He had said: ". . . then they gathered together their necklaces and diadems, their bracelets and rings, and they said to the captain, 'It's only right that we should pay you. Here, take all this. You've traveled the world up and down. Come, show us the way to paradise . . .' " And the first collection had begun even before his tale was over. Gourd bowls in hand, the totem's monster minions wormed their way through the crowd. These wretches, more used to taunts and blows than to alms and compassion, these beggars with their ever-empty bowls, hands open onto the void, now found themselves pouring out piles of treasure at the prophet's feet, then trotting back on their twisted legs for more, as the crowd kept calling, "Over here! Over here!" In no time, once it was started, the money changers had the affair in hand. They set up impromptu networks, organized an army of collectors. Most incredible of all, the crowd didn't even distrust them! At the sight of the gold and rupees heaped up like the sand in a giant hourglass, everyone saw himself playing a part in the legend. And when the turd eater pictured the fleet of the gods at the gates of the West, and described the people singing on the deck of the *India Star,* they all turned and looked at the *India Star,* and reached out their arms to paradise.

Ten

The turd eater went on board before all the rest. As the monster totem's rigid head traced its wake through the crowd, like a periscope poking up out of the water, they all fell still. The silence spread out from the dock in a wave, rolling on past the harbor, as far as the innermost streets of the quarter, where the hordes kept coming to join the swelling numbers. First the monster's head stood out against the side of the ship. Then his father's. And everyone could gaze at the symbolic pair slowly climbing up the gangplank. For the ones on the edge of the swarm—and those, even farther away, who couldn't see a thing, but who heard the description passed back to the outer reaches from mouth to mouth—the prophet's ascent became a god's ascension. Now no one could doubt that the enterprise must be divine. No one, that is, but the little commando bands, instigators all, who at that very moment were visiting the other ships in port, as well as every other port along the Ganges. Atheist though he was, Ballan himself began to have some second thoughts as he heard the sudden clamor rise out of the crowd. Up on the bridge of the *India Star*, the turd eater lifted his hands toward the sky. He grasped his son by his two twisted stumps, and when he raised him high in the air with a signal-like flourish, each soul in the numberless mass thought he heard himself summoned by name.

The rush that followed was peaceful enough, but it took its toll of dead: expendable dross on the fringe of the surging tide . . . The monster children had no trouble boarding. They were passed from hand to hand, over the heads of the crowd. But time and again the narrow, teeming gangplanks spilled over like brimming gutters into the pitch-black water between ship and pier. And many a soul sank down beneath the wooden pilings, to join those others who had gone before, the first to win the newfound paradise. Ballan was one. As the milling crowd picked up the monsters thronging about him, mouths still sticky from gorging on his sweets, he had tried to follow. But he kept falling farther and farther behind. And as he did, a link seemed to snap, that bond of flesh that had bound them to him. Now, suddenly, Ballan was just another white, spurned on all sides by those who knew him and those who didn't. He struggled to force his way into the torrent of bodies streaming up one of the gangplanks. But the torrent became a wall, a glass-chipped wall bristling with arms, and fists, and claws, and menacing teeth. . . . Ballan grasped at saris, clung to legs, felt his grip shaken loose. A pounding fist shut one of his eyes. Blood streamed down his mangled face and into his mouth. And all at once he clearly heard his lips pronounce these words:

"Forgive them, Lord, for they know not what they do."

So saying, he opened his fingers, let go of the soft, smooth calf he was clutching, and fell from the gangplank, halfway up, carrying off in his hand the feel of an alien flesh. His end was quick. As he sank down into the murky water, he realized how much he loved and missed the West. And that last awareness, that utter rejection of all he had stood for, so pained and distressed him, that he opened a willing mouth and took himself a healthy gulp of death.

Eleven

On that day and the days that followed, in all the ports along the Ganges, a hundred ships were stormed in the very same way, and not without a certain collusion by captains and crews. The turd eater had only to appear before the crowd and speak. On more than one occasion, local police had reported him standing on the bridges of two ships at once, which would tend to prove that even they were the victims of mob hysteria. To tell the truth, the human tide had swept this frenzied city clean of every vestige of authority. When one crack regiment, in fact, was ordered to shut off all roads to the port, the soldiers replied by throwing their rifles into the Ganges, and lost themselves deep in the crowd. The government wouldn't have risked even that token gesture if not for the pressure that all the Western consuls had brought to bear. Soon afterwards, the ministers holed themselves up, way out in their villas, and every department chief seemed to vanish from sight. All but one, that is, the head of Information, whom the Belgian consul, dean of the corps, managed to reach by telephone, one last time, before he too disappeared. That high official, a man of taste and breeding, seemed strangely composed, as if this assault on the Western World were as normal a thing as could be:

"Look here, my friend. Why cling to the hope that my government still has some say in all this? What's happening out on those docks is the fringe of the problem, the part we can see. Like the lava that shoots up out of the crater. Or the wave that breaks on the beach . . . Yes, that's what it is, a wave, with another one rolling behind it, and one behind that, and another, and another. And so on, out to sea, back to the storm that's the cause of it all. This mob of poor devils attacking the ships is just the first wave. You've seen their kind before. Their misery is nothing new, it doesn't upset you. But what about the second wave, the one right behind? Would it shock you to learn that thousands more are on the move? Half the country, in fact. Young ones, handsome ones, the ones that haven't even begun to starve . . . The second wave, my friend. The beautiful creatures. God's perfect specimens, these people of ours. Like statues, in all their naked glory, out of our temples and onto the road, streaming toward the port. Yes, ugliness bowing to beauty at last ... And behind them, the third wave, fear. And the fourth wave, famine. Two months, my friend, and five million dead already! ... Then the wave we call flood, stripping the country, destroying the crops, laying waste the land for five long years. And another one, off in the distance, the wave of war. More famine in its wake, more millions dead. And another, still nearer the storm, the wave of shame. The shame of those days when the West was master of our land ... But through it all, through wave after wave, these people of ours, rubbing bellies for all they're worth, to their bodies' and souls' content, to bring more millions into the world to die ... Yes, that's where it all begins. That's the eye of the storm, no matter how it's hidden. And you know, it's really not a storm at all, but a great, triumphant surge of life. . . . . There's no Third World. No, not anymore. That's only a phrase you coined to keep us in our place. There's one world, only one, and it's going to be flooded with life, submerged. This country of mine is a roaring river. A river of sperm. Now, all of a sudden, it's shifting course, my friend, and heading west . . ."

As he held the phone, the Consul's hand was so close to his nose that he gave it a quick, unthinking sniff. And he thought of those many times—press conferences, cocktails, and such—when this same official would shake his hand and steep his palm and fingers in a heavy scent, so stubborn that it took three days and twenty scrubbings with a good strong soap to wash it out. "The stink of the East!" the Consul would murmur to himself as he rubbed his hands under the tap. And he used to wonder if, just at that moment, his counterpart too wasn't washing his hands for the twentieth time, and thinking, "Good God, the stink of the West!"

"May I ask you something, my friend?" the Consul interjected. "What kind of cologne do you use?"

The official let out a surprised little gasp. Then something of a laugh, as if he had caught the meaning behind the question. And he had, in fact, subtle mind that he was.

"Do you really think that's a burning issue at a time like this, my friend?"

"Frankly," the Consul laughed back, "at the moment I can't think of any more burning."

"In that case, I'll tell you. I never use cologne. None at all ... And you, if you don't mind my asking?"

"I don't either. None at all."

"I thought as much."

"I thought so too," the Consul replied.

Their laughter subsided. For a moment there was silence. Then the Consul continued:

"Well now, there's a good solid fact I can wire my government. Uncoded, of course! It should satisfy their frantic need to know what's going on here, and why. Aside from that, though, there's not too much point to our chat, I'm afraid. Not that I really expected there would be. As always, you've tried to explain away that congenital habit you people have of closing your eyes . . . Oh, you're a bright, clever man, I'm sure. Your whole country is bursting with bright, clever men. Men who knew what was going to happen. Your nice little speech laid it all out pat: the famines, wars, floods, epidemics, the mighty myths and superstitions, the population growing by leaps and bounds . . . No need for a computer to predict the future here —though you people do have computers, I'm sure. . . . Oh no, you knew! You saw all those waves that you described so well. You knew they were coming! And what did you do? Not a thing!"

"Now, now, you're just being nasty!" the official interrupted. "But I don't mind, I understand. You're getting a taste of fear, that's all. Yes, fear—you bright, clever man! Well, five minutes more and I'll hang up the phone, and that will be that. Then you can go shift for yourself, my friend, with your precious Western future behind you. Nobody here will give a good goddamn—myself, any more than our outcast scum! And I'll thumb my nose good-bye, if you want to know, even though I can't see you. If my government still cared, that's one thing I'd be sure to tell them. It would be the neatest way to wrap up the whole affair. . . . You say we didn't do a thing? And what about you? God knows, we begged you for help, but that wasn't enough! You wanted to see us fall at your feet, you wanted to make us grovel. Besides, you couldn't have stopped it. The world had plenty of warning. . . . Your part of the world, that is. The only part that mattered . . . All those times, wherever they had me stationed—London, Paris —those times I'd be sitting over a drink with friends, and have to watch your television screens and see my own people dying! Or open your high-class papers and read the reporters who knew what was going on, but didn't let it spoil their dinner or keep them up at night. With headlines like: 'Affluent Nations' Conscience Unmoved by Third World Plight . . . Western and UN Aid Falling Far Short . . . Future of Third World Seen at Stake . . .' You people all know how to read. You're not deaf. You've heard the same tune for ten years now, in every key. But only from all your bleeding hearts, and plenty of them at that. So what did you do? You treated your conscience to a dose of guilt and then prayed to someone or other that things would stay the way they were as long as they could. That's where you went wrong. You should have held fast to your Western contempt. It might have steeled you against disaster. Because that's what's brewing for you now, my friend, and you can't do a thing about it. When all is said and done, it will serve you right, and no one will stand up and fight it. Not even your own. Which just goes to show what a decadent lot you really are."

"My conscience is clear," the Consul replied. "No guilt, I assure you. And no contempt either. I won't deny a few pangs of fear, but fear is the only emotion this country of yours has ever made me feel. That's why I'm going to rout it out by doing my duty, pure and simple. Will I see you at the docks?"

"My good man, you must be joking . . ."

It wasn't a joking matter, but the conversation did break off, in fact, with a kind of laugh. From that moment on, until the fleet was about to set sail, every last official from around the Ganges seemed to dissolve and disappear in silence.

Twelve

Later, when the world learned that the fleet had sailed, and heard the circumstances surrounding the Consul's death, not a single voice was raised to explain or defend his action. People talked about "Consul Himmans and his foolish heroics," but without the slightest concern for the little man trampled by the mob until he was nothing but a puddle of blood on the Ganges shore. The word "pathetic," which would have been far more fitting, never even so much as rose to the lips of the antiracists out beating the drum. Yes, the fleet was pathetic. The passengers were pathetic. But the Consul was foolish. One journalist, and only one, came close to the truth, and then on a sadly humorous note. His article was entitled: "Last Popgun Blast from a Dying Regime." It reviewed the major times that the West had sent its armies meddling in the lives of once-second-class nations, and traced its progressively weakening role down to that single symbolic shot from the Consul's rifle, fired in the name of a superiority that was no more.

In its outward appearance, at least, the Consul's heroic gesture was something of a prototype after the fact; an epitome, synthesis, conclusion all in one, as perfect and pure as the final creation of some terribly famous artist, who paints a single line on his canvas, or dabs one dot, and calls it his crowning achievement. The Consul, poor man, didn't know what a pose he had struck. He had looked for no models to follow. He had felt no epic grandeur in his soul, no taste for theatrics. And yet, his death was theater at its best. His army, for example, reduced to a single soldier—the faithful Sikh—was one of those comic theatrical symbols, the shabby, half-starved actor loping across the stage and awkwardly showing a sign with the words: "His Excellency the Western Consul's Troops." Worth noting, too, was the fact that the army in question respected the age-old tradition that, over the years, had cemented the power and might of the West beyond its borders: it was a native army, conditioned to abhor its own the way the white man's dog abhors the black's. More noteworthy still, the fact that this army—venal to the core, hired out to maintain the Western hold on a worldwide domain—was reduced to a single man. And so, with one soldier behind him, the Consul stepped for-

46

ward, a wizened figure in his English shorts, his half-sleeve shirt
flapping over a gaunt, gray chest, to confront a million flailing savages. Not that there really was, to be sure, in that crowd as we know
it, a single wildly flailing savage, but simply because in all the glorious
tales of Western conquerors—from Cortés and Pizarro to our own
Bournazel and his African exploits—the white man is pictured alone
(or almost), advancing against the unbridled, menacing hordes, and
putting them all to flight by his imposing presence. The charm,
however, had long since been broken. The poor little Consul looked
rather like a tired old magician, who knows that he's going to bungle
his trick, and does, but who tries it on the audience all the same, not
for his honor or anything of the sort, but because even a worn-out
magician deserves an orderly end, however absurd, just as a worn-out
hero of the Western World deserves to perform one last bizarre,
eccentric feat for the public that used to applaud him. Once admira-
tion gives way to disdain, the bizarre, after all, is the only way out
that makes much sense. And why not? Weren't jesters always clev-
erer than their kings? So be it. In this new swarthy reign, the white
man will be the jester. It's as simple as that . . .

High noon, and there by the docks the little Western Consul appeared, at the head of his army. To say that the army's morale was
low would be rather an understatement; it was catastrophic. The
army was in utter disarray. Its antique rifle trembled in time with its
panic. But careful to refrain from introspection, and strutting, puppet like, close behind its cadaverous, knobby-kneed commander, it
still caused enough of a stir—with its Belgian drill step, English style,
head high and vacant stare ("Whatever you do, never look at a
thing!")—that it made the crowd give way and let them through. The
mob was sizzling in the noonday sun, and the Consul sniffed. Then
he took a big white kerchief from his pocket and tied it around his
nose and mouth, like Marshal Bugeaud and his desert legionnaires.
No doubt this act of instinctive revulsion, quite unintended, struck
those up front as openly hostile. It was in that spirit that they described it to the ones behind them, who passed it down the line, and
into the heart of the crowd. In no time a murderous cry had gone up.
The army tightened ranks. That is to say, the Sikh guard tightened
his rump, and felt a cold sweat trickling down his thighs, as his gun
barrel trembled madly against a sky turned black with shaking fists.
The Consul struggled to push his way through the mass of flesh,
growing denser and denser, and managed to reach the pier. A big
ship sat at her moorings, almost as high as the *India Star.* Three

gangplanks connected her to land. Three teeming human anthills on the move. At the foot of one, with his back to the crowd and his face toward the sea, stood a mournful-looking white man, arms upraised.

"What are you doing here?" the Consul asked the bishop. "Do you think it's time for us relics to die? . . . On different sides, of course! . . ."

The bishop smiled and completed his blessing.

"You remind me of Christ," the Consul went on, "but a dead Christ at that. I've lost my job, but I'm willing to admit it. That's where we're different, you and I. You want to keep fooling yourself in the name of some meaningless God. A God that's in your head, and nowhere else . . . Well, take a good look at the rabble around us, then draw your own conclusions. You're nothing to them. Just a broken-down padre spreading a useless gospel. Whereas I . . . Well, at least for a moment they'll know I exist, and sooner than they think! . . . No, Your Grace, I'm afraid you're all alone. They don't have the vaguest idea what you're up to. But you go ahead and bless them all the same. That was what I saw you doing, wasn't it? You were actually giving that mob your blessing . . ."

"Quite so," said the bishop. "As prefect apostolic to the entire Ganges region, I'm wishing my flock a bon voyage, and praying for God's help to speed them on their way."

"What meaningless mumbo jumbo!" the Consul replied. "Bishop or not, you're still a simple priest at heart! Time was when bishops were born, not made, and priests were just priests. Now nobody draws any lines anymore, and it's all mixed up. . . . Really, who do you think will fall for such talk? A bishop for this Ganges scum! That's just what they needed! And you think God will bother to help the likes of them? Maybe yours, but not mine. I'm damn sure of that!"

The Sikh had turned a deathly green, twitching and squirming about, convulsed with fear. He looked toward the two men having their calm salon chat in the midst of the crowd, then pivoted around in a flash, like a tank's revolving turret in a slapstick film, his gun barrel grazing the wall of faces huddling thick about them. Then, completing his turn, he faced the Consul again, like a dervish whirling in a circle of fear, hoping that the next time around his master would finally listen:

"Consul Sahib! Please, let's go! They're not afraid of me anymore. They're almost on top of us. A few seconds, and they won't be afraid of you either. Then we'll never get out of here alive! Please, Consul Sahib! I've served your country all these years. Now save me! Please, for Heaven's sake, save me!"

"Is your rifle loaded?"

"No, Consul Sahib. What good would it do?"

"Well then, load it, you idiot!"

Shame on the Sikh guards, glory and pride of empires past! After four fruitless tries, the order was carried out, finally, by a warrior fallen from grace, beard and turban atremble, who looked like a drunkard struggling to find the keyhole with his key. It was then that the bishop replied to the Consul's remarks:

"God won't help them, you say? . . . Well, listen. He's doing just that! Impossible, but true. See? They're on their way!"

The whistle on the *India Star* gave out such a mournful wail that it would have brought a shudder to even the most mildly superstitious of captains. It was like the orgasmic groaning of some deaf-mute colossus, some giant in heat, unaware of the frenzy of sounds he was forcing from his throat. First a few short blasts, some high, some low. Then all of them blending into one immense gasp, each note of the scale scraping against the next without snuffing it out. The great organ pipe of the *India Star,* rusted through here and there in holes of various sizes, booming out the chant of its last divine office. After which, it proceeded to burst, just as the monster totem, up on the bridge, was closing his toothless mouth . . . The *Calcutta Star* sat at dockside—decayed, once-shining symbol of a decaying city. Her captain had draped himself in a kind of pilgrim cloak, but still had on his braided cap. He looked for all the world like a glove puppet, standing there on board, arms waving at the sailors hauling up the gangplanks. Two of them were up already. The Western Consul and his army had taken their positions at the foot of the third. At the top, a small patch of empty deck appeared to the waiting hordes on the pier quite able to hold them all. And so they began to edge forward, slowly at first, in a single, solid mass, like some gigantic beast with a million legs and a hundred heads, the closest of which was a handsome young man's, the picture of sublime inspiration, whose face seemed consumed by a pair of shining eyes, and who found himself suddenly barrel to brow with the Western artillery, such as it was.

"Fire!" the Consul ordered.

He had never used that word before in similar context, and it startled him a little to hear himself utter it now for the very first time. It was then, on the threshold of death, that the poor little man discovered the joy of personal contact with soldierly lore. . . . Fire! One more colony falls at your feet, Sir! Fire! Tahiti surrenders, run up the colors! Fire! The Sultan of Patakahuet implores the Republic's protection! Fire! Fire! Fire! The Arab rebel bastards bite the dust of the desert stockades. . . . We're a great and generous people, after all, but still . . . So ready, aim, fire! . . .

The Consul emerged from his daydream, jarred awake as the army drew back without a shot.

"What are you waiting for? Fire, you idiot!"

At which point the army deserted. It did so in the disarray of utter defeat, in its usual cowardly manner. Will God ever show us a conquering army turn tail and desert? No doubt, especially if the shabby lot that pretend to speak in His name ever get their way. . . . The Sikh thrust his rifle into the Consul's hands, and dove into the Ganges.

"You're not really going to shoot!" said the bishop.

"Oh yes I am! And I'm going to shoot to kill," said the Consul, leveling his gun at the doe-eyed multi-beast before him.

"But what on earth for?"

The Consul was staring right into the eyes of the handsome, dark young man at the end of his rifle. The crowd paused a moment before the final push.

"What do you want me to say?" the Consul answered. "For glory? Honor? Some principle or other? For Christian civilization, or nonsense like that? Well, not at all! I'm going to turn off those bright, shining eyes just for the pleasure it gives me! I have no brothers in this mob of Martians. They're nothing to me. And now, finally, I'm going to prove it!"

He fired. One of the beast's hundred heads disappeared, a bloody hole between its eyes. But it grew right back in the shape of a square, black face, with massive jaws and a hate-filled look. The Consul was thrown to the ground in a frenzy of blows. The bishop bent over his scrawny, prostrate form.

"In the name of the Lord, I forgive you," he said.

"In the name of the Lord, eat shit!" the Consul gasped.

Then the hundred heads plunged forward, as the surging beast, compressed within the confines of the gangplank, climbed on its thousands of legs to the deck of the *Calcutta Star.* Swept along in the tide, absorbed and digested, the bishop found himself lifted aboard and dropped down in place by the great human wave, alive but inert, like a shipwrecked sailor who, by some miracle, washes ashore on the sands of an unknown island. In that crushing welter of flesh, however, that horde exuding its mystic fervor through each of its pores, he had lost almost all sense of who and what he was. And when, in turn, the *Calcutta Star* sailed out of port, the bishop thought he saw, there on the deserted dock by the Ganges, a score of stray dogs lapping up a shining pool of blood, with a hundred others racing through the empty streets to join in the feast. "Really! Is that all that's left of the Consul?" he wondered—the only coherent idea that managed to muddle its way through his head. He even thought he saw one of the dogs spelling words in the blood with his tongue. But the ship was already out too far, and he couldn't read what they said, or even be sure that they really were words (though it seemed for a moment he could make out a few Latin syllables). For days on end he would sit transfixed on deck, in the stench of a yogi-style squat, racking his brain to the rhythmic swish of the water along the hull, trying to recall what his eyes had dimly seen. So doing, he soon took leave of his senses.

Thirteen

At the mouth of the Ganges, the delta's reddened waters paled abruptly as they emptied into the vast Gulf of Bengal, and the hundred ships of the refugee fleet steered a sluggish southwesterly course toward the Straits of Ceylon. The captains had agreed to limp feebly along for the sake of one moribund vessel, the shoddiest of the lot, a big river tugboat used to far calmer waters, the most pitiful cripple in this whole floating slum. Like the rest of her flat deck, her low-slung bow was piled white with pilgrims. With every wave it plunged into the water, paying the sea a ransom of surplus souls, carried off in the mists. A kind of pathetic Hop-o'-my-thumb, struggling to keep pace, and strewing a store of human pebbles over a path of no return. On the lead ship, the *India Star,* the captain's fancy cap had changed heads, and sat perched now on a bald, shapeless stump. Gold braid wreathed the monster's brow; the polished visor shaded his frozen gaze from the ocean sun, as he stood on board commanding the ship and, indeed, the whole fleet. He was like some oracle, consulted before any weighty decision, dispensing his orders. So long as someone could read the flash and flicker of his lidless eyes. In time it became quite clear that, more than once, the fleet owed much to those silent commands . . .

Some of the actors in the drama were soon to learn how superfluous they were. From the moment the *India Star* blew her very first blast, in fact. And it came as something of a shock. Ostracized, victims of racial hate or simple indifference—especially indifference—they found themselves prisoners unpenned, yet hemmed in by walls of human flesh deep in the mazes belowdecks, or stuck in some dark, stifling, cubby hole next to the engines. Forgotten outsiders, like captives won in battle, destined now only for the last triumphal march. A few helpless Chinese, and even some whites, squatting on their haunches, huddling together like primitive tribes, alone and hungry. Talking and talking, for a week on end . . . The event they had shared in, the event they were forced to sit idly by and watch, plunged them deep into raptures of reasoned delight, heightened no doubt by fatigue, and filled with each one's concept of a bright new world, like something from the glossy pages of any leftist weekly in the West. Experts one and all among themselves, always on the verge, despite their woeful state, of taking self-indulgent credit for their harangues, like satisfied signers of innocuous petitions, ready to bandy back and forth their names, their ideals, their principles—things that mean terribly little, really, when someone is wallowing down in a ship's dark hold. With no food to sink their teeth into, they chewed the West to shreds with words. Hunger was turning them mean. Already they saw it their mission to guide the flock's first steps on Western soil. One would empty out all our hospital beds so that cholera-ridden and leprous wretches could sprawl between their clean white sheets. Another would cram our brightest, cheeriest nurseries full of monster children. Another would preach unlimited sex, in the name of the one, single race of the future—"a simple matter," he added, "since unlike skins attract," which was something he claimed to know all about. Still another would turn our supermarkets over to the barefoot, swarthy horde: "Can't you see it now! Hundreds of thousands of women and children, smashing their way through those gigantic stores, stuffing their mouths with food, beside themselves with pleasure . . ."

Now and then one of those viperous tongues stopped wagging long enough to lick a few droplets of moisture condensed on the sheet-iron wall. "Nothing to drink, poor devils!" cried the renegade writer. "Well, decadent world, get ready to share your treasure! Your tubs will be filled to the brim, and the water boy, poor crook-necked bugger, will splash around to his heart's content, and maybe he'll even go out of his mind just thinking how heavy it all would be, hanging in buckets from a stick across his shoulders. And you know what? You'll have to knock at your door, your very own door, to beg for a glass of water!" So saying, he collapsed, not to be heard from again. By the ninth day they had all stopped talking, one by one: militants with a cause, lay missionaries, apostate priests, idealist quacks, activist thinkers, the whole brigade of antiworld thugs that had set sail with the fleet. Somehow they managed to keep alive. From time to time a child brought them rice, prompted, more than likely, by the memory of Ballan and his pocketful of sticky sweets...

It was only when the fleet sailed into the Straits of Ceylon, around the tip of India and then northwest toward the Red Sea and Suez, that the whole world sat up all at once and began to take notice. From that point on, words flowed and flowed from every thoughtful mouth—streaming over radio, coursing over television, and flooding in a swelling tide of print.

Fourteen

" . . . In a communiqué from Paris received just moments ago, the French government confirms the earlier announcement that a state of emergency has been declared in the four departments bordering the coast, and that reinforcements are being deployed to the south. It has also been confirmed that the President of the Republic will address the French people at midnight, tonight, Paris time, with a message of grave concern. The Soviet government has decided to make public the statements contained in that message, as soon as they have all been reviewed by the Central Committee of the Party, presently meeting in Moscow, in extraordinary plenary session . . ."

"Ah, Zackaroff! I can see myself now. Hero of the Soviet Union, from grenadier cadet at Stalingrad to general in the artillery, commander of the northern bank of this blasted Amur . . . And all of a sudden, a year before I'm supposed to retire, they're going to turn me into a butcher of women and children! . . . Well, all we can do now is figure how much vodka we'll need to make those Chinese look as if they all have uniforms. Then we can shoot them without a second thought. . . . What do you see? What's happening over there?"

Colonel Zackaroff replied without turning his head. Through the peephole in the command-post bunker, he had his sights trained across the river, watching the Chinese swarming in silence since morning along the Amur's southern bank.

"We're going to have our hands full, General! We knew what to expect, but it's still pretty hard to believe! So many of them, squatting on the ground, lined up in rows as far as the eye can see. Like a giant collective, with Chinamen sprouting wherever you look. On the right, the babies. In the middle, the women. On the left, the young ones. And behind them all, the men. From here, if you count them in squares, like cabbage, I'd say there are two or three million. From a plane, maybe five. And still they keep coming! . . . Are they just going to pile up in the river? Or do you think they can swim?"

"They're like dogs, these Chinese," the general answered. "They know how to swim from the minute they're born. . . . Listen, Zackaroff, don't stop watching. You've got to be my eyes. I can't bear to look. I never could pull the trigger when an animal looked me in the face. . . . Anyway, don't waste your pity. Don't be fooled by those sweet little tots, those clean-cut girls and boys, those helpless-looking women! You can bet when we shoot up that crowd each one we kill will find just the right dramatic pose before they fall in a heap. Anything to impress us. With that faraway look in their eyes that they do so well. And the wounded ones will writhe at our feet, like no other wounded bastard you ever saw. Twenty lessons to learn the whole act, with group drills and practice sessions, and special instructors in make-believe. They love all that. And the ones that put on the biggest show, the ones that seem to be hurting the most, maybe won't have a scratch. You won't know who's wounded and who isn't. A real Chinese opera! You'll see how much fun it's going to be! . . . What are they up to now, Zackaroff?"

"Nothing's moving over there. No talking. No singing. No laughing. No nothing. I haven't seen one of them take a bite to eat all day. Or even move their jaws . . . You know, there's one thing that puzzles me: do they pee while they're squatting like that?"

"Tell a Chinaman 'don't,' and he won't eat, or drink, or piss, or screw, or think. . . . Give me the vodka, Zackaroff. Those characters are beginning to get me down. I think I'll put them all in the Chinese army."

"I can see something else, General. Every hundred yards or so . . . Trucks, with loudspeakers on top, aimed this way."

"Of course. And in each one there's a damn little Chinaman who speaks Russian, and thinks he's the star of some second-rate play. A few words from him, and we're all going to burst into tears! 'Proletarian comrades of the great Soviet Union, the time has come to return to the Chinese people, in a spirit of brotherly love, these Siberian lands so long a part of their sacred ancestral home. Our women, our children, our peasants stand before you, helpless and unprotected, your brothers and sisters, here to open your eyes, to show you the truth and reclaim what is theirs. Please don't shoot. We're unarmed. We're just poor, humble folk trying to make our way . . .' And blahblahblah, and more of the same! . . . Well I'll tell you, you have to watch out when you talk about poor, humble folk to other poor, humble folk who haven't heard anything else but poor, humble folk for some sixty-odd years. You might just take in a few, don't you know! Then all of a sudden we'll be sitting by the Urals, across from an unarmed army of pathetic old men, all ten years old, and yellow peons squatting on their haunches! . . . Give me my bottle, Zackaroff. I've got to get uniforms on them all, and stripes!"

"I'm not worried about you," said the colonel. "I know you can do it. Just like in Berlin, when your vodka turned that crowd of young fraüleins into an SS company of panzer grenadiers. . . . I remember . . . But here you have two hundred thousand men, General. If the order comes down to shoot, what will you do? Will you get them all drunk? All two hundred thousand?"

"It wouldn't be the first time. The armies of Peter the Great weren't sober for a second. The sailors on board the *Potemkin* were terrible drunkards. Stalin himself used to dictate his finest maneuvers while he rolled around under the table each night. Yes, I've given it some thought, my friend. But the drunk soldier has no prestige anymore. Not in this world of ours, mucked up with brotherly love the way it is. Or the soldier, period. We're caught in the clutches of the great hermaphrodite, Zackaroff. We're all its serfs. And we can't even cut off its balls!"

"Sir?" the colonel queried. "I'm not sure I . . ."

"World conscience, illiterate prole! World conscience! Imagine how shocked it would be at a piece of news like this: 'Drunk Russian army slaughters five million unarmed peasants, women and children . . .' Anyway, if the French decide to shoot, that mob over there will take the hint and stay where they are. But frankly I don't think the French can do it. They've always been the fair-haired boys of something or other—of the Church, of logic, of love, of revolution. And now, of that blasted hermaphrodite, the dears! So it's going to be up to us. We'll have to be the ones to shoot. Thank Heaven our garden-variety muzhik is still the same good-natured oaf he's always been. Both feet on the ground, head screwed on straight. You see, being slaves to tradition isn't all that bad! By the time I show up, the hunt will be over. They'll have bagged themselves five or six thousand Chinese, maybe more. Unfortunately, on an empty stomach, even a muzhik gets tired of splashing around in blood . . ."

The general closed his eyes and rubbed his lids, as if he were trying to shake off a weariness, heavy and deep.

"Zackaroff," he said, in a strangely different voice, "tell me again what you see over there. Are there really women and children? Women with breasts? With long, slender necks, and delicate wrists? With pants that hug their bellies and outline their sex? And children too, with those great big eyes? So serious-looking, the way only children can be . . . You know what I mean, don't you, Zackaroff? You know how serious children can be when they make up their minds, and play it for all it's worth . . ."

"There are women and children, all right! And the way they look from here, General, you're going to need plenty of vodka. Just like Berlin."

All at once a voice boomed over from the southern bank, the metallic voice of the damn little Chinaman, star of the second-rate play, mouthing the opening lines of his part:

"Proletarian comrades of the great Soviet Union . . ."

"What did I tell you!" the general smirked. "Time was, we would soften the enemy up with a few rounds of fire. Today they just pound you to hell with their bullshit. The world has had enough of us, Zackaroff. I think it's time we quit . . ."

The roaring voice rolled across the river, from one bank to the other:

"You see here before you our women, our children, our peasants, helpless and unprotected, your brothers and sisters, here to open your eyes, to show you the truth. Soon we'll start to cross the river. Please don't shoot. We have no arms. We're just poor, humble folk trying to make our way . . ."

"What time is it, Zackaroff?"

"Three-ten, General."

"Then it's ten past midnight in Paris. That means their president has just finished his speech, and Peking has made up its mind. They'll be at it like this for the rest of the day, and all through the night, until morning. Call the field marshal, Zackaroff. Ask him for permission to shut up those loudspeakers once and for all . . ."

"Permission denied," said the colonel, setting the general's red phone back on his desk. "Not a drop of blood, except on specific orders from the Kremlin," he added, with a laugh.

"And you think that's funny? Can't you see that those windbags in Moscow have decided not to act, but to keep on arguing, back and forth, in the name of a bunch of principles they think it's their sacred duty to protect! We're caught in a crossfire of words, Zackaroff. That's no good for a soldier. It spoils his final bow!"

"I'm laughing at something else he said, General. He told me to tell you that 'no blood' doesn't mean 'no vodka'!"

"Ah, him too!" he sighed. "He must wonder what in hell he was doing in China when the first war was over. You should have known him then. A rabble-rousing cutthroat if ever there was one! Well, choke down your regrets, old friend! Come dawn, we'll all be plastered!" He shook his fist. "Three sensible drunks at your service, Mother Russia! . . . Come, Zackaroff, let's drink! And close up that peephole. I don't want to have to hear that loudmouth! He sounds like a priest, and he's getting on my nerves. Now that every last padre has his pen or his mike, you can't even hear yourself drink anymore. Yes, it's padre time, Zackaroff, that's what it is. All over the world. They're oozing out of every country. Thousands of everyday priests, ready and willing to poison the minds of millions of idiots. Bleeding hearts puking out gospels galore . . . Ready, Zackaroff! Forward, march! One, two! One, two! One, two! Keep in step! Head up! Eyes front! Stare vacant! Head empty! Amen!"

"If you don't mind, General, I'll pour myself a drink first. I can see we're in for a good long night."

Fifteen

To claim that the news of the fleet's departure caused any great alarm in the Western World when it first became known, would be plainly untrue. Which is doubtless why there was no lack of clever folk, willing, from the start, to spread endless layers of verbal cream, spurting thick and unctuous from the udders of their minds. The obliging bovines of contemporary Western thought, tails all aquiver, acquiesced with delight to the daily milking, especially since, for the moment, there was no cause to think that a serious problem was actually at hand. To appreciate the West's opinion of the refugee fleet—or, for that matter, of anything new and unfamiliar—one essential fact must be borne in mind: it really couldn't give less of a damn. Incredible but true. The more it discovers about such things, the more fathomless its ignorance, feeble its interest, and vulgar its own self-concern. The more crass and tasteless, too, its sporadic outbursts, fewer and farther between. Oh yes, to be sure, it indulges in flights of sentiment now and again, but cinema style, like watching a film, or sitting in front of the TV screen, poised for the serial's weekly installment. Always those spur-of-the-moment emotions or secondhand feelings, pandered by middlemen. Real-world drama, served in the comfort of home by that whore called Mass Media, only stirs up the void where Western opinion has long been submerged. Someone drools at a current event, and mistakes his drivel for meaningful thought. Still, let's not be too quick to spit our scorn its way. Empty drivel indeed, but it shows nonetheless how reading the papers or watching the news can provoke at least the appearance of thinking. Like Pavlov's dog, whose slobber revealed the mechanics of instinct. Opinion shakes up its sloth, nothing more. Does anyone really believe that the average Western man, coming home from his office or factory job, and faced with the world's great upheavals, can eke out much more than a moment's pause in the monumental boredom of his daily routine? Even Worker Power, that saving grace of our society today, is nothing but a parlor game, and played in a parlor too shabby and worn to stand up to more serious frolics. Risk a few, and the floor will cave in and go crashing to bits. The Moon, Biafra, a murderous earthquake, a campaign against pollution, a six-

59

day war, a Bay of Pigs, the death of a Mao—mere Christmas parties
one and all, with the great thoughtless void suddenly wreathed in
flowers, and tooting its two-penny whistle. For a little while no one
is bored, which is something at least. Quite a bit, in fact, if only it
would last! But life isn't always Sunday, and we can't have famine in
Pakistan or war in Israel every day of the week. (Thank Heaven, by
the way, for the Israelis, those entertainers of the Western World. No
danger of getting bored as long as they're on stage. Our jokers can
all go to bed and rest easy. When they wake up next morning their
café au lait will be steaming, brisk and fresh, to the boom of Israeli
guns . . .) But give a damn? Never! What for? And so, when the first
news helicopter flew low over the fleet, off Ceylon, and got a worldwide scoop with a series of staggering pictures, what do you suppose
our Western joker thought? That his life was in danger? That time
had just started his countdown to death? Not a bit. All he thought was
that now, as the fleet limped along on its hopeless course, strewing
corpses in its wake, he would finally be able to watch a first-rate serial,
week after week.

But now let's imagine a rude awakening, a plunge into reality, with
everyone caught in the soup, like nothing since World War II. The
serial suddenly breaks through the screen, smashing it to pieces into
the steak and fries. And all at once the hordes of characters stream
into the living room, looking the way they did in the fishbowl, doing
their tricks a few moments before, only now they're not acting, and
the glass wall is shattered, and they're armed with their woes, their
wounds, their groans, their grievance, their hate. Their machine
guns too. Now they rip through the apartment, jar it out of its orderly
calm, stun the families caught short in mid-digestion, spread through
the town, the country, the world, pictures come to life, living, breathing problems on the march, newsfilm actors turning on their director
in unbridled frenzy, suddenly telling him "shit!" to his face. . . . Now
our poor little friend sees only too well that he should have paid
closer attention. He read it all wrong, he heard it all wrong. The
story, this time, wasn't published and aired for his leisurely, private
delight. In fact, what he's going to hear now is this: "A million refugees from the banks of the Ganges set to invade France in the
morning. Five more fleets on the way, from Africa, India and Asia."
Then he'll run off to lay in supplies, to stock up on sugar, and oil, and
sausage, and noodles. And he'll stick a sockful of gold coins under a
board in the floor. He'll go to his local garage and lick His Lordship's
greasy boots for two jerrycans full, set aside for the periodic evacua-
tion. Then, eyes moist with manly tenderness, he'll look at his wife,

his daughter, his aged mother, and see them already haloed in the nasty aura of self-sacrifice. After which, having belched up the last gaseous echo of the last sumptuous banquet of the Veterans of Gourmet Dining, he'll declare himself "ready to confront the situation." With the look on his face somewhat changed, a little more sly and resigned. Prepared to sell out, if need be . . . But things haven't gone quite that far for our little friend yet. For the moment, with millions of others, he's dozing off, ready to drown in the drivel, ears peacefully cocked toward his mind master's tinkling bells.

What a concert! What talent! All solidly classic, steeped in the noblest tradition of the music of brotherly love. With maestros too numerous to name, loosing a flood of notes, those first few days, a torrent of heavenly voices, angelic enough to make you weep. But still, let's try. We'll get tired of reading about them in no time—much sooner than they themselves got tired of their broadsides and speeches—but we mustn't forget the weight of blame they bear. They took our poor little friend and twisted him around their finger. Not many on purpose, to be sure. But the minions who fawned on the monster, though few, knew what they were doing. And they did their job well. The rest of them spewed out their words and their ink for other irksome reasons; most common of which, a certain aversion to violence, like the beast on the edge of his lush, fragrant forest, threatened with attack, but suddenly loath to growl or bare his fangs, when the merest snarl would be more than enough to protect him. Try to figure it out! Then too, there was more than a goodly dose of moral misgivings—or cowardice, if you will—in the spreading contagion of their spineless pronouncements. Like the fear of not sneering in tune with the other hyenas, of not weeping in time with the pharisee chorus, of not bleating with the fools, of unwittingly proving you can think for yourself; or the fear, above all, that world conscience would point its accusing finger, and single you out as the spoilsport troubling their treasonous revels. Oh what fine scribblers and spouters we had back then, in those early days of borrowed calm before the storm!

One name on the roll of honor has to stand out above the rest: the unspeakable Jean Orelle. Official spokesman of the French Republic, it was he whose babblings broke the silence, in charge, as he was, of starting the auction off. Everyone hoped he would set the bidding high. And he did. Eternal France, in keeping with time-honored custom, owed it to herself to stand up, solo, and squeal out sublime and noble notes of love, with no thought of how she would get off the hook once the die had been cast . . .

Sixteen

"Without meaning to exaggerate the seriousness of the situation," the minister began, placing a slim sheaf of documents in front of the microphones . . .

The ministers had, in fact, seemed rather nonplussed by the whole affair. "What if they get all the way to Europe and decide to land in France?" asked one. "Never make it," replied an admiral. "I've taken a look at the pictures. One good stiff wind, and that's all there is to it!" Just like that. A million wretches, drowning on the ground floor of the Élysée Palace, while the breeze gently rustles the trees in the park outside, clothed in their tender, young green. "In other words," the President observed, with his usual festive, postprandial smile, "we can sit back and just let the storm gods take over. Old Aeolus and Neptune, if I'm not mistaken?" Someone cleared his throat, trying to come up with a simple idea: "Why not ask all the governments on the Indian subcontinent to stop them while they still have time?" A snicker from the end of the table. "Is there any such animal?" asked some undersecretary or other, one who usually never opened his mouth. "A government on the Indian subcontinent!" Sighs from the distinguished seats. "I can give you their answer right now," said the Minister of Foreign Affairs. "The governments of the Indian subcontinent, gravely concerned with domestic conditions and the worsening crisis in food distribution . . ." Another snicker. "Balls!" exclaimed the undersecretary of this or that . . . Now, the President is hardly one to frown on after-dinner banter. Still, he finds the expletive somewhat out of order. "Please," he says sharply, "a little decorum. This is a serious matter." Then, turning to Foreign Affairs, "You were saying . . ." Another sigh. "The governments of the Indian subcontinent wish to make it clear, at this time, that any action on their part is quite out of the question, and they wish to disclaim any and all responsibility . . ." So, back to the beginning. "Yes, I'm afraid you're right," the President agrees. "A fine way to run a country! Isn't there a government on the face of the earth that's willing to be responsible for anything these days? . . . Well, what if the admiral is wrong? Couldn't we still try to work something out? Something official, I mean. Through diplomatic channels. Maybe the United Nations . . ."

The undersecretary springs to his feet, like a jack-in-the-box, beside himself with glee. "Listen, I have a perfect idea. We put this fleet of nomads under the UN, blue flag and all, with sailors from Sweden, Ethiopia, and Paraguay to act as observers. Then we let their Relief Agency send out helicopters once in a while to feed the people and take care of the ships. And the fleet goes round and round, from ocean to ocean, all over the world, for the next twenty years. That should satisfy everybody. Besides, it's hardly a new idea. Remember Palestine? . . . Just one thing: in twenty years there'll be twice as many on board as there are today. What with the heat, and nothing to do . . . We'll have to build floating camps and attach them to the fleet. Believe me, gentlemen, it could go on like that for a long, long time! In two generations they won't even know why there's nothing out there but ocean, far as they can see, or why the deck of a ship is their only homeland. . . . That's right, their homeland. Because, in time, they'll even come to feel a kind of national pride. The heat, after all, and nothing else to do . . . Then they'll ask for independence. They'll damn well demand it. And why not? The UN has delegates today from a hundred countries that have no excuse for existing. We'll invent a hundred and first, that's all! The Floating Republic of the High Seas, we'll call it. Naturally, there'll have to be a partition, the way there always is. We'll split the fleet in two, and make sure both halves turn in opposite directions. That way they'll never have to meet. Of course, it's going to cost us something. The West will have to be dunned for the upkeep. The richer we are, the more jealous they'll be, and the more we'll be billed. But so what? We're used to all that. Don't we do the same thing now when the Third World kicks up and we want to make peace? We pay. We bitch a little, but we pay. And we get our peace for a couple of food packages from UN Relief and some aspirin from World Health. Cheap enough, don't you think? Isn't that what you want? A nice, quiet, lasting little peace, and one that won't cost us too much or worry our neighbors . . ." He turned to the President. "There's my idea, Your Excellency. It's yours for the asking!"

The President flashed him a quizzical scowl. "What's your background, Monsieur Perret?" "Marginal majority." "No, I mean what school?" "École Normale Supérieure, degree in letters." "I could have guessed . . . You're joking, I hope." A look of disapproval furrowed every brow, frozen in a painful mask of fruitless thought. "Gentlemen," the President went on, "you're worse than a bunch of tongue-tied schoolboys flunking their orals! Whereas you, Monsieur Perret . . ." A smile passed between them. "Yes, Your Excellency, you're right, I'm joking. Still, I seem to be the only one here who sees what an absolute farce this whole business is! To threaten the West with a bloodless invasion! Indeed! Did you ever see the lamb attack the wolf and gobble it down?" A flurry of portfolios, and cries of "Shame! Shame! No heart! No soul!" Yes, when the mind is missing, a soul will do. "Your Excellency," he continued, "when my colleagues decide to discuss the subject rationally, I'll be only too happy to suggest twenty serious ways of solving this ludicrous problem." "For example?" the President queried. The undersecretary sat up straight, pointed his hands like a child with a make-believe gun, swept them in an arc around the table. "Bang bang! Bang bang! Bang bang bang! You're all dead!" he shouted. A wave of shocked dismay ran through the room. As it reached its height, the admiral, half hidden behind his minister's chair, went "Boom! Boom! Boom!" "What's that?" the minister blurted, wheeling around, eyes aglare. "The cannon," the admiral replied. . . . Three ministers were sitting, heads in hands. Another was mopping his brow. Two more were choking back their anger, while three were trying to stir theirs up. One of them even sat there weeping discreet and worthy tears. It was he, in fact, who finally broke the siege of silence, as he slowly raised his head and gazed at the council through disheveled locks, with the tragic mask of a grand vizier. "Are we the government of France," he began, "assembled in extraordinary session with His Excellency, the President of the Republic, to discuss, humanely, a drama that has no precedent since deep in the Middle Ages? A drama that shows the way to man's loftiest transformation, as he stands, at last, at this hour of materialism's ultimate upheaval? Or are we some petty village council, called by the mayor to tighten the ban against gypsies camping on our public lands?"

The speaker was Jean Orelle. The President, rather sheepish, felt obliged to soften his attack. "Aha! My thoughts exactly," he said. "My very words to the council last year, during the general strike: 'Gentlemen, are we the government of France?' And later, too, when we had to devalue the franc." Satisfied with his defense, he added, "Please, Monsieur Orelle, continue." Whereupon the wind of the past rose up from across the ages, gathering all the derelict fleets, the prophetic peoples, the militant armies, the nations drunk on trumpets and drums, the Kingdoms of God, and sweeping them off toward the calm and fathomless deeps, where even the boldest of storms will blow themselves out in the end. Its great historic gusts pushed back the slumping shoulders, raised up the bowed heads circling the Elysian table, and turned all eyes toward the vast perspective of humanity unbounded. Proof, once again, that when the mind is minute and the heart misplaced, we have to invent a soul to answer for all our foul transgressions . . . Off in his corner, the undersecretary sat smirking to himself. No one gave him a second thought, except the President, perhaps, in his own bizarre way. . . . "The spirit of France, her particular genius," minister Jean Orelle went on, "has always guided her path through the great waves of modern thought, like the noble flagship whose instinct shows her the way to go, as she plies resolutely forward, colors flying for all to see, at the head of the fleet of enlightened nations, setting their course, now left, now right, showing them how to sail into the storms spawned by the great compassionate gales of human progress . . ."

And so the thinking machine whined on, guaranteed authentic, hundred percent Orelle, last word in modern technology, with chrome-plated psyche, plastic-coated, rustproof, antidoubt brain, and prefab heart clicking its clockwork claptrap a mile a minute, available on easy budget terms, perfected model for high-class personnel, and special reinforced model, ultra de luxe, for millionaire social lions and potentates of the press. "Could we get to the point?" the President mumbled, discreetly winking at the stenotypist to keep the remark off the record. The point was finally reached a quarter of an hour later, but only after a stratospheric flight beginning at feudalism's dying gasp, through the Declaration of the Rights of Man, the abolition of slavery, universal suffrage, state-run education, the antifascist gains of '36, the liberation of Paris, the liberation of Algiers, Third World relief, and French-style socialism. "Gentlemen," said the minister, "what difference does it make if this fleet, heading west, inching its way through our conscience with its last ounce of strength, like a dying indictment, lands on the shores of France, or Germany, or England? What difference indeed? All the privileged nations must stand up as one, must lend one solemn ear to the eternal question, 'Cain, where is Abel thy brother . . . What hast thou done . . . ?' Can any among you fail to perceive that France owes it to herself to respond in a clear, compassionate voice, and to plan a heartfelt welcome, here and now, in keeping with both our material wealth and our moral resources? At the moment of truth, how urgent it will be to know how to read the signs and symbols, and master our own selfish interests!" Ah yes, what a lovely tune! How that breed puffs and struts when there's nothing to do but sing! These days, with its swelling cliché chorus, how expert it is in feigning concern with-

out taking a stand; in basking in the trumpet's blare while marking
time in place; in pouring out into the street to beat the drum for the
revolution, yet never leaving the pavement hallowed with a single
corpse for a single cause; in cherishing its heroic illusions, bought for
a song! In no time the Council of Ministers gave their approval. Plan
a welcome? Why not! With the universe all eyes and ears, think how
awed and impressed it would be!

"Isn't that rushing things a little?" the President ventured to suggest. "Spontaneity," replied the minister, "is the mark of true
generosity. France owes it to herself . . ." "Yes," echoed the President, loud and clear, "France owes it to herself . . ." Then silence. But
his thought marched on: "France owes it to herself to speak the truth.
No more, no less. When will she finally stop playing along with fate,
and decide to put her foot down! She'd find it so refreshing!" And he
gave a hint of a shrug with his shoulders, meant for himself. After all,
wasn't he the first citizen of France, up to his neck in the monster's
slimy jaws, playing both sides at once like all the rest: antiracist and
racist; protester and patriot; Marxist and libertine; democrat and
fascist; Communist and landlord; ecumenist and Catholic; unionized,
socialized, subsidized conservative; humanitarian and hedonist,
rolled up in one? "Yes, France owes it to herself," the President
repeated, "to present the world with a clear, coherent view of the
whole event. For that reason, I'm authorizing Monsieur Orelle, as
spokesman for the government, to explain our position to the press,
and—taking into account the distant vantage point we still enjoy
vis-à-vis the refugee fleet, and its uncertain future, and within the
bounds of common sense, of course—to sketch out for them, in very
broad terms, some kind of general welcome, in a framework of international cooperation, I would hope, to allow us, if need be, to share
the burden of a generosity which, frankly, I fear we could come to
regret. In fact, if you want my thoughts on the matter . . ." He caught
himself raising both hands hip-high, in what promised to be an eloquent gesture; then stopped in midair, thought better of it, and shook
them from side to side in mute negation, as if to say that this probably
wasn't the time to be giving his thoughts on the matter, all things
considered. . . . Off at his end of the table, the undersecretary wasn't
taken in by the maneuver. He looked the President square in the eye,
and formed four short, silent words with his lips: bang bang bang
bang. "Gentlemen, that will be all for today," the President said,
standing up. Then he went to his office, gave orders not to be disturbed, poured himself a good strong whiskey, loosened his tie, un-

buttoned his collar, turned on the giant television set, and settled his everyday, round-shouldered bulk deep into his armchair. Then, live and in color, Monsieur Jean Orelle:

"Without meaning to exaggerate the seriousness of the situation," the minister began, placing a slim sheaf of documents in front of the microphones, "the government of France perceives it as a sign of things to come, a symbol of the rising worldwide socialist movement. Suddenly the symbol has grazed the tip of its wing against our worn-out world, and the old world, whether afraid or proud, shudders at the touch. Gentlemen, in an effort to clarify our position in regard to this momentous decision, I have come here this evening to answer your questions . . ."

Seventeen

"Monsieur Orelle, without jumping to conclusions as to their final destination, may I ask if the government has any plans to ease the plight of these poor, suffering souls? It's reaching a point where we can't sit idly by . . ."

The speaker was one Ben Suad, alias Clément Dio, one of the monster's most faithful minions, concoctor in chief of the poisonous slops poured piping hot each Monday into the feeble, comatose brains of the six hundred thousand readers of his weekly rag, served up in its fancy sauces. Citizen of France, North African by blood, with an elegant crop of kinky hair and swarthy skin—doubtless passed down from a certain black harem slavegirl, sold to a brothel for French officers in Rabat (as he learned from the bill of sale in his family papers)—married to a Eurasian woman officially declared Chinese and author of several best-selling novels, Dio possessed a belligerent intellect that thrived on springs of racial hatred barely below the surface, and far more intense than anyone imagined. Like a spider deep in the midst of French public opinion, he had webbed it over so thick with fine gossamer strands that it scarcely clung to life. A cordial type all the same, given to great informative bursts if he chose, though always one-way, sincere enough to put his convictions on the line and draw the occasional fire of intelligent colleagues —of whom there were fewer and fewer, alas!, and whom people had all long since stopped reading. In those topsy-turvy days the Left sprawled out in abundance, while the rightist press, in a hopeless muddle, languished alone in its trenches, deserted. The home front, meanwhile, true to form, fraternized high and low, unabashed and unrestrained. Politically, Dio's columns were something of a hash, whipped up with a proper dose of utopian pap. But most dangerous of all was his very special talent—unrivaled, in fact—for planting his mines through the waters of current French life, far and wide, just surface-deep, always finding those areas still intact, and larding them through with the deadly devices, spewed mass-produced from his prolific brain. Jean Orelle, we should note, was one of his most devout readers, never missing the weekly pause in the journey along his ageing imagination, and confiding to his intimates, with a chuckle,

that "this Dio chap" reminded him so of the fearless reformer he
himself used to be. "Lots of nerve! Plenty of new ideas! And a real,
burning passion for the everyday man, the citizen of the world!" Yes,
this Dio chap's citizen of the world, in all his glory! Ah, what a dismal,
repulsive creature! The journalist's pen gave him many a size and
shape, but one thing never changed: his contempt for tradition, his
scorn for Western Man per se, and above all the patriotic Frenchman. Like a kind of anti-Joan of Arc, charged by King Dio with a
thousandfold mission. To wit, to crush with the weight of shame and
remorse the common, foot-slogging soldier of the Western World,
lord of its ancient battles, deserted by all his generals to a man, but
a powerful force all the same. In column after column, the anti-Joan
became, by turns, an Arab workman, snubbed and insulted; a publisher of smut, hauled into court; a black bricklayer, exploited by his
boss; a theater director with a censored play; a young Madonna from
some leftist slum; a rioter, beaten for ripping up the streets; a café
tough, shot in his tracks; a student terrorist; a schoolgirl on the pill;
the head of a people's culture center, summarily fired; a marijuana
prophet; a rebel leader dispensing guerrilla justice; a married priest;
an adolescent lecher; an incestuous author; a guru of pop; a female
dead from an overdose of love; a pummeled Egyptian, a poisoned
Greek, a Spaniard, gunned down; a reporter, attacked and beaten;
a protester crapping on the Unknown Soldier; a hunger striker, soft
in the head; a Vietnam deserter; a big-chief thug from the wrong side
of town; a faggot with a medical excuse; a sadistic schoolboy tormenting his teacher; a rapist, mind twisted by racks of hard-core porn; a
kidnapper, sure of his righteous cause; an incurable delinquent, victim of his genes or society's pressures; an abortionist butcher, screaming for his human rights; a Brazilian backwoods wench, sold into
São Paulo salons; an Indian dying from a tourist's measles; a murderer
calling for prison reform; a bishop spouting Marx in his pastoral
letters; a car thief, mad for speed; a bank thief, mad for publicity's
easy life; a maidenhead thief, mad for free and easy sex; a Bengali
dead of starvation . . . And so many more. So many crusading heroes,
skillfully chosen to please and persuade. Which they usually did. And
why not? When the heart gives way, it's a Turkish bazaar. Freedom
is all or nothing. With the likes of this would-be heartrending rabble,
these pseudopathetic peons beating his battering rams against the
gates, Dio knew that, in time, he was sure to smash them down.
When freedom expands to mean freedom of instinct and social destruction, then freedom is dead. And all the slimy Dio-larvae teem

on its corpse, ready to burst into great black moths, heralding angels
of the antiworld.

To appreciate the scope of Dio's power, we could look to a hundred
examples. One will suffice: the Saint-Favier swimming-pool scandal.
Saint-Favier is a dull, sleepy town stuck away in the Jura, that decided one day to indulge its wild fancy and present itself with a gift
sure to rouse an industrious populace lulled by the pipemaker's
lathes. Namely, a swimming pool. Olympic, Hiltonesque, covered in
the winter, basking in mountain sun in the summer, a billionaire's
pool on a communal scale, a fabulous toy for the people, democratic
to a fault, and always jam-packed (God knows how those French love
the water!) . . . Well, it just so happened that, in one of the weekly
analyses required by law, a lab technician discovered a troop of
bacteria—gonococci, to be precise—living on a corner of the metal
plate marked "Saint-Favier Municipal Swimming Pool," happy as
could be with their new surroundings, and, in a word, thriving. So
well, in fact, that the hospital, much to the doctors' disbelief and
indignation, found itself treating three youngsters with ophthalmic
gonorrhea: two girls and a boy—not even related—and one of whom,
it should be noted, was a pupil with the Sisters of Perpetual Help.
Now, in France, no schooltot does anything much with her eyes but
open them wide, agog at the wonders of the world. There had to be
an explanation. And it soon came to light in the files of the hospital,
the national health plan, and the factory infirmary, where the records showed that a thousand Arabs—first-rate workers notwithstanding, and socially accepted if not socially absorbed—had been showing
up time after time, to the tune of some ten percent, with the after-
maths of a stubborn case of North African clap. To be utterly fair and
unbiased, the authorities proceeded to check through the files of all
the Jura natives too. A time-consuming task, but one which the West,
personified there in Saint-Favier, felt obliged to perform in the
worthy effort to subdue its prejudices. The result, unhappily, merely
confirmed them. They turned up a total of two rich young brats, both
terribly spoiled, who wouldn't have dreamed of using the public
pool, and one dirty old derelict, who never bathed and didn't know
how to swim. What a blow for the poor town fathers! Such fine folk,
too, these laborers, pensioners, railroaders, politicized peasants, placing their leftist ballots in the box, like Eucharists laid on the communion plate, and scratching their chins, deep in thought . . . One of
them, a delegate from the Communist trade-union party, in a highly
emotional search through his papers, brought out a mimeographed

document proving that the Arabs were essential to the economic well-being of the nation, and that the sudden resurgence of racism had to be nipped in the bud. Of course, they all agreed. The point was well taken. They were all for the worldwide solidarity of the masses. But still! If their kids' eyes were going to catch the clap, after all—and in their nice new pool, to boot, that they scrimped their pennies together to pay for—and a dose like you wouldn't pick up from some army-camp whore, well, Arabs or not, they couldn't just let the thing get out of hand, and besides, doesn't everyone know it's an Arab disease? . . . The fine folk believed it was only common sense to vote as they did, and to reach their unanimous decision: namely, that thereafter the only Arabs to use the municipal swimming pool at Saint-Favier would be those with a medical certificate proving that they had no contagious diseases that might be spread by water. The decree was posted at the entrance to the pool, and in all the Arab cafés and haunts in town. It was, in fact, rather clumsily worded. But that's hardly a surprise. In times when a spade has ceased to be called a spade, it's no wonder that thirty-two town fathers—each one a family man, but none with an excess of schooling—should let themselves be trapped by the subtleties of language. . . . Dio rubbed his hands with glee, and proceeded to use the Saint-Favier edict as his cover of the week, spread over the newsstands in all its glory (by ultracapitalist distributors, no less), with a big title splashed across, proclaiming: "Anti-Arab Racism Alive and Well!" Six hundred thousand copies. Rather hard to miss! . . . In Paris, His Excellency the Algerian ambassador demanded an audience and got it on the spot. The North African press let loose volleys of hate, and the French press picked up the tune, albeit in a minor key. Somewhere there was even the observation that plenty of Frenchwomen jumped into bed with those poor, slandered Arabs, without once insisting to see their bill of health. . . . Retaliation took many forms. Oil, for example, was an issue again, as three tankers returned bone dry. And a hundred nice French girls, teaching school in Algeria, were suddenly hauled into the hospital and spread on the stirrups to be plumbed and explored by a squad of medical student commandos, whipped up to a frenzy. Two of them died as a result, but the inquest didn't last. On his minister's orders, the prefect of the Jura quickly reversed the Saint-Favier decree, first for certain technical flaws, and also for its breach of human rights. Dio was exultant, crowing his triumph in one of his best editorials. Because, when all was said and done, he was right. And any time that man was right—which he often was, since

he chose his pretexts with diabolical skill—the walls of the ancient
citadel were sure to crumble. So the Arabs of Saint-Favier returned
en masse to the pool, victorious. And they had it all to themselves.
No townsfolk were seen there again. There wasn't even talk about
building another one, separate from the first. What would be the
sense? ... And all at once whole sections of New York are deserted,
a score of American cities watch the flight to the suburbs—and half
the historic Paris pavement too—American tots in their integrated
schools fall five years behind, tubercular Gauls flee in droves from our
open-air clinics. ... Tally-ho! Tally-ho! Just listen to that battering ram
smash at the southern gate!

And so, into the pressroom of the Élysée Palace, amid five hundred
reporters all concerned more with rhetoric than truth, slipped the
battering ram's most recent recruit: the starving passenger of the
pathetic fleet. The question was very well put. Not the principal
question, to be sure. No frontal attack that might frighten off the faint
of heart. But a question that checked the big issues at the door, and
subtly aimed at the hidden, most vulnerable spot: ". . . may I ask if
the government has any plans to ease the plight of these poor, suffering souls? It's reaching a point where we can't sit idly by . . ." True,
the West can't sit idly by anymore. Not for anything. It had better
get that fact through its skull, no matter how many induced neuroses
it takes to sink in. Out of all the world's billions, let one Indian from
the Andes croak from famine, or one black from Chad, or one Pakistani—all citizens, by the way, of free and independent states, proud
of their self-determination—and suddenly the Western World feels
obliged to fly into raptures of repentance. The agitators know its
reactions. It's not even money they're after. No appeal to the breast-
beating West to thump on its wallets, once and for all, and adopt the
four-fifths of the globe trailing dimly in its wake. No, they aim for the
head. Those remote lobes of the brain where remorse, self-reproach,
and self-hate, pricked by thousands of barbs, come bursting out,
spreading their leukemia cells through a once healthy body. It's
reaching a point where we can't sit idly by! Of course not! Sit idly by?
What a thought! The minister's voice was so choked, he could hardly
speak:

"Gentlemen, we have to think in tune with worldwide conscience.
Or perhaps the word should be 'throb,' not 'think,' since our hearts
are at issue, I'm sure you agree, not our heads. The moment this fleet
set sail, a million human beings chose to cut themselves off from their
homeland. Far be it from us to pass judgment. Far better to think of

these poor, homeless souls as citizens of the world, in search of their promised land. At first the government of France felt compelled to approach the governments of India, in an effort to persuade them to hold back the fleet, to keep it from plunging out onto the deep. It will come as no surprise, when we think of the wretched conditions that engulf that unhappy part of the earth, to learn that our efforts were fruitless. What power, after all, can stem the force of fate? . . . And so, let me assure you, Gentlemen, that the government of France, having once done its duty, is nonetheless ready and willing—indeed, all the more so—to assume the humanitarian obligations incumbent upon all men of good will in these truly unprecedented times. France will take her place in the forefront, make no mistake. She asks only one thing, and we venture to say that her past actions give her the right to insist: that is, that she not stand alone. With that in mind, she has proposed to her Western partners that an international commission be formed, for the purpose of providing the fleet with urgently needed food and supplies. Whatever qualms some of us may have about the outcome of an affair unparalleled in its desperation, we are duty-bound to keep them to ourselves, and to say for all to hear: 'These men are my brothers!' "

"Typical!" the President said to himself. "The old son of a bitch has to throw in a headline!"

Also in front of their color TV screens were most of the magnates of the French shipping industry, watching the press conference from their presidential suites. They were doing their job, nothing more, merely keeping abreast of whatever concerned the sea, and whatever might hinder the speed of their ships and the profits they reaped. Their reactions—against the general tide—are well worth noting. First, consultation by phone among themselves. Then coded messages buzzing from antennas, haughty and high atop their company roofs, to all their ships in the Indian Ocean: "Ordered to change direction, earliest convenience. Avoid all possible contact with refugee fleet. Present position assumed as follows . . ." Of all the captains who received that command, not one failed to see that this forced retreat was a retreat of the conscience. Theirs was being protected, and they rushed to obey. Seafarers that they were, they knew the impossible and hopeless when they saw it. Let one typhoon blast those rotting wrecks, with their million starving creatures strewn over the water, tangling in their tunics and waiting to die, and every last ship in the Western World, brought together by some kind of miracle, still couldn't save even the hundredth part! And at what a

price to try! All useful commercial traffic halted. Crews stunned by
the sight of an ocean of corpses. Fine merchant ships turned Samari-
tan craft, floating hospitals left to days on end of aimless drifting. And
for what? For life? Not even! For death. Death, seeping its way deep
into the Western marrow . . . In other countries too the same orders
were sent. In England, Germany, Italy, and more. And from that day
on, the refugee fleet had the sea to itself. Off on the horizon, no
billows of smoke marked the presence of man, no beating heart
. . . Such was the first response to the minister's exhortations. Kept
secret for the sake of human dignity, it did little to alter the course
of events . . .

"Monsieur Orelle," asked another reporter, "are we to understand
that you plan to reimpose censorship?"

"Really, Monsieur Machefer! Aren't you embarrassed to sound so
foolish? What on earth could make you ask such nonsense?"

This verbal jousting between these two was a common occurrence.
It livened things up, and sometimes they even enjoyed it. But this
time they seemed quite determined to loathe each other in earnest.
In short, the moment of real confrontation that had to come sooner
or later.

"Why, you said so yourself, Monsieur Orelle. We're duty-bound, as
you put it, to keep to ourselves any qualms we might have about the
outcome of this affair. Aren't you suggesting a kind of moral self-
censorship, in fact? With all the clear consciences on one side, and
on the other . . ."

"And on the other, yours! Yes, we know, Monsieur Machefer. Well,
don't worry. You can go on just as you have, writing anything you
please."

"Good, that's exactly what I'll do," said the journalist, "first thing
in the morning."

"And I'll be sure to read you, too, Monsieur Machefer," the minister replied. "I'm one of your most faithful readers. Of course, I have
no choice. It's my job. But still, that should make you happy. After
all, there aren't many of us left . . ."

An obsequious smile ran through the pressroom. Everyone knew
about Machefer's paper. They knew what a time it was having to
keep its head above water, and most of them gloated to watch it
struggle. A poor, eight-page daily, with no pictures, practically no
ads, badly printed, and more badly sold, it owed its survival to the
combined efforts of a few anonymous benefactors, no one of whom
gave very much, but who, taken together, got the moribund rag

through the end of each month, like the Cavalry in any good Western, galloping up in the nick of time to save the beleaguered forces. Each month, just as all hope seemed lost, the bugle would blare its salvation. No one ever knew that the President himself was one of the unknown troopers.

Machefer's paper was neither right nor left, nor even lukewarm middle of the road. It would lash out, often where least expected, tilting at the windmills of hackneyed opinion, rather dogmatically sometimes, to be sure, though Machefer's followers always felt that he hit the mark. And he probably did, judging by the hatred he never failed to stir, far out of proportion with his real importance. But the press takes great pride in its objectivity—no personal hate, just personal opinion!—and so it pretended to treat Machefer's paper like a kind of journalistic joke, the Punch and Judy show of the trade. When all of them had had their laugh in Machefer's direction—no Punch-puppet he, this tall old man with the deep-blue eyes, nattily dressed, white close-cropped hair, white drooping mustache—the minister called the class to order, making it clear that their playtime was over:

"Well I think that's enough of that!" he announced. "Monsieur Machefer, I assume that you didn't raise your hand to subject us to your petty quibbles. If you don't mind, please get to your question."

"Monsieur Orelle," Machefer began, "let's suppose that the Western nations go along with the government's proposal and provide for the refugee fleet as long as it's off in mid-ocean. Can't you see that you'll simply be feeding your enemy, fattening up a million invaders? And if this fleet . . ." (His tone, deliberately businesslike at first, grew more and more accusing, and shut up the lingering laughs of the last few fools) ". . . should reach the coast of France, and throw those million invaders out onto the beach, would the government have the courage to stand up against the very same hordes that its kindness had rescued?"

"Now that's the real question!" thought Dio, who had tossed out the first only to provoke the second. And he knew that Machefer wouldn't fail him. But he also knew, when he launched the debate on a lofty, altruistic note, that any other point of view would be seen as revolting, or at least overruled on the spot. For, when man is convinced of his noble nature, he'll never so much as flirt with evil —which usually does him in, in the end, ripped apart by both sides, like Buridan's ass, forced to choose between his water and his oats.

"Monsieur Machefer," the minister replied, "your question is revolting! Do you ask a drowning man where he was going and why, before you pull him out of the water? Do you throw him back in if, assuming the worst, he admits he was swimming to your private beach to break into your cottage?"

"No, you pull him out and hand him over to the police," Machefer answered. "With a million thieves pulled out of the water, how many police do you think you can muster?"

Monsieur Jean Orelle, the writer, beat an orderly retreat, as the minister in him came back to the fore:

"There's no reason to suppose," he said, "that the fleet will come anywhere near the coast of France, or even near Europe, for that matter. But assuming the possibility of such a hypothesis, and since nothing on earth could give us the right to stand in its way—even if we conceivably could—the government has decided, as it says here in the communiqué, to work out, with its Western partners, some kind of appropriate welcome, in a framework of international cooperation, to allow us, should the need arise, to share the burden of our generosity."

"At five knots," Machefer argued, "they could sail around Africa and still reach the coast of Provence in roughly a month and a half. That should give your commission just enough time to study such vital matters as when and where to meet, and how to proceed. They won't be in any hurry, you can bet. They'll take their sweet time to see where the fleet is heading. Then each one will tiptoe out, and leave the lucky winner to shift for himself. And what if we pick the right number? What then, Monsieur Orelle? Believe me, our friends will be simply delighted to see us left with that crowd on our hands! No, I repeat my question . . ."

"You won't repeat anything, Monsieur Machefer. You don't have the floor!"

"But for God's sake, a million immigrants!" Machefer shouted, over the rising commotion.

Back in the twentieth row, unobtrusive, Clément Dio sat calmly by, quite still except for the rhythmic clack of his heels on the floor. And in no time five hundred reporters sat stamping their feet. Well, let's be exact. There were at least seven abstainers, with a total readership of forty-two thousand.

"You don't have the floor anymore, Monsieur Machefer! Now don't force me to have you ejected. It would be the first time in a press conference, I assure you! Your attitude is intolerable. Wholly out of keeping with our goals, with our mission of humanity and mercy. The mission that the government of France has entrusted me to set forth to you here, this evening. ("Drumroll, please!" said the President to himself.) I trust that the gentlemen of the Third World press will do France the honor of ignoring the comments—so utterly at odds with the unanimous views of her people—that I'm sure you'll be printing tomorrow, in no uncertain terms."

"We're in for quite a match," Dio whispered to his aide. "Gentlemen, pens in place! And let the one who beats his breast the loudest come out the winner!"

All at once the minister's voice dropped down a few notches, as if something were draining him of his faith, like the blood ebbing out of a wounded man. And, indeed, something was. He was being drained dry to the sound of a word, a lovely word spoken just moments before, now echoing back in his brain, like water, dripping, dripping, constant and tormenting: Provence, Provence, Provence ... Yes, there in Provence, nestled against a sweet-smelling hill, an old country farmhouse, transformed by the Nobel millions into a touch of paradise, welcomed the minister summer after summer, and Christmas, and Easter, and Trinity Sunday. . . . But when your name is Jean Orelle, prophet of your time, hero of great revolutions past, friend of the fallen leaders, adviser to the worthies of this world, and when age is upon you, ready to rub the slate clean in the name of a well-earned rest—when the moment has come to stop dealing in great ideas, and to loll in the shade of a hundred-year pine—don't you owe it to yourself to raise your head one last time, faithful to your image of yourself, that image so hazy and naïve that you almost have to smile at the thought, but a smile mixed with tears at the emptiness of it all ... The minister raised his head:

"Any more questions?" he asked in a weary voice.

And there were a few more, in fact, though none very important, since everything really had already been said. The only one to attract some attention came from a Gabonese reporter, anxious to learn what they planned to feed "our brothers in the refugee fleet, since, Monsieur Orelle, the important thing isn't just giving, but knowing the right things to give." Someone, at least, had understood ...

Dio made sure that he had the last word:

"Monsieur Orelle, all other questions aside, do you think they have a chance?"

"A chance! A chance!" the minister exclaimed. "Can we ever be sure whether man has a chance?"

It was a clever dodge. And Dio picked it up, past master that he was:

"It's the Last Chance Armada . . ."

Pronounced in a murmur, just loud enough to be heard, the expression struck home. Repeated thousands and thousands of times, can it be that its impact paralyzed the West? Is a last chance something to turn your back on? Perhaps that might be one explanation . . .

Eighteen

Contrary to what he had told the minister, Machefer didn't write a word in his paper the next morning, or, indeed, any of the mornings that followed, throughout those endless days while the armada inched its way toward the entrance to the Mediterranean. On that morning and not before, when the danger is real, and close at hand, Machefer will wake from his self-imposed slumber. But we'll have to wait patiently till then to hear, at last, the first discordant notes in the great altruistic revel. . . . It was while listening to the radio that night that he made up his mind to keep quiet. He was tuned to the evening's early editorials, presented by a pair of talented reporters, each one the permanent holder of a daily ticket to ride the prime-time kilocycles from the two main commercial stations just over the border. In the war of the wavelengths, an event must always be couched in commentary, according to the principle that a listener hanging on his mind master's every word, convinced that he's deep in meaningful thought, is much easier to sway in the long run than the one left to think for himself. Result: the commercials plunge in through the breach, and sweep over his poor, feeble brain. Which is why the sponsors paid exorbitant prices for the precious seconds just before and after the editorials in question, aired by two of the monster's obedient servants: Albert Durfort, at 7:30, and Boris Vilsberg, at 7:45. Machefer had time to switch from one to the other and catch them both.

Albert Durfort was full of the milk of human kindness. (Machefer would have used a rather more vulgar expression. He always said the professional do-gooders turned his stomach. A little too harsh, perhaps, for Durfort, not a bad sort, really.) Constant crusader, he would gallop through radioland to the rescue, looking for supposedly desperate causes, barely taking the time to change horses between two campaigns, always panting for breath as he came on the scene just in time to deliver the downtrodden victim, expose a scandal, and lash out at injustice. A Zorro of the airwaves. And the public adored it. So much so, in fact, that some—the most obtuse—saw each nightly editorial as a serial installment: Durfort on skid row, Durfort and the Arabs, Durfort vs. the racists, Durfort and the police, Durfort against

79

brutality, Durfort for prison reform, Durfort and capital punishment, etc., etc. But no one, not even Durfort himself, could see that our Zorro was flogging dead horses, flying off to the rescue of issues long since won. Something else, strange but true: he was looked on as the model of the free, objective thinker. He would have been shocked and surprised to learn that he was, in fact, a captive of fashion, bound by all the new taboos, conditioned by thirty years of intellectual terrorism; and that, if the owner and general manager of the station that employed him entrusted ten million good Frenchmen to his care each night, it certainly wasn't to use his talents to tell them the opposite of what they supposed they believed in. As for the plush publicity that surrounded Durfort and flanked his little gems of moral indignation, it brought truly awesome results, though no one was awed in the slightest anymore, so long had the public soul steeped in this system of self-contradiction, like a turd in a toilet bowl, rotting away. All the press, or almost, played this curious poker, and won every hand. And Dio's paper led the pack, with its glossy, full-color spreads.... Men, get into the swing, wear suede this season! Your banker is your friend, invest with confidence! For a whole new *art* of living, Trianon Towers, five rooms, patio, barbecue, 480,000 francs! Vacation club, private beach, pool, 10,000 francs a share . . . Enough to make you suspect the capitalists of abysmal stupidity, or make you wonder if their show of good will was a payoff in advance to some Mafia of the future! It all paid for the inserts in those catalogues called newspapers, whose editors, decked out in suede, and barbecue-fed, with their Riviera tans, cried out for human liberation through an end to profits, preached rejection of money, that enslaver and corrupter of souls, called for doing away with all social constraints and for abject equality, all lines and bars down. It hit the spot. It sold. Whereas nothing else did. Why stand on ceremony? Go along with the times and sell out your conscience! In this world of ours, clearly, opinion-mongers the likes of Durfort, Dio, Orelle, Vilsberg and Co. have to live on their ideas since that's all they have. But if they seem to be sawing the limbs where they're sitting, egged on for some senseless reason by the man who owns the tree, please don't worry! They've already got their eyes on another nearby branch, one they'll grab at the very last moment, because surely you don't think the new world can come into being without them, after all! Their kind doesn't work for nothing. In the stew they're churning up before our eyes, you can bet they'll keep afloat, decked out in leather, with their Riviera tans.... And so, as he spoke of the armada, sitting

astride his branch already sawed more than halfway through, Durfort was his most convincing self, finding just the right words to hit
home, to sink into the muck of each heart with a soft little plop. With
appropriate variations, he played out the same master hands that had
made him famous: the case of the Greek deportees, and the more
recent one of the Algerian laborer accused of the rape and murder
of a little girl, and victim—perhaps—of a miscarriage of justice. With
relish and talent, Durfort reenlisted his Greeks, and pressed the
miscarriage of justice back into active service. And he made no bones
about it:

"You, my faithful supporters and listeners, know that I never
mince words. There's no compromise with despair. There's no compromise with evil. So I'm sure you won't mind if my talk gets rough.
Don't forget, if I did my bit, with your help, to change the fate of the
Greek deportees, and if I saved us all from putting an innocent man
to death—the most odious crime a society can commit—it's only
because I talked rough when I had to. Well, friends, the time has
come now for me to bring into your homes, with the sound of my
voice, a million more deported, exiled souls, exiled this time of their
own free will, but victims no less of the worst, most heinous miscarriage of justice since the world began. So I'm going to talk straight
from the shoulder again, and let the chips fall where they may. If you
want to eat supper in peace, good friends, I suggest you turn your
radios off for the next five minutes!"

"Hear that, Marcel? Durfort is onto something else!" "Josiane, tell
the kid to keep quiet!" In the low-rent flats a quick shot of red wine
washed down the news, since the heart's mawkish pleasure goes
sliding down better with something to chase it. It was washed down
with Scotch in the salon nooks of the patio suites, but ever so more
subtly; that is, instead of a few quick gulps to help swill down the food
for thought, the glass will be poised with a well-planned gesture, long
enough to listen, holding back to let the tastebuds build to exquisite
heights of thirst, then letting go all at once in a crowning orgasmic
burst between mind and event. . . . Three thousand two hundred
sixty-seven priests started frantically scribbling with an eye toward
the following Sunday—ready-made sermon, delivered to the door,
nothing to do with the gospel for the day, but who worries anymore
about such minor details? (Among the cast of thousands we should
note the presence of a certain married priest, Catholic and cuckold,
wearing a pair of Christian horns, and aware of the fact—a situation
so utterly new to the poor man, and muddling his mind into such

disarray, that for over a month his Sunday sermons seemed to leave him at a loss. Durfort's strong dose saved him from total silence. The therapy worked so well, in fact, that the antlered, oil-fingered gent forgot all about his sanctified horns and recovered that gift of thunderous fire and brimstone that made him the shepherd of the largest flock of masochists in the diocese. Perhaps we'll see him again bye and bye . . .) At the very same moment thirty-two thousand seven hundred forty-two schoolteachers hit on the subject for the next day's theme: "Describe the life of the poor, suffering souls on board the ships, and express your feelings toward their plight in detail, by imagining, for example, that one of the desperate families comes to your home and asks you to take them in." Irresistible, really! And the dear little angel—all simple, childish soul and tender heart—will spread four pages' worth of infantile pathos, enough to melt a concierge to tears, and his paper will be the best, the teacher will read it in class, and all his little friends will kick themselves for having been much too stingy with their whines and whimpers. That's how we mold our men nowadays. Because even the tough, hardhearted little brat, the one with all he needs to succeed in this life, is forced to take part, since children abhor standing out from the crowd. So he'll have to play along too, and work himself into a hypocritical sweat over the same philanthropic rubbish. And he'll probably write just as brilliant a theme, clever child that he is, and he may even wind up believing what he writes, because youngsters like this are never really bad, just different, that's all, just untapped potential. Then he'll go home, like his classmate, both of them proud of their fine compositions. And father, who knows what life is all about, will read the A-plus masterpiece, terrified (if he has the slightest imagination) at the notion of that foreign family of eight coming to live in his three rooms and kitchen, but he'll sit back and keep his big mouth shut. Mustn't frustrate the little angels, mustn't shock them, mustn't sully their innocent thoughts and risk turning them later into hopeless prigs. No, he'll wallow, ensnared, in his gutless affection, and chuck his little angel on a cheek flushed with pleasure, telling himself that he's really a dear, and besides, "out of the mouths of babes," isn't that what they say? . . . The mother will snivel in her handkerchief, eye moist with maternal affection rewarded. But let the famished Ganges horde show up some morning at their door—assuming, of course, that such a thing could happen—and there's one damn family that's bloody well had it! Perhaps instead of an open-armed welcome, despite the prophetic prose of the little remote-controlled angel, they'll take to their heels. The Western heart, down deep, is all sham. In any event, they'll have lost the strength and the will to say no! Now, multiply that by a million mindless themes, applauded by a million milksop fathers, and you get some idea of the climate of total decay. Could that be one explanation? . . . At the very same instant, some seven thousand two hundred and twelve lycée professors decided to begin their next day's classes with a discussion of racism. It didn't make the slightest difference what they taught: math, English, chemistry, geography, even Latin. After all, whatever his field, isn't the professor's role to develop his students' minds and force them to think? And so, they would have them speak their piece. The subject was there, ideal, made to order, too good to pass up: the fleet and its mission to cleanse and redeem the capitalist West! A fine topic, politically charged, with something for everyone, a limitless script in that ongoing cinema of the masses, spontaneous and unrehearsed, whose feeble and trite ideas, hashed over again and again, swallowed up any sense of reality, any notion of personal obligation. Here too, we need keep in mind only the negative side of these vapid and fuzzy debates. Let the Ganges invader finally set foot on the Côte d'Azur, and except for the warped, misguided few whom we'll see dashing south, like pyromaniacs to a fire, the brawling little robot brats will be more than content to pull down their pants, like daddy, howling, according to their imbecilic logic, that they've needed a kick in the ass for a good long time, and they really deserve what they get! The beast's obedient servants were counting on just such delightful results. . . . Well, there's no need to go through and count up the millions and millions of Durfort's faithful listeners. The whole of France gulped down the narcotic: when the time would come to cut off her legs, she was sure to be ready for the operation . . .

"True enough," Durfort's voice rang out over the air, sharp and clear, and so sure of itself, "the exile we're witnessing now is self-imposed. True too, the miscarriage of justice stems from no courtroom verdict. But the first is the offspring of poverty and neglect. And I'm sorry to have to tell you, my friends, that we all share the blame for the second. You see, we wealthy nations condemned our Third World brothers. We set up our walls, walls of every description —political, moral, economic. We sentenced three-quarters of the earth's population, imprisoned them, put them away, not for life, but for lives. Yes, for countless lives on end. Now, all at once, this gigantic prison is rising up in peaceful revolt. Our captives have begun to escape. A million strong, they're on their way, bearing no arms, no malice, and seeking just one thing: justice! So long as this planet of ours, this speck of a planet, shrunken to nothing by a hundred years of incredible progress, still bears two kinds of men, a scant five hours apart by plane, one whose average yearly income is no more than fifty dollars, and the other, some fifteen or twenty thousand—so long as that's the case, my friends, nothing will convince me, with all due respect, that one isn't an exploiter, and the other, his victim . . ."

"Exploiter, my ass!" Marcel exclaimed to Josiane. "That's a good one! What's for supper tonight?" (He squinted toward the oilcloth on the table, proletarian throne in the middle of what passed for a living room.) "Noodles, headcheese, a few scrambled eggs. What's that to brag about? And the TV payment? And the payment on the car? And how about my shoes? Look, nothing but goddamn holes!"

"Oh, not you," said Josiane. "He means all the ones with money."

"Oh yeah? Then let 'em shove some of it my way, why don't they! I don't go around barefoot. I work for a living . . ."

Let's give ear, in passing, to this discordant note. Good, canny common sense, a little uncouth and harsh—in other words, healthy —draws itself up to its dignified height and kicks up a fuss. Just a bit more effort and it could save the day. Marcel is no fugitive from the Ganges. He works, he wears shoes. He's a hundred percent man, and make no mistake! With some prodding you could get him to admit that he's part of a civilized country, that he's proud of it too, and why not? Peekaboo, it's our little white friend again, our foot-slogging soldier of the Western World, hero and victim of all its battles, whose sweat and flesh seep through all the joys of Western life. But he's hardly the man he used to be. He only goes through the motions now. This volley won't hit the mark. And there won't be another. When the time comes, he'll sit back and watch, as if none of it makes any difference to him. When he suddenly finds that it does, it will be too late. They'll have made him believe it's no skin off his nose, and that only the others—all the ones with money—will cough up and pay, in the name of equality, and brotherhood, and justice, or some such nonsense that no one dares question. And of course, in the name of the beast. But that's something they won't tell Marcel. Would he know what they meant? . . . In the name of the beast, Durfort stood guard, manning the ramparts of radioland. Nothing escaped his watchful eye. Soon he was at it again, sharpening up his aim:

"I believe in premonitions," the oracle's voice continued. "And it seems I'm not the only one. Like all of you just now, I heard Monsieur Jean Orelle. Well, something tells me that this warmhearted man has the same feeling I have, the same premonition, though he can't come

out and say so. The feeling, my friends, that the refugee fleet is
heading for Europe, for France. Yes, our very own paradise. And I
don't mind admitting that I hope I'm right. . . . Let me read the
official communiqué once more, the finest document France has
given the world since the Declaration of the Rights of Man. I quote:
'Since nothing on earth could give us the right to stand in the way
of this pathetic fleet, the government of France has decided to work
out, with its Western partners, an appropriate welcome in a framework of international cooperation, socialistically structured . . .' End
of quote . . . And there we are! Yes, there we are, my friends, with
hope and justice for all mankind! At long, long last! The earth's most
dispossessed and wretched souls begin to stir, and finally the mighty
West takes note. Finally she turns a willing eye and looks despair and
misery square in the face. Ah yes, my friends, what a day this is! What
a wonderful day! For all mankind! Because who can believe—with
our talk of welcome, our plans for cooperation—who can believe that
the time hasn't come for our own victims, too? Time to give our poor,
numberless masses a share in that affluent life that they see being
lived all around them, while they barely survive? No, clearly, we're
going to be forced to revise our thinking, reexamine the ties that bind
us, man to man. We're going to have to share our profits, invest them
in the social good, conceive our economy in terms of love, not personal gain, so that each one among us, even the lowliest outcast from
the Ganges shore, can finally claim his right to a rich, full life. There's
more to be said, my friends, and we'll say it in all good time. For the
moment I'll only say this: we're all from the Ganges now, and let's
not forget it! . . . Good night, until tomorrow."

"You've been listening to Albert Durfort and his nightly view of
the news . . . And now, men, a word of advice. For those weekends
in the country, those hunting trips, those long romantic walks
through the woods . . . Or just for those quiet evenings by the fire,
crackling and dancing on a fine old hearth . . . It's suede for the
well-dressed man! Yes, suede. More than just for your casual wear,
more than just to relax in, suede lifts you up to the heights of
fashion . . ."

Marcel felt reassured. Drill-press machinist at the Citroën plant, he
never wore suede; he never went hunting; he never took walks with
his pals in the woods, only sat by the highway, feeding his face,
watching the cars and waiting to see whether one would crack up;
he couldn't care less about sitting by the fire, finding all his aesthetic
delights in the beauties of the four-burner stove. Still, he wasn't the
sort to turn up his nose at fancy slogans. In fact, he enjoyed them.

That suede to relax in, to lift you up to the heights of fashion ... Well, that stuff wasn't for him, but it gave him a good-natured chuckle. And somehow he felt better knowing that such things existed. Straightforward radical, barroom debater when the spirit moved him, he blew up the system left and right with his verbal blasts. But have a few honest-to-goodness crises, and all of a sudden, deep down inside, he began to get worried, wondering if maybe the crumbs that fell from the hands of the bosses and profiteers, decked out in their suede, weren't better than no crumbs at all. He wouldn't admit it, not even to himself, but the idea had struck him that, as long as the bosses are rolling in money, and killing themselves to make more—between two hunting trips, of course, or two elegant evenings by that fine old hearth—the people manage to get their share, even if, sometimes, it may take a little squawking. . . . Yes, in his heart of hearts Marcel adored the suede way of life. You could think what you wanted about it and no one could stop you. But blow it to pieces? Bring it toppling down, if the chance ever came? No, never! At least, not Marcel! Then defend it, maybe? No, not damn likely! You don't defend social injustice, not even when you're much better off than the ones who have justice to spare. There it is in a nutshell. Could that be one explanation? Marcel is the people, his mind is their mind, half Durfort and half suede, not exactly the most compatible couple, but getting along by and large. And the people won't lift a finger to help. Not in either direction. We're not still back in the Middle Ages, when the poor exploited serfs would take cover behind His Lordship's walls the minute the tocsin pealed its warning that bands of marauders were loose in the land. If the boss—sorry, I mean the seigneur—didn't have enough troops, then the workers themselves—excuse me, the serfs—would take to the ramparts, while their wives went bustling about, preparing the cauldrons of boiling pitch. When you worked for His Lordship, you may have lived badly, but at least you lived. Not so when the lawless bands came plundering through, and left you with nothing to do but starve. Marcel isn't any less bright than his forebear the serf. But the monster has eaten away his brain, and he never even felt it. No, Marcel won't go running to man the ramparts against the Ganges horde, the latest marauders to pillage Fortress West. Let the troops fight it out by themselves. That's their job! And if they retreat, if they turn tail and run, it's not up to Marcel to bring up the rear and rush into the breach! He'll sit by and watch today's forts being sacked, watch them loot today's castles: the steel and concrete walls; the cellars, stuffed to the rafters with food; the store-

rooms, crammed with supplies; the workrooms, never idle; the para-
pet walks, the drawbridges, thundering under the constant tread of
feet; the fertile lands; the tower strongholds, filled with gold and
silver. Yes, he'll let them all go. He can't think anymore. They've
gelded his will of its instinct for self-preservation. . . . That night,
having heard his Durfort, Marcel would fall asleep with an easy
mind. "You see," said Josiane, "like I told you, it's the bosses who'll
pay for that gang. All the ones with money. Besides, so they're heading this way in their boats, all million of them. What's the fuss?
They're not going to get here so quick, don't worry! Take my word,
that . . . that armada, like they call it, won't come anywhere near us.
And even if they do, if they're such poor things, like everyone says,
well . . ." And on, and on, and on. . . . Hook, line, and sinker. Thank
you, Durfort!

At one point, however, there was almost a chance that Durfort
might lose his program. Of course, the chance was muffed. We'll go
through it in detail, though, and add it to our list of bungled oppor-
tunities, along with all the others. What happened was this. Right
after his famous "We're all from the Ganges now!," Durfort got a call
in the studio. The owner and general manager of Radio-East asked
him into his office:

"Really, my friend, don't you think you've gone just a little too far?
I appreciate your eloquence, and your generosity certainly is admir-
able . . . ("And generously admired!" he added, to himself. "A million
a month for five minutes a day! Talk about generosity!") . . . But this
time it's not some trivial issue, like the Ben Mohammed trial. It's not
even off at the end of the world, like another Biafra. No, it's big, it's
close to home. Just think. Once you bring us your million Indians,
once they move in to stay—I mean, assuming their ships could get
here, and assuming I don't take you off the air first!—why, the country will never be the same."

"Exactly what I have in mind! Do you think I'm talking to hear
myself talk, or just to make a living?"

"Perish the thought, my friend! . . . ("Self-righteous bastard!" he
said to himself. "I think he may even believe what he's saying!")
. . . But don't you ever ask yourself what something like this would
mean? The mixture of races, and cultures, and life-styles. The different levels of ability, different standards of education. Why, it would
mean the end of France as we know it, the end of the French as a
nation . . ."

"Yes, the rebirth of man."

"Don't give me that rubbish! The rebirth of man! Do you really believe that? For almost two years I've had you do the seven-thirty broadcast, right? Now seriously, in all that time, do you think your noble thoughts have done the least little bit to make man any better? Not damn likely, believe me!"

"Then why keep me on?"

"All right, I'll tell you, if you really want to know. I keep you on to amuse the crowd. After the psychics, the faith healers, the confessors, psychiatrists, advisers to the lovelorn, and all that bunch, what the public likes best are the great white knights, the righters of wrongs. Your type, that is. Well, right all the wrongs you want, we've got more than enough. A good ten years' worth, if you're smart and space them out. And as long as the public doesn't suddenly fall for some other kind of clown. But hands off the country, you hear? And hands off the economy that manages somehow to run it. They may not be perfect, but they're made for each other, those two. . . . And as long as I'm at it, I'll tell you something else. You live damn well yourself, much better than any of the downtrodden masses you serve up over the air every night. So take my advice. Be satisfied to expose our vices. That's enough. Maybe one day, if we can wait that long, it will do us some good."

"I knew you were callous, contemptuous, heartless . . ."

"Thanks! You mean 'realistic.' "

". . . but I never dreamed you were so disgusting! When I think it's a handful of men like you who pull all the strings, and run the whole show, I know it's damn well time to change our society!"

"Yes, well, you'll have to go change it on somebody else's station, not mine. That is, unless you cut out this crusade for your refugee friends from the Ganges."

"Not a chance."

"All right, then. Let's get out your contract. It'll cost me the usual arm and a leg to break it. You're good with figures! But never mind, we'll pay . . ."

"You won't pay a thing. I'm staying. You've forgotten the most important part. Read the contract through, if you please. . . . You see? The big suede promotion, the investment funds, Horizon Vacations, Pertal Gas and Oil, Tip Watches, Joie de Vivre Condominiums, the National Bank, et cetera, et cetera. . . . I know my accounts. And I know that every last one of those sponsors signed with you to get air time just before or after my broadcast. I got you each one of them, and don't you forget it. Tens and tens of millions of francs! You think you can afford it? Things aren't too hot right now . . ."

"I'll get someone else. You're not the only one in the business."

"No, that's true. But my name is the only one on the contract. And anyway, when it comes to our famous armada, every one of my colleagues worth his salt will sing the same tune."

"I'll hire Pierre Senconac."

"Senconac! That reactionary? My dear friend, learn your business! You know that in advertising, today, it's only the Left that sells. The Right is finished. The sponsors aren't crazy, they all know it too. . . . So Senconac takes my place. What do you suppose he'll say? I can hear him now! Save the race, save the country. Whatever the price, inhuman or not. Ship them back where they came from, back to their wastelands. Or sink them to the bottom. Or put them all in camps. Pretty words! Not quite what times like ours want to hear! And great for your competition! You'll see, your sales will hit rock bottom. . . . No, there's a moral to all this: nothing pays like generosity. If you don't believe me, pick up the phone. Call the National Bank, or Horizon Vacations. See what they say . . ."

The owner and general manager didn't make any calls. He didn't have to. He knew Durfort was right.

"In other words," he mused, "you're kind of a Trojan horse. You and all the rest. We've let in a whole damn cavalry of you. Including that bunch of first-class nags trying to run the government. I called the Élysée just before you came. They confirmed Orelle's communiqué. It's the official position, all right. But I still have hope. First, that my country can be saved, and second, that I'll send you packing, now that I finally see you for what you are. The press secretary stressed the word 'official.' Subtly, of course. But I think it's safe to assume that there's an unofficial position too. The President's, probably. Of course, it's hard to hear it over all the neighs and whinnies. Who knows, when all is said and done, maybe the sensible people will come out on top. If there are any left. God help us, there aren't very many . . . As for you, Durfort, stay out of my sight. I don't want to see you. But be careful, I'll be listening to every word you say. Step one inch out of line, one hair beyond the official position, and you're out on your ear, sponsors or no! For the moment, you're right, I can't touch you. You've got a reprieve. My board wants money, and they want it in a hurry. It's true, they've sold out to the Left. They're a slimy bunch, but maybe when they get good and scared they'll start thinking. And maybe the government will change its mind, and ask us to spread the word. The minute they do, you're out and Senconac is in, believe me! And the sooner the better!"

Yes, maybe. But it would be too late. France wasn't to hear a change of tune until the Ganges million were streaming off their ships. Even then the countercurrent had little or no effect on the drug-deadened brains. The capitalists themselves were no better off. Having lined their pockets hawking the drug, they had finally succumbed to it too. That could be one explanation . . .

At the end of Durfort's broadcast, Machefer heaved a sigh:

"Ah, gentlemen, ten more minutes and we get an earful of Boris Vilsberg on RTZ! . . . Someone go get the Juliénas. Only a good Beaujolais will help! . . . You're all too young to remember, but once upon a time we used to take care of guys like that!"

He was talking to three young men, huddled in his minuscule office. The sum total of his staff. Three literature students, very talented, earnest, and badly paid. Most of the time, not paid at all. What with rent for the office—three garret rooms on the rue du Sentier—and the cost of paper, typesetting, printing, distribution, and the telephone, the receipts from the sales of *La Pensée Nationale* didn't go very far. Ten thousand copies printed, four thousand sold, if that. For a daily, the brink of despair. What few ads there were barely paid for the Juliénas. As for food, old Machefer lived on noodles, or got himself invited to the Medical School canteen. . . . The four lower floors housed the offices and presses of *La Grenouille,* a satirical weekly of the altruistic Left, whose company owned the building. Late in the evening, when no one else was on the stairs, and when a little too much Juliénas inspired him to heights of derring-do, Machefer would make it a rule to empty the contents of his bladder on the mat in front of their office. A ritual, of sorts, and hardly a well-kept secret. The managing editor would shake his head, have someone clean up the landing, and send the office boy hiking to the garret with a pro forma complaint. And that would be that. His forbearance appeared to defy comprehension. Not only did he pass off Machefer's little prank with a stoical sniff; not only did he give his paper a roof over its head; but he actually printed *La Pensée Nationale* on his very own presses—title and opinions notwithstanding, and in spite of a rather capricious way with unpaid bills! Such tolerance from a doctrinaire thinker, even one with a sense of humor, might well cause a few jaws to drop. But not Machefer's. He wasn't taken in. One day, with more Juliénas than usual under his belt, he had given the mat an especially copious soaking—and in mid-afternoon, to boot!—only to find himself suddenly cornered by the managing editor of *La*

Grenouille: "Ah, no, Monsieur Machefer!" he had shouted. "This time I've had enough!" "How's that?" Machefer had answered, with a none-too-agile tongue. "I can't see why you're complaining! It's the same old smell your rag always has, isn't it? Now it stinks as bad outside as in. What's the difference?" The editor had replied in his surliest of tones, "Now look here! You know you have no lease, no press. I could throw you out tonight if I wanted! . . . Sometimes I wonder why I haven't already!" And Machefer, his mind much steadier than his legs, jibed back: "Well I'll tell you why, old chum! It's because, thanks to freedom of the press, you can print any trash you want, and poison the heads of a million damn fools. It's because, thanks to freedom of the press, you can go your merry way, sapping the strength of the nation, quietly tearing it down brick by brick, behind your convenient satirical mask. Well, the fact is, old friend, the people aren't all blind just yet, no matter how low they've sunk. To get them to swallow what you feed them, you need something vaguely resembling an opposition. For the moment, as long as you and your kind haven't won hands down, you can't let me go. I'm your excuse. Without me and a handful of other survivors not much better off, poof!, no more difference of opinion, no more freedom of the press! When the time comes, you won't think twice. But you still have a while to wait. Why, I bet you a case of Moulin-à-Vent, the best there is, that if I decided to fold up today, and stick the keys under your door, you'd buy up my paper on the sly, and keep it running yourself, just to make sure you had something to sneer at! It wouldn't be the first time. To 'hold the line against fascism,' or some bullshit like that, you've got to be sure there are still a few good pseudofascists handy. You have no kick! As demagogues go, you couldn't do better. I'm a pretty good buy—efficient, convincing, cheap. And I save you doing the job yourself. That's the price I pay for my innocent little whim. So leave me alone and let me piss on your mat in peace! You know damn well, when the time comes, you won't have to make a move to shut me down, except maybe walk up the three flights to tell me. And even then, you'll send your boy . . . Good day, Monsieur, it's been a pleasure!"

Worth noting, simply, was the rather surprised and thoughtful look on the editor's face as he went back inside. Buy up *La Pensée Nationale?* As a matter of fact, the idea had crossed his mind. . . . Worth noting, too, that on D Day, when the Ganges masses begin to leave their ships, run aground on the beach, and come streaming off by the hundreds of thousands, the office boy from *La Grenouille* will, in-

deed, climb up the three flights, and inform *La Pensée Nationale* that
its days are over, and that its editor has ten minutes to get his ass out
of the building and go jump in the lake. Because, throughout this
dark and seamy tale of often hidden motives, we should call attention, as we go along, to any perceptible chain of events that meets
the eye. When a mole shows his presence by burrowing close to the
surface, we mustn't fail to track him down. Of course, it won't do any
good. Still, maybe it will help us understand . . .

"No," Machefer went on, still sighing, "no chance that Vilsberg or
Durfort will find a hired killer or two in their bedrooms tonight. No
such luck. The Right has no killers anymore. We lost all we had
defending our last few colonies. What a pity! And besides, you can't
touch the bastards nowadays. The Left is so full of traitors, packed
in so tight, that no one can tell how they're selling us out, lock, stock,
and barrel. I guess the goddamn jig is up. Gentlemen, we're screwed!

Well, it's time to hear Vilsberg, and find out how hopeless things
really are . . ."

Boris Vilsberg was no Zorro. Unlike Durfort, who had no doubts
as he pondered the world, Vilsberg had doubts about everything in
sight. Which made both men very typical of the times, since dog-
matic, relentless doubt, these days, has the strength of assertion.
From the moment he took up the thinking profession, Vilsberg—a
man of vast culture, unmatched curiosity, and a clever, discerning
mind—bore his doubts like a cross of redemption. He moved his
audiences all the more, as they sensed a kind of personal anguish
each time he was forced to give up certain basic ideas that he seemed
to hold dear. Much too subtle to deal in such standard clichés as: "We
have no choice. . . . Times change, we have to change with them, no
matter how it hurts. . . . We have to find new modes of thought, more
in tune with the times . . ." etc., etc.—still, when all was said and
done, this sort of thing was precisely what most of his listeners in-
ferred. Many of them saw themselves reflected, especially those who
thought they were clever (or wished they were), which, in this day
and age, is a rather fair number. In private, Vilsberg complained that
he was misunderstood, that he only meant to voice his doubts.
Strange type, this man whom no one understood, and who nonetheless persisted in his mind master's role! Shrewd servant of the monster, prisoner of the sin against the intellect, drugged with his own
narcotic doubt, but probably not to blame. Day by day, month by
month, doubt by doubt, law and order became fascism; education,
constraint; work, alienation; revolution, mere sport; leisure, a privi-

lege of class; marijuana, a harmless weed; family, a stifling hothouse; affluence, oppression; success, a social disease; sex, an innocent pastime; youth, a permanent tribunal; maturity, the new senility; discipline, an attack on personality; Christianity . . . and the West . . . and white skin . . . Boris Vilsberg probed. Boris Vilsberg doubted. For years on end. And heaped at his feet, an ancient country, lying in rubble. Could that be one explanation? . . .

"At the tone, the time will be seven forty-five, brought to you on RTZ by Alpha, the watch that sets the tone for the times . . . And now, Boris Vilsberg and his nightly opinion . . ."

"Juliénas," said Machefer simply, holding out his glass.

Out of the radio, slow and calm, came Vilsberg's voice:

"As I read and listen to the first reports and comments on the Ganges armada, and its staggering exodus westward, I'm struck by the depth of human feeling that seems to pervade them all, and the candid appeals for a wholehearted welcome. Indeed, have we time for a choice? But through it all, one thing appalls me: the fact that nobody yet has pointed to the danger, the risk inherent in the white man's meager numbers, and his utter vulnerability as a result. I'm white. White and Western. So are you. But what do we amount to in the aggregate? Some seven hundred million souls, most of us packed into Europe, as against the billions and billions of nonwhites, so many we can't even keep up the count. In the past we could manage some kind of a balance, more precarious daily. But now, as this fleet heads toward our shores, it seems to be saying that, like it or not, the time for ignoring the Third World is past. How will we answer? What will we do? Are these the questions you're asking yourselves? I hope so. It's high time you did!"

"There, the work's cut out!" Machefer broke in, over Vilsberg's voice. "The usual bear hug! Nice and clear. Right up close. Enough to scare their pants off! Now, if only he'd go the next step, and tell them to shoot, tell them to blast the crowd to hell! But no! Not our Vilsberg!"

"I can tell," Vilsberg continued, "that you really don't believe how serious the situation is. After all, we lived side by side with the Third World, convinced that our hermetic coexistence, our global segregation, would last forever. What a deadly illusion! Now we see that the Third World is a great unbridled mass, obeying only those impulsive urges that well up when millions of hapless wills come together in the grip of despair. More than once in the past, from Bandung to Addis Ababa, attempts to organize and mobilize that mass had failed. But

today, since morning, we're witnessing a mighty surge, seeing it take
shape, for once, and roll on. And nothing—nothing, take my word—
is going to stop it! We're going to have to come to terms . . . But again,
I can tell, you don't really believe me. You'd rather not think. It's a
long, long way from the Ganges to Europe. Maybe our country won't
get involved. Maybe the Western nations will come up with a miracle
just in time. . . . Well, you're welcome to close your eyes and hope.
But later, when you open them up, if you find a million dark-skinned
refugees swarming ashore, tell me, what will you do? Of course,
we're merely supposing, granted. All right then, let's suppose some
more . . ."

"Now watch, kiddies," Machefer interjected, "here comes the pir-
ouette!"

"As long as we're at it, let's assume that we're going to take in these
wanderers. Yes, like it or not, cordial or begrudging, we're going to
take them in. We have no choice. Unless, that is, we want to kill them
all, or put them away in camps. Perhaps we have forty days left,
perhaps two months at best, before their peaceful and bloodless
invasion. That's why I want to suggest, in this time for conjecture,
that we all do our utmost to accept the idea, to grow used to the
thought of living side by side with human beings who seem to be so
different from ourselves. And so, I'm inviting you all to join us here
on RTZ, beginning tomorrow, at this same time each day, for our
new, forty-five-minute feature, 'Armada Special.' We'll try to answer
your questions frankly, all the questions you'll be asking yourselves
—and us—about how a million refugees, fresh from the Ganges, can
live together, in harmony and understanding, with fifty-two million
Frenchmen. I say 'we,' because, happily, Rosemonde Réal has agreed
to join me in this staggering task. You know her well for her percep-
tive thinking, her passion for life, her trust in mankind, her profound
awareness of the human soul and its innermost workings . . ."

"Good God, not her again!" Machefer exclaimed. "Isn't there anything that hag won't do to get on the air?"

"Needless to say, we won't be alone. Rosemonde and I have spared
no effort to bring in specialists from every field to answer your questions: doctors, sociologists, teachers, economists, anthropologists,
priests, historians, journalists, industrialists, administrators . . . Of
course, I don't claim that we'll have all the answers. Certain more
delicate problems—perhaps in the sexual or psychological realms—
certain problems that strike at the heart of that lingering racism
present in us all, may demand more thought and more specialized

experts. But we promise to strive for the truth, as the sensible, clear-headed people we hope we are, and we trust that we'll find the truth worthy of you, and of us. Later, when all is said and done, at the end of the gripping adventure begun this morning on the banks of the Ganges, if not one single hopeless wretch has come our way, then we, the public, will simply have played in the greatest radio game in history: the antiracism game. And believe me, we won't have been playing in vain! At least we'll have played for the honor of mankind. Then too, who knows but what, in some dim, distant future, we may have to play it again, and for keeps? . . . And now, until tomorrow, good night . . ."

"Rabble!" Machefer snarled. "It serves you all right. You've got the kind of radio you deserve! Hear that? A game! That's what they come up with! 'Bread and Circuses!' But who remembers Juvenal's contempt? No, antiracism is right in style, but they know it's not much fun to hear, they know it won't pay, so they make it a game! The way they've done so long with all the important issues. So long, that the people are used to it already. The fight against cancer? A game. Biafra? A game. Pollution? A game. Famine? A game. I could go on and on. You're incredible, all of you! You take the peons, bored to tears, and drag them out into the streets to buy their tickets and support the cause. You have them blink their lights to show they've got the spirit. You turn whole neighborhoods, whole towns into teams, competing to see who can get the most pledges. Then the monster telethon, day and night, flashing the results, with plenty of songs and show to liven it up . . . At midnight it's over. That's that. A good time was had by all. And what did it all accomplish? You dangled the fish on the line, frittered the issue away with fuss and fanfare. Over and done with. Then on to the next. And nothing ever changed. But no one was any the wiser. Well, this time the issue is us. We're the issue. But you'll see, no one will bother to notice. Just another game, that's all, only longer, because this time the fish is much bigger, and we'll have to keep him dangling for weeks and weeks. And when playtime is over, suddenly we'll come out of our daze and realize that it's too damn late, that nothing can save us. Too late! You should have been thinking, and not playing games! . . . Well, kiddies, don't miss the 'Armada Special,' it's going to be a ball! A whole army of fathead assholes, streaming out over the air, and drowning the country in a flood of their drivel! Oh yes, they know what they're doing, all right!"

"But Monsieur Machefer," piped up one of the students, "we've

got to speak out and expose the conspiracy! We've got to do something to smash it, dismantle it piece by piece, display it piece by piece
for all to see, to warn those who haven't rolled over and played dead
yet. We've got to fight this thing tooth and nail . . ."

"With a sale of four thousand copies? You've got to be joking!"

Just then the telephone rang.

"Hello, *La Pensée Nationale?* This is the news office at the Ministry
of Foreign Affairs . . ." Machefer couldn't place the voice, although
in fact, it belonged to Jean Perret, our little undersecretary friend,
disguising it as best he could.

"This is Machefer, editor in chief. What can I do for you?"

"We're taking a survey of the press," the voice continued. "Not to
influence anyone, of course. But we're anxious to get some idea of the
growing reactions to the fleet from the Ganges . . ."

"I see," said Machefer. "What you mean is, you're shaking in your
boots!"

The undersecretary choked back a laugh. Maybe so. But Machefer
didn't really see at all. The fact is, there was no survey, only one
solitary call to one solitary man, Machefer.

"Just an informal poll," Jean Perret replied, straining to sound
offhand. "Could you give us some idea, Monsieur Machefer, what
position *La Pensée Nationale* intends to take?"

At the Élysée Palace, the President of the Republic was waiting for
the answer. He had run the gamut in a single day: the Council of
Ministers meeting, which he had deplored; the press conference of
Monsieur Jean Orelle; and finally, the Durfort and Vilsberg broadcasts, heard in the privacy of his own apartment, where he vented
his rage to his heart's content. He had judged, with horror, the terrifying disproportion in the views presented. He had expected it, of
course, but not to that degree. All on one side, nothing on the other.
It was then that he had called Jean Perret, dialing his personal number himself: "Monsieur Perret," he had told him, "you're probably
surprised to hear from me, and I'll ask you to keep my call in the
strictest confidence. Frankly, in this whole Ganges business, you're
the only one I trust. No need to tell you why, I'm sure. . . . What I
want you to do is to call Machefer—discreetly, on some pretext or
other, I'll let you decide—and try to find out if his paper is planning
to take a position. It's simply inconceivable that certain things
shouldn't be said, and I think, the way things stand, that he's the only
one with the courage to say them . . ."

"It'll be an honor," Machefer answered, in a tone that suggested a sneaking suspicion. "Do I gather that your question is serious?"

"You do indeed," the voice replied. "Well then?"

"Well then, no position at all," said Machefer. "Not a word. There's only one of me, and there are lots of them. I'm weak and they're strong. I only have one round to fire, and it won't carry very far at that, I'm sorry to say! If I want it to hit the mark, I'll have to wait for the moment of truth, and then shoot last."

"And nothing until then? Really?" asked the voice, a little disappointed.

"Nothing . . . No, I take that back. Each day there'll be a front-page map—Asia, Africa, Europe—with a dotted line showing their probable route to France, and a heavy line showing how far they've come. No text. Just a caption: 'Only x more kilometers to the moment of truth.' That's all."

"Thank you," the voice said, simply.

The next day, just before noon, a messenger came rushing into the garret offices of *La Pensée Nationale*, and asked to speak to Jules Machefer in person. "I'm Machefer," the editor answered, surprised. "Just a minute," the messenger told him. And he took out a photo from his pocket, and compared the face with Machefer's. "All right," he said. Then he placed a package on the desk, and left without a word. In the package Machefer found two hundred thousand francs, in worn hundred-franc notes, and a sheet of white paper, unsigned, with these simple typewritten words: "Don't wait too long."

Nineteen

Back in the days of great national wars, among peoples who cared, the citizens used to tack up battlefield maps in their kitchens or parlors, with little flag pins marking out the front, and every night they would move them, or not, depending on the news. In France, at least, the practice died out as early as 1940, when the little paper flags were swept away, first by the winds of debacle, and then by the winds of indifference. At the height of that war, not a soul, or almost, showed the slightest concern—an attitude piously passed down, father to son, from then on. The daily map in *La Pensée Nationale*—clearly suggesting a vast battlefield under attack by an advancing army—made so feeble an impression on the minds of the masses, that the paper's sales increased by not one single copy. At the end of a few days, the student assistant editor in chief proposed that they change the daily caption, by adding something like: "Full-Scale War! Follow the Front!" "Damn right it's war," said Machefer, "but who's going to believe us? War? When our helpless enemies are dying left and right, thousands and thousands of miles away! No, the people can't think, their minds have been put to sleep. For them, there's only one kind of war, the kind they lay their stupid wreaths for, year after year. You can spread your word 'war' in black and white, in an eight-column headline, and the Frenchman won't much care one way or the other. That is, unless he's seen the enemy face to face, or heard the guns, or gotten his ration book! All it would get us is a bunch of housewives rushing to stock up on coffee, and oil, and sugar, and a bunch of snot-nosed brats rushing into the streets of the Latin Quarter. No, forget it. Let's wait. When the starving bastards show up off our shores, then we'll use the word 'war,' and hope it hits home. In the meantime let's leave the caption as is. 'Truth' is the word that counts. Nowadays nothing is as frightening as the truth. It's such a mysterious word. No one knows what's behind it. No one wants to. They avoid it. But it frightens them all the same. In a healthy country, when the chips are down, there are always at least a few who'll get so scared that they'll turn and look their fear in the eye, instead of running. And they'll pounce on it, and try to destroy it. That's what I'd like to see. But I don't have much hope. Is our country still healthy enough? That's the question . . ."

As best he could judge, Machefer wasn't alone. The shrewdest minds in the opposite camp had adopted an identical position, but for very different reasons. Confrontation, invasion, struggle between the races, penance by the West, end of imperialism—and other disquieting notions, put forward the first day without much reflection —vanished from the lips of the monster's most faithful servants. They too began speaking of truth. And how sweet it was to hear! They made no bones about it, spelled it out to the letter, blithely forgetting their twenty years' worth of hammer and tongs (and sickle), aimed at the shameful paradise of the Western World. Paradise? Why of course, why not? (It was even the title of one of Clément Dio's brilliant columns.) A paradise not so shameful anymore, all things considered, and one that we Westerners could suddenly take pride in. An immense, expansive paradise, limitless in its bounty, where finally we could reach out, in a spirit of brotherhood and peace, and take in those pathetic, starving souls from the Ganges, so desperately searching for a happier life . . . We should note here, too, for the record, a most interesting sidelight. Namely, that all through the country, every strike and social protest seemed to come to a most abrupt halt. After all, the Western worker was living in paradise all of a sudden. Do they have strikes in paradise? Certainly not. At least, so decreed the brains of the leading unions, two or three of whom knew precisely what they were doing. Weak-kneed as ever, the other unions—giants with feet of clay—wobbled meekly behind them. Could that be one explanation? . . .

By the second day even Durfort had changed his aim. It almost seemed that the word had gone out, that everyone had agreed. (Of course, the strings were all pulled by the beast, and the puppets never knew what moved them.) No more did he speak of the "gigantic prison rising up in peaceful revolt," or the need to "reexamine the ties that bind us, man to man." He picked simple stories from his file-card brain. Often even true ones. Stories about Third World children, adopted not so long ago, and now caring for their aged French parents. Stories about dark-skinned immigrants, model citizens today, some even with seats on town councils. Josiane and Marcel were moved to tears. . . . As for Vilsberg and Rosemonde Réal, they injected their own special hypos into the flabby and copious rumps of public opinion. With barely a squawk. Everyone on the "Armada Special," questioners and questionees, seemed to be of one mind. Judging by those good people of France screened by the switchboard at RTZ, skin colors are mere illusions, and everyone's soul is the same underneath.

During all those early broadcasts, in fact, there was only a single discordant note. It sounded when a certain listener insisted on getting on the air: "Hamadura . . . Indian and Frenchman, or Frenchman from India, if you like . . . Ex-deputy from Pondicherry, while it still belonged to France . . ." "Welcome to our program, Monsieur Hamadura," clucked Rosemonde the magnificent, "we're delighted to have you. In a sense, you represent the spearhead of the movement, the living proof of what can be accomplished when . . ." "Ha ha!" broke in the welcome Monsieur Hamadura. "Thank you just the same! You make me laugh, only it's no laughing matter. Spearhead indeed! I'd rather be the last of the last in that Indian mob! You don't know my people—the squalor, the superstitions, the fatalistic sloth they've wallowed in for generations. You don't know what you're in for if that fleet of brutes ever lands in your lap! Everything will change in this country of yours. My country now too. They'll swallow you up, they'll . . ." When Rosemonde had recovered from the first moment of shock, she pressed the red button in front of her, the emergency switch that let them get rid of a bothersome caller. "Obviously not a typical case!" Vilsberg cut in, calmly. "At any rate, Rosemonde, I imagine the gentleman said all he had to say. What strikes me as strange is the fact that he's an Indian. But I'm sure there's a reason. Perhaps our sociologist friend would venture an opinion . . ." The sociologist stopped to think. It was irrefutable: "An acute sense of repeated frustration, expressed in the rejection of one's own race . . . Caste prejudice . . . A common phenomenon in India . . . It wouldn't surprise me to learn that the gentleman's skin is quite light, and that he belongs to the Brahman aristocracy . . ." A tactical slip at the switchboard, and all of a sudden Monsieur Hamadura's voice came bounding over the air again: "I'm as black as a nigger!" he laughed. "Even worse," the sociologist countered, as Rosemonde dispatched the gentleman for good. "What we have here then is the classic case, so typical of the colonial context, of assimilation into the host culture's power elite, with a subsequent revulsion against one's own roots. The case of the white man's dog that hates the black. It's a very common syndrome . . ." And that was that. No more was said. But we haven't seen the last of Monsieur Hamadura . . .

As usual, it was Clément Dio, in *La Pensée Nouvelle*, who scored the most points. His spectacular special on "The Civilization of the

Ganges" had something for all those who thought they could think. Arts, letters, philosophy, history, medicine, morality, the family and society—everything found its way into the issue, signed by the best names in the business. Considering all the wonders that the Ganges had bestowed on us already—sacred music, theater, dance, yoga, mysticism, arts and crafts, jewelry, new style in dress—the burning question, by the end of the issue, was how we could manage to do without these folk any longer! As for the rest of us—spiritual sons of the Latins and Greeks, of Judeo-Christian monks and Barbarians from the East—could it be that what we needed to perfect our work of art was to throw our doors open to the Ganges, even if only to balance the materialism of our present-day life? The thought was advanced with caution, of course, but it came from Clément Dio, and nobody found it the least bit surprising. . . . And so, the press settled down to its cruising speed, cleverly playing on three basic themes, in varying combinations: the paradise of the West, the Last Chance Armada, and the role of Ganges culture in mankind's ultimate perfection. Meanwhile, public opinion went sailing off unconcerned, especially since three days had gone by with no word of the fleet, last seen by some fishermen from Madras, somewhere along the twelfth parallel north. Sole item of front-page news. Not much, but something the press could go to town on. No visible connection with any earthshaking event—if "visible" applies in the case of such blind opinion. But the beast gloated and rubbed its claws. The Pope published a tear-jerking message. A few social-minded bishops made something of a stir (in the spirit of Vatican III, they explained), along with the various world committees and philanthropic leagues, worked up by the usual troop of the beast's unflagging faithful. Just enough to fill out the prologue. At which point the International Ganges Refugee Commission, springing fully armed from the brain of the minister, Jean Orelle, held its opening meeting in Paris. Its members were veterans in the rat race to gnaw at the UN cheese, old hands with UNESCO and UNICEF, with Food and Agriculture, World Health, and UN Relief. They all knew their trade inside and out, and the dictates of their own gilt-edged existence. In short, they decided to sit back and wait . . .

The only distant reaction worth noting comes to us from Australia. Set off by themselves in their remote corner of the planet, the Australians have the distinction of belonging to the white race. They live like nabobs in that vast, empty land, assured of the limitless wealth of their mines and their flocks. One thing they do quite well is read maps. The armada, when it left the mouth of the Ganges, appeared to head south. To the south lies Indonesia. Skirt it as far as the Straits of Timor, and suddenly, there's Australia—precisely the route the Japanese were taking through the Pacific in World War II, before they were stopped just in time at the straits. Meeting in Canberra, as it did every Tuesday, for supposedly "routine deliberations"—a prosperous and vulnerable nation knows how to conceal its panic—the government published a communiqué, which, though buried in a mass of other texts, didn't pass unnoticed. "The Australian government," it stated, "considers it necessary to call attention to the fact that entry of all foreign nationals into the country is subject to the provisions of the Immigration Act, and that under no circumstances will these provisions be abated or rescinded." Plain and simple. Now, when you consider the model severity of the Australian Immigration Act, encouraging, as it does, the entry of Greeks, Italians, Spaniards, English, French—in short, all those white of skin and Christian of soul, while relentlessly excluding any trace of yellow, black, or brown —you will understand that, for the Australians, champions of the Western World stuck away in the farflung hinterlands of Asia, this reminder was intended to rally public sentiment. It encouraged the Australians, in rather veiled terms, to steel themselves against undue compassion, and served notice on the Ganges fleet to keep its distance.

Australia is a free country, and its press releases aren't censored. In no time the news had circled the globe. In the sickest of the Western nations, it crackled through the air like a racist manifesto, to a caustic accompaniment of slur and aspersion. It was clear to the beast that the battle had at last been joined. In London, Paris, Washington, Rome, The Hague, great mobs of young people, shaggy but well behaved, laid peaceful siege to the Australian embassies, with rhythmic chants of "Ra-cists Fas-cists We're-All-from-the-Ganges-Now!" Except in Washington, where the "pigs" still clung to some of their nasty, brutal habits left over from the "long, hot summers," the police were satisfied just to cordon off the embassies with massive but motionless detachments. It had been a long time since any democratic regime had been willing to lift its clubs in a racist cause. Besides, it would have been pointless. The demonstrators were content to demonstrate, careful not to endanger property, life, or limb. Some had even been seen waiting patiently in line for a red light to change before stepping off at a crosswalk. The beast had long since understood that violence was counterproductive, that it frightened public opinion, and risked waking it up with a start. The only violence it had let itself commit over the past few years—and that, more and more—had been in the name of wholesome, unassailable, and utterly selfless causes: art works stolen, then ransomed to aid some suffering people or other; airplanes hijacked, and hostage passengers released in exchange for medicines, food, and clothing; banks held up to benefit victims of some natural disaster, or some civil war . . . That kind of thing. Good, altruistic violence. Just another way of raising money, of giving to charity on a worldwide scale. Reasonable people took their heads in their hands, unable to cope with the moral upheaval. If they came to the conclusion that altruism doesn't justify out-and-out brutality, they made sure not to spread the word. Besides, who would have listened? Even when the beast directed its violence at inequalities of lesser dimension: when grocers in some poor part of town were attacked and beaten; apartments, left vacant for the summer, invaded by African squatters; shops looted, and their merchandise scattered through the slums; shady financiers grilled by guerrilla tribunals and convicted; abusive bosses, cleverly chosen, kidnapped and held . . . No, not a soul protested! And justice itself, shaken to the roots of its majestic calm, uncertain whether its laws had been made to bully society or defend it, never failed to agree that, indeed, there had been extenuating circumstances, never failed to free its prisoners, who would leave the courtroom in a cloud of glory. Enough to demoralize those men and women who considered themselves good law-abiding citizens; in other words, almost the entire population. In short, through its own diabolical devices, the beast had tucked cops and courts of the Western World safely away in its pocket, and was free now to indulge in what it termed "the shaping of opinion." And so, once again, opinion was shaped to believe that racism in the cause of self-defense is the scourge of humanity.

As for the shape that Western opinion should really have taken—namely, the realization of the mortal threat to its very existence—the Australian government's action served no purpose whatever. Trumped up, doctored, wrenched out of context—an excellent example is the photo of the Immigration Act splashed across the cover of Dio's *La Pensée Nouvelle*—it turned out to harm that same white world that it meant to protect. Much like that other defensive maneuver, when the Western shipping magnates—rather cruelly, perhaps, but in their own best interests—rerouted their vessels to keep them a good two days away from the refugee fleet. And that, just after the press conference of Minister Jean Orelle. It must have been written in the Book of Fate, in the chapter on the white man, that flashes of good sense, twitches of courage, or simple reflexes of self-preservation, were destined to remain rare exceptions, hidden or deformed, never able to add up to a meaningful whole. That could be one explanation . . .

In no time the Australian government's Immigration Act was forgotten, no longer relevant as the fleet changed course and headed southwest. The world learned the news when the armada, entering the Straits of Ceylon, between that large island and the tip of India, was spotted halfway between both coasts at the western end of the straits, just off Tuticorin. An Associated Press helicopter, bristling with telephoto and wide-angle lenses, flew over it some twenty times, at different altitudes. Among the photos that were published in the press the world over, certain ones were appropriately overwhelming, just enough to move sensitive souls without terrifying them unduly. One curious detail, however: the close-up shot of the monster child, perched on the bridge of the *India Star*, astride the shoulders of a gigantic Hindu, gazing out at the sea through his motionless eyes—that bloodcurdling photo, realistic beyond endurance, was published a mere six times in all. And then, only by papers of piddling circulation and infamous political stripe, like *La Pensée Nationale*. Are we, perhaps, to think that a few of the beast's devotees, in high, key places, guessed how devastating such a photo would be, and pulled the plug before it could make all the rounds? Or that, somehow, the editors in chief of the major Western papers decided against it on their own? Be that as it may, the fact remains that public opinion, for the most part, didn't even know it existed. That could be one explanation . . .

Another sidelight in passing, for the record. In Paris, our friend Mohammed—the one they called "Cadi One-Eye"—ran across a copy of *La Pensée Nationale* on a newsstand, with the monster child spread across page one. He bought the paper, cut out the picture, tacked it up on the wall in his kitchen, and chortled to his wife Élise: "Isn't he something, our ugly little brother! Some fun if he ever lands here! Then, by God, you'll see the shit fly!" The same thought went through the minds of assorted Third World diplomats and students, despite the fact that, thanks to their Mercedes cars, their fancy dormitories, double-breasted suits, embassies, white sheets and social successes, they were worlds apart from the half-starved monstrosity on the *India Star*. They pounced on their maps of the world, the lot of them, zealously planting their little paper flags, as if to mark out the route of their own revenge. Curious reflex, and one that would have plunged Boris Vilsberg's whole team of sociologists into hopeless confusion. These people who spent their vacations at the Vichy spas, whose sole contact now with their homelands was the peanuts they nibbled with their drinks, who refused to visit their poor old mothers, off in their villages, because they persisted in squatting on their haunches, yet who, with all their heart and soul, cried out for the destruction of a world where they had finally made their way! How unbending, the deep-hidden burden of envy and hate! The dogs of the whites were changing sides, that's all. They barked a lot, enough to help deafen opinion. But come the moment of truth, and we'll see them cowering in their kennels, trying to hide the feelings of hatred finally turning against themselves . . .

The Last Chance Armada sailed out of the Straits of Ceylon, and the world lost track of it once again.

Twenty

In the lengthy dispatch that he filed with his pictures from the helicopter, the Associated Press reporter spoke of a horrible stench rising
up from the water, in a kind of thick layer. "It gags you!" he wrote.
"The pilot and I soaked our handkerchiefs in gin and covered our
faces. It smelled just like shit!" (That last sentence never got published . . .) The fleet was already some forty-eight hours into the
Indian Ocean, sailing along the tenth parallel, toward the channel
between the Laccadives and the mainland, when a west wind suddenly swept in off the sea and over the whole of the Malabar coast,
as far south as Cape Comorin, bequeathing the stench to the land in
a long and lingering trail. The startled masses that peopled the region
lifted their heads, noses heavenward in pious pose, and sniffed in
terrified disbelief at the putrid cloud hovering above them. It clung,
reeking, to countryside and town alike, so strong that it quite overwhelmed the everyday smell of dried droppings, burned daily in
millions of earthen ovens and open fires, by millions of women cooking their meager dole, as they did the length and breadth of the land
. . . In short, the nomad Ganges stunk to the skies, as all of fleshpot
India had never stunk before.

Which brings us to a question of prime concern throughout the
armada. Namely, the problem of what to cook with. There was plenty
of rice, at least by frugal native standards. There was plenty of water
to prepare it. But each day they needed enough for a hundred boat-
loads, or a million mouths in all. From the first day out it was chaos.
The galleys were no match for the task, powerless to feed the thousands of teeming souls, milling about at one another's throats, outside
their doors. In time clans formed. Fortuitous families, chance geographical tribes that would last throughout the voyage, staking out
their spaces: forward, aft, belowdecks, by the workrooms, all over.
And each of these random tribes set up its own improvised galley. On
the biggest of the ships, like the *India Star* and the *Calcutta Star,* by
the time the fleet was off Ceylon, there were more than a hundred,
crammed in from stem to stern and from deck to hold, with rice
boiling day in day out, in saucepans, pots, steel drums, tin cans,
containers of every kind, over fires made from anything on board

that would burn. From the start, wood was scarce on these makeshift craft. Everything was fair game: the last few lifeboats, the bunk frames, the timbers in the holds, the paneling in the officers' chart rooms and cabins, even the handful of books from the libraries, such as they were. If not for the turd eater's prestige and persuasion, the charts, and logs, and sextant cases too would have gone up with all the rest. By consuming its vitals in smoke and flame, thousands and thousands of times, the fleet might have kept its fires burning to the end. That is, were it not for the need to feed the pyres as well . . .

India burns her dead. No sooner out to sea, the armada did likewise. Those who died on board, of course. Not the ones who fell into the water, like paltry vermin shaken from the flanks of the wave-tossed ships. And they died in droves, especially the very old and very young, worn out before they began, half-starved and barely clinging to life, and done in for good by a frenzy of expectation. On each deck the nomad Ganges relived the horrible cremations of Benares. Mass pauper cremations, economy style. Shapeless pyres heaped up from a few scraggy oars, old crates, rusty planks, hatchway covers. Endless piles of burning bodies—dank, slimy entrails, mostly —overspreading the sea with a noxious stench. Arms and legs tumbling from the pyres, too narrow for their loads. Heads of scorched hair, rolling at the feet of the squatting multitude . . . The cremators would poke long boathooks into the mass of molten, dripping flesh, and try to push it neatly back in place. Others would stir up the ashes with shovels, looking for chunks of unburned wood to revive the dwindling flames. Until the day, just out of the Straits of Ceylon, when the pyres burned their last, for lack of fuel, and the last glowing embers died out under hundreds of pots, and pans, and cans, and drums of rice . . . India is a sister to death, and mother of her dead. A hush fell over the fleet as the turd eater turned to consult the silent oracle. A bluish trickle drooled down the corner of the monster child's gaping mouth. . . . "Throw the dead into the sea!" the turd eater commanded. But what about the rice?

For the rice, no problem, no need to be told. There was only one solution. Every Indian knew it well. With no cow droppings at hand, our seagoing horde would have to burn its own, prepared by a tried and true peasant technique known for three thousand years. And so, the decks became weird workshops, where hands deft at molding this curious coal—children, for the most part, down on their haunches—took each new batch of turds, kneaded and shaped them, pressing out the liquid, and rolling them out into little round briquettes, like the kind we used to burn in our stoves not very long ago. The tropical sun did the rest, heating the sheet-metal decks, where the crowd had left great spaces, like giant drying racks, with thousands of the putrid mounds spread out to bake and harden into fuel. Other children, quick and clever, kept them supplied, eyes peeled for anyone, man or woman, poised in the humanoid fecal position. Zip! zip! There they were, hands flashing between two outspread thighs, grabbing the precious substance and trotting it off to the dung rollers while it was hot . . . All of which explains how the fleet kept cooking its rice, and why it spread the horrible stench our reporter friend mentioned (and which, by the way, caused many a head to be scratched on certain foreign vessels miles downwind).

Life on board had turned vegetal, at best. They ate, they slept, they saved their strength. They pondered their hopes for the future, and their paradise of milk and honey, with its gentle rivers thick with fish, whose waters washed fields fairly bursting with crops, growing wild for the taking . . . Only the children, the turd runners—darting, dashing, hands cupped, in and out—gave any signs of life in that stagnant throng, lying on deck like battlefield corpses laid out at day's end. But in time, very slowly, the flesh began to seethe. Perhaps it was the heat, the inertia. Perhaps the sun, pouring druglike against the skin and into the brain, or that tide of mystical fervor it swam in. Most of all, the natural drive of a people who never found sex to be sin. And little by little, the mass began to move. Imperceptibly at first. Then more and more, in every direction . . . Soon the decks came to look like those temple friezes so highly prized by tourists, prurient or prudish, but rarely touched by the beauty of the sculpture and the grace of the pose. And everywhere, a mass of hands and mouths, of phalluses and rumps. White tunics billowing over fondling, exploring fingers. Young boys, passed from hand to hand. Young girls, barely ripe, lying together cheek to thigh, asleep in a languid maze of arms, and legs, and flowing hair, waking to the silent play of eager lips. Male organs mouthed to the hilt, tongues pointing their way into scabbards of flesh, men shooting their sperm into women's nimble hands. Everywhere, rivers of sperm. Streaming over bodies, oozing between breasts, and buttocks, and thighs, and lips, and fingers. Bodies together, not in twos, but in threes, in fours, whole families of flesh gripped in gentle frenzies and subtle raptures. Men with women, men with men, women with women, men with children, children with each other, their slender fingers playing the eternal games of carnal pleasure. Fleshless old men reliving their long-lost vigor. And on every face, eyes closed, the same smile, calm and blissful. No sounds but the ocean breezes, the panting breaths, and, from time to time, a cry, a groan, a call to waken other sprawling figures and bring them into the communion of the flesh . . .

And so, in a welter of dung and debauch—and hope as well—the Last Chance Armada pushed on toward the West.

Twenty-one

The sea was quite placid for that time of year, just a broad swell of leisurely, crestless waves, good-naturedly nudging the pathetic fleet along. Among the frequent explanations we have seen fit to offer in the course of the present account, one, perhaps, is of greater importance than all the rest combined. Namely, the fact that the waters remained so incredibly calm throughout the nearly sixty days of the great ocean trek. One has to believe that God had taken the hundred ships in hand, let one (and only one) fall by the wayside—just to prove to His faithful the power of His dominion—and set the other ninety-nine down safely on the Western shore. And that, for one of two reasons: to prove to the whites of the world that they had triumphed long enough, or—perhaps we'll find out in the next world, who knows?—to show them that the time had come to steel their souls once more, cast out all pity in a single night, if they wanted to merit the protection and favor rightfully due the chosen people.

Out in the middle of the Indian Ocean, between the Laccadive archipelago and the island of Socotra, the big river tugboat straggling along behind was suddenly sucked down into the calm blue water. Laboring under an impossible load, unfit for the surge of the open sea, she had struggled to keep pace since the fleet left the Ganges, always making the others slow down to let her catch up. Whenever the engines of the *India Star* would stop, whenever the shudder of her ancient turbines died, as they did each time the tug strayed from view, the monster child—whose ears were sharp despite his silent tongue and frozen gaze—would begin to fidget, his face and body alive with tics and twitches. The turd eater would grow anxious, and so would the rest of the armada's high command, at their permanent posts on the bridge of the *India Star*. Too bad for the tug! Loaded down with the sorriest of the lot—the outcasts, the pariahs—she had already paid the sea a heavy toll. Her length and excess weight had turned her into a kind of driftwood wreck, barely rising from the surface of the water. Each time a giant wave came along, it would wash nonchalantly over her deck, from stem to stern, with no special fury, choosing its victims as it passed, and sweeping them off in the wake of the fleet. From time to time a foreign vessel would spot some of the corpses, circle them slowly at a cautious distance, and dash off, full speed ahead, as the shipping lines had ordered. Each day the tugboat's rail had dipped deeper, in spite of a load growing lighter and lighter as more and more outcasts were served up to the sea. Until that moment, finally, when, heading through a wave scarcely bigger than the rest, she simply went under and never came up, strewing the surface with her only remains: some three thousand drowning wretches, flapping and flailing their arms and hands in a forest of brown. One by one, the ships flashed the message forward to the *India Star*, and one by one, they ground to a halt. But the pause was brief. On the bridge, when the turd eater went to turn around toward the distant disaster to see what he could see, the monster child, still perched on his shoulders, began to shake and quiver. Tears streamed from his eyes. His stumps came to life and thrashed at the air like the wings of a wounded bird gasping its last. His father turned back, facing the west, toward the prow of the ship and the corpse-free seas beyond. The monster stopped shaking. Twice more the same maneuver, twice more the same result. A clear command that the fleet was to proceed. Which it did . . . When the floundering castaways saw that they were being left behind to die in the middle of the ocean, the forest of arms and hands fell suddenly still in a gesture of submission. From then on, once rid of the poor little Hop-o'-my-thumb hanging on its coattails and begging it to wait, the fleet was able to make better time. In fact, it was this extra speed that saved it from disaster. On Easter Monday morning, the very day after the fleet had run aground along our southern shores, and the very moment that the last refugee, waist-deep in the water, was leaving the last ship and heading for the beach, a murderous storm blew up over the Mediterranean. A few hours later, and the whole armada would have gone down for sure, and everyone and everything on board along with it. Could that be one explanation? . . .

The world learned about the lost tugboat some ten days later. Indeed, it need never have learned at all, since the fleet, without radios, was utterly silent. (Besides, it wasn't about to ask anyone for help, or anything else for that matter.) The story would never have come to light, were it not for a drunken Greek sailor talking to himself at a table in a waterfront bar in Marseille, and an overly eager reporter, back from his daily cat-up-a-tree. The reporter spoke Greek, for the simple reason that he too was a Greek, living in self-imposed exile since the days of the colonels' coup, along with a number of musicians, actors, and writers, now all but forgotten. He had had his moment of glory. Then Greece went out of style, replaced on page one by other victims of oppression. (Because the important thing about oppression, if you're going to keep it panting in the public eye without killing it outright, is to make sure there's plenty of variety.) And so, he had a score to settle, which he did that very day, worth noting, because the results must also be counted among our explanations . . . "There were thousands of them in the water," the sailor sniveled, eyes riveted to the bottom of his glass. "All black, and dressed in white . . . So many . . . And lots of them still alive, take my word! . . . And we plowed right through them, twenty knots, just like that!" A sudden sweep of his arm across the table sent his glass smashing to the ground. The reporter had plucked his remarks out of the general hubbub. He went over to sound out more details. Shocked by the enormity of what the sailor told him, he took him home, sobered him up, fed him some supper, and got him to tell all he knew. No doubt his officers had given the strictest orders not to breathe a word. But he gave in, more than likely, to a sizable offer of cash, not to mention the pangs of his conscience, staggered by the hideous spectacle he had witnessed, and in which he had played a part.

What came out of his story was this: the Greek freighter *Isle of Naxos*, skippered by Captain Notaras, was en route from Colombo to Marseille through the Suez Canal, with a cargo of precious wood. She had crossed the tenth parallel, halfway between Ceylon and Socotra —the sailor, a qualified helmsman, had just taken his turn at the wheel—when she came across a first half-dead victim, who seemed to come back to life as the ship approached, waving a feeble hand out of the water. The sea was calm, there was no wind. The captain ordered the engines cut, and called for a boat to be lowered. At just that moment, the officer on watch, spotting the poor devil in his glasses, noticed that the water all around him was teeming with corpses, just below the surface. The captain grabbed his binoculars. There, spread out before him, far as the eye could see, was an ocean of bodies, some floating on top, some slightly submerged, depending on whether they were living or dead. "The mob from the Ganges!" he exclaimed. And he called back the lifeboat, already being lowered, and gave orders to start up the engines, easy astern. The drowning man, seeing the ship pull away, closed his eyes without a murmur, and let himself sink. "Captain!" the officer shouted. "Are you just going to leave them to drown?" He was a very young man, pale with shock and on the verge of tears. "You know the orders," Captain Notaras replied, "they're pretty damn clear. Besides, what if I took on that crowd, what then? What would we do with them all? My job is to haul a load of wood, not to help that mob invade Europe!" By now the officer was openly weeping: "But you're sending them to their death! You don't have the right!" "Oh, don't I?" the captain answered. "Well, that's where you're wrong!" And, turning the pointer to "Full Speed Ahead," he called down to the engine room: "Give me all you've got!" And he snapped at the helmsman, "Steady as she goes! Half a degree, to the left or right, and I'll have you tossed in irons for mutiny at sea!"

"Steady as she goes" meant straight ahead. And straight ahead stretched the seascape of black, white-petaled flowers, some dead, more alive, bobbing like human seaweed on the surging, swelling tide. At twenty-five knots, the Greek freighter *Isle of Naxos*, thanks to its captain's will and the passive complicity of its crew, cut down a thousand souls in the space of five minutes. Probably the greatest one-man crime since the world began, except for acts of war. And it was precisely as an act of war that Captain Notaras, rightly or wrongly, envisioned his crime, driven on, no doubt, by the name he bore and its long, noble history.

In Greece, the Notaras family prided itself on belonging to an ancient and honorable clan, though they may well have merely been namesakes. A portrait in the captain's cabin pictured a dark-eyed, deep-gazed giant of a man, in a suit of tooled armor, with a tuft of white plumes streaming from his helmet's golden crest: Luke Notaras, archduke and admiral of the Byzantine fleet, commander in chief of the last Christian galleons just before the fall of Constantinople to the Grand Turk, Mahomet. Escaping from the massacre and captured by the janissaries, he was brought to Mahomet with two of his sons, two young boys of unusual beauty, "that Grecian beauty," wrote the historian Doukas, "that inspired so many centuries of artists and poets." Now, the Grand Turk had a liking for young boys in general, and the two sons of Notaras in particular. But for some strange reason, in the midst of the carnage, he wanted them willing, and brought to his great silk bed by their father. An aesthete's whim? The ultimate refinement of voluptuary pleasure? Be that as it may, the Notaras trio, standing proud and erect among their captors, were quick to refuse. The two boys were beheaded on the spot, while their father looked on, and the admiral himself laid his head on the block. Since then, every Greek with the name of Notaras—and a goodly number they are—is fiercely proud of the memory of that tragic triple murder. Oddly enough, the name was far more common outside of Greece than within its borders, in the Hellenic colonies of Smyrna, Damascus, Alexandria, Istanbul, or on Cyprus and along the Black Sea coast, as if the Notaras clan—of disputable ancestry—still clung to its taste for a life in the farflung outposts of Christendom. One finds a Colonel Notaras in the Greek armies of Asia Minor, during the war against the Turks in 1922, and an urban guerrilla named Notaras on Cyprus, both of them guilty of their share of atrocities. Captain Luke Notaras, skipper of the Greek freighter *Isle of Naxos*, simply added his name to the list . . .

Clutching the bridge rail and looking out over the water, the young officer on watch had gazed in horror at the dismembered bodies, tossed like balls against the hull of the ship by the swift-churning water. "I felt like I was hypnotized," said the helmsman. "It was like driving a great big tank, rolling over a bunch of bodies, lying on the ground, and crushing them to death. I only hope they all died quick, before they got caught on the propellers in back. I didn't get a look in back, but I heard from some of the others that it was full of chunks of flesh, all bloody. . . . And the whole time, the whole five minutes it lasted, she didn't go an inch off course. Not an inch. I can't explain it. All I know is, I did my damnedest to keep her heading straight. It was awful. . . . Once in a while I'd look over at the captain, thinking maybe he'd yell out, 'All right, that's enough!' But he didn't! He just stood there, with his eyes wide open, and a smile on his face . . ."

As might be expected, the affair caused a stir. Shipwreck and massacre, both at once? Too much for the fragile Western World to bear! Published by a Marseille daily, picked up next morning by the whole French press, and by every major paper in the West, the sailor's story circled the globe. The least one can say is that it ravaged public opinion. Convinced that it was guilty of everything in general—having had it drummed home for so long—the West now saw itself guilty in particular, and with a good, concrete reason to boot. The beast had a new, unhoped-for symbol—Captain Luke Notaras—and it trumpeted the name far and wide. Luke Notaras took his place on the infamous roll of current events, in the chapter on the cutthroat whites, a chapter kept zealously up to date by the lackeys of the beast, who never missed a chance to spout out all the most evil names, wholesale and en masse, like a threat, a warning, a hideous reminder. No Dreyfus case here, with its violent pros and cons.

Arrested in Marseille and thrown into prison, Captain Notaras had everyone against him. In this day and age, let a rapist hack a little girl to bits, let a murderer bash in an old man's skull for a hundred francs, or any such horrible crime of the sort, and modern justice will always trot out psychiatry to the rescue, or at least the excuse that our nasty, perverted society is really the culprit. But not so in the case of Captain Notaras and his dastardly deed. No one bothered to delve for profound explanations. Captain Notaras was the white race incarnate, convicted of blind racist hatred. Period, new paragraph. Why that hatred? Yes, that was the question, and the psychiatrists might have asked it, had there been a real inquest and trial. (But the inquest, thanks to public pressure, was rushed through, one two three. And the trial, scheduled for Aix-en-Provence, the Tuesday after Easter, never got to take place, for obvious reasons. Besides, on Easter Sunday evening, the captain had already escaped, just after his guards had gone running off themselves . . .) What memories, what forebodings could have shed light on such a crime? A crime so hard to fathom, in fact, that a whole new understanding, a whole new mentality would be needed to assess it. Instead, there was talk about making an "exception," and bringing back the death penalty just for Luke Notaras! The staunchest enemies of capital punishment supported the suggestion in their papers. And heading the list, Clément Dio, of course; the same Clément Dio who had been so vocal in defending many a no less heinous crime committed in the name of this Third World cause or that, by countless "guerrilla liberation units" of any and every kind. Clearly, it never occurred to anyone that perhaps Captain Notaras, gripped by some bloodthirsty madness or other, had "liberated" himself from something too. Even Machefer kept quiet. Yes, even Machefer! For a moment he had toyed with the thought of heading a column with Talleyrand's celebrated mot on the murder of the Duc d'Enghien: "Worse than a crime, a blunder!" But he dropped the idea. Who would have understood? It was far too subtle, and public opinion had only one thing in mind now: to bay with the wolves.

Yes indeed, a blunder . . . Two notions essential to any spirit of Western resistance were torn down that day, or at least badly shaken. The first, the notion of attack, of invasion—beginning to make some headway in a few minds here and there, despite the obvious nonviolence of the Ganges fleet, and the constant bludgeoning by the press —sank to the bottom with the ill-fated tug. Such pathos, such weakness would never be a threat. After all, how *could* it! As for the second, the notion of self-defense—even less acceptable to Western opinion, bound up in its complexes—it was nipped in the bud, having found only one antichampion for its cause, in the person of Luke Notaras, the man with the red hands, dripping with the blood of his innocent victims. At his microphone, Albert Durfort summed it up: "There's no Luke Notaras among us, my friends! And there never will be, believe me!" Marcel and Josiane were convinced. That could well be one explanation . . .

The Notaras affair had at least two practical results. For one thing, it permitted the world to locate the fleet, last spotted as it passed through the Straits of Ceylon. (Hundreds of little flags, stuck into hundreds of maps, made a leap of two thousand kilometers westward. In all of Third World officialdom, hands were rubbed with glee —except for the Arab world, that is, where exultation froze aborning, the moment it was plain that the fleet was heading for the Red Sea and Suez . . .) For another, it prompted the International Ganges Refugee Commission—having moved its headquarters to Rome in the meantime, where the winters are warmer—to start showing signs of life. From the first stage of droning discussions and Platonic hopes and dreams, it moved to the second, the on-site inspection; which, besides giving the impression of action, often provides for a pleasant vacation at UN expense, and never matters in the slightest, since so much time goes by between inspection and report, that the problem in question has already changed shape many times over. But this time, no pleasant vacation for the members of the commission. The Ganges armada—with no de luxe hotels, no pools, no beaches— clearly had little to attract these good folk. And so, the inspection was assigned to a wing of the French air force, based in Djibouti, and pompously dubbed for the occasion the "I.G.R.C. Friendship Flight," with UN markings, and the whole shooting match. Plenty to fill out the numerous press releases that were bound to follow . . . The pilots of the "Friendship Flight" returned to their base, perplexed, to say the least. They had never seen anything like it. After several low passes over the fleet, looping and dipping their wings as a sign of good will, they were finally obliged to accept the facts: not a single face had looked up, not a single arm had been waved, not a single fluttering handkerchief or scrap of cloth had displayed the slightest interest. "And yet," the wing commander radioed, "they're alive, I'm sure of that! I can see them from here . . . Eating, moving around, cooking . . . Some walking up and down on deck, some . . . Yes, that too! . . . But not so much as a look in our direction! They couldn't give less of a damn if we're here or not!" No doubt the monster child had set the proud example. The Last Chance Armada intended to go it alone. Some saw that as all the more of a threat. But for most, that pride in the midst of despair shone forth with epic grandeur. "They're not coming here as beggars, but as men," noted Boris Vilsberg on "Armada Special." And he went on to ask: "How will we respond to this splendid example of human dignity?"

The communiqué from the I.G.R.C. was a model of tact: "It would seem, for the moment, that there need be no concern for the fate of the Ganges armada. The ships have been located at such-and-such latitude and such-and-such longitude, sailing in calm waters, at a speed of ten knots, with no apparent difficulty. Conditions on board appear perfectly normal. No request for aid or assistance was received by our planes, which flew over the fleet throughout the day. The long-range forecast for that part of the globe predicts an extended period of clement weather. Reconnaissance missions will continue to be flown at regular intervals, to be ready to offer immediate help should the need arise. At this time no precise information is available regarding the ultimate destination of the fleet, inasmuch as no government spokesmen, attachés, or representatives have as yet set foot on any of the ships of the fleet, nor will they do so, pending an express request. The governments participating in the International Ganges Relief Commission have decided to respect the sovereign will of the refugees, in accordance with the right of all peoples to self-determination, as set forth in the charter of the United Nations."

Damn hypocrites! What government in its right mind would have dared lay a hand on such a deadly gift, except, of course, to pass it on to its neighbor! And then, what a diplomatic battle, what sordid maneuvers, what pleas of poverty, while blessed opinion would watch and weep! The West was nothing but a game of roulette, with a little black ball in the middle, bobbing and bouncing, still waiting to make its choice. And all those who understood gazed at the ball in terror . . .

Twenty-two

While everyone assumed that the fleet was about to sail into the Gulf of Aden, en route to Suez, it was spotted some seven days later off the Comoro Islands, sailing into the Mozambique Channel, heading south toward the Cape of Good Hope. There could be no doubt in the minds of the French pilots, flying back from a routine patrol to their base in Diégo-Suarez. What they saw was the Last Chance Armada, no question. Ninety-nine ships in two long lines, strung out behind two big, rusty, lop-stacked steamers—the *India Star* and the *Calcutta Star*—whose description had been sent to every navy and air force in the Western World. The weather was holding fair. The sea was strangely calm. Nothing, in fact, seemed to threaten the relentless course of the fleet from the Ganges. But if no explanation could be found, there was no less surprise at the shift in its course, which apparently had taken place—figuring an average speed of ten knots—somewhere to the east of the island of Socotra, the outpost guarding the Gulf of Aden.

Although it was careful to keep the news secret and not leak it out to official circles or the press, the fact is that the government of Egypt had taken a hand in the matter. It had done so by itself, without consulting its Arab partners, without informing the appropriate world bodies or foreign powers, in an atmosphere of intrigue and alarm bordering on sheer panic. The mere thought of a million desperately impoverished refugees stuck in the Suez Canal through some sailing mishap, or perhaps through some move by the Western nations, was enough to strike terror in the ministers' hearts. Understandably so. Egyptian indigence has long since proved its powers of elasticity, but accepting the impossible is quite another matter. Diplomatically, politically, economically unthinkable! And so, in total secrecy and total confusion, orders were radioed to the last Egyptian torpedo boat still left intact from the wars with Israel, to proceed to confront the armada, and persuade it to alter its course. "Just how?" asked the Egyptian admiral. "Should I use my guns if I have to? And if so, how much?" The reply was as terse as it was ambiguous: "You have a free hand. May Allah guide you! Bon voyage! Over and out." The Egyptian ministers, obviously, had no wish to go into detail.

Besides, what could they have said? Still, one mustn't conclude that they were speaking idly. In those unprecedented times, when divine will made itself felt at every turn, they were placing their faith in Allah, fervent Moslems that they were. And Allah heard them. Who knows how things might have worked out if the peoples of the West, in similar straits, had put their faith in God, by name, and stormed their churches the way they did in those blessed ages past, when plagues and invasions buttressed their faith?

The confrontation took place some six hundred kilometers east of Socotra. It didn't last long. The admiral was up on the bridge, relaxing, amber prayer beads in hand. All at once, the first clouds of smoke puffed over the horizon, closely followed by that first noxious whiff, growing thicker by the minute. With all the speed still left in her engines after twenty-five years of service and three unsuccessful wars, the Egyptian craft headed straight for the fleet. Once she was abeam of the *India Star*, she hauled around in a broad arc and came up abreast of the steamer, cutting her speed to let her sail side by side, just long enough to send a message over. As for what went through the actors' minds in this drama of confrontation between the two ships, there isn't much to tell. It was noon, and the sun, in a cloudless sky, flared like the fires in a blazing furnace. On board the *India Star*, the mob lay drowsing. Nothing could have wrenched it from its torpor. Nothing, that is, but the news that the long-promised paradise was at last in view. Now then, the Egyptian sailors, with their dark skin, their black hair and eyes, were surely no harbingers of the white man's Promised Land. A few of the passengers lifted their heads, only to let them droop, next moment, back to the deadening stupor of sleep. Two or three children waved a friendly hello, but they soon gave up: every Egyptian eye, transfixed, was gazing at the bridge of the *India Star*, where some kind of hideous pygmy, perched on a giant's shoulders, and wearing a gold-braided cap, was waving a pair of twisted, handless arms. These men were no strangers to woe and despair; and grotesque, misshapen bodies were a common enough sight the length and breadth of Egypt. Still, they were staggered by what they saw. Never, in Egypt's darkest hours of suffering and shame, had they seen the fearsome likes of that monster's face, epitome of woes untold, but of woes infused with a kind of sacred fire, peopled by strange, dark powers, supreme and unbending. The admiral shuddered in spite of himself, in the presence of this nemesis incarnate. "Allah preserve us!" he murmured. "Praised be his name for making us poor! Now send the message!

There must be someone over there who understands Arabic . . ." An officer put the megaphone to his lips. "Aim at the bridge of the *India Star,*" the admiral added. "That's where the brain and the soul of the fleet are, believe me!"

"The admiral and commander in chief of the Egyptian navy sends greetings to you, his brothers from the Ganges, and wishes you a safe voyage. The government of Egypt, however, is concerned for your security, and strongly advises against your attempting to pass through the Suez Canal. Some of your larger vessels run the risk of sinking. Our country is poor. We can be of no help. The admiral has orders to make sure that you receive this message, and that you give it your utmost attention. Good luck and Godspeed!"

His binoculars trained on the bridge of the *India Star*, the admiral watched and waited. As if, by some miracle, a ship unlike any that had ever sailed the seas could play by the rules and send back an answer. Any kind of answer—by megaphone, signal flags, semaphore, or just an old-fashioned hand-to-mouth shout. Did these people have the slightest idea of such things? He felt a kind of deep distress well up within him, a feeling he had never known, not even in the thick of battle, like a sudden awareness of how helpless we are to cope with the superhuman. And that message? Absurd! Just so much official jargon, meaning little, saying nothing concrete, and with no teeth whatever . . . All at once, on the *India Star*, the mob seemed to rise up from their sleep, in a body. The monster was still waving his arms, high atop the bridge, and thousands of pairs of eyes were watching in rapt attention.

"Repeat the message," the admiral commanded. "This time tell them they've got five minutes to change course. Or else . . ."

"Or else what?" asked the officer.

"Or else . . . Or else, nothing! . . . No, wait. Just say this: 'May God show you the way . . .' No, damn it! Strike that! . . . Let's stop playing games. That's not our style or theirs. Make it plain and simple. Tell them: 'You've got five minutes to turn around. If not, I open fire. So God damn well better show you the way!' "

On the bridge of the steamer a man made a sign as if he had understood. He was wearing a blue pea jacket with four gold stripes on the sleeves, but his head was bare. The captain, most likely. He pointed to the monster, astride the giant's shoulders, then disappeared into the wheelhouse.

"Load the anti-aircraft guns," said the admiral. "Tracers. One round. Aim them over the bridge, up between the mast and the smokestack. Forty-five degrees. Then stand by to fire."

He shook his wrist free and looked at his watch. As the seconds ticked past, the *India Star* and the Egyptian craft sailed on, side by side, due west, toward Socotra and Suez. The endless fleet trailed on behind, meek as lambs, blind, dumb, and unthinking . . .

The fourth minute went by.

"Open fire!" the admiral shouted.

He was used to the guns, but never before had he heard them make such a deafening din! Could it be that his nerves, stretched taut, made them seem all the louder? Or perhaps . . . Perhaps they had thundered from some unknown sky, in some other dimension, bouncing off some mysterious reflector . . . The admiral pulled himself together. The volley traced its streaks of fire over the bridge of the *India Star*, and disappeared into the sea. Seconds later, a noise burst up from an unearthly silence, a howling wail unlike any sound of man or beast. A kind of spasmodic pant, like gusts of wind moaning through some vast, sepulchral cavern. The monster child was bellowing out his cry! More incredible still, he turned his head! Just once, but he actually turned it! When you realize that he had no neck, that he couldn't move a muscle in his misshapen body, except to thrash his truncated arms and twitch his contorted, featureless face; when you realize, too, that the flap of skin that passed for a mouth had opened just once in a similar cry—on the banks of the Ganges, when the *India Star* was stormed by the mob—then you have to believe this was something of a miracle. At least, such was the thought of the thousands teeming on deck. And such was the decision of the fleet's high command, up on the bridge, as they gathered around the latter-day Christopher, towering above them. Of course, there must be another, more rational explanation. No doubt, when the shells went whizzing through the air, booming overhead, the creature's sudden terror, for just a split second, shook up centers in his feeble brain disconnected since birth. Hence the cry. Hence the twist of the head. In this day and age, that's how we explain, quite simply, such miracles as the ones at Lourdes, for example. The sun at Fátima? Mass hypnosis. And so on and so forth . . . Perhaps there's a clue to be found in this basic disparity in viewing the marvelous. Two opposing camps. One still believes. One doesn't. The one that still has faith will move mountains. That's the side that will win. Deadly doubt has destroyed all incentive in the other. That's the side that will lose.

The monster had turned his head toward the south. A moment

later, the man in blue came out of the wheelhouse, where he must
have gone to consult his maps and chart his course. Again he gestured, and his eyes met the admiral's. Despite the distance, both men
seemed surprised to discover a look of relief in their glances. The
tension fell. The mob settled back, like grass in the wind. . . . Little
by little the channel between the two ships grew wider, broadening
to a river, and finally to the open sea. The *India Star* was pulling
away, and behind her, ninety-nine wakes, describing a great, sweeping arc, a quarter of a circle, heading due south. An hour later, the
fleet had vanished beyond the horizon. At which point the torpedo
boat sailed off full tilt, as if to escape the armada's path, like those
Western ships that had fled at its approach, before they could be
snared in the traps of compassion. On board, an admiral, deep in
thought. Feeling rather like someone who has seen a ghost, wondering if he really did, and knowing that no one will believe
him.

At this point in our story, it's clear that the fate of the West has just
been sealed. Let's take stock and see why. Had the fleet passed
through Suez, the West might perhaps have been saved. On the
shores of the narrow canal, at the gates of the white world, in fact,
there would have been no dearth of objective observers to describe
the bare truth, see it for the threat that it was, and bear witness
against the unnatural marriage about to take place; no lack of diplomats stationed in Egypt, tourists, businessmen, foreign nationals,
reporters, photographers—all there to watch the antiworld sail by,
and get themselves an eyeful, almost close enough to touch it. Just
imagine them cheek by jowl with the fleet. Picture them confronted
by that floating debauch. Seen from a plane, in cleverly captioned
pictures, that suffering, stinking mob was a pitiful sight indeed. But
seen up close, on its nightmarish ships, passing one by one just a few
yards off shore, it would have caused more than a little dose of fear.
A good, healthy fear, and one that certain observers—partisan blindness and conventional ethics notwithstanding—could have injected
just in time into the flesh of our Western World. It would have been
hard to quash their stories, to rub out their panic before it could
spread. We might have remembered poor Consul Himmans and his
lonely death by the banks of the Ganges, killed for being the first to
see the light. We might have understood the crime of Captain Notaras a little better, or paid more attention to the warnings of a man
like Hamadura, gagged for his high taboo-treason. If only the Last
Chance Armada had passed through the Suez Canal . . .

But no, it turned south, and headed for the Cape. If a last chance was lost, it was the West that lost it. And if the slightest flicker of a flame still remained, the affair of the so-called South African threat would put it out once and for all.

Twenty-three

The Notaras affair had died down—too quickly for the mind masters' liking, to be sure—when the South African scandal broke. The first had seen bloodshed. The second saw only threats, explicit enough, but not followed through. "Too bad about those South African bastards," Clément Dio observed, at a meeting of his board. "What a shame they couldn't give us a real good massacre while they were at it! Why couldn't they play it the way it was written?" But the two affairs do have a good deal in common, especially the uses they were put to, and the incurable effects they both had on public opinion. Another point worth noting: if the fleet had passed through Suez, world conscience would have had far less time and incentive to set the West up for the kill. That could be one explanation . . .

The fleet was crossing the Tropic of Capricorn, into the waters off the Republic of South Africa, when certain moderate Western papers, most likely at the instigation of their respective governments —in France, it was a well-known evening daily—came up with an observation of geographic and economic import hitherto unnoticed. The Ganges fleet had been looking for a paradise. Fine! We were waiting with open arms, ready and willing to help. We weren't heartless, after all! But why should they take such risks, why bear the martyr's cross from sea to sea, with torments untold, when, after all, just one look at the map would show that paradise was a stone's throw away: South Africa, of course! There ensued a round of unctuous mouthings in praise of South Africa's numerous advantages: her area (almost three times that of France), her small population (one-third that of France), a climate made to order, a high level of technical and economic life, a huge store of untapped resources . . . Such being the case, why ask poor old Europe, far away as she was, to come to the aid of the armada, when certain basic climatic and demographic problems—not insurmountable, perhaps, but no less real—might very well prevent her, despite her best intentions, from offering adequate assistance? (For the record, in passing: the "climatic and demographic problems," subtly euphemistic, were a direct, though top-secret inspiration of the President of the Republic. A timid attempt at moral backfire to stem the conflagration, but without success.) Then came the flood of figures, assessments, statistics, plans of all kinds: the computers can answer whatever we ask them. Financing? No problem. Europe would foot the bill. We would send them money, machines, technicians, entrepreneurs, doctors, teachers—whatever the South Africans thought they would need! (Notice: the first signs of panic. "Whatever you want, only keep them away! Away from us!" But panic isn't the same as that good, healthy fear. It turns you to jelly, it melts you to nothing, as we'll see before long . . .) At the end of his column, our editor had dispatched utopia southward, with a few flicks of the pen. A plausible hypothesis. Reasonable, humane, full of hope for the future. Of course, the first thing was to consult the South African government, and put out some feelers to the leaders of the fleet. Perhaps the International Ganges Refugee Commission . . .

What a hue and cry!

The servants of the beast flew into a rage. Apartheid! Blacks with passes! Racist dictatorship! Shame of the human race! The whole verbal barrage. With South Africa, that limitless scapegoat, that convenient target for the self-righteous conscience, the world had stopped wearing kid gloves long since. Entrust a million poor dark-skinned devils to protectors like that! Slavery, no less! Avast, you wishy-washy moderates! The Ganges rose up of its own free will, of its own free will it's going to choose its fate! . . . There was only one danger: that the constant cries of welcome to our shores might frighten public opinion, and force it to take sides too soon. Better to do what was done in the past, get it softened up slowly, little by little, for its ultimate, fatal surrender. The prima-donna pros had sensed the danger. Following Clément Dio's example, they shut their mouths, calmed down their rash and overanxious troops—another feeble chance that the Western World missed!—and bet on a violent South African reaction that had to pay off in their favor. Which is just what happened. Like the Australians and their Immigration Act, only magnified a hundredfold, and served up by the whites on a platter, this time with no mincing of words!

Under siege in their rightful homeland, the Afrikaners had turned their backs on Britain and the Commonwealth, and burned all their bridges behind them. With the buffer state of Rhodesia washed away in a sea of blood, with the weight of Africa pressing against their gates and the weight of world scorn bearing down on their conscience, sapped from within by armies of pastors and priests, singers and writers, the Afrikaners had stopped wearing kid gloves too. As the twentieth century wore itself out in an unremitting hatred of white supremacy, they persisted in offering up one atrocity after another. And they did it on purpose. They seemed to enjoy it. As long as they were going to be heaped with insults, they might as well deserve them! A planet apart, no question! ... As for their reaction to the plan, no official communiqué was forthcoming, but the President did hold a brief news conference in person. We can only quote the highlights of it here. From the outset he was plainly on the offensive, as he spoke to the tightly packed crowd of foreign correspondents from the Western press:

"As always, gentlemen, I know that you've come here as enemies. In a few moments our telephones and teletypes will be at your disposal to let you spout your usual loathing of us to the rest of the world. Just let me make one thing clear: the Republic of South Africa is a white nation with eighty percent blacks, and not—as the world would like to think of us, in the name of some mythical equality— a black nation with twenty percent whites. That's the subtle difference. And it's one that we insist on. It's a question of background, of outlook. You'll never understand . . . But let's get to the point. At this very moment there's a fleet of Third World invaders heading for the Cape, a hundred miles off our shores. Just off Durban, to be exact, according to last reports. Its only arms are weakness, misery, a faculty for inspiring pity, and its strength as a symbol in the eyes of the world. A symbol of revenge. What puzzles us Afrikaners is the masochistic way the white world seems bent on taking revenge against itself. . . . No, I take that back, we're not puzzled at all. It's only too clear. That's why we reject this symbol out of hand, because that's all it is: a symbol . . . Gentlemen, not a single refugee from the Ganges will set foot alive on South African soil, under any pretext whatever. Now I'll take your questions . . ."

Q.—"Are you suggesting, Mister President, that you won't hesitate to open fire on defenseless women and children?"

A.—"I expected that question. No, of course we won't hesitate. We'll shoot without giving it a second thought. In this high-minded racial war, all the rage these days, nonviolence is the weapon of the masses. Violence is all the attacked minority has to fight back with. Yes, we'll defend ourselves. And yes, we'll use violence."

Q.—"Supposing the fleet has decided, in fact, to land en masse on the shores of your country. Will you give orders to have it blown up?"

A.—"I think that the threat will discourage an invasion. Frankly, gentlemen, it's my impression that the fleet is heading for Europe, and that you'll have to be asking yourselves that question in just a few weeks. But I'm willing to answer in principle, since I'm sure that's what you want. . . . Yes, if need be, we would bomb the fleet out of the water. Hiroshima, Nagasaki, Dresden, Hamburg . . . Think of all the cities razed to the ground back then. . . . Who cared what it cost to pry victory loose? Who worried then about the price, the millions of unarmed civilians—yes, women and children then, too—burned, dismembered, buried in the rubble! War was war! I was only a baby, but I remember. Everyone cheered! . . . Well, today it's still war, just a different kind! All I can say is, if we have to do it, we won't enjoy it, believe me . . ."

That last was probably the one spontaneous comment the President let slip, once his temper had cooled. And he meant it sincerely. Like the sensitive man complaining that he's going to have to kill his rabid dog. The phrase circled the globe. *Clunch,* the satirical English weekly—especially nasty—published its best cartoon in years. It pictured a dungeon cell, and in the middle, the President, butcher knife in hand, bending over a naked Hindu, all skin and bones, stretched out on the rack. On the walls of the cell, an array of giant pincers, cat-o'-nine-tails, spiked collars, thumbscrews, an electrical device, and a soldering iron. On the ground, a tub, a wheel, and an iron cage crawling with rats. The prisoner, dripping with blood, his one good eye staring in terror at the knife-wielding white. Tears streaming down the President's face. And underneath, the caption: "Tsk, tsk, poor thing! War is war! Now I've got to kill you, but believe me, I won't enjoy it . . ." Reprinted in color, the *Clunch* cartoon spent a week spread over every newsstand in France, on the cover of *La Pensée Nouvelle. La Grenouille* went one better, with a cartoon plastered across page one. The President appeared as a jaunty, bearded peasant, in a Boer general's uniform, potbelly spangled with cartridges and loaded down with guns, pipe between his lips, brimmed hat turned up on one side. Sitting by the ocean, looking out at the water. All around, behind him, the landscape strewn with corpses. Bodies hanging from gallows galore. Black figures huddled behind barbed-wire fences. The President, big and fat, sitting on a mound of living creatures, smothering them under his bulk. In the background, off in the distance, the Ganges fleet sailing by, caricatures of ships, with human arms stretching toward the shore. And the caption: "So sorry we can't let you in. But we already have our share of happy blacks!"

Enlarged and put on posters, the two cartoons made the rounds of
the South African embassies in all the capitals of the Western World,
draped in black crepe and held up by demonstrators who, this time,
added silence to their nonviolent arsenal. No slogans, no shouts. Just
long lines, filing past, slowly, without a word. Some had even tied up
their arms and legs, like the chaingangs of years gone by. In Paris,
at an official reception, Jean Orelle refused to shake hands with the
South African ambassador, and made quite a point of turning his
back. "What a shame," murmured the ambassador, who spoke our
language like a native, "that the minister from France should be such
a deadly boor!" The quip was picked up, and it soon spread through
Paris, blown out of proportion by the media. It had already begun to
set off a diplomatic row, when Albert Durfort saw fit to reply, "And
what a shame, Mister Ambassador, that the Boer from South Africa
should be so deadly too!" Boris Vilsberg, of course, tossed in his two
cents' worth: "Our faces will always be white with shame!" ("White?"
Marcel objected. "He means red! Doesn't that guy know how to
talk?" "No, no," Josiane explained a moment later, "that's what he
means. White with shame. Because after a terrible thing like this, we
should all be ashamed that we're white!" And that's that . . .) Three
of the best-known salons, in the city's most fashionable quarter,
closed their doors to South African diplomats. One of the hostesses
shrugged off the problem in these charming terms: "Bah! We'll take
in some blacks instead, that's all! Do you think there are any in Paris
who are poor enough to help us? To teach us, I mean? Really, I think
their diplomats here dress much too nicely. They should be more
careful of their image. Frankly, I'm beginning to find them a little
shocking . . ." Even old Esther Bacouba sprang up fully armed from
the depths of her bygone vogue. By now she no longer sang, only
warbled, her golden voice cracking with age. But her head of tight
white ringlets, and her handsome, stately face worked miracles. At
the Palais des Sports people came in droves to hear her. Just for her,
Clément Dio came out of artistic retirement. Known once upon a
time for his lyrics of a certain social bent, he had written such popular
ditties as "Paris, You're a Bitch!" or "I'm the Guy They Call Dirty Old
Ahmed," not to mention the lilting little samba "My Milk-White
Breasts, Your Coffee-Brown Thighs" . . . For Esther Bacouba's return,
he penned "The Ballad of Man's Last Chance," set to a three-note
melody by a certain Indian sitarist. Twenty-five verses. A good fifteen
minutes, beginning to end . . . A Palais des Sports gripped in silence,
stock-still with emotion, plunged in darkness. And, standing alone on

the platform, as if suspended in a thin beam of light, the aged black
singer, eyes closed, hands joined together, warbling:

"Buddha and Allah went off to visit
The nice little god of the Christians
Pulled out the nails
Took him down from his cross
Mopped his disappointed brow
Sat him in their midst.
'You owe us your life, you nice little god
What will you give us in return?'
'In return I'll give you my kingdom
For now the thousand years are ended
Yes, the thousand years are ended now ...'
... Pulled the nice little god into a circle
A circle around the empty cross
Then carpenters three
They all went to work
With the pieces of the cross
Built themselves a boat
For now the thousand years are ended
Yes, the thousand years are ended now ..."

And so the thousand years ended, and the Ganges armada wafted
its way on the hoarse three-note twang of a sitar, and a broken,
breathy, once-great voice, through a hundred thousand jukeboxes,
prize-winning song, number-one record all over the world, ingenious
(and infamous) hit, sailing out in the neon glare of supermarket drug-
stores and over the hi-fi's of weary bourgeois, chanted in vaulted
cathedrals by choirs of guitar-strumming pagans (as the old priest
looks up at the band of young toughs, resignation in his eye), danced
to the nighttime rhythms of melancholy love, smoked to the puffs of
hashish and pot, droned by young beggars haunting streets and sub-
ways, floating the airwaves' prevailing winds ten times a day, and at
night hummed along on the lips of long-distance truckers, of children
about to fall asleep, of couples undressing without a glance: "Yes, the
thousand years are ended now ..." Ah! The power of a beautiful song!
Lyrics by the Great Unknown, as set down by the inspired pen of our
own Clément Dio. That could be one explanation ...

What chance, after that, of ferreting out from some inner recess
of the self, from the deep maze of ready-made thoughts and emo-

tions, some hateful remnant of a dauntless courage to throw against pity? No need to rehearse all the pastoral letters, the newspaper columns, the group petitions, the students' themes, the professors' sermons, the moral stands of every description, the panels of blithering fools, the parlor chitchat, the salon clichés, the weeping and wailing: it's all there, in one giant swell, even more than after the Australian affair or the case of Captain Notaras. But the beast is careful to keep hands off, and not jostle public opinion unduly. Just let it go on, content with itself, in passive acceptance. If it grows too active and lets itself think, who knows how it might be shocked into panic? The South African affair has played its role, doctored up and deformed like the ones before it, wrenched out of its context. The monster's minions gloat behind the scenes. Now everything is ready for the final act . . .

And yet, well oiled though it was, the machine did misfire. But only once, and with no real damage. Which shows how clever the beast can be when nasty little obstacles spring up in its path. After their President's violent declarations, what on earth made those same Afrikaners, a few days later, try to pass for Sisters of Charity, out of a clear blue sky? The fleet was rounding the Cape of Good Hope, heading north-northwest up into the Atlantic, leaving the coast behind, when all of a sudden it was peacefully intercepted by a flotilla of barges from the South African navy. At the government's invitation, reporters and photographers were watching the maneuver. It lasted no more than a quarter of an hour. On strictest orders from the South African admiral, not a soul set foot on the ships of the armada, not a word was exchanged. (And besides, the apathy of the refugees, and their unbending silence, would have doomed any contact from the start.) No, South Africa, quite simply, was furnishing the Ganges fleet with provisions! The operation had been worked out to the letter: sacks of rice hoisted up in great loads, giant tanks of fresh water, crates full of medical supplies—all placed on board in record time. After which each side proceeded on its way, the armada out to sea and heading toward Senegal, the South African craft back to port on the Cape . . . And then the incredible happened. It took every officer, every reporter, training all their binoculars on the Ganges fleet, to admit the impossible: the armada was dumping everything into the water! The anthill, suddenly roused, had been stirred up to almost a frenzy. On deck the crowds formed human chains. Sacks of rice passed down the line, from hand to hand, and plunged into the sea, one after another. Groups of men by the dozens pitted shoulders and crowbars against the huge tanks, and toppled them overboard, one by one. And everything sank to the bottom, except for the crates of medicines, lighter than the rest, bobbing along on the waves like a dotted line marking the wake of the fleet. Then the dotted line stopped. There was nothing left to dump. . . . On board the South African craft, jaws dropped and hung agape in disbelief. Was that any way for a starving mob to act? Of all the explanations offered on the spot, the South African admiral's probably made the most sense. Landing at the Cape, surrounded by a pack of reporters bombarding him with questions, the admiral, hands in pockets, could only shrug his shoulders with a look of profound disgust . . .

But you have to give the beast credit. You have to admire its cleverness and skill! All at once it gets wind of something unpleasant, something barring its route. An act of charity, of all things! Conscience money? Long overdue? Ulterior motives? Say what you like, it was still a humane gesture. With some kind of contact, or at least an attempt. A helping hand held out, in the flesh. Enough to risk making those Afrikaner types seem like downright nice people to a flabby world opinion! . . . Those racists, nice people? Careful now! Enough is enough! After fifty-odd years of flimflam and claptrap, the West could slide back to its racist past, throw up new defenses against the present peril . . . The beast smells disaster, sees its prey escaping! . . . The whites could wake up, surprised and relieved to find themselves drawn to those once loathsome racists, so much like themselves! . . . Oh no, not a chance! Wouldn't that be just lovely! . . . But the West is no phoenix rising from its ashes. Hardly more than a fragile fly, buzzing on the loose. With one flick of its claw, the beast catches it, crushes it to death. South Africans? Nice people? . . . Just enough for one gulp! . . .

The Western press, at its eloquent best, makes sure we get the word. No need to read through all the small print. The headlines will suffice: "South African Generosity, True or False? Five Questions and Answers" (moderate, London). "Bon Voyage, Pretoria! Good-bye and Good Riddance!" (moderate, Paris). "Blackmail in Human Despair" (left of center, The Hague). "Was Poison Their Real Motive?" (lurid left, Paris). "Handouts Won't Help" (moderate, Turin). "Charity South African Style: A Slap in the Face" (far left, Paris). "Go Peddle Your Stuff Somewhere Else!" (left of center, Frankfurt). "Armada: Poison Plot Fails" (far left, Rome). "Lunch à la Pontius Pilate" (moderate, Brussels). "Armada Dumps South African Rice, Keeps Self-Respect" (moderate, New York). "No Compromise for the Ganges Refugees" (Paris, far left) . . .

The last was the headline over Clément Dio's column. Not a word in his paper about the poison nonsense. That wasn't his cup of tea. But he didn't mind a bit if, through no fault of his own, it sent shockwaves through the low-rent flats. As usual, he hewed pretty close to the truth. (Though, of course, not too close. The unvarnished truth isn't something you publish. Just enough to keep his reporter's conscience all in one piece. A delicate balance that he played really well, and that made him so deadly whenever he turned his sincerity loose . . .) He had hit on the truth. He alone, or almost. He had flushed it out with no trouble at all, since it sprang from the very same source as his hatred. Yes, that was it. The Last Chance Armada, en route to the West, was feeding on hatred. A hatred of almost philosophical proportions, so utter, so absolute, that it had no thoughts of revenge, or blood, or death, but merely consigned its objects to the ultimate void. In this case, the whites. For the Ganges refugees, on their way to Europe, the whites had simply ceased to be. They no longer existed. Paradise had already changed hands, and hatred made faith all the stronger. Which was what Clément Dio was trying to suggest, without showing his colors or theirs: "No Compromise for the Ganges Refugees . . ."

That same day, Jules Machefer got another anonymous packet. One hundred thousand francs this time. A note was pinned to the first sheaf of bills. A slip of white paper, unsigned, with four typed words: "Don't wait too long!" Added at the bottom, a hastily handwritten "Please!" And he wasn't alone. The new underground was bristling with many such efforts, all secret of course. The owner of Radio-East, for example, where Albert Durfort held forth in all his glory, was sent two hundred thousand francs at home. (It came as no surprise, we might add.) Inside, a note asked, "Will we have to pay through the nose to hear a different tune?" But he couldn't do anything either. Not yet. And he hinted as much, as subtly as he could.

As for Machefer, he kept playing dead in his foxhole, according to plan. That day, the front page of *La Pensée Nationale* showed its usual map of the fleet's itinerary: a solid line for the distance covered, a dotted line for the route still ahead. And above it, a boldface eight-column caption:

ONLY 10,000 KILOMETERS TO THE MOMENT OF TRUTH!

Ten thousand kilometers . . .
How far is that, really? Very? Not too? One day? Maybe never?
. . What's on TV tonight? A good comedy, maybe? . . .

Twenty-four

Two weeks later, just the caption had changed: "Only 5,000 Kilometers to the Moment of Truth!" In the meantime, nothing new. Total silence. Clear, blue skies. Off in the distance, the armada, plying its unseen path over sea-lanes long deserted. An old friend by now. And world opinion, cruising on course, taken in by the universal brotherhood myth, singing "The Ballad of Man's Last Chance," and listening to Rosemonde Réal as she chirped the results of her children's art contest, based on the theme "Our Guests from the Ganges." Under the aegis of Monsieur Jean Orelle—Nobel laureate in literature, Minister of Information, and official government spokesman—the best of the entries were put on exhibit. At the Petit Palais, no less. Framed, lighted, catalogued on vellum, titled in gold, arranged by subject: at home, at school, in the hospital, the factory, the country, the street ... It cost a small fortune. Mammoth publicity. With every important voice in Paris dying to chime in. The opening was the social event of the season. Thick with celebrities, everywhere you looked. Five famous recluse painters, millionaire Marxists, aloof from the honors heaped on their work, even left their châteaux in the sun for that one special night. The Petit Palais, acrawl with reporters and their ever-present mikes, rang to the rafters with their chorus of "oohs" and "ahs." The young artists had outdone themselves! Never had youth, by nature so flighty, poured forth such a wealth of talent! ... And no one with enough good sense to observe that these masterly works from the brushes of children, grotesque little gnomes, were the proper concern of psychiatry, not art. The Minister set the tone, standing in rapt attention before a gouache, particularly garish. Against a red background, it pictured a kind of arm-waving harlequin, one black foot, one white, one white calf, one black, one black thigh, one white, and so on, up to the face, divided in quarters. "Ah!" he exclaimed. "Now there's a painting! See? All talent comes from the heart. It takes soul to produce real genius. ... Yes, we should ponder the lesson these children want to teach us ..." And Jean Orelle pondered. Monsieur Jean Orelle. Minister, winner of the Nobel millions, adviser to the worthies of this world. And all the while, that deep, gnawing ache, that twinge in the pit of his stomach, re-

133

minding him of his farmhouse in Provence, with its twelve rooms
furnished in his image, its shaded garden, the chaise longue under
the tamarisk trees, and a million fist-shaking skeletons ready to storm
the gate . . . He fell suddenly silent. But no one thought it strange.
They were used to his moods. The press described him as "speechless
with emotion, true to his lofty ideals." His ideals indeed! At the price
of what anguish! Standing there ready to chuck it all over and finally
speak his mind, yet faced with his past, armed sentinel guarding the
narrow pathway from brain to tongue, holding back the words, not
letting them break . . . As for the painting, it was sold for a hundred
thousand francs, to help raise money for the Ganges refugees. And
at that, there were twenty collectors at each other's throats to get it.
God knows where it might be today, and how its lucky owner views
it now . . .

From that point on, not much to report. Until the São Tomé airlift,
that is. Airlift: specialty of the Western World, for use whenever it
gets the urge to take up the cause of a neighbor in distress. Presents
the great advantage of bridging the vast expanse between the hard-
put neighbor in question, beside himself with gratitude, and the
generous West, safely ensconced, cheering the planes on their way
with gestures of friendly concern. Very useful, especially in serious
cases, since it salves the conscience. Might even conceivably do some
good, though that wasn't the profound intent of its inventors. As for
the São Tomé airlift, it did no good at all, and only sent world opinion
plunging into confusion. It was spawned by the Rome Commission,
tired of chasing its tail around sterile debates, and deciding that the
time was ripe to risk making a move. It was now or never. The UN
was talking about taking the matter in hand. And who knows what
mischief those types might whip up, if left to themselves and their
Third World majority, with toys like imperialism, racism, and such
to play with! Only Western nations sat on the Rome Commission, and
they were the ones who were holding the ball. Hot as it was, the time
hadn't come to pass it to the Third World just yet! . . . At any rate,
the São Tomé airlift ought to go down in history. A useless monument, like a kind of Eiffel Tower . . .

It had become clear that, as it crossed the equator, the Ganges fleet
would pass close to the African coast. Or, more precisely, to the island
republic of São Tomé, that former Portuguese colony that the United
States Air Force had used until recently as a base, and whose airport
was still pretty much intact. The Commission decided that supplies
would be airlifted out of São Tomé, and dropped to the armada.

Where South Africa had failed, there would be another try, but this time by selfless and generous people, acting in good faith. They would show those poor wretches—and the whole world, in fact—what the white race was really like! In no time the São Tomé airport was buzzing, besieged from all sides. The great mercy-go-round. A hundred planes circling the leaden equatorial sky, waiting their turn to land. The mad scramble was on! Choice morsel of noble emotions. Monumental confection of selfless ideals. Magnificent antiracist pastry, filled with the cream of human kindness, spread with a sweet egalitarian frosting, sprinkled with bits of vanilla remorse, and on top, this graceful inscription, in flowery caramel arabesques: "Mea Culpa!" A cake to tug at the heartstrings, if ever there was one. And everyone wanted to get the first bite ... Don't push! There's enough to go around! ... What a party! As long as you were there, as long as you were seen, that's all that really counted ...

The white Vatican plane was the first to touch down, winner by several lengths. No matter where or when, it always managed to get there first. As if they kept it ready, night and day, for instant takeoff, loaded with medicines, with Dominicans in jeans, and with pious pronouncements. It must have flown faster than sound, at the speed of symbols, no doubt. To equip it, Pope Benedict XVI, impoverished by his predecessor's whim, would sell his tiara and his Cadillac. But there still were places, here and there, full of simple, superstitious Catholics who couldn't conceive of a pope without a tiara or a fancy car—the really backward parishes of Corsica, Brittany, Ireland, Louisiana, Galicia, Calabria, and the like—and it never took long for the money to pour in. The Pope, dejected, would give in to those poor, dear souls, and buy back his car and tiara, only to sell them again with great delight—humble saint that he was—the moment world opinion or the pressure of events called for the white plane to fly a new mission. But alas! They kept making him rich. How distressing. He did so truly want to be poor! Lucky for him that the white plane was there to help him out in his hour of need! ... A pope in tune with the times, congenial to the press. What a fine front-page story! They described him living on a can of sardines, eating with a plain tin fork, in a makeshift kitchenette up under the Vatican eaves. When you realize that he was living in Rome, that city bursting with health and wealth, chock-full of centuries' worth of well-gotten gain, you have to admit that this one and only malnourished Roman was giving his all for the cause. (A few diehards in the city even held it against him, for some vague reason ...) And so, his plane was the first to arrive at São Tomé. And the Breton villages, with their roadside shrines and their crosses of stone, took up a collection to buy him a tiara even finer than the rest.

Coming in second, but not far behind, the eternal runner-up: the gray World Council of Churches plane. Unlike its papist counterpart, the Protestant craft was very selective in its choice of flights. Each one was a battle, with its planeload of shock-troop pastors, righteous in their loathing of anything and everything that smacked of present-day Western society, and boundless in their love of whatever might destroy it. In a recent message that caused something of a stir, the Council had voiced its conviction that "present-day Western society can't be saved, but has to be torn down so that we can build a new world of justice on its ruins, with the help of God . . ." Charity is a very convenient weapon, especially when used with singleness of purpose. You never saw the pastors fly their missions of mercy when no radical issue was at stake. For an earthquake in Turkey, say, or a flood in Tunisia. But they would always be there to answer the call, with supplies for the Palestine refugee camps, the Angola freedom fighters, the Bantu liberation armies—in fact, wherever the voice of hate was as loud as the voice of distress. And if most of the pastors had long since stopped packing in copies of the Gospels with their cases of food, they didn't bat an eye. No, this was their Gospel. They were living it now. As the Council explained, "Christ spent his life in a struggle against established religion and temporal power." So the pastors, too. Espousing vicarious woe and despair. Marching against white power and the Church. While off São Tomé an army was sailing to wage a great war . . . The Protestant plane touched down with a thump, crammed full of calories to the tips of its rudders . . .

Next came the aircraft of neutral persuasion, flying in the name of universal conscience. First and foremost, the Red Cross plane, then the Swiss and Swedish duo—charity unbounded: gilt-edged neutrality's surest defense—and the big air freighters of the European powers, whose minions were really all agents on the same secret mission. Namely, to spy on the fleet and see where it was heading. ("Anywhere they want, only not near us!") And bringing up the rear, closing the circle, the eccentrics, the wags of the flying flotilla. The best of the lot: a Boeing from the sovereign and benevolent Order of Malta, shining like a knight in armor, four-triangled cross emblazoned on tail and wings, and the Grand Master's crest, in all its colors, spread like a mustache under the nose. As the black customs men of the Republic of São Tomé were checking its cargo with a somewhat wary eye, enjoying their moment of glory to the fullest, there alighted from the plane—rather spryly, all in all—a lieutenant-general (fugitive from the Jockey Club of Paris), a commander of the order (forgoing his weekend on the links), three officers, including one old duke (all titled like Spanish grandees), and a princess of the blood, nurse's kerchief on her head (noble and pious lady, lips lit in a radiant smile), whose first words, as her delicate foot touched African soil, expressed her unselfish impatience: "Take me to the poor dears! I want to hug and kiss each one!" It had to be explained that the poor dears were sailing the vast ocean deep, somewhere off the coast. "Good Heavens," she replied, "I do hope they're not seasick!" And she turned to the old duke. "You see, Georges, we always forget something! All that medicine, and not a single package of dramamine!" Good-hearted for all her naïveté, she was known the world over, turning up here and there, anywhere suffering reared its aching head, always perfectly at ease, dashing after "the poor dears" like the game hunter, off on safari, mad for a kill. As for the touching knights-errant along with her, no question in their minds what they were after. No more charity, no more sovereign and benevolent Order of Malta! Simple as that! Eight centuries of tradition and a caste to preserve. As good a reason as any, Georges old man! Yes, innocents and clowns. The salt of humanity. That is, if humanity lasts . . .

And speaking of clowns . . . That airplane, covered with painted flowers and Hindu sayings, like a neighborhood hippie's cheap little buggy! A twin-engine rig, flown in by an English singing group . . . The young millionaire performers, unloading the cartons and crates themselves. A cargo beyond belief! "Everyone else is bringing them life," they said, as they took off from London. "We're bringing them pleasure!" And so, piled up along the runway on São Tomé: two cases of tricks and jokes, a box of harmonicas, fifty Indian sitars, a load of portable tape recorders, perfume for the women, incense, thirty kilos of marijuana, fancy chocolates from London Candies and Co., a box of erotic picture books, another full of comic strips, and a complete supply of fireworks (with instructions in Hindi) "to set off on board when you catch sight of Europe." The young idols ran from crate to crate, beaming with joy. Publicity stunt of a juvenile mind? Fruit of sober reflection? No one ever found out why they really had come. In no time, the West had more serious fish to fry . . . But just for the record, a few words about the high point of the São Tomé air show: last but not least, in all its glory, the four-engine Air France jet, decked out with the colors and letters of the French National Radio and Television Network!

Ah, the endless talk about that plane! Paid for, lock, stock, and barrel, in just one night! Trip and all. One wild, unbelievable night. Madness en masse. Two hundred film stars, singers, orchestras, writers, actors, skiers, designers, playboys, dancers—even that bishop who was all the rage, the one who had found himself a wife in Saint-Germain—they were all there, swarming through the streets, in Paris and provinces alike, to the deafening din of a circus parade, complete with battalions of pretty girls taking up collections, patriotic style. (Tricolors spread out flat, under a rain of money, pitched from all sides...) Never had there been such a fine time in the streets, especially in Paris. At least, not since the fall of the Bastille! Meanwhile, that night, on every radio station and television channel in the country, one program and only one: the handsome and talented Léo Béon—idol of the airwaves, toast of every living room in France—giving his crowning performance. Just for the record again, we took down his kickoff remarks: "Yes, friends, our government is sending its planes to São Tomé. And it's only right that it should. It's doing its duty. But duty is dry as dust. Now it's up to us to go one step further. It's up to us to send brotherhood and love! That's right, my friends. We, the people of France ... We're going to send our own plane to São Tomé. Yes, the people's plane! ... We have two hours to raise the money. And two hours to say what's in our hearts. So please ... Please, friends, send in what you can, no matter how little. And add a message, of twenty-five words or less, telling just how you feel. The writer of the best message will win an all-expense trip to São Tomé ..." (Ah! Léo Béon! How he does let himself get carried away!) " ...to present, in person, to our friends from the Ganges, a collection of all your choicest sentiments, specially translated ... It's one thing to give. It's something else to tell why ..." And on and on. Drumroll, please! ... Of course, it was a triumph. A million people out in the streets. Traffic tied up in the heart of twenty cities. While Léo the handsome sat in front of his ten white phones ... ("Place de la Bastille? ... Huge crowd, you say? A regular stampede? Tremendous! Fantastic! Our old Bastille, still the beating pulse of Paris! ... Hello, Marseille? ... Up and down the Canebière? In every direction? Fantastic! The pulse of Marseille, beating right in time!") ... and read some of the choicest sentiments in question over the air between calls. Weeping, no less. Yes, weeping real tears, the swine! And up in his garret, Machefer was weeping too. But only because he was laughing so hard! . . . By ten o'clock it was over. France will always come through! And a hoarse-voiced Léo Béon, a dozen pounds thinner, sent everyone beddy-bye, tucking them in with "thanks from the bottom of my heart, you didn't let me down," taking himself for the conscience of the nation (which, alas, he probably was!). But not before one Monsieur Poupas (Stéphane-Patrice) had appeared on the screen, hair stylist de luxe from Saint-Tropez, and the lucky winner: "There are no more Hindus, no more Frenchmen. Only Man, and that's all that matters!" Hurrah! Now there's a deep thought! . . . Poor dumb bastard! On Easter Monday morning, a petrified Monsieur Poupas (Stéphane-Patrice), shaking too hard to find the ignition, will take off on foot from Saint-Tropez, run twenty kilometers north, and fall in a heap, rolled over by thousands of streaming cars, driven by thousands of desperate Frenchmen, for whom only two weeks before nothing mattered but Man, with a capital M! . . . Marcel and Josiane went to bed, worn to a frazzle. They had seen the whole show, run the length and breadth of Paris, shaken hands with a hundred stars. Cheap enough for a couple of coins tossed into the flag! But now, lying thoughtful and still, with the TV off and the lights turned out, covers up to their chins, they're taken aback by the sudden, vague feeling that somehow something is wrong. Too much noise! Too much fuss! Too much talk! Too much love, drooling like syrup from too many famous mouths! What if things have gone too far? Can it be that good common sense, led astray in the forest of lies and illusions, deeper and deeper, is finding its way out at last? No, not quite. Josiane and Marcel just lie there, hugging each other to sleep. They don't know it, but that vague little feeling of theirs is going to turn to panic . . .

On São Tomé, Monsieur Poupas (Stéphane-Patrice) holds forth for the press, along with the millionaire singers. For the twentieth time he repeats his gem: "There are no more Hindus, no more Frenchmen. Only Man, and that's all that matters!" Applause and cheers. But he doesn't stop there: "There are no more English, no more Swiss . . ." Etc. etc. He's ecstatic . . . Meanwhile, Léo Béon is kissing the princess's hand and gazing at the tents that have sprung up along the runway. It's time for another of his memorable mots: " 'Operation Heart of Gold,' that's what they should call us!" The phrase is picked up by twenty special correspondents. The mercy-mongers pat each other on the back. They decide on an emblem: a yellow cloth badge in the shape of a heart. Five hundred chests sporting five hundred yellow hearts. Even the secret agents, close by on the beach with their glasses, scanning the horizon, or bargaining away their eyeteeth for the last few fishing boats still to be found. (The Rome Commission has commandeered everything on São Tomé that has a motor and can stay afloat.) Everyone is ready. The atmosphere is tense. Dominicans and pastors agree on a common service. The island blacks, unwittingly ecumenical, wiggle their rumps to the pop group's impromptu hymns. Monsieur Poupas (Stéphane-Patrice) reads a passage from the Gospels. Asked to comment on the text, he draws this moral: "There are no more Hindus . . . Only Man, and that's all that matters. . . ." The crowd begins to sing ("With the pieces of the cross/Built themselves a boat/For now the thousand years are ended/Yes, the thousand years are ended now . . ."), while the old duke, the princess, and most of the Catholics present, take communion at the hands of a Methodist preacher, who views the Host as a symbol and no more. But every heart soars up as one in a Heavenward surge, every face is wreathed in smiles or moist with tears, every soul feels the swell of emotion, ripe in the tropical heat, like a fruit about to burst. So much so that, finally, when a lookout on the beach cries "Here comes the fleet! Here comes the armada!," every voice rings out in one single reply: "Thank God!"

What happened after that was like something from a nightmare, or at least a bad dream. The long-awaited encounter took place two miles off the coast of São Tomé. But it soon became clear that the Ganges fleet had no intention whatever of stopping. The *India Star* even seemed to change course, heading straight to ram one of the barges! Indeed, the Knights of Malta owed their lives to the presence of mind of their pilot, who was able to throw the engine into emergency reverse practically under the steamer's prow. For a moment the old duke imagined he was back in the days of the Order's intrepid galleons, doing battle with the Turk. As for the "poor dears" the princess was after, the only thing she saw, as she thought herself doomed, was a hideous, misshapen, convulsive dwarf, with a sailor's cap, and two stumps outstretched, as if ready to open the gates of Hell. She murmured a *mea culpa* and fell forthwith into a graceful swoon. At this point, since none of the mercy-mongers would dare to imagine the impossible—to wit, an openly hostile act on the part of the Ganges armada—they assumed it was an accident, happily avoided, and sent their barges off once more to pull alongside the ships and board with their provisions. Attempt abandoned no sooner than begun. Three boxes of rice, deposited somehow on the low-slung deck of a rusty old torpedo boat, lasted less than ten seconds,

as hundreds of arms sprung up and flung them back into the water.
And little doubt this time that the act was deliberate. On another
ship, one of the French secret agents was received in a forest of fists,
some brandishing knives. He had hoisted himself up on deck by a
cable dangling over the side, and managed to save his skin thanks
only to his commando training, with a fancy jackknife flip back into
the water. Meanwhile, English fireworks fell thick and fast on the
pop group that had so generously supplied them, thwacking the
drummer square on the head, and cutting a gash in the lead singer's
shoulder. Persistent, the papal barge held out longer than the rest,
like a stubborn sheep dog prodding the flock. Abreast of the *Calcutta
Star*, she was making her third attempt to board, when a naked
cadaver, hurtling down from the deck, fell with a heavy, sickening
thud at the feet of the Dominican friars. It was still soft and warm.
White skin, blue eyes, blond beard and hair. The man had been
strangled. When they loosened the rope eating into his neck and took
a good look at his face, they were stunned at the sight: it was one of
the great Catholic writers of the decade, lay member of the Council
of Vatican III (at the Pope's own invitation), outstanding reformer,
and religious intellect par excellence, known far and wide. Convert-
ing to Buddhism one fine day, he had vanished from the Western
World without a word, and never wrote another line. From then on,
he was known in some quarters as "the renegade writer." The last
white man to see him alive had been Consul Himmans, at the Consulate General of Belgium in Calcutta, a few days before the fleet had
set sail. All we need add here is that, as soon as it was dark, they
buried him in secret—the Dominicans, that is—on one of the island's
deserted beaches, and that news of his death was never made public,
on São Tomé or anywhere else. Such was the decision of the handful
who had witnessed his murder. The Vatican, consulted in code,
wholeheartedly concurred. Could it be that the Pope was afraid? Did
he feel that so foul and unprovoked a deed, against one of the century's most intelligent figures, whom the whole world had followed
in his staggering quest for Truth, might change Western opinion, and
turn that distressing demise into a crime of collective proportions?
Indeed, we might well assume that a surge of spontaneous indignation would have roused the Western World to condemn the thoughtless wretches in toto, to turn its Christian love to hate, and to close
its doors to them once and for all. . . . No, the Pope had prayed God
so long and hard to enlighten the West. He couldn't be wrong. That
could be one explanation . . .

When the last ship of the armada dipped below the horizon, leaving São Tomé behind, every tent by the runway was engulfed in that bewildered silence that comes in the wake of an unexplained defeat. Everyone agonized to find the answer. Actually, it was staring them in the face. But minds back then were too warped and worn to admit the inevitable truth when they saw it. It never occurred to a soul that the Ganges fleet had just waged the first battle in an implacable racial war, and that nothing on earth now could stem the power of weakness triumphant. From this point on, it would give no quarter. . . . And so, the discussions in the tents on São Tomé gave rise, above all, to a vast confusion. But not for long. Suddenly there it was: the explanation! Inspired, more than likely, by the Protestant pastors (or maybe the Catholic priests), and welcomed as a kind of deliverance, as an end to the torturous round of banal clichés and barren solutions: "Of course! It's obvious! The poor devils didn't trust us! They thought we wanted to poison them! Of course, that's it! How pathetic!" No one went on to say it was all the South Africans' fault, but some thought so, and some even hinted rather broadly. And if many, in their heart of hearts, had glimpsed the gaping chasm, waiting to swallow them, conscience and all, still, once back in the West, each one in his respective country gave the selfsame account of the event. Yes, surely it had confused them. That much they admitted. But now it was clear that only a nasty misunderstanding had held back the outpouring of brotherly love. At the airport at Roissy, before the members of the press assembled, Léo Béon tossed off yet another of his mots. Managing to flash his famous smile, with just the appropriate tinge of sadness, he told them:

"We'll have to bring the poor souls to their senses."

Thanks to that idiot and his constant need to shine, the beast got a new—and unlimited—lease on life. We'll see what it did with it shortly. In the meantime, once again for the record, let's note the instinctive reaction of our own Clément Dio:

"That stupid twat!" he exclaimed.

And he hit on the title of his next week's cover story: "Let's Bring the Poor Souls to Their Senses!"

Twenty-five

For two whole days Machefer went back on his vow of silence. The first day, two pages, in spare, straightforward prose, but crammed full of facts and precise detail, with the headline: "Frenchmen, Don't Be Fooled! The Truth About São Tomé. Eyewitness Account of the Duc d'Uras . . ." The old duke had been a subscriber to *La Pensée Nationale* since the year one. Back from the trip only twenty-four hours, he came bursting into Machefer's office, with a fistful of all the morning papers, and the evening editions from the day before. "It's a scandal!" he shouted, shaking with excitement. "What are they trying to do to us? I've never in all my life seen anything so distorted! Or so clever! They make it sound true, but they've twisted it all around. I had to read it twice before I saw through it. Why, I was on the Malta boat myself. I was even in command . . . It's 'Captain d'Uras,' you know. Retired . . . And what do I read? That my pilot lost control and almost ran us into their lead ship, and that they barely swerved out of our way in time! Why, that's preposterous! That wasn't it at all, it was just the other way around! I wasn't dreaming, I know what I saw! The *India Star* was heading straight for us, with that goddamn dwarf, wiggling and squirming on the bridge, and all those other characters on deck, staring down on us with murder in their eyes! . . . And what about the knives, and the fists? How come nobody mentions the knives? . . . Bring the poor souls to their senses, my foot! I saw those 'poor souls,' and I'll tell you, I couldn't believe my eyes! They hate us, plain and simple . . . And that poison nonsense! Really, what do the papers take us for? Why, not one of us even came close to getting a dialogue started. Anyone who tried to set foot on board wound up in the water, before they could open their mouth, tossed over like boxes. I told them all that on São Tomé, but no one would listen. 'You're tired, Monsieur d'Uras. Why don't you go lie down?' That's the answer I got! . . . I knew one of the Dominicans in the Vatican group. He was my wife's confessor back when I was naval attaché in Rome. A crafty little padre if ever there was one. Sly as a fox, with a name like a lamb: Fra Muttone. He's come a long way since then! . . . Well, you know what he told me? 'This is God's way of testing our charity'! That's what he said! 'The divine scheme is

143

clear. It's all or nothing. We can't stop halfway. We have to do our
Christian duty. Of course,' he went on, 'there are some who might
not understand. So we'd better keep certain things quiet, things that
might seem unpleasant, but that God put before us to help us deserve
salvation . . .' How do you like that for twisting things around! I was
flabbergasted. Next morning, before he left, he gave us all a little
sermon on the subject, and if you ask me, everyone swallowed it
whole. Divine scheme indeed! You wonder who on earth—or beyond
—put an idea like that in his head! . . . Anyway, I began to see the
light. But there was still one piece of the puzzle missing. And then,
yesterday morning, at the airport at Roissy, I took Fra Muttone aside,
and I said to him, 'Just one thing, Father. How about that nice little
present you almost got hit on the head with? That naked corpse, I
mean. The white man with the long blond beard?' That shook him
up a little. I knew what I was talking about, too. I've still got my
midshipman's eyes, and a first-rate pair of binoculars to boot! . . . Well,
he pulled himself together. 'You must have been seeing things, Monsieur d'Uras! There was nothing of the sort, I assure you.' Just like
that! With a wide-eyed, innocent look that would put a choirboy to
shame. So I said, 'Do you swear to that?' I was sure that would get
him, but no such luck! 'Monsieur d'Uras,' he answered, 'I'm willing
to forgive your whims. At your age you have the right. Yes, of course
I swear.' And that's how it ended. But I saw that corpse a second time,
Monsieur Machefer. That night, way down at the end of the beach.
They were burying it. Muttone mumbled something, blessed the
grave, and they all ran off as fast as they could. I went over to take
a look. It was pretty well hidden. I have no stomach for that sort of
thing, so I said a little prayer and left. . . . And in case you're wondering what I was doing there so late, it's very simple. I was taking
myself a quiet little pee. At my age I get up a lot at night. . . . Anyway,
that gave me the missing piece: it was plain that the padre was lying
through his teeth, Dominican or no! Since then I've been putting all
kinds of strange things together. With so many priests going off the
deep end, and taking us with them, how many are just plain liars, I
wonder? Monsieur Machefer, I'm afraid!"

"All right, kiddies!" said Machefer to his youthful crew. "I want you
to take down Monsieur d'Uras's story. Ask him anything you like.
That's what he's here for. And give me a good straight text, no frills.
We'll print up a hundred thousand copies . . ."

"A hundred thousand!" exclaimed the press foreman of *La Grenouille*, a short while later. "How are you going to pay for it? You
know my orders."

"In advance!" Machefer replied. And he took a roll of bills from his pocket.

The hundred thousand copies were sold, hawked through the streets by newsboys, the way they used to be, back when. It wasn't much, but it was a beginning. Machefer took heart. The next day the second installment appeared. This time with a bombshell headline: "White Strangled on *Calcutta Star,* Thrown Overboard. Racism Seen as Motive!"

Fifteen minutes later, the presses of *La Grenouille* rolled to a halt. Machefer went down to see why.

"Well, what's the matter? Why have you stopped?"

"I'm sorry, Monsieur Machefer," the foreman told him. "The men are on strike."

"On strike? Really?"

And he went from one to the other, looking each one in the eye. Not one of them moved, not one said a word.

"You're only hurting yourselves, can't you get that through your heads? Didn't you read my article? Don't you understand?"

"We're on strike," the foreman repeated. "I'm sorry, but you know our union rules."

"Your union? That's a good one! Your union is downstairs in the boss's office, right?"

"We're on strike," he echoed. "Period. That's it. Don't complain, you've got your ten thousand copies, same as always. What more do you want?"

"And tomorrow?"

"Tomorrow? Same thing. Our local took a vote. We'll print you ten thousand copies. One more, and we go out on strike."

"But that's a political strike," Machefer protested. "You can't do that!"

"Political? Not at all! Your rag always ran ten thousand, and that was just fine with us. But we won't go overtime, that's all. Overtime is slavery. The slavery of the proletariat."

"I can't tell," Machefer replied, "if you're all a gang of bastards, or just stupid assholes!"

He shrugged his shoulders, and added as he left: "Just assholes I guess! Too bad!"

A few moments later, he was upstairs, talking to his crew. "Well, kiddies, that's that! It was too good to last. We surfaced too soon, and they mowed us down like a bunch of schoolboys! We should have held back until the last minute. I've said so since the beginning. I never should have gone ahead with it. Now they've practically shut us up. We'll have to look for another printer, if there is one around that's not a union shop. In the meantime, until Gibraltar, we proceed as usual. Run this headline tomorrow: 'Only 4,000 Kilometers to the Moment of Truth!' "

That could be one explanation . . .

This time, the beast let loose with a roar, and strode boldly out of its lair for all to see. The country echoed to its every growl: "Senile Old Man Tells Story . . ." "Those Maltese Clowns . . ." "Aristocrats Fight to Preserve Race Supremacy . . ." "Exclusive Interview with Fra Muttone . . ." "Archbishop of Paris Chides Duc d'Uras . . ." "Peaceful Demonstration at Order of Malta Headquarters . . ." The same day, the string of petitions began, calling on the public to "welcome the Ganges armada," with thousands of signatures, collected by hundreds of committees, from the Council of Christian Mothers and the Gay Liberation Alliance, to the Union of Former Draft Resisters, through movements of every stripe and persuasion —intellectual, political, and religious. And heading the lists, all the most familiar names of that petition-happy mob who, for years, had been sapping the conscience of the Western World. "Useless!" they had thought. "What good does it do!" Oh really? Drop by drop, the painless poison does its job, until, in the end, it kills . . .

On Saturday morning, the day before Easter, as the Ganges fleet approached the coast of France, about to run aground that night, the press was still printing those lists. Funny, when you stop and think, that most of those last-minute signers—ears glued to the radio, sitting at home behind double-locked doors, or crowding the escape routes in their cars, if they lived down south—had the same revelation, one simple, terrifying phrase, ringing like a deathknell in their brain: "If I only knew . . ."

Posthumous signers, in a sense. At death's door, done in by their own last will and testament.

Twenty-six

The São Tomé relief attempt was never repeated. Advised by the secret agents' reports—much closer to the truth than the stories in the press, and stripped of the hearts and flowers—the gentlemen of the Rome Commission threw up their hands. It was too late, they had waited too long. With their governments' tacit approval, they had let the time slip by, still hoping, hoping . . . For what, exactly? The most astute among them would sooner have been hacked to bits than admit it. In international bodies formed to deal with Third World problems, careers don't get built on the truth . . .

On the eve of Palm Sunday, they had met behind closed doors. The fleet had been spotted off the coast of Senegal, heading north through calm and windless waters. Only two routes to choose from: up through the Atlantic and the Bay of Biscay, along the coast of Portugal, Spain, and France, and perhaps through the Channel to England; or, more likely, a right-angle turn through the Straits of Gibraltar, and into the Mediterranean. In either case, Western Europe. Unless . . . The British delegate rose from his seat. He began by giving a discreet little cough. (One of those English coughs that remove any doubt as to the gravity of what follows.)

"Gentlemen," he began, "as we all know, our commission was formed for the express purpose of giving aid to the Ganges refugees, and welcoming them to our shores. Now then, on the question of aid, I . . . ahem . . . shan't say too much. As for welcoming them to our shores . . . Well (cough, cough . . . stammer . . .) it . . . it seems to me that . . . perhaps it wouldn't be terribly wise, just now, to . . . to throw open our . . . how shall I put it? . . . our modest little flat to so large a family! Perhaps we should try to make them see that we're simply not equipped, just now, to . . . ahem . . . to take them in, and give them room and board, as it were. Perhaps, all in all, they'd best go back where they came from, and give us more time to set things up, don't you know . . . to receive them the way they deserve, the way the world expects us to do, with all our resources . . . Yes, a gala welcome. That's what we're planning . . . Of course, we haven't had time to . . . ahem . . . to work it out just yet, since . . . Well, I mean, after all, we really didn't invite them, now did we? . . . And . . . Well, gentlemen, I propose that we extend them a formal and earnest invitation, for some time in the future, to be determined in consultation with all governments concerned, ours and theirs . . ." (Having represented Great Britain on the Permanent Atomic Disarmament Commission, the Englishman knew what "some time in the future" really meant . . .) "Meanwhile," he continued, "until conditions permit—and we hope with all our hearts that they will—we respectfully request that the fleet return home. Via Suez and the Indian Ocean it's not very far. Needless to say, we'll help in every way we can. Supplies, escort craft, hygienic and technical assistance, replacement of unfit vessels with our own. Simply a question of expediency . . ."

The commission approved. Certain governments, the ones that felt most threatened—like Spain and France—were secretly terrified. Up to Senegal, they could still hope for an accident, a verdict dealt by fate, that a tearful public opinion would have to accept, then the solemn services "in memory of," the airlift to ferry the survivors back home, the pledges of increased aid, the endless, breast-beating grief, and life goes on . . . But day after day, that water, so strangely calm. That sky, so clear, as never before in the annals of the sea! No, there wasn't a chance. May as well stop hoping! The Ganges fleet and the flood of words would soon come together. And the meeting would cost an exorbitant price, unless . . .

"The main thing," the English delegate went on, "is to convince our guests. If you don't mind a comparison . . . At home, in our better public schools, when a rowdy youngster simply won't behave, we resort to a little physical persuasion. Why, how many times, when I myself was a child, did they tweak my ears to make me toe the mark! Yes, when conditions demand it, and nothing else will do, I'm all for that kind of persuasion."

So, they were finally getting down to business! But in what a roundabout, two-faced way! Heaven help the white race the day it refuses to voice its basic truths—even mumble them under its breath—for lack of anything better! That day was about to dawn.

"Given the circumstances," asked one of the delegates, "just how do you see us 'tweaking their ears'?"

The Englishman wasn't coughing now.

"We challenge their ships," he answered. "Threaten to fire, if need be. Then put armed men aboard, and take over, like it or not . . ."

"And what if the children won't let us tweak their ears?" asked the delegate from France. "What if they pounce on the teacher, in a fit of rage, and try to bash his head in? Will he have to use his gun?'"

"Quite likely," the Englishman answered.

"And what if he hasn't the heart to harm his pupils?'"

There was a long silence.

"I'm not saying it will work. I'm saying we've got to give it a go. If we don't do a trial run now, next week we won't know our own strength."

"And who's going to do that 'trial run,' may I ask?"

"Well, actually, Great Britain doesn't feel she should. I'm authorized to make the proposal, but considering the special, long-standing relations we've enjoyed with the governments of the Indian subcontinent . . ."

"Italy," said another delegate, "has to take into account the opinion of His Holiness the Pope . . ."

No need to rehash all the coded wires feverishly exchanged between the Rome Commission and the governments of the West. In France, the President of the Republic made a hasty, secret decision, consulting no one but the chief of naval affairs and Undersecretary Jean Perret. (To appreciate the reasons behind this collusion, one must only refer to the meeting of ministers that took place just after the fleet had set sail from the Ganges delta . . .)

"We'll give it a try," the French delegate announced. "Of course, it goes without saying that this has to be kept in the strictest confidence. Only the heads of your governments will be informed of the results. An order has already gone out to our destroyer escort 322, on patrol off the Canaries, to proceed south for a top-secret mission. She's receiving detailed instructions at this very moment."

"And if your trial run fails?" someone asked.

"Well then," replied the Englishman, properly phlegmatic, "we'll have to have another meeting. We've got to make some kind of decision . . ."

On Holy Saturday, when the Rome Commission had met for the very last time, no one worried anymore about decisions. What kind? For whom? Everything was coming apart at the seams. Save your skin! Every man for himself! . . .

Twenty-seven

On Palm Sunday, around four in the afternoon, returning from a mission termed "routine" on the papers presented to the Senegalese authorities, destroyer escort 322 entered the port of Dakar. It stayed no more than five minutes, just long enough for its launch to put the captain ashore—one Commander de Poudis—then skirted around the harbor and turned back out to sea. (Let's note, for the record, that four days later, destroyer escort 322 was back riding at anchor off Toulon. Quarantined, crew confined on board, no visitors allowed, total radio blackout . . .) In Dakar, an unmarked auto, naval attaché in mufti at the wheel, whisked Commander de Poudis off to the airport. A French Air Force Mystère 30 was waiting on the runway. Six that evening, the air base at Villacoublay. The captain, in civilian clothes, got out of the plane, walked some ten yards, and disappeared into another unmarked car. With him, Undersecretary Jean Perret . . . Down the highway, through the Bois de Boulogne, up Avenue Foch, to the Élysée Palace. And into the President's office, spirited in through the back, instead of the usual anterooms and chambers. There, alone, standing up to greet him, the President of the Republic:

"Captain, I'm so glad to see you! I've been waiting . . . You understand, I'm sure. I felt a coded message wouldn't do, no matter how detailed. We really had to bring you in from Dakar in person. Under the circumstances, it's not so much the facts we're after, as the . . . how shall I put it? . . . the general atmosphere . . ."

"Yes, monsieur, I understand."

"Now then, I'll try not to let myself get carried away. . . . I want you to take your time, and be perfectly frank. Just tell us what you know, as simply as you can. We can skip the big words and fancy phrases that usually hide the truth hereabouts. Please, sit down . . . No, here, in this big chair . . . Make yourself comfortable . . . Can I offer you a Scotch?"

"Thank you. That would help."

"Yes, you're right. In these Third World discussions, I find that a good shot of whiskey is the only official response that makes much sense. It's the one I invariably turn to. These people! They rant and rave at the UN, they treat themselves to jets, and coups d'état, and wars, and epidemics. And still they reproduce like ants. Not even their deadly famines can seem to keep them down. It's frightening! . . . Well, here's to their health! Figuratively speaking, of course! Though I'm afraid the three of us may need another drink when we hear what you have to say."

"Yes, monsieur, I'm afraid so too."

"Monsieur Perret here will take a few notes while we chat. In this whole Ganges affair, he's the only one I trust. All the rest . . ." (The President gave a vague little flip of the hand.) "Well, let's just say we're quite alone."

"More alone than you realize, monsieur," replied Commander de Poudis, simply.

"Before you begin, Captain, there's one essential point you can clarify for me, if you will. It's about the makeup of your ship. When I decided on this mission, it was all we had in the area, close at hand. The admiral tells me we couldn't have hit on a better one. All career men in the crew. Crack officers. Right?"

"Well, more or less, monsieur. Out of a hundred sixty-five petty officers and seamen, only thirty-two were drafted, forty-eight are on five-year enlistment, and the rest are specialists. In for life. Bretons, mainly. A really first-rate crew, much more spirit and discipline than you usually find. Of course, it's not like it was in my own midshipman days. But still, with the way things are today, an old navy man like me can't complain . . ."

"You understand, Captain, if I ask you about them, it's only because I go back a ways! I remember a few things. Like how we lost Algeria, for instance. There were dozens of good reasons, but the most important was that we sent our draftees. Except for the paratroopers and the Legion, it was really no army at all. Just a bunch of ghosts, not sure why they were there, full of hidden motives. A shadow of an army. Why, I can still hear one of my predecessors in this very office. I was a young man, just starting out. Minister of this or that. And he took me aside, and he said: 'The army? Forget it! Is there still any kind of war you can get them to fight in? Ideological war? Lost cause. Popular war? Civil war? Certainly not. Colonial war? Racial war? Even less. Atomic war? You don't need the army for that! You don't need anyone! Old-fashioned national war? Maybe, but I'd be surprised. Besides, before long there won't be any national wars. So what good is an army of draftees, will you tell me? All it does is turn people against the military, and fatten up the pacifists' conscience. Not to mention the excuses it gives for all kinds of subversive behavior! No,' he told me, 'if ever you find yourself in my place, I only hope you won't have to turn to the army. Except maybe to march in parades on Bastille Day! And even then, you'll see. They don't even march right anymore!' Unfortunately, Captain," the President added, "I'm afraid I need the army now . . ."

"I know exactly what you mean, monsieur. My crew was mainly career men. And the few draftees there were never stepped out of line. Maybe a handful who read *La Grenouille* or *La Pensée Nouvelle*, but no more than in other units. No conscientious objectors disguised as medics. No anarchist militants. At least, not that I know of. Certainly no more than anywhere else. And no chaplain on board, you can be sure! . . . Still, even with a crew like that, things were a little rough. Believe me, monsieur, they were rough!"

"Tell me about it."

"Well, to begin with, I had no trouble finding the fleet on radar. Five minutes past eight that morning, twenty degrees latitude, a hundred forty-two miles off the coast of Mauritania. I could have found it just as easily by the smell. The whole ocean was like one big festering sore . . . Anyway, I pulled up behind that squadron, if you can call it that, ready for my first maneuver. The instructions said: 'Contact Ganges fleet. Initiate confrontation.' Now, I wasn't too sure just what that meant I should do. 'Confrontation' can mean a lot of things. So I checked in the dictionary. (I always keep one handy. They're very helpful in the navy, when you want to say something in a couple of words . . .) For 'confront,' one of the meanings was, 'To bring face to face, to subject to lengthy examination.' That seemed like a good one. So I started examining. With my glasses I could begin to make out a lot of details. And believe me, what I saw set me back on my heels. Even someone like me, who's rubbed elbows with every race on earth, and seen all the worst there is. It was pretty clear to me then, monsieur, what the spirit of my mission was supposed to be. So I got the whole crew out on deck, over toward starboard. Except for maybe twenty or so who had to stay below and make sure the engines kept running, and the electricity, and all. Then I pulled within fifty yards of them, to our right, and we sailed up the line, alongside, from the last one all the way up to the lead boat. An old steamer, the *India Star*. They were doing ten knots. I was down to sixteen. And still, it took us better than an hour. It was like a review! The whole of the Ganges fleet, sailing by like one of those dioramas, you know? . . . Well, monsieur, that's what I assumed it meant by a 'lengthy examination.' And that's how I 'confronted' them . . ."

"Yes, well done. You understood precisely. I'm big on the dictionary too . . . Please, go on."

"What we saw . . . It's impossible to describe it. How should I begin?
The over-all effect? Each separate detail? Maybe first just the numbers . . . Believe it or not, my executive officer stood there the whole
time counting heads. He made a mark for every thousand. At the end
of an hour he was out of his mind: he had nine hundred marks
. . . And then, when we got a good look, up close! Like those old
Pasolini films, remember? Starvation on every face. All skin and
bones. Pale, glassy-eyed stares . . . Now and then, other figures rising
from the heap. Tall, proud-looking athlete types, standing there
calmly, staring us down. And scratching. Yes, scratching. Until they
would bleed. To mortify the flesh, I suppose . . . My duty officer was
standing next to me. I heard him mutter: 'Gladiators . . . A pack of
naked gladiators! . . . Like Spartacus!' Yes, they were naked, all right.
Almost all of them. Well, not the way you might think. I mean, not
really without anything on. Like in a morgue, or on the beach, lying
in the sun. Much more casual. Suddenly a body moves, a tunic comes
open, and the flesh gets a breath of fresh air. No shame, no shock. No
one cares, one way or the other. Not as if they're showing themselves
on purpose. Just the natural way, I guess, after a thousand years of
free and easy sex . . . An old woman bends over, and her scrawny
breast brushes the deck . . . A bandage full of pus comes loose, and
you see a knee half eaten away . . . A pair of shoulders. An old man's?
A child's? Who knows? . . . Two rattleboned children, so skinny you
can count their ribs. Boys or girls? Who can tell? Then you see them
get up to piss, and you know they're one of each. Pretty little faces.
Smiling at each other, then back down on deck . . . A woman, dragging through the pile of bodies. A dwarf, with her two heavy breasts
barely bobbing above the heap . . . Someone sitting. Two thighs,
gnarled like stumps. And I wondered at the time if he'd sat like that,
stock-still, all the way from the Ganges delta . . . Another woman, flat
on her back, gazing up at the sky. Never blinking. She was dead. I
could tell because, the moment we sailed alongside, two men came
and grabbed her by the hands and feet, and tossed her overboard,
just like that. She couldn't have been very heavy. Up on the bridge,
I saw my Breton crewmen cross themselves for all they were worth.
. . . And bellies, and butts, and everywhere, sex. Everywhere you
looked . . . I remember one young woman, picking between her
thighs, through the thick, black wool, looking for lice, I imagine

. . . Not to mention all the ones with their tunics pulled up, squatting down with their rumps in the air, not giving us a second thought. Who were we, after all? We didn't exist. Not for any of them, in fact . . . Still, don't think it was all sheer horror. Not really. There were lovely bodies to look at too. Perfect bodies. Lots of them. Quick glimpses, flashing by. Maybe all the more striking just because of the ugliness and misery around them. I really can't explain it. . . . Like something I saw on the *Calcutta Star*, up toward the front of the line. A back. A magnificent naked back. Up by the bow, away from the crowd sprawled on deck. With stunning black skin, and hair streaming down, and a white sari draped on the hips. Then the sari fell, and the girl turned around to pick it up. It must have been some kind of game, I suppose, because right near by, a horrible little monster was laughing his head off. The girl stood up, and five seconds later she was wrapped in the white cloth, from head to foot. But for those five seconds I couldn't stop staring. I've never laid eyes on such a beautiful body. And she looked at me too. The only one out of all those thousands and thousands. It just lasted a second. But the look on her face made me wish she had never turned around . . . Well, so much for details, monsieur. The over-all impression hit me even harder. It was deeper, tougher to fathom. I can't really express it without sounding trite. All that teeming, steaming squalor. Absolute squalor. The countless souls, the depths of despair, the nightmarish visions. Flesh for the taking, sex on the loose. One swarming, miserable mass. But beautiful too . . . A whole other world passing before our eyes. But that doesn't tell half the story. I'm afraid we weren't in much shape to judge it. . . . Well, monsieur, you see what it did to the captain. You can guess what it did to the crew, career men or no! I brought a few pictures, if you'd like to have a look. We developed them on board . . ."

There were twenty or so. The President flipped through them, without a word.

"If it weren't too late for pranks," he said, finally, "I'd have one of the Garde Républicaine hop on his motorcycle and run these over to our friend Jean Orelle, with a note. A few words like: 'These are your guests. I hope you enjoy them when they visit you in Provence!' . . . Oh, I see you got a picture of that creature, too! The one on the *India Star*, with the cap! I was sent one just like it about six weeks ago. It was snapped by the photographer from Associated Press, just past Ceylon. Unfortunately, not many papers bothered to print it."

He slipped the photo into the frame of the big Louis XVI mirror

above the fireplace, between the glass and the wood. The monster
child took on a new dimension, as if he had just come in and joined
the three of them in the office.

"There," said the President. "My colleague from the Ganges!
... You know, they say that back in World War Two, in the North
African campaign, Montgomery kept a picture of Rommel. Never
parted with it. And before every big decision, he would study his face
long and hard. I guess the trick worked. But a lot of good it's going
to do me! What on earth can you read in a face like that! Cap and all!
Believe me, I've had my share of motorcades up the Champs Élysées,
with ugly jokers in fancier caps than that! But this time I need more
to go on!"

Then, changing his tone:

"Good God, what a horror! ... Please, Captain, continue. Tell me
about your crew. How did they react?"

"Badly, monsieur! At least, from our point of view, yours and mine.
I had put all the officers and mates I could spare up on deck, and had
them mix in with the seamen. That way I could get a pretty clear
idea. As we passed alongside the first boat, suddenly you couldn't
hear a sound. Then one man piped up, as if to be funny: 'Boy, take
a look at that! They sure don't give a damn what they do over there!'
A few moments later, the same one again, but this time his voice was
very different: 'Poor devils!' And for the next hour, that's all you
seemed to hear on board. Things like, 'I can't believe it!' or 'My God,
those poor bastards!' or 'Lieutenant, what are we waiting for? Why
don't we get those buggers some food?' or 'What's going to happen
to all those little kids?' There was only one man with a different
reaction, a simple old salt, with the lowest IQ on board. I know,
because I checked out his papers. 'Lieutenant,' he said, 'is it true that
gang is heading our way for a little rest and recuperation?' He must
have found that hard to swallow. By the time we got up to the *India
Star*, the ship with the biggest load of all, you didn't hear a word. The
crew stood rooted to the spot. And that was that. End of confrontation ... Then I did what I was supposed to for the second phase of
the mission. I called for all hands to man their battle stations. I'm sure
you know the signal, monsieur: a series of short, sharp blasts over all
the loudspeakers on board. It makes for a pretty dramatic effect.
Really insistent. But I never saw the crew so upset. Some of them
began to swear. Others asked questions that my officers had orders
not to answer. Strictly a reflex action, I imagine. But there I was, in
command of a warship unlike any other, with a crew that, I'm willing

to bet, despised its captain, its uniforms, the navy, themselves, and everything else to boot!"

"Go on, Captain," Perret interrupted. "This was all my idea. I remember exactly what your orders were: 'Simulate combat alert. Proceed in utter earnest until the moment before you would normally open fire.'"

"There too, monsieur," the captain replied, "I think I understood what was expected. I gave my men the full treatment. Imagine you've got a helmet on your head and a lifebelt around your middle, and you're doing your damnedest to load the torpedoes into the tubes. Or you're clinging to the rocket launchers, too tight to let go, or your eyes are glued to the sights of the big guns, and the gun crew is yelling out the elevations, getting ready to fire. And the whole time the ship is shaking like mad, creaking in every joint of her armor, full speed ahead at thirty-five knots . . . Well, at times like that, believe me, you turn into a different person! Isn't that what you were wondering, monsieur?"

"Very true," the President answered. "We were wondering . . . But that's not the same as hoping, now is it? Just what were we hoping? . . Nothing, I imagine. What was there to hope for?"

"Nothing, you're right," said the captain. "The machine worked to perfection, just like on maneuvers. After all, we're a first-class ship, the cream of the fleet! But there's just one catch: on a combat vessel, the last thing you do before opening fire is to raise all the artillery to the proper elevations. And even if the men only have to push a button, when they're up that close they know damn well what it is they'll be shooting at. Well, that was the moment, monsieur, when I found myself with a full-blown mutiny on my hands. The men were in tears, they went all to pieces. Polite, respectful . . . But still, it was a mutiny. My act was too convincing! They really thought I meant to fire! Up on the bridge, it was one call after another. From every battle station on the ship. Messages that left no doubt. Words no combat captain had ever heard before! 'Turret, here, Captain. We're not going to fire! We're sorry, we can't!' 'Forward machine guns, here. Don't give the order, Captain. We can't obey it! We won't!' Of course, with a machine gun I can understand. You can see what you're killing. . . . Just one consolation. They sounded really torn. Like poor, lost children! So I picked up the mike and went out over the intercom: 'Drill concluded, men. Drill concluded.' Not quite by the book. But, frankly, I was as shaken up as they were . . ."

"One other thing, Captain. There was a third phase, if I'm not mistaken."

"Yes, monsieur, I was coming to that. Unfortunately! . . . Fifteen minutes later, I went out over the intercom again, as per your instructions. This time I had a little more leeway. I did my best. What I told them was something like this: 'Men, this is your captain speaking. The drill you've just taken part in was a psychological test, unlike anything before in all our naval history. For that reason, none of you will be held responsible for your outbursts of insubordination. They've already been forgotten. Which is only right, since, in a sense, they were part of the test. I'll try to explain . . . We're faced with a situation that's also unlike anything before in our history. I mean this fleet full of refugees from the Ganges, sailing toward Europe, peacefully enough, but with nobody's permission, after all, and nobody's invitation. You've all had a chance now to see them close up, and maybe even judge for yourselves. Your job, men—our job—is to sound the fleet out. Destroyer escort 322 is going to be a kind of guinea pig. We don't know what they're up to. This might well be some new, sophisticated form of warfare: a pathetic enemy, who attacks without firing a shot, and who counts on our pity to protect him. If so, we have to work out our defense. And that, men, is the mission of destroyer escort 322 . . . Let's imagine that the fleet has decided to land in France. For reasons that may well have become clear a few moments ago, and that the government is obliged to consider, it's possible that our naval forces could be ordered to board these ships and reroute them toward Suez, and back to India, where they should have stayed in the first place. Obviously, any such move on our part would be carried out with all the humanitarian precautions you would certainly want to see. . . . Now, in case the government decides—as it very well might—that our country's security is at stake, and that we do have to intercept the fleet, we've been asked to carry out another very sensitive preliminary maneuver, one that would serve as something of a test. In fifteen minutes, a force of marines and commandos will attempt to board one of the ships in the fleet as peacefully as possible. If the operation succeeds, the task force will leave the occupied ship at once, and no further action will be taken. It will be a kind of dress rehearsal . . .' Well, that's more or less what I told them, monsieur," Commander de Poudis continued. "I finished up by saying something like, 'I'm counting on all of you, men . . .' Pretty dull, I know! But what else could I say? Can you imagine the usual military talk making sense with the kind of enemy we were facing? Besides, monsieur, military talk doesn't make much sense at all anymore. Nowadays it just makes everyone laugh, military men included . . ''

"I know," the President replied. "And not only military talk! Why, today, when I pay my respects to the nation, they almost make fun of me right to my face! What used to be clear, and concise, and from the heart, has turned into one big, ludicrous cliché. . . . Well, enough of that. Let's get on! Tell me, Captain, how did the operation conclude?"

"Badly, monsieur! Very badly! The ship I chose for our operation was a broken-down old torpedo boat, not too big, not too small, something I thought my men would be at home with. I figured she was good for the test, because they'd be more comfortable with a warship, even one that was out of commission. . . . Anyway, she had about two thousand people on her. My strike force was a pair of motor launches, three officers, and forty men armed for close action. But with strict orders not to kill or wound anyone, except in self-defense. Besides, even if I'd ordered them to, they never would have obeyed. . . . Well, for a minute I thought it was going to be easy. The men moved right in, without a hitch, and took up positions at the foot of the bridge. The crowd just fell back and stood there, watching. But when they started for the hatchways that led up to the bridge and the engines, all of a sudden the crowd tightened up—'crammed together like a solid wall of flesh,' one of my officers told me. The men tried to grab a couple and elbow their way in. Impossible. They would have needed three thousand arms to wade through that mass. So the officer in command had the men take aim. Then the usual orders, very slow and deliberate. Something you can understand in any language . . . Well, the crowd didn't give an inch. And all those submachine guns, aimed just high enough to point at a sea of children's faces, staring wide-eyed, not even afraid . . . The crew seemed to appreciate the importance of its mission. In fact, we went farther than I ever thought we could. We even shot off a volley. Over their heads, of course. But still, we were taking a risk! Believe me, monsieur . . ." (The captain flashed a sad little smile.) . . . "you can be proud of your navy! What training, what discipline! No one like them when it comes to firing off the target! A great deterrent, this navy of yours! But deterrents only work when both sides know the rules. And our friends from the Ganges don't. Not even a trace of panic. They didn't so much as flinch! Far from it. Instead, that wall of flesh began to move forward, and close in on my unit. My men punched, and kicked, and fought them off with the butts of their guns. And the others didn't even fight back. They just pushed and swarmed ahead. Two thousand swarming bodies! Against forty-three! The ones that my men knocked down were swept up into the crowd. In no time others took their place. To hold their ground my men would have had to fire. Really fire, I mean, and kill them . . . By some kind of miracle, they made it back to the ship. All but two seamen, that is. And those two were thrown overboard, dead. Not a sign of violence on their bodies. No stab wounds, no choke marks. Just trampled to death, that's all. Not by anyone in particular. But by everyone in general, which amounts to the same thing. Drowned in a flood of flesh and bone. Yes, drowned, that's the word . . . Well, that's about all I can tell you, monsieur, except that from now on you'd better not count on destroyer escort 322. She's a sick ship. A body without a soul, I'm afraid . . ."

"And her captain?"

"Not much better, monsieur. It's driving me crazy just thinking about it. We have to make a choice. Either we open our doors to these people and take them in. Or we torpedo every one of their boats, at night, when it's too dark to see their faces as we kill them. Then we get out as fast as we can, before we're tempted to save the survivors, and we put a bullet through our brain. Quick and clean. Mission accomplished."

"The pilot who dropped the bomb on Hiroshima died quietly in his bed at eighty-three."

"Maybe, Monsieur Perret, but those were different times. The armies of the West have learned a lot about guilt since then . . ."

"Captain," the President interrupted, "if I gave you that order, would you carry it out?"

"I've given that question a lot of thought, monsieur. My answer would have to be no. But I suppose that's part of the 'psychological test'!"

"Yes, quite . . . Thank you, Captain. Be sure to take a few days' rest before you rejoin your ship in Toulon. It goes without saying, this is all in the strictest of confidence."

"Believe me, monsieur, it was bad enough living through it. I don't much feel like talking about it too. You see, one of those seamen was Marc de Poudis. He was my son . . ."

He got up and left the room.

"Well, Monsieur Perret, what do you think?"

"That you're going to have to fight without a navy. And since the home front deserted you long ago, it's going to be up to the army. I suppose if we stir up a few of the regular units—career men, I mean —there may still be a chance."

" 'Career men'? You saw just now what happened to 'career men'!"

"Yes, but we should be able to find a hundred thousand or so who aren't built to go all to pieces. The army must still have a few good tough battalions. Or maybe the police? The important thing is to change the nature of the confrontation. If you publicly and solemnly deny the refugees permission to land, then, the minute they set foot on our shores, unarmed or not, they'll be committing an act of aggression. At least, that's how the army will see it. The enemy will change from a hypothesis to a fact. On the water he's on his own, we can't touch him. But once he lands, he'll have gone too far."

"You think so?"

"Well, I'm not really convinced, but it's worth a try."

"Monsieur Perret, I'm giving you a free hand. Contact the general staff as soon as possible. Draw up your plans. Feel out all the major unit commanders. And don't breathe a word to the press. The public mustn't know. According to the admiral's figures, we're lucky if we have a week. Keep me informed. My door is open to you around the clock . . ."

Twenty-eight

At three in the afternoon, on Good Friday, the Last Chance Armada passed through the Straits of Gibraltar, and into the waters of the Mediterranean. The moment the coast of Europe appeared, sharply outlined in the sun, the deck of every ship in the fleet came suddenly to life. Thousands of arms began waving and shaking, like a forest in the wind. And a slow, singsong chant welled up to the heavens, in mystic incantation or prayer of thanksgiving. Not until Easter Monday morning would arms and voices finally grow still . . . It had been at precisely three o'clock that Friday, that the monster child, sitting astride the turd eater's shoulders, was gripped by a violent spasm, that contorted his body and his twisted stumps, and appeared, indeed, to leave him lifeless. At the same time his neckless head drooped ever so slightly. Incredible though it seems, that movement was caught by all eyes in the fleet, and it set off the surge of triumphant chanting on every deck at the selfsame moment. . . . A cataleptic seizure, nothing more. And one minute after midnight, into Easter Sunday morning, in the clatter of ninety-nine hulls plowing headlong onto the rocks and beaches of the coast of France, the dwarf will wake up and let out a shriek, that old Monsieur Calguès, in his house on the hill, will hear loud and clear, as he crosses himself and mutters: "Vade retro, Satanas . . ."

Twenty-nine

The news that the fleet had passed through Gibraltar quickly spread throughout Europe. It was Spain, though, that suffered the most drastic shock. Of the famous Good Friday processions that had long lined the streets of every Spanish town, only the folklore and traditional pomp remained, as colorful as ever—hooded penitents, brass bands, priests dressed in vestments of a bygone day—all for the greater glory and profit of the chambers of commerce. People brought their children. Everyone took pictures. And only a few old women would still kneel in prayer as the cross was borne past. On that particular Good Friday, as the news blared out over every transistor, again and again, the processions, strangely, found the spirit they had long since lost. The transformation wouldn't last. But as long as it did, the crowds fell to their knees and sang the old hymns. Those who didn't remember the Latin words weren't ashamed just to hum. Rosaries, long ornamental, took on new life, as their beads passed, one by one, between the joined hands and trembling fingers of black-garbed penitents. Then, in no time, the streets were deserted. Everyone went back home, shutters closed, as whole families huddled around their TVs and radios. Bishops proclaimed their messages of charity, and the ruling leftist cliques droned on in the name of universal harmony and brotherly love. But even as the Spanish government spoke of peace and calm, the highways out of every city along the Mediterranean—Málaga, Almería, Cartagena, Alicante, Valencia, all the way to Barcelona—were jammed with cars packed with baggage and children. Two streams, in fact, were cutting across Spain, in opposite directions. One, a river of words, rolling down to the sea and the Ganges fleet beyond. The other, a river of life, flowing inland, away from the coast. On Good Friday evening, the second stream dwindled and died: the fleet had gone by and kept its distance. It was then that the stream of words swelled into a gushing torrent, one that wouldn't subside until Easter Monday, when, clearly, it was France that was going to be invaded . . .

The evening of that same day, a band of Andalusian fishermen from the little village of Gata, near Almería, came upon some twenty naked corpses on the beach. Around each neck, biting into the flesh, each body still bore the tight-knotted cord that had choked off its life. Could it be that the fishermen turned and fled in panic, afraid of an epidemic? Or that the police, with the whole of the coast to patrol, simply couldn't get involved in Gata at the moment? Be that as it may, the inquest was delayed. For reasons hard to fathom at the time. Before jumping to conclusions, the Spanish authorities insisted on bringing a team of medico-legal experts to Gata, some all the way from Madrid, which took a whole day. It wasn't until Easter Sunday morning that they finally came out with the facts. Namely, that the corpses weren't Hindus at all. According to the experts, most of them were white, with three Chinese thrown in, and one Afro-American mulatto. One of the whites was identified by a bracelet, which his killers had apparently forgotten to remove. He was a young Frenchman, a lay missionary and agricultural adviser in a village along the Ganges, who had joined the fleet and dragged all his villagers with him. The last white to see him alive had been Consul Himmans, in his office at the Belgian Consulate General, in Calcutta, a few days before the fleet would sail. But nobody knew. As with Ballan, the philosopher, murdered by the crowd on the docks by the Ganges. And the renegade writer, strangled and thrown into the sea, off São Tomé. Before the gates of the Western World, the armada sloughed off those wheeling, dealing traitors who had served it all too well. It had used them in much the same way an occupying enemy subverts and exploits its native collaborators, all judged and condemned, sooner or later. A classic situation, in which basic human justice will invariably prevail. The armada was standing forth alone now, cleansed in advance of all compromise, steeled against all illusion, its racial diamond pure and unflawed. Xenophobia, in a word.

And the word was pronounced, and written, and published. Because finally, at long last, the foes of the beast were raising their voices. And people were listening. At noon on Easter Sunday, it was Pierre Senconac, not Albert Durfort, whose voice was heard over Radio-East. The change had been smooth, with no pressure from above. Albert Durfort had merely failed to appear for his broadcast the previous evening. His telephone didn't answer. His friends were at a loss to imagine where he was ... (For the record, let's note what actually happened, and how Zorro of the Airwaves, erstwhile idol of millions, bowed out, leaving public and microphone behind. Quite simply, by running off to Switzerland. With a few tens of thousands of francs' worth of gold in his luggage, and a young Antillean mistress, of whom he was terribly fond, and who clung to him like glue since that moment a few days before, when he picked her up at the Martinican embassy, sticking her last little flag in the map. Since the Swiss would be slow and deliberate, as usual, in marshaling their forces, Durfort made tracks for the south, hoping to reach Geneva before the inevitable closing of the borders. Let's add that he wasn't alone that day, and that others, too, were speeding in the same direction . . .) And so, it was Pierre Senconac whose voice was heard. A sharp voice, curt and biting, almost unpleasant:

"The time has come," he began, "to call the roll of our dead. And there's one in particular to whom I want to pay tribute, one who died for us all some two months ago. I'm speaking of Consul Himmans, Consul General of Belgium, in the city of Calcutta. People said he was mad! They screamed it from the rooftops! You remember, I'm sure. That one man, Consul Himmans, on the docks in Calcutta, standing up to the crowd to keep them off the ships. And they trampled him to death. Mad? Consul Himmans? Then it's time we were all acting mad, I'm afraid! . . . And the others? The ones killed at Gata, in Spain? A few moments ago, on another station, I heard Boris Vilsberg call them 'martyrs to the cause of brotherhood'! That just shows you how blind we've become. The enemy's henchmen have your brains in their clutches! Birdbrains, I'm sorry to say! Stop listening to them. See them for what they are, fight them off if you still have the strength. The monster is here. He's aground off our shores, but he's still full of life. And everywhere, the same plea to throw your doors open, to take him in. Even from the Pope. That feeble voice of the sick Christian world. Well, listen to me. For Heaven's sake, shut them! Shut your doors! Shut them tight, if it's not too late! Be hard, be tough. Turn a deaf ear to your heart. Remember Consul Himmans. Remember Luke Notaras . . ."

At noon on Easter Sunday! After so many words, and sentences, and statements, piled up over so many years . . . May as well try to grab at a river, and make it flow back from its mouth to its source. Too late! Too late! That too is one explanation . . . And who really knew what Senconac meant? Well, at least let's admire the good people for trying. They manage to lift an enormous weight, like a corpse come suddenly to life, budging his tombstone for a moment, enough to let in a sliver of light, then plunged back into endless darkness . . . Josiane asks Marcel: "You know those Arabs up on the sixth floor? The eight of them in two rooms . . . Like, you wonder sometimes how the kids can keep so clean? . . . Well, all day they've been outside our door. The minute I open up, there's one of them out there, staring. With our three rooms, I mean, and only the two of us . . . You think that's what Senconac meant when he yelled about keeping our doors closed, Marcel? . . . What if we can't keep ours closed? We'll never be alone. Unless we move up to the sixth floor, maybe, and change places with the Arabs . . . But where would we put all our things? We'd never be able to fit them all in there!"

That sliver of light, as the tombstone moves a crack, then falls back in place with all its weight. Too heavy, Marcel! Much, much too heavy!

Thirty

They died in great numbers on the ships of the refugee fleet, although not so many more, when you stop and think, than in Ganges villages ravaged by wars, epidemics, famines, and floods. The Last Chance Armada had simply brought with it the death rate of the Indian subcontinent. Since fuel to cremate the bodies had run out very early, it will be recalled that the fleet, once into the Straits of Ceylon, had begun to strew the sea with its cadavers, like a Hop-o'-my-thumb of tragic dimensions. Then Cape Gata, and only a score of corpses. All foreign, at that. Because, past Gibraltar, they were saving their dead. And plenty of them, too. In the last three days of the improbable epic, they were dying on board left and right. On the big ships, especially, like the *India Star* and the *Calcutta Star*. Malnutrition, sheer exhaustion—both of body and soul—at the end of so long a crossing . . . It's safe to assume that the sick and the dying who had held out only by clinging to their hope, gave up the ghost during those three days once they saw the shores of Europe and realized their dream. Others merely died of hunger and thirst, the feeblest of the lot: the old, the infirm, the misshapen little children. (Except, that is, for the dwarfs and utter monsters, treated as they were with very special care.) Indeed, by the end of the voyage, the rice and fresh water were probably so scarce, that some choice must have had to be made who would get them. Perhaps some chose to let themselves die, or perhaps they were marked out for death in the name of the general good. Cruel though it was, in any event, the plan succeeded. (We are told that the hardiest races are the ones pruned down by natural selection, today as in the past . . .) And so, in due time—very shortly, in fact—there will pour out over the soil of France a flood of hungry, scrawny creatures, but solid and healthy no less, and ready to pounce with all their might. The others, the dead of the last few days, thrown ashore by the thousands once the fleet runs aground, will be gently borne on the waves, and land at last in paradise as well. In the eyes of their living companions, they won't have lost out one iota. Since ideas are the stuff that keeps man alive, death makes no great difference once the mission is fulfilled.

There was only one white still left on board the fleet, one and one only, spared no doubt because he was mad, and because he had spent a long life of charity serving a people who had learned to trust him if not to love him. He lay on the deck of the *Calcutta Star,* day in, day out, lying in the shadow of one of her smokestacks. Everyone knew him. Madness and decay, striking little by little, couldn't wipe from the minds of the ones embarked with him the knowledge of who this man was. But seeing this sort of deranged ascetic, half naked in his filth-stained rags, who else would have known that a mere two months before he was still His Grace the Catholic bishop, prefect apostolic to the entire Ganges region? He could hardly remember himself. Although once in a great while he would sit up from his litter and bless the crowd around him. The crowd would laugh. His former flock would laugh too, but a few of them, just to make him happy, would trace out a sign of the cross in reply. Then he would lie back and dredge from his muddled senses those curious Latin syllables he had thought he could read in a puddle of blood on a dock by the Ganges. He wanted for nothing. He was brought food and drink. Kindhearted children would sit by at his meals and encourage him to eat, for fear that he might slip off into death, or bring him some scraps when his meal had been forgotten. Serenely insane, with each passing day he seemed to grow happy, as if some strange harmony had sprung up within him, bringing him peace. Sometimes, in the morning, he would mutter and mumble, on and on. Snatches of prayers, or verses from the Vedas. Because, after all, he had always professed—holy, broad-minded man that he was—that Truth can shine forth in many a different form. And at night, while the whole deck slept in the grip of a heavy, dank heat, old women would slither to his side. Through a fold in his rags, a hand would gently grasp at his phallus and slowly caress it, until it would swell, between shadow fingers, to spasms of pleasure, pleasure given and received, that kind of pleasure that India abounds in, and one that the old women doubtless believed the poor man should share. One woman would leave. Another would come, in the dark, silent stillness. In time, as soon as night would fall, the poor mad bishop would get an erection, as easily as others get religion, so to speak. On board, his phallus became, first, a subject of conversation, then of curiosity, and, finally, almost of reverence. Lines would form by the light of the stars to inspect it up close. Much like those secret Hindu temples, where ages on end have seen lingams carved in stone offer themselves for the crowds' veneration. When the fleet passed through the Straits of Gibraltar, the bishop from the Ganges had become a holy man. Twice in one lifetime. God's will be done! . . .

Thirty-one

Early Good Friday evening, Monsieur Jean Perret, Undersecretary for Foreign Affairs and personal adviser to the President of the Republic, arrived at the Élysée Palace and was immediately ushered into the executive office. The President was alone, doing nothing, apparently, but smoking a cigar and drinking a highball in gluttonous little gulps. Beside him, on a low table, the wires that an aide had been bringing in every fifteen minutes were piling up higher and higher. Certain passages were underlined in red. On the same table, a radio, volume turned down, was playing the Mozart Requiem.

"Please have a seat, Monsieur Perret," the President told him. "One might imagine that time is of the essence, that we have to make thousands of decisions, and that our minutes are numbered. If my cabinet had its way, and the other frantic old women I have running the country, that's how I'd be spending my time. And I'd never even notice that it's slipping by for good. Well, that's not how things are at all. One simple decision is all we're going to need, and we still have lots of time to make it. History must be full of heads of state who have lived through just such moments, and who never felt calmer or more relaxed than before they pronounced that fateful word 'war.' It takes in so much, it puts so many lives on the line. Actually, when you think about it, it's much more a philosophical question than a physical or moral one. There's nothing as stark, as concise as that word, when you really understand it. . . . Anyway, you see we still have time. Now I suggest we sit here and listen to the news. Obviously, we're not going to learn anything, you and I . . ." (He tossed an offhand gesture at the pile of wires beside him.) "But I'd like to put myself in the shoes of an average citizen, who realizes all of a sudden, after six weeks of altruistic frenzy, that his Easter weekend is ruined, and who even begins to suspect that the rest of his weekends are in for a change, and that life will just never be the same as it was. I want to feel the shock of it myself, like my humblest constituent. I'm going to have to address the nation, probably on Sunday. Maybe that way I'll find the right tone for my speech. . . . You'll notice, since this morning we've been swimming in Mozart. That means Jean Orelle has finally seen the light. When you own a magnificent place in Provence, on the water, right in the thick of where the action's going to be, it has to make you stop and think! Well, let's not be mean. He was in here just now, in an absolute daze, poor man!"

"I know, monsieur. I ran into him in the Gray Room and we chatted for a moment. I hardly knew him. His ideas, that is. Wild, weird ideas! Like a nationwide draft, only no arms, no guns. And including the women and children! A huge peace offensive into the south. 'Nonviolent aggression,' he called it. He was babbling."

"Poor thing!" said the President. "Such an elegant, refined guerrilla! Put yourself in his place. Artist and warrior, rolled into one. Every 'war of liberation,' no matter where ... Suddenly there he was. Fifty years, fighting the battle. And sometimes with a lot of courage, too. Though lately they seemed to be holding him back, to keep him out of danger. I guess a Nobel Prize is worth more to the cause alive than dead.... And each time he would come back more famous than before, ready to write his magnificent books, and go chasing around from salon to salon, collecting his art, inviting his select little circle to his lady friends' fancy châteaux. Playing both ends for all he was worth, the best of two worlds! Then, all of a sudden, things have changed, and his game is no good. It won't work anymore. But the warrior can't bring himself to wring the artist's neck. At the end of his life, he sees the light at last, sees what it was all about ... Unlike most people, I think old age is the time when man finds himself, when he finally—and sadly—learns the truth. That's what happened just now to Jean Orelle. The man who left here a few moments ago was terribly sincere, and terribly sad. He had been through it all. Which explains the Mozart Requiem, I suppose. After all that time poisoning the airwaves, he finds that he's really all Western Man at heart. You can trust him now to be sure we go out in style. Berlin came tumbling down to Wagner. With Orelle it will be more elegant, more refined ..."

A voice broke softly through the silence that followed:

"Seven fifty-nine and thirty seconds ..."

The President leaned over and turned up the volume ...

"The time is exactly eight o'clock. And now, the news. According to rather confused reports reaching us from several Third World countries, it would seem that refugee fleets are currently forming all over the globe. The governments in question admit their powerlessness to stem the apparently spontaneous uprisings. In Indonesia, notably, in the capital of Jakarta, the port has been overrun, and a number of foreign vessels have been seized without bloodshed. The government of Australia, Indonesia's closest Western neighbor, has officially declared that, quote, 'the situation must be considered as extremely grave,' end of quote. In Manila, the Philippines, the police have been unable to prevent a large mob from invading a trio of cruise ships, among them the giant French liner *Normandie,* all of whose passengers have been removed to several of the city's hotels. In the cities of Conakry, in Africa, Karachi, in Pakistan, and, again in Calcutta, the docks have been virtually taken over by crowds estimated to number in the tens of thousands, milling aimlessly about. . . . Meanwhile, the government of China has officially denied a report, originating in Moscow, stating that millions of Chinese civilians have been massing along the Siberian border. . . . In addition, it was learned two hours ago that, in London, where the labor force includes some eight hundred thousand Commonwealth nationals, a group calling itself the 'Non-European Commonwealth Committee' is planning a peaceful demonstration Monday evening, in order to, quote, 'demand British citizenship, full voting rights and human rights, equal salaries, equal employment, and equality in housing, recreational facilities, and social welfare,' end of quote. The British government has, as yet, had no official reaction . . ."

"I hope there are lots of Zulus in London," the President muttered. "There's something I'd like to see! A Zulu, citizen of Great Britain!"

"As we announced in our three o'clock newsflash," the voice went on, "the Last Chance Armada was seen passing through the Straits of Gibraltar at that time, heading in a northeasterly direction. Reconnaissance aircraft of England, France, and Spain immediately flew over the fleet. The skies were clear; the seas, calm. We have a special report from our correspondent on the scene, aboard one of those planes. It was phoned in shortly after his return to Gibraltar, and is rebroadcast for you now":

"I'm speaking to you from the airbase on Gibraltar, where I landed ten minutes ago in a Royal Navy Vulture. What I saw as we circled the fleet defies the imagination. The ocean is covered. There must be a good hundred ships. Almost no wind, no waves to speak of. Still, the decks barely show above the water. I don't think I saw one ship intact. Every hull is rusting away. Some have holes below the waterline . . . This is what miracles are made of, and it's a miracle they've made it all the way. . . . We circled low several times. The smell was unbearable. The decks are, literally, a solid maze of black and white. Black skin, white tunics. Thousands of poor souls. You simply can't imagine what it's like. You'd think you were flying over one huge mass grave, except that the corpses are still alive. I could see them waving their arms in the air. As close as I could figure, there must be eight hundred thousand survivors on those ships. . . . The fleet is sailing northeast, which means that it's heading straight for the Côte d'Azur. The ships are bound to run aground, I think it's safe to say, since none of them even has an anchor. No mooring lines, nothing. And I'm sure that, judging by what I saw, there's no way they could go back where they came from. Or even stay afloat another week, for that matter. According to my rapid calculations, if they hold their present speed, and if the weather doesn't change, they'll be running aground sometime Saturday night, or early Easter Sunday morning. In other words, in about a day . . . I should mention, too, that up and down the Spanish coast the prevalent feeling is one of great relief. Everywhere people are speaking again of the need for compassion and brotherly love. . . . This report has come to you direct from Gibraltar. We return you now to Paris."

The Parisian announcer broke in:

"This has been an eyewitness account from our special correspondent, recorded at four o'clock this afternoon. Subsequent reports confirm that the refugee fleet is, indeed, sailing toward France and the Côte d'Azur. In addition, Arab radio stations throughout North Africa have stepped up their broadcasts in Hindi, urging their brothers to keep heading north, since, quote, 'that's where the West begins, and where milk flows like water,' end of quote. It should be added, too, that a note of alarm can be detected in the announcers' voices. . . . Meanwhile, throughout the south, recent appeals by press and local officials to remain calm and present a united front have gone largely unheeded. An exodus is already under way toward the cities of the north. Since morning, trains and planes have been filled to capacity, and traffic on Highway A7 was already bumper-to-bumper by four o'clock. Large numbers of homes and businesses have closed their doors. Transport companies throughout the area have announced that their vans are unable to handle any further calls. . . . At five o'clock, Monsieur Jean Orelle, Minister of Information and spokesman for the government, read the following statement to the press, rebroadcast at this time":

"In the face of the report, officially confirmed, that the fleet from the Ganges is, indeed, sailing toward the southern coast of France . . ." (The ageing minister's voice sounded firm but muted, as if he were fighting off a feeling of great fatigue.) ". . . the government has decided to adopt a number of tentative measures vis-à-vis the refugees themselves. The four departments along the coast have been placed under the command of Monsieur Jean Perret, Undersecretary for Foreign Affairs, and personal representative of the President of the Republic for the entire southern region. Should circumstances demand, the government will not hesitate to declare a state of emergency. Army and police units have been ordered to set up a quarantine line along the coast, to guard against possible epidemic, and have been ordered to prevent any unauthorized landing that might prove detrimental to one of our nation's most prosperous areas. The government pledges to make every effort to find humane solutions to the present problem, in keeping with its unprecedented nature, and will not hesitate to impose them, if need be. The President of the Republic wishes to reaffirm his respect for those citizens, sizable in number, who have expressed their support and sympathy for the refugees, but he feels obliged to alert them against certain excesses antagonistic to the preservation of law and order, so essential at this time. Attempts at individual action will not be tolerated. In addition, all residents of the southern areas of the country are requested to remain calm, to cooperate with the government, and to go about their daily business . . ."

"When he left me a few moments ago," the President observed, "that wasn't at all how he felt. We'd worked out that statement at about four, the two of us. But things happen fast. Like that story that some Italian writer dreamed up once upon a time. Buzzati, I think it was. Someone accidentally rips a shutter off one of the windows, and the whole house comes tumbling down, bit by bit, and kills everyone inside . . . Well, it seems as if our starving friends have ripped off the shutter. Buzzati, if I remember, didn't try to explain it. He just described what happened. I'm afraid we can't do much better . . ."

"You have just heard the statement," the announcer's voice went on, "read by the Minister of Information at five o'clock this afternoon. Since that time, however, the number of people leaving the south has considerably increased. A mass migration would seem to be in the making. At the same time, a modest current has been noted in the opposite direction, composed of the most diverse elements. Whole hippie and Christian communes have been seen heading south. Along with them, groups recruited from the outskirts of Paris, young industrial workers, bands of students from the several disciplines, as well as large numbers of clergymen and nonviolent militants of varying persuasions. One serious confrontation has already been reported. It took place on Highway A6, at tollbooth number 3, when police tried to turn back one of the groups in question. Monsieur Clément Dio, editor in chief of *La Pensée Nouvelle*, has voiced a formal protest against what he terms 'this vicious attempt to prohibit freedom of movement,' and has let it be known that he too is heading south, as a symbolic gesture. Our reporter interviewed him outside the offices of *La Pensée Nouvelle* only moments before he drove off . . ."

(Then Dio's voice. In the background, street sounds, and frequent cheers and applause.)

"People are leaving the south in droves, and that doesn't surprise me one bit. The West is having conscience pangs. It can't stand the sight of misery on the march. And so, instead of waiting to face it, to welcome it with open arms, it sneaks off without a word. Too bad! Let it go! If the south turns into one great big desert, all the better for the armada! All the more room to put our poor devils and give them that last chance they're after. I'll tell you the truth: that's why I'm leaving Paris myself and heading south. And right here and now I'm inviting everyone who feels the way I do—everyone who puts human ideals above governments, and economic systems, and religions, and races—to come and join me. I'd like to see us turn out in force. Who cares how many soldiers they send? And as for Perret, that fascist puppet . . . Listen, I heard Jean Orelle too. I heard him talk about his 'tentative measures,' and his 'imposed solutions,' and his 'quarantine line'! Quarantine my foot! It's a battle line, that's what they're drawing! Are they going to order our troops to fire on poor, starving bastards? Are they going to set up concentration camps? Are they going to . . ."

"He's getting on my nerves," said the President, turning down the volume. "But at least," he added wistfully, "there's someone who knows what he's after!"

"Whose idea was that 'quarantine line,' monsieur?" asked Jean Perret.

"Mine," the President sighed. "I hesitated quite a while. But as soon as I saw the exodus begin in earnest, I realized nothing could stop it. It's a long-standing national habit of ours, especially the richer and better off we are. May as well speed it along, I thought, and make the most of it. I figured if we cleaned out the home front, so to speak, and got rid of all that fear and trembling, the army might have a chance to do its job. All the rest—the part about remaining calm and going about their business—well, that was so much window dressing."

"But everyone knows there are no more epidemics, monsieur, no more medieval plagues!"

"Well then," said the President, "the ones who want an excuse to turn and run, instead of defending their property, can pretend there still are, if they want to. I owe my constituents that much, don't I?"

And he bent over the radio dial.

"Immediately after making his statement," the announcer's voice continued, "Monsieur Clément Dio left Paris, accompanied by his wife—the well-known writer Iris Nan-Chan—and a number of friends, inviting the cheering crowd to come join him on the coast . . ."

Thirty-two

Hurtling southward goes Clément Dio, fast as his powerful car will take him. He speeds past long infantry convoys, truck after truck, their canvas flaps open in back, and sitting inside, young soldiers lined up on benches. The army has certainly changed. It reeks of gloom. The soldiers don't even lean out to admire his magnificent, sleek red bomb, with its endless hood. And Iris Nan-Chan, that beautiful lady . . . Why, they don't even blow her kisses, or laugh to catch her eye, or slap their thighs in a flurry of off-color comments. Not so much as one dawdling private flashing an obscene gesture, as that strictly untouchable ivory flesh passes close to his truck. "The army looks good!" says Dio. "Not exactly singing their way to the front!" He's delighted. His handiwork, partly. How well he remembers his noble battle, dragging the army through the courts, forcing it to lift its ban on publications of a certain persuasion. And winning the case, hands down! For ten years now *La Pensée Nouvelle, La Grenouille,* and the rest, had been read in the barracks of every French regiment under the sun. Prisons, too, for that matter. They had taken advantage and gotten into the act. Our friend Ben Suad, alias Dio, had had his revenge. Revenge for that bill of sale, found in his family papers. The one that showed his grandmother, a black harem slavegirl, sold to a brothel for French officers in Rabat. Why on earth had his Moroccan father, mild-mannered civil servant under the French, held on to that odious proof of his past? To keep his hatred alive, that's why! . . .

At the tollbooths, squadrons of security police in black, helmeted and massive, and not in too good a mood either: "I wouldn't go south if I were you." "You wouldn't? What do you mean, Lieutenant?" "Just what I said!" growls the bemedaled lieutenant, eyeing the long red hood, the beautiful Eurasian, the driver's swarthy skin and elegant crop of kinky hair. "Back where you came from, and on the double!" "You wouldn't be a racist, would you, Lieutenant?" "Me? A racist? You've got to be kidding!" No, no one is a racist today anymore. That's the official word, everyone agrees. The police even less so than the rest. They're paid to remember . . . A glimpse of the press card, and open sesame: "Go ahead, monsieur. Sorry for the trouble!"

(A press card works wonders in the right hands these days. Though
not that it came without a struggle, mind you! . . .) Across the highway, traffic is on the move. Dio looks at his watch: a few hours until
Saturday. The day before Easter! And the road is crammed with cars
streaming up from the south, away from the sun! A weekend turned
around. Clément Dio loathes that crowd of sheep, as much as he
loathed them before, in reverse, when they flocked to the sun, like
convicts to their feed. He smiles. His wife smiles. Their hands meet
for a moment. They're bucking the current, turning the tide. The
south is draining dry, spewing its stinking, self-indulgent slime. And
soon a different kind of slime will surge in to take its place. All
perfectly clear? Apocalypse or birth? A new breed of man, a new
social order? Or the death of all bearable life as we know it? Dio
couldn't give less of a damn. He admits it. ". . . human ideals, above
governments, and economic systems, and religions, and races . . ."
Yes, that's what he said. But what does it mean? Not a blessed thing,
really. There's nothing at all above those things. An absolute void,
like the splitting of the atom, or a great empty nothingness, let loose
all at once. A show too good to miss. A sight to send even the horrible
mushroom back to the prop room . . . Through the Morvan. Bur-
gundy. And Dio, crooning as he drives, "For now the thousand years
are ended, yes, the thousand years are ended now . . ." Master of
mankind, even for a moment. Enough to make a whole life worth
living. Like the killer at Sarajevo, but suddenly with the gift to see
into the future, going through with his action instead of holding back,
spellbound by the vision of the cataclysm he's unleashing . . .

Beyond Mâcon, a rest area with a lot of bright lights, and a column
of tanks, standing still, lined up like huge toys. Dio slows down, turns
off the road, and pulls up next to the tank at the head of the line. "Get
the fuck out of here!" cries a voice. A colonel, none too pleased.
Second Hussars, Chamborant Regiment. Three centuries of military
tradition. Grouped around him, in silence, a few flustered officers.
In front of the tanks, the men, much more vocal. Arguing back and
forth. "Let's take a vote," says one of the hussars . . . Chamborant!
Three centuries of glory! And this is how it ends: in a mutiny, no less!
"Press," explains Dio. "Kiss my ass!" replies the colonel. Great khaki
colossus, lumbering toward him, murder in his eye, fists clenched. An
officer comes between them, with all due respect. "Drop dead!" roars
the colonel, and he turns and climbs into his tank. Only his chest,
ablaze with ribbons, and his glowering, helmeted face, stick up from
the turret. Lovely military tableau, washed in a flood of almost eerie

light. The tank bears the name Bir Hacheim. Relic of battle glories past! Suddenly its motor begins to growl. An officer shouts out, "But Colonel, they're still there! You can't do it! You can't!" "Bullshit I can't!" cries the colonel, in his frontline voice. "If the bastards don't get up, I'll run them all over!" Dio moves around to the front of the tank. He sees "the bastards," some twenty or so, lying across the exit ramp leading back to the highway. Most of them are in uniform. Red shoulder braid, Chamborant, three centuries, etc. Five are in civilian clothes. One, stretched out almost under the tracks of the tank. Long beard, curly hair, the face of a sculptured Italian Christ. "Who are you?" Dio asks him. "G.L.A.," the prone figure replies. Gay Liberation Alliance. "And you?" he asks another. "Just people," is the answer. "Proletarians. No special name." The purest of the pure in Dio's book. "He's going to mow you all down," he tells them. "Not a chance, he won't dare," the homosexual answers. "Me, he wouldn't mind, but not his own men." "For God's sake, get up!" an officer pleads. "Can't you see, here he comes!" The mass of steel has started to move. Imperceptibly at first, as the tracks nibble forward, inch by inch. "Colonel!" screams the officer. "Balls!" replies the colonel. Iris Nan-Chan shuts her eyes. Her Western half can't take any more. A few moments later, when she opens them again—to please her Oriental half—the Italian Christ has disappeared, and the tank tracks are dragging chunks of shredded, bloody flesh. And all without a sound . . . One after another, each one of the figures gets out of the way, but only at the very last moment. The bullfighter's elegant dodge, just out of reach of the metallic beast. Quick and agile, one by one, the soldiers roll over on their sides. Like a training maneuver, an obstacle course. Crack regiment! The best! . . . The tank, Bir Hacheim, has begun to speed up and head for the highway. The colonel doesn't even turn around. Three tanks roll along behind it with a roar. Then a fourth. And that's all. Back from the Russian campaign, in 1813, the Chamborant Hussars had twice that many survivors . . . Dio can't take his eyes off the patch of bloody muck on the pavement. Beside him, an officer is silently choking back his tears. "And what's that hero's name?" Dio asks him. The officer misunderstands. "Him?" he asks, shaken, pointing to the pool of blood. "I'm not sure . . . I think he said his name was Paul." "No, not him. Not Paul. The other one, the one who just left. The killer with all the stripes!" "Oh, you mean the colonel? Colonel Constantine Dragasès . . ." "Strange name," thinks Dio, and he muses to himself: "Fall of Constantinople . . . May 29, 1453 . . . Constantine XI Palaeologus, last emperor of Byzantium . . . Known as Dragasès . . ." The officer hadn't flinched at the epithet "killer." Why should he? Why not call the colonel a killer, after all? And the notion begins to make the rounds . . . The officer, meanwhile, as if on maneuvers too, hurdles the barrier, and plunges, on foot, headlong into the moonlit country-side before him . . .

Dio is back behind the wheel. Straight ahead, full speed. The car is flying. But this is no night to wind up dead in a stupid pile of twisted wreckage! Oh no! Tonight he feels he could live forever . . . Not far down the road, he passes Colonel Dragasès, five tanks and all. He laughs. He's happy. The Villefranche tollbooth looms up into view, oasis of harsh, raw light. Lots of motorcycles parked in a row. Shadow figures with helmets and boots. Strange helmets for police! White, red, bright blue. Colorful, phosphorescent stripes. "Who are you, gents?" "We're the Rhodio-Chemical People's Strike Force." The purest of the pure, all out on this glorious night of nights. Sit-down strikes, hunger strikes, ransom demands, sabotage, laboratory smash-ups, antiracist purges, anti-antiprotest pogroms, ready to loot shops, to struggle against all forms of oppression, available for all kinds of action, running on nothing but cycles, girls, tobacco, and slogans, ready to break up everything in sight when they lose their temper, often fired but always rehired, because, after all, they have everyone terrified, political delinquents, since that's the term we found that fits them best, and that covers—and excuses—their multitude of sins . . . "And what are you doing here? Where are the cops?" "Left an hour ago," a magnificent specimen answers. (Tall young man in jeans and surplus U.S. Army jacket, with a sleeve full of stripes and a shoulder patch marked "Panama Rangers.") "Not too many of them. But . . ." (He sweeps his arm around in an arc.) ". . . like, there's two hundred of us, maybe more! Besides, they're all a bunch of pussies. No guts. Company Three, out of Mâcon. Old pals of ours! They're the ones who shot us up last year. Like I mean, it was just a peaceful demonstration, you know? Of course, they had it tough I guess. Kind of outnumbered, the stupid assholes! Anyway, they got two of us. But man, what a funeral! I mean, great! A hundred thousand people, all the plants and factories shut down, and the workers marching behind the bodies. Since then, people spit when they go by their barracks. Like, when they go into a store in town, they get treated worse than a black in South Africa. And their kids don't have any friends. No-body'll talk to them at school. And their women can't walk out in the street. There's even this priest who says from now on he'll go say mass at their place, so as not to screw things up in his church. Like, their captain even got the boot, you know? Poor bastards! They've had it. All they can do now is wait to retire. Not even much good for directing traffic. So, I mean, when they saw us coming this time, they turned around and split. Said they'd come back with more men. Meantime we're having a ball!" When Panama Ranger laughs, he's charming beyond belief. Like a handsome young god, striding free and victorious, from the deep, dark forest of machines. Of the race of conquering heroes. Who cares what conquest, what cause? No difference! . . . Dio tells him who he is. And again he asks, "What are you doing here?" "All kinds of stuff," Panama Ranger answers. "To-day's our day to have a blast! Like first, scrounge up a little bread. We've got ourselves a tollbooth, so, I mean, people have to pay us, right? For everyone leaving the south and going up north, it's ten times the price. Two hundred francs. A real bargain! They cough it up and never even bitch. Too much of a hurry to get the hell out. For the ones going south, we've got ways to slow them down. I mean, unless they're some of ours. Like, we found a roadblock the cops left behind. The kind that folds out. You know, with long spikes. The first batch of army trucks managed to slip right by, they were going so damn fast. Before we could get set up, I mean. But the second one was something else! We got them, but good! The officer's jeep and the first three trucks plunked down right on the spikes. All four wheels. So I said: 'Chowtime, folks. Everybody out!' The soldiers thought it was funny, but the officer was a tough-assed son of a bitch. He had his men line up, like for real, and he yelled, 'Clear out this crap!' Then I piped up and said, 'Listen, you guys. Take a look at us. We're just about your age. Let's see all you factory workers step forward, and all you farmers, and students. All you laborers in the struggle of the people against oppression!' Well, you should have seen the rush! When it was over, the officer stood there with five poor bastards. And in no time they ran off and left him high and dry. They're probably still running!" "And the officer?" Dio asks. "He's down the road trying to thumb a ride. But I don't think he's going to have much luck. Like I mean, before he left, we ripped off all his clothes!" Dio laughs a hearty laugh . . . In the midst of the parking area, in front of the police building, a crowd of young men—in chaotic array of uniforms and jackets, helmets ajumble in fraternal mélange—sit warming themselves around giant campfires. On all sides, the sounds of joy, voices singing, jokes about "the captain's big, bare ass," raised to Rabelaisian proportions. No harm intended. Wooden benches and panels, stripped from the trucks, standing idle, crackle gaily in the flames. "I guess we'll pull out and take the backroads south," says Panama Ranger. "Like, they say the cops down there are pretty tough. But we've made out our will, and we're leaving it behind." He raises his arm and points to the tollbooth. "See?" Spread across the façade, a broad streamer, shining in the light. And on it the words:

WORKERS, SOLDIERS, GANGES REFUGEES
UNITED AGAINST OPPRESSION

"Beautiful!" Dio exclaims. "But you'd better get going. In a little while five tanks will be coming this way, with a colonel who's out of his head. And believe me, he won't think twice about shooting." "Thanks," says the young man, "see you on the Riviera!" "When?" Dio asks him. Panama Ranger smiles back his reply: "No rush. With so many pigs running north, we'll have our pick of fancy places to take ourselves a vacation in the sun! I just hope they haven't emptied their pools. Like I mean, now that the revolution's finally here, the first thing to do is enjoy ourselves, right?" Dio's thoughts exactly ... In a moment, a great, friendly hubbub, a couple of fenders merrily scraped in a flurry of pretended insults, hurled back and forth from driver to driver, in the best French style, then off into the darkness, young men, trucks, and all, as a tune goes running through Clément Dio's brain, lyrics by himself: "For now the thousand years are ended, yes, the thousand years are ended now . . ." For a few moments, silence, only to be broken by the ominous rumble of Dragasès's tanks looming out of the shadows and into the light of the tollbooth. The gun on the lead tank points up a few degrees and fires off four rounds. In a cloud of dust the façade comes crumbling down, and with it the pretty streamer, Panama Ranger's last will and testament. The colonel was never a big one for slogans. And the five tanks roll on, pushing doggedly forward, up over the mound of debris, and off into the night, further south, further south . . .

On the outskirts of Lyon, Dio takes the boulevard circling the city —deserted in these wee, small hours, while convoys of army trucks rattle along the river, through the heart of town—and turns left on the road to Grenoble. Via the "Tourist Route," as a sign announces. Toward Nice, on the road Napoleon took when he came back from Elba, and marched up to Paris. Iris Nan-Chan finds it rather amusing, and drawls out a long, exultant laugh. "Napoleon Dio! My own little eagle! Flying in triumph from steeple to steeple. Only we're going to land in the plush Negresco towers!" When they reach Grenoble,

one of the suburbs by the banks of the Isère is aglow with flames.
"Press!" declares Iris Nan-Chan's little eagle. "What's up?" A captain
of the security police is standing in the highway, in front of a roadblock of trucks, lined up zigzag. "The prison. It's on fire." "And the
prisoners?" "Escaped, every damn one. At least two thousand. If you
folks are driving farther down, watch out. From Grenoble on we
can't be responsible." "How did it happen?" Dio asks him. "Oh, it
wasn't hard," the captain replies. Standing there with his fifty-odd
years behind him, his drooping gray mustache, and the downcast
look of a faithful public servant who suddenly feels the trap door of
anarchy fall open beneath his big booted feet. "I was sure it would
end this way," he says. "I was sure too," echoes Dio, in his most
concerned voice. "It happened just like I expected. A hundred guys
come and attack, blow in the doors, knock them down . . . Yelling
something like: 'Workers, prisoners, Ganges refugees, united!' Then
all of a sudden fire breaks out in the section where they keep the
political prisoners. And the guards just open up the gates and take
off. Put yourself in their shoes, after all. For ten years now everyone's
been down on them, blaming them for everything. The same with
us. So why risk their necks? If you want to know, I think it was a
put-up job. The Ganges, that's all they ever talked about. This idea
they had that when the fleet finally got here, all the prisons would
fall in a heap. Last year it was the Pope! They were sure he was going
to show up at Christmas, in person, and open all the gates. And why
not, with things the way they are! You don't know what to expect
these days. Everything's upside down. The world's on its head."
"Exactly, captain," Dio replies, the picture of composure. "That's
why you have to be careful whose head you're kicking." The captain
turns to ask him a question: "Say you, what paper do you write for
anyway?" But Dio has already gone speeding off . . . Gap. Sisteron.
Digne . . . In no special hurry, the mountain garrisons have come
down from their Vauban-built forts, and are combing the valleys for
the escapees. And when, in the fading darkness, the net closes
around an occasional catch, strange whispered dialogues take place:
"Who are you?" "Prisoners. Victims, just like you! Come on, you guys,
give us a break!" "Go on, beat it! You've sweated enough. School's
out, have a ball!" "A ball is right! Thanks a million . . ." Next morning,
a total of four have been recaptured, and put back under lock and
key. One of them, a famous criminal: twenty years at hard labor for
kidnapping the little daughter of a wealthy perfume magnate of the
region. The early risers stand around and cheer him on: "Don't

worry, Bébert, you won't be in long. Damn army pigs! They're working for the cops!" Deathly pale, an officer flings down his cap and
elbows his way through the crowd, suddenly hushed and still, as if
waiting for a funeral to pass . . .

At Barrême, Dio stops at a station and fills his tank. "You're my last
customer," the attendant tells him. "After you, I'm closing up and
getting the hell out. It's too dangerous. Between here and Grasse,
five stations I know of have already been hit, and the cops won't even
answer when you call anymore. I had a dog, but since last night he's
practically gone nuts. Like he could sniff out that gang already, all
eight hundred thousand . . . Oh, you mean you're paying? Say, thanks!
The last car, the one before you, ran out on the bill. Just like that. No
bones about it. Eight of them inside, dressed like a bunch of tramps,
crammed in like sardines. The kind you see heading for the coast in
the summer. The driver looks at me and says: 'Listen, man, no sweat
about the bread! From now on everything belongs to the people!'
Does that make sense? Anyway, I'm getting out. I'll come back later
when things settle down . . ." In the dim light of dawn, as he shifts
into gear, Dio spots a big German shepherd, like a sentinel at his post,
left behind in the debacle. He's trembling all over. And whining.
Then, all at once, rearing up on his hind legs, he faces the south,
opens his jaws, and lets out a long, mournful wail. "Nasty dog!" Iris
Nan-Chan remarks with a shudder. "Let's hurry, darling, or that
dreadful beast is going to spoil my whole day . . ."

At the La Faye Pass, another stop. More trucks blocking the road.
The army this time. Dio recognizes the insignia of the marine commandos. A unit never seen in France, but one that the reporters of
La Pensée Nouvelle follow step by step all over the world, like a dung
beetle sticking to the bull that feeds it. An uprising to put down in
Chad, or Guiana, or Djibouti, or Madagascar? They're the spearhead
sent on loan overseas, to those presidents beset by the hatred of their
people . . . An officer steps forward. Elegant and polite. The living
image of that soldier in the posters, the ones ripped to shreds so often
of late: "Young Men With Ideals! Enlist! Reenlist!" Dio really has
forgotten that such creatures still exist. "Your press card, please," the
officer asks. "Well, well!" he exclaims, "Monsieur Clément Dio! After
loathing you all these years, I finally get to meet you in the flesh!"
Some paratroopers come over. They surround the red car and stare
silently at Dio. They haven't forgotten that such creatures still exist,
but off on their distant campaigns they've never seen one in person,
that's all. "Take a good look, men," the officer tells them. "If you've

never seen a swine close up, here's your chance. Now maybe you can see why we're crawling with assholes." His voice is so matter-of-fact and calm, that Dio, past master himself at composure, wonders if this is the end of the road. "Impossible!" he thinks, stifling the urge to laugh at the thought. "Not here! It would be too stupid!" Meanwhile, Iris Nan-Chan has turned toward the officer, trying to taunt him in her most honeyed tones: "Why, Monsieur Brontosaurus! We thought your breed died out eons ago, and now here you are. And you can even talk! My, my!" But the confrontation doesn't last long. Strangely enough, it's the soldiers who lose interest, like a living organism that begins to reject a foreign body. "You see?" says the officer. "They don't give a damn about you. All right, you can go. I have no orders to do anything with you. In fact, I have no orders at all, and that's how I like it. My unit is all alone in the world, and that suits us fine. Just one word of advice. From here south the country is dead. The people who should have stayed, left. And the ones who did stay, or the ones who are coming, shouldn't be here at all. You'll find plenty of friends in Saint-Vallier, down over the pass. But I'm not too sure you'll like them. Especially Madame Nan-Chan. There's a little bit of everything. The whole of the Draguignan prison, in fact. Sex criminals and baby-killers included. Not to mention the pack of striking workers from some stinking factory in Nice, a bunch of Arabs from Boumedienne Village, a few dyed-in-the-wool blacks who can only speak Wolof, and, just for good measure, some student unionist cell or other, though I really couldn't tell you what they stand for. You can't miss them all. They've taken over the Hotel Préjoly—forty rooms, baths and toilets, bar, elevator, grill, phone in every room, heated pool, tennis courts. At least, that's what it says in the *Guide Michelin*. Of course, now . . ." (He gives a doubtful shrug.) "Well, at least I can tell you that your friends are nice and clean. With my glasses it's easy to see the pool. They've all been bathing, and the water is filthy. I should really go in there and clear them out, so my men can move on. . . . Oh yes, I forgot to tell you: they all have sawed-off shotguns. There isn't a gun store for miles around that hasn't been broken into. . . . But I'd rather wait until they're all dead drunk. It won't take long. You can hear them from here. . . . Well, my friends—monsieur, madame—so much for our chat. I hope you have a delightful trip!"

And what do you do after that, when your name is Clément Dio?

Shift into gear and drive off, resolutely, to Saint-Vallier. Which is just what he did . . .

Thirty-three

The President had just turned his radio up again:

"... Immediately after making his statement," the reporter's voice was saying, "Monsieur Clément Dio left Paris, accompanied by his wife—the well-known writer Iris Nan-Chan—and a number of friends, inviting the cheering crowd to come join him on the coast. Interesting too is the marked difference between the reaction of the evening press, in its late editorials, and the spontaneous reaction of public opinion, apparent in the mass migration from the south. While all roads leading north are quickly becoming the scene of huge tie-ups, growing worse by the hour, the press, both right and left, is virtually of one voice in calling for a humane solution to this unprecedented problem. The conservative *Le Monde*, in an article signed by . . ."

"Yes," the President observed, " 'marked difference' indeed! Go try and explain it. And yet, who here in the government didn't suspect it? Even those who wouldn't admit it. Not even to themselves."

"Accepted notions die hard, monsieur," said Jean Perret. "Like straitjackets, stifling our minds. You remember the national poll they took two weeks ago? You remember the questions? 'To maintain a proper balance in present-day society, do you consider racism to be: (1) Essential? (4%), (2) Somewhat necessary? (17%), (3) Moderately objectionable? (32%), (4) Revolting and inhuman? (43%), (5) No opinion? (4%). Would you be willing, if need be, to take the consequences of your opinion? Yes (67%), No (18%), No opinion (15%) . . .' And yet, monsieur, no one is pressured to answer one way or the other. And the people they poll come from every social class, across the board. If there is any pressure, I suppose it comes from what people are made to believe they should think. But certainly that's nothing new. What is new, though, is the kind of prestige, the status these polls give a weak, lazy mind."

"Yes, I know," the President replied. "Then again, maybe I've been a little weak and lazy myself. Until now we've been governing by what the polls told us. It was all very easy. But maybe we've really been governing in thin air. I'm afraid it's too late to find out . . .'"

"... It's true," the reporter's voice went on, "that none of these journalists has, as yet, gone beyond mere words, to offer any concrete proposals. Only Monsieur Jules Machefer, editor in chief of *La Pensée Nationale*, has, in fact, come forward with a serious suggestion. I quote: 'Unless the government orders the army to take all possible steps to prevent this landing, it's the duty of every citizen with any feeling for his culture, his race, his religion and traditions, not to think twice, but to take up arms himself. Even Paris, our own beloved Paris, has already been besieged by the henchmen of the invader. My offices have been ransacked by bands of mindless thugs, among them the vilest dregs of the capital's foreign populations. My newsboys have been harassed, day in day out, chased through the streets by groups of extremists, without the police even lifting a finger, and before the very eyes of an unconcerned public. Under such conditions, I have no choice but to suspend publication of *La Pensée Nationale* until better days. But I'm not going to give up the fight. I'm just changing my style. Peace-loving old man that I am, I serve notice nonetheless, here and now, that I'm going to be waiting down south, hunting rifle in hand, to welcome those threadbare legions of the Antichrist. And I hope that a lot of you will join me!' End of quote ..."

"They've finally gotten to him," the President murmured. "Well what's the difference ... 'Before the very eyes of an unconcerned public ...' Thin air. Thin air ..."

"... In another development," the voice continued, "Vatican sources have just released to the media, no more than ten minutes ago, a statement by His Holiness, Pope Benedict XVI, the official text of which reads as follows. I quote: 'On this Good Friday, day of hope for Christians the world over, we beseech our brethren in Jesus Christ to open their hearts, souls, and worldly wealth to all these poor unfortunates whom God has sent knocking at our doors. There is no road save charity for a Christian to follow. And charity is no vain word. Nor can it be divided, or meted out little by little. It is all, or it is nothing. Now, at last, the hour is upon us. The hour when all of us must cast aside that halfway spirit that has long caused our faith to founder. The hour when all of us must answer the call of that universal love for which Our Lord died on the cross, and in whose name He rose from the dead.' End of quote ... It has also been learned that His Holiness has ordered all objects of value still contained in the palaces and museums of the Vatican to be placed on immediate sale, with the proceeds going entirely to aid and settle the

Ganges refugees once they have landed. . . . This concludes our eight o'clock summary of the news. Our next bulletin in fifteen minutes . . ."

"How do you like that!" the President exclaimed, over the concerto that followed. "I can just hear the good Lord above, complaining: *'Et tu, fili?'* What else could you expect from a Brazilian? The cardinals wanted a new-style pope. For the universal Church, they said. Well, they certainly got one! I knew him well when he was still a bishop, badgering Europe with his pitiful tales of Third World despair. I remember telling him one day that by wearing down the wayward mother he would only harm the children all the more. You know what he answered? That poverty is all there is worth sharing! Well, he's keeping his promise. . . . Are you a Christian, Monsieur Perret?"

"Not a Christian, monsieur, a Catholic. It's a basic nuance I insist on."

"I guess I don't believe in much myself. Maybe a mass from time to time. Like Henry IV. That's why I need you. Now that I have to make a choice, I need something to base it on, something to believe in. I'm afraid my choice is bound to be wrong. . . . And something else too. Now that you've become 'that fascist puppet' there's one thing you can count on. With this pope in the Vatican, you'll be excommunicated for sure."

"I couldn't care less, monsieur. In the Middle Ages they would have kicked a few cardinals in the rump, elected a new pope, and declared this one an antipope, just like that. Which is just what I'm doing in my own heart of hearts. Besides, it's all nothing but words. For six weeks now we've been drowning in a flood of words. Your staff is up to their necks, monsieur. Look, in just the last hour alone . . ." (He was holding up a sheaf of wires.) "This one is from thirty Nobel winners, in support of the armada. Without Jean Orelle, by the way, but who cares about him anymore? They whipped together all the peace prize names they could find, with old Kenyatta and Fra Muttone leading the pack! . . . Here's one from Boris Vilsberg and ten thousand intellectuals, with a petition calling for equal justice . . . One from the French National Committee for the Encouragement of Immigration from the Ganges, to let you know they've got more than two million signatures . . . The Archbishop of Aix is offering to empty out his schools to house the refugees, and his seminaries too—which, between you and me, are empty already. . . . And this one from the UN, where they've just passed a unanimous resolution to abolish the concept of race. Which means ours, you can bet. And we voted for that? Well, I'm not surprised, what with everything else we've voted for in that three-ring circus! . . . One from Geneva. A hunger strike by the founder of The Brotherhood of Man. Listen to this: 'Edgar Wentzwiller, Calvinist leader and eminent humanitarian, continuing the hunger strike he began after the disaster at São Tomé, has stated that he will abstain from all nourishment until such time as Western Europe has taken in all of the Ganges refugees, to provide them with food, with care, and salvation . . .' This is his third starvation campaign, monsieur. Remember Gandhi and his endless hunger strikes? Still, he lived to a ripe old age, and it took an assassin to get him, after all! . . . Here's another good one: 'Ten thousand souls spent the day Good Friday in fasting and prayer, with Dom Vincent Laréole, at the people's abbey at Boquen. Dom Vincent, returning from a Buddhist congress in Kyoto expressly for the occasion, recalled a quotation from Gandhi . . .' Immortal, monsieur, no doubt about it! . . . ' "How can one bask in the warmth of divine sunlight when so many human beings are starving to death?" At the end of the session, a motion was passed by acclamation requesting the government of France to make a firm commitment to the Ganges refugees, and to welcome them en masse . . .' The wire doesn't tell us, monsieur, if, after their flesh was properly scourged, our pilgrims went back home for supper . . . Well, I'll spare you the rest . . ." (The wires went flying all over the carpet.) "Suffice it to say, everyone's atwitter. Church leaders, labor leaders, groups of every sort. Why, we've even had word from a nursery school in Sarcelles. The brats are staging a marble strike, if you can imagine! 'In sympathy with all those poor little Ganges children, who can't feel very much like playing . . .' And just one more. The last one, monsieur. It's worth its weight in God, so to speak: 'His Eminence the Cardinal, Archbishop of Paris, the President of the Council of Protestant Churches, the Grand Rabbi of Paris, and the Mufti of the great mosque Si Hadj El Kebir, wish to announce that they have formed themselves into a permanent committee . . .' "

"Oh, that bunch!" said the President. "I had to put up with them this morning. The Moslem was the only one who managed to keep still. He seemed very uncomfortable, as if he knew more than the others. But not a word out of him. Not like the Cardinal. He rattled on and on about all the injustices here in Paris. As if I didn't have my hands full in the south! 'Hundreds of thousands of foreigners . . .,' he told me. 'Laborers, workers, waiting to be treated like human beings

... Suddenly feeling their patience running out ...' He even quoted that remark of Sartre's—yes, Sartre from a Prince of the Church, if you can believe it!—that quotation that caused such a stir not long ago, and that gave rise to so many avant-garde theatrics, all subsidized of course. You remember: 'There are two and a half billion people in the world: five hundred million human beings, and two billion natives...' And even through that the Mufti didn't bat an eye. He just sat with the same impenetrable expression. A moment or two later, the Cardinal stuffed a paper in my hand, with a statement their permanent committee had cooked up ...'"

Perret went digging through the wires.

"Yes, I think this is it, monsieur. It came out at noon: '...Their only crime is that they belong to a different race. Therefore, it becomes no mere question of basic human charity to accord them our respect, but a question of justice. Whatever violence we do them, great or small, whatever breach of respect we commit, it is all the more appalling, in the light of the painful and difficult position the various hardships of their refugee status have imposed upon them ...'"

"Yes, that's it. That's it. That's the one. I felt like screaming: 'And how about us, Your Eminence? How about our painful and difficult position!'" (The President seldom, if ever, raised his voice, but now he was clearly enraged.) "It was all so absurd! I kept watching the Mufti's inscrutable gaze. And I said to myself, 'If that hypocrite could sign a thing like that, such a solemn admission that the races are unequal, he certainly must have had other things in mind.' I suppose he feels they're unequal all right, but with different ones on top at different times. Just a question of rotation ... Well, finally I couldn't keep quiet anymore, and I said to the Cardinal, 'Who's the patron saint of Paris?' He mumbled something. I'm not too sure what. 'Saint Genevieve,' I told him, in case there was any doubt. And I said, 'When the Huns attacked Paris, she showed up at the gates, in style. And your precursor, the archbishop, was with her, delighted to get such unexpected help, and such holy help at that!' Do you know what he told me? That there never really was a Saint Genevieve. That all that was only a fairy tale, a myth, and that Rome had scratched her name off long ago. 'Officially nonexistent,' it seems. I'd forgotten all about it. It's true that, at the time, no one in Paris raised much of a fuss, except for one of the City Fathers. A pleasant, wide-eyed dreamer type whose name hasn't even come down ... Well, anyway, at that point I showed the four holy gentlemen the door. I was absolutely beside myself. There's only one consolation, I'm afraid.

The fact that this permanent committee of theirs meets at the arch-bishop's palace. Since the Cardinal sold all the furniture for some worthy cause or other, he's been living in a hovel that even our friend the Red Bishop of Bahía would turn up his nose at. It's got to be the most uncomfortable place in Paris. I just hope those wooden stools they sit on, day after day, give them all a good pain you know where. Some consolation! But we have to grasp at straws . . . Well, anything else, Monsieur Perret?"

"Everything and nothing, monsieur. It's all over, and yet it goes on. For six weeks now all those who thought that they knew how to think have been taking a stand. Always the same one. Governments, too. Madly trying to work out some scheme or other. And all for what? For nothing! We live in an age when language corrupts. Words absolved us from actions, and we sat back and waited for what was bound to happen, what we knew was beyond the power of our words. Now we're faced with the only actions that matter, the ones that point out a very basic fact: Christian or not, they're all calling it quits. They're all giving up. And unless you and I can make do with words too, I'm afraid we're all alone, monsieur, just the two of us."

"Well, not quite alone. We still have that old madman Machefer. And Pierre Senconac, who's at Radio-East, now, according to what the owner tells me. Even Jean Orelle has come over, though there's not much left of his sanity, poor man. Of course, on the other side there's Clément Dio, that activist of the intellect. And all those bar-room idealists, those campus and cloister visionaries, heading down south, finally practicing what they've preached for so long . . . I almost envy them for it, too. . . . And don't forget the army. The professionals, I mean. The finest, crack units. Since morning, on my orders, they've begun to dig in . . ."

"Ah yes, the army! All those thousands of men, and officers, and generals! Words, monsieur, that's all! Words dressed in uniforms, hiding their weakness behind that veneer of soldierly steel, and ready to run at the first sign of action. For ages it's been nothing but a make-believe army. No one really knows what it can or can't do. Because no one dares use it, for fear of showing up what a worthless farce it is. You'll see, monsieur, the army will let you down too."

"You weren't talking this way last Sunday, Monsieur Perret."

"No, monsieur. But all this week I've had secret meetings with the handful of generals who still know how to think, and I've had my eyes opened on a big, gaping void. The West thinks it has great, powerful armies. Well, it hasn't. It has no armies at all anymore. For years now, our people have been taught to despise their armies. Every possible way. Take the films, for example. All those films seen by millions and millions, based on massacres long since forgotten, and dug up after a hundred years for the sake of the cause. Blacks, Indians, Arabs, biting the dust, scene after scene. Wars of survival, but changed for the occasion into merciless attempts to impose the white man's rule. Even though, in the long run, the West lost them all. There weren't enough flesh and blood soldiers left to hate, so they fell back on phantoms from the past. All you could want, no limit to how many. And what's more, too dead to protest. Served up for public indictment with no risk at all . . . Forget the serious works of art—the fiction, the plays, the music—things aimed at a small intellectual elite. Let's just talk about the media, so called, and the shameless way certain people, under the guise of freedom, took a tool meant for mass communication, twisted and warped it, and used it to bully the minds of the public. The few clear thinkers left tried to warn us. But we wouldn't listen. We gave way to one huge masochistic frenzy, dragged from nightmare to nightmare. We never said no. We wanted to show how permissive we could be, despite the foolish risk that, one day, we would have to face everything, all at once, and all alone. You remember, monsieur! You remember those clever campaigns worked out with such devilish skill to demoralize the nation and break down its spirit. No more colonial wars. Vietnam and all that. But that was just the beginning. We've come a long way, and there's no turning back. The people despise their army. They've heard it accused of genocide too often. And as for the police . . . Well, ever since Punch first felt the policeman's club, their fate has been sealed. You wonder how they managed to last this long without making themselves sick. Now, finally, they have. And the army right behind them. Enlistees or not, career men or not, they can't stomach themselves. So don't count on the army, monsieur. Not if you've got more genocide in mind."

"Who then?"

"No one, monsieur. We've had it."

"Then it just means another kind of genocide, that's all. Our own. It's the end."

"Yes, I'm afraid you're right, monsieur. But you'll never be able to get the word out, because no one's in any condition to listen. We're going to die slowly, eaten away from the inside by millions of microbes injected into our body. Little by little. Easily, quietly. No pain, no blood. Which is what makes the difference between our death and theirs . . . But it seems that our mental midgets in the West see it all in terms of the rights of man. Just try to explain to the people, or the army—or to world opinion and the universal conscience—that on Easter Sunday, or maybe the day after, they're going to have to butcher a million black-skinned refugees, or else they'll all die themselves, only later, much later . . ."

"Maybe so, Monsieur Perret, but that's just what I'm going to say. And it's up to you to go down south and help me. Now tell me, when are you leaving?"

"Tonight, monsieur. I managed to lay my hands on a jet—a fighter —whose pilot wasn't on retreat, or at prayer, or doing some other mental or moral gymnastics, painfully trying to square his career in the military with the existence of the Ganges fleet. My pilot isn't too squeamish yet. He's agreed to fly me down south, straight to the headquarters of the regional prefect. The poor man just called a little while ago. He was out of his mind. He's practically all alone down there. Most of his staff ran out on him this afternoon. I'm taking Commander de Poudis along, to act as my aide. He seems to have thought things over. I think he looks on his son's death now as something of a score to settle. If we had a few more men like him, stirred up by good, constructive grief, who knows?, maybe we could still be saved. Unfortunately, grief doesn't stir up much these days. Just labor demands and things like that . . ."

"I've been thinking a lot too, Monsieur Perret," the President broke in. "In the long run, whatever I do, I certainly can't let that starving mob come and land on our shores. We could put them in camps, we could try to assimilate them. But the result would be the same: they would be here to stay. And once we had opened the door and shown how weak we are, others would come. Then more, and more. In fact, it's already beginning . . ."

"They'll come, monsieur, no matter what you do."

"Yes, I know. But I'll tell you something. Something that's going to sound very old hat, so trite that no politician today would dare say it, not even the most inept. But for a change, it's the absolute truth: my conscience is clear. Good-bye, Monsieur Perret. I don't know if we're going to be meeting again, you and I . . ."

Thirty-four

At midnight, as Saturday passed into Sunday, the first minute of Easter, the day of the Resurrection, a great noise was heard along the coast, somewhere between Nice and Saint-Tropez. The prows of ninety-nine ships plunged headlong onto the beaches and between the rocks, as the monster child, waking from his cataleptic sleep, let out a triumphant cry. Throughout the whole day that followed, and part of the night, nothing stirred on board those ships. Nothing, that is, but the forest of black, waving, snakelike arms, upraised by the thousands; the corpses thrown into the sea and washed in by the waves; and the myriad mouths, intoning, in almost a whisper, an endless singsong chant blown ashore on the wind . . .

At about ten-thirty that night, the national chain broadcast its nth special bulletin of the day. Each time, as the announcer read through the news, his voice would grow more and more concerned, as if he were reading reports of his own declining state of health and impending demise:

"The President of the Republic has been meeting all day at the Élysée Palace with government leaders. Also present, in view of the gravity of the situation, are the chiefs of staff of the three branches of the armed forces, as well as the heads of the local and state police, the prefects of the departments of Var and Alpes-Maritimes, and, in a strictly advisory capacity, the papal nuncio, and most of the Western ambassadors currently stationed in the capital. At present the meeting is still in progress. A government spokesman, however, has just announced that this evening, at about midnight, the President of the Republic will go on the air with an address of utmost importance to the nation . . ."

It was just at that moment, in fact, that the President was bringing the meeting to a close with remarks such as these, more or less:

"For almost ten hours now I've listened to what you've all had to say. You two, for instance . . ." (He turned toward the prefects.) "You've filled my head with your mad plans to welcome that mob, with your lists and lists of places to house them. I've sat through your babble about setting up work camps to 'weather the storm.' Tomorrow, if not sooner! And I know that you don't believe a word of what you're saying. No one asked you to come here. You left your posts down south to come running where it's safe. Safe for you, and your families, and above all your precious conscience! Oh no, they'll never point a finger at you! Well, I'll tell you, my friends. You're fired! I'm relieving you of your duties, as they say. Not that it matters. I'm just getting a head start. By tomorrow, when all hell breaks loose, there won't be many governmental duties left, if any. . . . And you! Our heroes!. . . " (He turned to the chiefs of staff.) "You have the gall to show me your maps and play me your make-believe war, with your phantom divisions and your paper brigades! Do you take me for a Hitler, raving mad in his Berlin bunker? Don't you know that of the two hundred thousand men sent south in the last two days and a half, only twenty thousand ever joined their units? And not exactly glad to be there, either! The rest? Disappeared. Carried off in the land-slide. The nameless, faceless mass. An army that came from the people, you told us? Well, now it's gone back to the people! In Mâcon, they're dancing in the barracks. In Montélimar, some regiment or other deserted to a man, with all their guns and gear, and went into the factory slums to set up a workingman's commune, racially mixed, for the first time ever. In Romans, a people's committee, Soviet style, took over the sub-prefect's office. It's made up of students, and work-ers, of course, and—yes—soldiers too. And all without firing a shot. Not a shot! But for most of them, it's just plain back home, back where they came from, scot-free at last. Every man for himself. No fuss. no fanfare. So stop telling me these tales about your 'mobilized units' and your 'columns on the march.' Anyone would think you still be-lieved in your own importance, even now, as the country goes under. Or maybe you think it will help your careers! Well, you're all fired too. Relieved of your duties. I've taken Monsieur Jean Perret's ad-vice, and put Colonel Dragasès in complete control of all our security forces throughout the south, and I've named him chief of staff of what's left of the army. You're free to go join him and swell his ranks, if you think you can take it. But you'd better bring some submachine guns with you, because fighting men are what we need down there, nothing else! . . . As for you, my trusted cabinet . . ." (He turned to the ministers.) ". . . I've had to put up with you too. Sitting here, listening to you take me to task. But I understand why. I can hear your own fears and ambitions through the flood of your meaningless drivel. Some of you, I know, have already packed your bags, already squared your consciences with your Swiss bank accounts. All very shortsighted, I'm afraid. But still, there you are, ready to sell out, to

come to terms, feathering your nests with this contact and that. I
know there's a provisional government of sorts already in the making. Because you feel—and you're right—that once the inevitable
happens, some kind of order will have to be imposed, and that's
where you, the experts, will save the day. You'll be welcomed with
open arms, to assure a smooth transition. Then you'll do your
damnedest to stay in power. Who cares what kind of power it is, as
long as you wield it! Well, maybe you'll succeed. Who knows? Others
have done it before, saving what they could from a fire that they'd
helped to start themselves. And sometimes it's worked out for the
best. But that's where we differ. I can't resign myself to your view
of France, safe and sound, but deformed. You see, unlike you, I have
no more ambitions. Thanks to Colonel Dragasès, and Monsieur Jean
Perret, and the remnants of our army, I'm still in official control for
the moment. All the action will take place with them, down south.
Messieurs, I accept your resignations too, at least until tomorrow.
. . . And as for you, my friends . . ." (He was speaking now to the
Western ambassadors.) ". . . there's little I can do but take note of
your heartfelt sympathy, useless though it is. Your government leaders will have plenty to chew on tonight, if the rather disturbing news
from your capitals is any indication. I know that they all have their
eyes glued on France, hoping that a massacre by the country that
gave us the Rights of Man, after all, will excuse whatever horrors they
may have to commit themselves. Well, you're just like the rest of us.
You'll have to wait for tomorrow to see how the question is answered.
The one real question in the world today: whether those rights of
man that we hold so dear—of certain men, that is—can be preserved
at the expense of others. I'll let you think that one over. . . . And as
for you, my holy friend . . ." (He turned to the papal nuncio.)
". . . just a word or two. I can see now that Stalin was wrong, years
ago, when he smirked and asked how many divisions the Pope could
muster. Your boss has no end of divisions. Though, of course, it's true
that he's hired a lot of extras . . ."

At eleven that night, after the playing of Mozart's Second Symphony, the same announcer came back on the air:

"All still seems quiet on board the ships of the refugee fleet. A
communiqué from army headquarters confirms that two divisions
have been deployed along the coast, and that three divisions of reinforcements are heading south at this moment, despite considerable
difficulty of movement. Five minutes ago, army chief of staff Colonel
Dragasès reported that troops under his command have begun set-

ting fire to some twenty immense wooden piles along the shore, in order to burn the thousands of dead bodies thrown overboard from all the ships. . . . Finally, government sources note with some dismay the mass exodus of population currently under way throughout the south. While they view this movement with concern, they do not feel justified in advising against it, given the unprecedented nature of the situation. Army and police have been put on maximum alert to help maintain order, and to see to it that the migration does not interfere with the flow of essential military matériel en route from the north. A state of emergency has been declared in the four departments bordering the coast, under the command of the undersecretary, Monsieur Jean Perret, personal representative of the President of the Republic. The army will make every effort to protect all property left behind, insofar as its other duties permit. Government sources confirm that the President of the Republic will address the nation at midnight, tonight, with a message of grave concern . . ."

And that was all. It will be remembered that old Monsieur Calguès, sitting alone by the terrace of his house—perched like an outpost, guarding his old village, high above the sea—had asked himself if windbags, perhaps, always died without a word, since, in a world long exposed to verbal frenzy, such terseness was most impressive. Then he had opened a book, lit up his pipe, and poured himself another healthy glass of wine, as he waited for midnight . . .

Thirty-five

Three other Western governments, not to mention the United States and the Soviet Union, conferred that night too. In London, Pretoria, and Canberra, to be precise. Despite their respective reactions— dismay in London, determination in Pretoria, and a sense of tragic isolation in Canberra—they had all arrived at the same conclusion, after hours of feverish consultation. To wit, that, since the Ganges armada had first set sail, the West had assumed the precarious posture of a house of cards, in the midst of a great Third World upheaval, and that, if the card marked "France," at the base of the uneasy structure, should suddenly give, all the rest would go toppling, one after the other. At half-past eleven, on the night of that same Easter Sunday, the President of the French Republic received three pitiful wires, one from each of the capitals in question, imploring him to take a firm stand, even if it meant the spilling of innocent blood. (For the record, we should note that, today, all three of those wires form the central exhibit at the Antiracism Museum in the UN's new Hanoi headquarters, as the dying examples of a racial hatred that wouldn't go unpunished. Schoolchildren the world over know the texts by heart, and have to be able to recite and discuss them on demand, whatever their age or class, for fear that we may let down our guard, and allow a rebirth of those loathsome sentiments so much at odds with man's true nature . . .)

In London, during those last three days, the situation had become what official jargon would describe as "confused and uncertain." Nothing disastrous. No riots, no brawls. Not the slightest incident of a racial nature. No threats whatsoever of real or verbal violence. Nothing but a silent and orderly march on London, by tens of thousands of Third World workers from every corner of England, at the urging of the Non-European Commonwealth Committee. A good example of the curious lethargy that seemed to engulf the country was the incident at the Manchester station—if "incident" is even the proper term for an event whose actors and spectators alike never once lost their calm or composure. At least on the surface. No anger on anyone's face, no insult on anyone's lips, no hostile reactions on either side. What happened was this. On Easter Sunday evening, some thirty thousand Pakistanis, Bengalis, and Indians, reinforced by Jamaicans, Guyanans, Nigerians, and such, swarmed into the Manchester railroad station, on their way to take part in the demonstration planned for the following morning in London. The tide of black flesh flooded over the lobby and onto the sidewalks, as endless lines stood waiting at the windows. Because, strangely enough, no one had the slightest intention of traveling without a ticket. This detail, and several others of the sort—not due to mere chance—sealed England's fate. After all, in the land of the habeas corpus and the unarmed bobby, who could possibly object to even a mass migration, when everyone paid his way, nice as you please! One after another, without a word, the whites in the station began to leave, assuming no doubt that space on the trains was a hopeless cause. But the ones who doggedly stuck it out in line—white ducklings among the black brood—were treated with the utmost respect. No one elbowed them aside, no one dreamed for a moment of using the force of numbers to push them away from the windows. Still, in no time, most of the whites seemed to find themselves feeling hemmed in, although they were quick to admit that their dark-skinned neighbors, pressing in on all sides, were polite to a fault. Some may have been put off by the rather pungent and unfamiliar smell. More likely, they merely decided—as they saw themselves suddenly becoming a minority—to step graciously out of the way and avoid complications. Simple lack of experience . . . The same strategic retreat took place once the trains had been boarded. With twelve to a compartment, two whites crammed in with ten blacks would quickly decide not to travel that day. They would hurry off, many of them, out the wrong side, usually with some excuse or other, for fear of offending, or of seeming to be racists uncomfortable with blacks. In one compartment, a British gentleman who had shown up well in advance, sat calmly in place as the seven other seats disappeared in a pile of fourteen black bodies, all terribly careful not to disturb him, sitting there reading his *Times.* Two minutes before the train was to leave, the gentleman stood up, mumbled something inaudible, and disappeared onto the platform. But no one had forced him out. He had left of his own accord. . . . In Liverpool, Birmingham, Cardiff, Sheffield, the stations and trains were every bit as crowded. So much so, in fact, that by midnight on Easter Sunday, as the world awaited the message of the President of the French Republic, two million foreigners were already camped out on the streets of London, as quiet—for all their mass—as a party of Bantu huntsmen stalking through the bush. At the height of the influx the British government had attempted a few discreet maneuvers: power failures along the electrified lines, last-minute layoffs of various conductors . . . But no use. The "Paks" formed better than half of the crews, and once the unions had gotten the word, many of them chose that particular day to work. No one ever quite figured out why. . . .

Africa, meanwhile, had turned herself loose over underbrush trail and forest pathway, rallying round one single cry: "On to the Limpopo!" Beyond the Limpopo River spread the detested Republic of South Africa, dagger in Africa's back, gaping wound in her proud heart, white rash on her tender black skin. An old score to settle, and one that the politicos, and gunrunners, and gangs of capitalist hoodlums had always been able to keep from erupting. Now cry no more, my beloved country! Your brothers and sisters are here, and their children with them, rising up from the depths of the African past, ancient and noble, to bring you your freedom in their bare, unarmed hands! . . . There were thought to be more than four million strong, massed by tribes and by peoples, along the Limpopo's northern bank, in Rhodesia, that next-to-last tomb of the white race in Africa. Certain contingents, from the furthermost points, were there in little but token strength. And yet they were all represented: Algerians, Libyans, Ethiopians, Sudanese, Congolese, Tanzanians, Namibians, Ghanaians, Somalis . . . All waiting for Easter evening to wipe away a world dead and done with, and let the dawning sun, at last, shine over an Africa cleansed of her shame. Along the Limpopo, the beating of tom-toms. And over the river, over the white man's vineyards, and fields, and mines, and skyscrapers, other tom-toms throbbing their reply, tom-toms held captive in prison cities, where nobody slept that night, all squatting on their haunches at the ghettos' rigid edge, facing the white man's army, gazing back now, for the first time, with eyes cast down in apprehension . . .

The Australian army had no one to face. Just the vast, barren sea, protecting their island continent on every side. But they all knew the threat: a peaceful fleet all ready in Jakarta, waiting for dawn to weigh anchor, and sail for the white man's paradise . . .

Marcel and Josiane weren't the only ones that night to read the truth in big, covetous eyes, agleam with hope, biding their time on the landing, outside the door that will open at last on a flat much too large just for two, as all the while, to the blare of justice, Jericho's worm-eaten walls will come tumbling . . .

Thirty-six

Clément Dio looked at his watch for the hundredth time. Ten minutes to midnight. It was five hours now since the last drunken songs had died down, petering out to the frequent thump of a body laid low by liquor and fatigue. But one of the thugs must have held out much longer, because at ten o'clock, or thereabouts, Iris Nan-Chan had uttered another feeble groan. At first, when it all began, she had let out a few quick screams, moments after her husband had been locked in that fourth-floor toilet where he lay now for more than a day and a half, in a state of exhaustion bordering on stupor. Then she had cried out again and again, but her cries couldn't cover the raucous guffaws of the men ganging round her, downstairs in the bar. Then she had begged, and snatches of her pleas had reached Dio's ears whenever the chorus of vile, drunken voices would stop for a moment. As time went by, she had started to laugh—no doubt they had forced her to drink—and the strange, unearthly sound of her laughter had stabbed Dio square in the heart, transfixed him, all but lifeless, on the cold toilet floor, eyes dry, no tears left. During the last few hours of the nightmare, her laughter had died away, gasp by gasp, and had turned to that low, plaintive groan that Dio could hear so clearly once the din had subsided. Like a hurricane, blown out, at last, from its savage excesses. And no other sound had troubled that deathly silence. Except for a column of trucks, rumbling by toward eleven, speeding down to the sea. (Most likely those marine commandos from the La Faye Pass, heading south to take up their positions . . .) Ten minutes to midnight. Dio heard footsteps on the stairs, then in the corridor leading to his prison . . .

And yet, things had all started out so well, despite the sarcastic warnings of that commando captain. To be sure, in Saint-Vallier their car had been stopped in front of the hotel. But only because it was red and shiny, covered with chrome, all studded with lights and bristling with antennas, and upholstered in leather. An elegant object, something the poor unfortunate prisoners could feast their hands on, too long deprived of all contact with refinement. Dio had introduced himself. Many knew who he was. His radical penal reform campaigns, waged with so much success, had made him a rather

well-known figure in most prison circles. They had even recalled his
famous editorial, the one that had shaken penology to the roots:
"From my point of view, our civil offenders are really no more than
political prisoners, innocent victims of a social system that first de-
stroys them, then refuses to save them, turning its back as they
languish in disgrace. No one of us can be sure that he won't land in
prison. Today more than ever, as the police web tightens its hold on
our lives. We're told that the prisons are all overcrowded. But isn't
the worst prison really our life outside?" After cheers and hurrahs,
they had offered him a drink, a toast to their freedom. He and his wife
had played right along. It was all quite amusing. Of course, a few of
the men had already drunk too much, especially some of the Arabs
and blacks, and the bar was a mass of puddles and stains, strewn with
broken glass and bottles. But the mood was good-natured, like a
Bastille Day of sorts, only this time a Bastille had really been taken.
"Tell me," Dio had asked, glass of rum in hand, "how did you manage
to take the place over?" It was easy to explain. The Ganges fleet was
the why and the how behind the operation. It was all they had talked
about while they were in prison. They had read every line. They had
stuck their pin in the map every night. And sometimes the chaplain
would join them, and lead the discussion, which was part of his job.
For him the fleet was something of a symbol, "a kind of mass messiah
with a million heads," he called it. A symbol the prisoners could
readily accept, set apart as they were, and easily moved. In time, the
atmosphere seemed almost devout. So strange, in fact, that the poor,
confused guards, superstitious at best, hardly stirred from their lairs,
skulking out like frightened shadows to tend to the barest essentials.
It was then that it happened. And all terribly simply. At the end of
the Good Friday vigil, while the guards were still sleeping in their
quarters, letting their worthy charges do likewise, none other than
the chaplain had flung open the gates, with the comment that Christ
may have died for all men, but for thieves first and foremost. . . . "He
always said he would do it some day, but it still sure was a surprise!
God knows where he is right now! I'll tell you one thing though. If
that crowd ever lands, there won't be one prisoner behind bars,
believe me . . ." Then they had chatted. About this and that. About
society, for instance, and how "fucked up it all is." About "filthy rich
bourgeois pigs," and workers brutalized by their machines. And the
more the men drank, the louder they got. But why not? They had
been reborn, and a little excitement seemed perfectly in order.
"Take me, for instance," one fellow explained. "I had to make a

choice. Either bust my balls on some job for forty more years, or take a chance on three minutes in the big time, and maybe hit the jackpot. Well, I gave it a try and I lost, so I got put away. Damn right society's all fucked up!" And the same one, an hour later, drunk and ugly: "Come on, guys, what do you say! This is no goddamn fun. Too damn much talk. Let's have a ball. You know what I mean, guys? Let's have a ball! Like, first we're going to dance!" He leered at Iris Nan-Chan. "Right, baby?" It was hardly the moment to beat a retreat. She was caught in the middle, with pairs of groping hands all fighting for her favors. They tugged her between them. Her dress was ripped to shreds. Dio struggled to reach her, tried to elbow through the pack. "Listen, you!" one of them shouted. "Talk about filthy bourgeois pigs! Did you guys see the car this bastard was driving? You think he gave a damn about us? Bullshit, he did! He was selling his goddamn paper, that's all. Just using us to fill his pockets. Now it's our turn, right? Come on, baby, one at a time!" A few of the men tried to stem the tide. But the rest of them beat the "revisionists" back. Maybe because there weren't very many. At which point Dio was kicked up four flights, and dragged into the toilet . . .

The footsteps stopped in front of the door. Dio heard the key turning. The man standing there still seemed drunk, but at least he was awake. "You can come out of there," he mumbled, none too sure of himself. "The party's over." Then he thought for a moment, and added: "I guess maybe I should say we're sorry. We shouldn't have locked you up like that. Not guys like us, I mean, who know what it's like. But you've got to understand. When the shoe's on the other foot, like they say . . . Anyway, your wife's downstairs. I guess maybe we were kind of rough at the beginning. But she's still in one piece, don't worry. She's sleeping. We gave her a good stiff drink. After that things calmed down . . . Well I mean, I never touched her myself . . ." And he left.

The hotel reeked of wine and tobacco, and stank of stale vomit. Most of the windows were smashed, no doubt by the bottles thrown through them. In the rooms, doors flung wide, men were flopped on the beds, on top of the covers, snoring, dead to the world. Dio picked his way over the landing, over bodies lying asleep where they had fallen. A radio still blared out a concerto. The last drunkard to fall hadn't thought to turn it off before biting the dust. Dio found Iris Nan-Chan at the bar, just where he had left her. She was sleeping, naked, stretched out on a bench. Someone had thrown up all over her chest. Someone else must have covered her, waist down, with a cloth from a dining-room table. She was sleeping very soundly. As if she had swallowed a whole bottle of pills. Which, in fact, was just what she had done. The vial of barbiturates lay empty at her feet. ... All of a sudden, the concerto stopped short. In the studios no one cared much anymore about smooth transitions. Then a voice:

"We bring you now an address by the President of the Republic . . ."

Midnight. And that was how, on Easter evening, Clément Dio found himself listening to the message that the whole world was waiting to hear.

Thirty-seven

Midnight. The President is about to speak. If only we could stop the flow of life for a moment, break down the moving film into stills, encompass the world in one vast panorama and catch all the actors at the moment of truth. Impossible task. The whole world is listening. Every relay station, every satellite, beamed onto the French transmission. The most we can do is shine a few spotlights here and there —through clouds, and rooftops, and cover of night—and ferret out this one and that, co-actors in our saga. Our curious epic. (We tried to come up with a more exact word. Something to describe an epic in reverse, or upside down, or loser-take-all. Like an anti-epic. Yes, perhaps that's the word . . .)

Albert Durfort, for example. He has stopped his car somewhere near Gex and pulled over to the side, too choked up with emotion to listen and drive, especially over the ice-glazed roads that wind through the La Faucille Pass. (He chose that dangerous route on purpose. Better to stick to untraveled paths when you're heading for gold . . .) And when his young Martinican lovely, beginning to wilt, languidly asks for the umpteenth time if "we're almost in Switzerland"—because she's simply dying to take a shower, and slip into bed with her precious Albert—Durfort barks back, "Shut up, goddammit!" This roadside stop will prove their undoing. Durfort is going to be attacked and robbed by one of those roving bands that own the darkness and give no quarter. His body, stabbed over and over, will be tossed in the ditch. And the pretty, black, sleek-haired miss will submit to the sexual fancies of savages rid of society's rules.

Like the reader, most likely, the chronicler of this drama has been struck by the simple Manichaean-style justice displayed by fate in meting out death. Well, maybe not all that simple, really. If we think the matter through, we see that this ethic, in fact, is a two-way street. The Good are at war with the Bad, true enough. But one man's "Bad" is another man's "Good," and vice versa. It's a question of sides. With this idea in mind, let's shine our spotlight on another pair of characters: Élise, the wife of our friend Cadi One-Eye, Frenchwoman-turned-Arab, and Pierre Senconac. Senconac, at the moment, sits musing in the studios of Radio-East, mulling over the impromptu comments he'll be making on the President's speech. He knows, of course, that he's going to preach violence. But exactly what grounds will the President give him? What precise rationale? And so he sits, waiting, like a knight before the fray. Useless waste of time, in fact, if we move the clock forward by a mere twenty minutes. Because that's when Élise, listening in the kitchen to Senconac's curt, biting voice, will *know* that, finally, the days of contempt are over, and that redemption by blood is at hand to purge its last traces. And she'll speed off in her car to the studios, all but deserted, with her husband's razor hidden inside her right stocking, flat against the thigh. Senconac will gasp his last, throat slit in mid-sentence, as the last few technicians take to their heels. Manichaean ethic. Just a question of sides . . . And yet, in the over-all conflict, such jungle vendettas affected no more than a handful. Again we would have to conclude that, apart from a modest elite, Manichaean however we view it, the white race was little more now than a few million sheep. That has to be one explanation . . .

On the shore, facing the armada, Colonel Dragasès has stopped stuffing black corpses into the bellies of the great wooden pyres. The time has come to confront the living. He's sitting in the garden of an abandoned seaside villa, on the low, columned railing just over the water, looking out at the ships, run aground in the darkness. Silhouette figures in a vast shadow show. "We bring you now an address by the President of the Republic . . ." Since nightfall, hour by hour, the colonel has been counting and re-counting his troops over this incredible front, some twenty kilometers long. From time to time, the radio crew, set up in the villa, fails to contact this unit or that. Yet another one lost. A day spent facing those million poor wretches. Then dusk, and the unit would still cling to life. But come night, by the light of the stars, it was dead. Phantom soldiers, already condemned for a crime not committed, running out on the scene of their would-be atrocities. Making off through grove and garden, fast as they could, for fear that daybreak might catch them still there . . . A little before midnight, Undersecretary Perret takes leave of the prefect—or the remnants thereof—and goes to join the colonel. Commander de Poudis is already there. They have only some ten thousand men left in all. Behind their lines stalk Panama Ranger and his motley band, their numbers swollen along the way. Here and there, on the fringes of the now deserted landscape—vague, shadowy battleground—dark, muted encounters have begun to take place. Low-whispered verbal duels, calls that rarely miss their mark.

Muffled calls to defect. And inside the ransacked houses, Panama Ranger himself greets each new defector with open arms, to the sounds of music and shouts of youthful joy. Sirens singing with a hi-fi voice, breath heavy with the best bourgeois Scotch. Things the colonel has no defense for. Still, Panama Ranger laments his five dead, shot down without warning when they opened their mouths. (Some units, it seems, have no taste for discussion. Especially certain marine commandos, just recently arrived, who plowed their way through his peace-loving legion. Their captain believes that rebirth and renewal can't take place if there isn't a good civil war, and that even if it's destined to fail from the start, that's all the more reason to give it a go. In a civil war, at least, you know whom you're killing, and probably why. Something the captain finds very rewarding . . .)

The tidal wave fleeing the south has paused briefly to catch its collective breath in the soft underbelly of the nation. From Valence to Mâcon, the hotels are packed. And so are the schoolhouses, barns, gymnasiums, cinemas, restaurants, town halls and people's culture centers. The prefects, caught in the flood, have appealed to their citizens for a show of cooperation. It's one thing to mouth high-sounding phrases about welcoming the Ganges refugees to our shores. Quite another to find yourself faced, in the flesh, with the hordes running off to escape them. No one counted on that! The local populations increase by leaps and bounds. And with them, their prices. Food suddenly costs ten times what it's worth. A bath goes for two hundred francs. A nursing bottle, for a hundred. Gasoline is as hard to come by as the local Beaujolais, itself so scarce that the desperate entreaties of the bistro imbiber—a familiar new sound—make the groveling pleas of the addict for his drug seem a dull, tasteless prank. Wherever they've been hiding, the black-market vermin, long dormant on their dungheaps, are abuzz and astir, puffing and swelling like a ravenous frog. Exploitation unabashed, man done in by his brother. And the real thing, finally: white skinning white. Now, at last, it's clear, in this fair Western land, that all we kept hearing about exploitation, all the whoop and the holler in every key, was nothing but so many meaningless words. Now we see it for what it is. And the victim pays. Without a peep. Soon the government moves in, decides it will have to ration bread. Like the good old days, isn't it! There's none to be had, but under the counter you can get all you want . . . Yes, France has come back to normal. Come to terms with herself. And what's more, with her police. Now that she needs them—and needs them in a hurry—doubled up with

that time-honored gnawing in the gut. Scared witless (or worse)
... Terror on the highways. Shakedowns left and right, kidnappings,
ransoms. This one's daughter, abducted ("Corporal, let me lick your
boots..."). This one's bride, hardly paid for, carried off by some gang
("Sergeant, let me kiss your ass . . ."), whisked off by young toughs,
like the rugged, handsome kind in the movies, and the whole scene
out of a porno-shop film, free for the paying. This one, held up at
gunpoint, robbed of his wallet, with all of his papers ("Captain, let me
slobber on your big, hairy hands . . . I repent! I repent!"). Oh, the
great rush policeward! Blessed minions of the law! ("No one's safe
anymore. Only you can protect us. Only strong, smart policemen,
who want to do their duty. Open up, let us in. How about a cigar.
Here, these are the best . . .") And suddenly the station houses,
headquarters, barracks—all yesterday's "pigpens," remember?—
loom up to the poor fleeced lamb like remote medieval monasteries,
secure and inviolate. The anti-epic, in all its glory! Time was, the
people used to huddle in their churches, while the nasty old seigneur
sent his surging tide of knighthood breaking over the lofty château
walls. Today it's the knights who are manning the ramparts, defending the refuge, while outside, the men of the cloth, with their latter-
day saints, bay like wolves on the prowl. But the knights aren't the
same. The spring inside has snapped. Even in difficult times like
these, you can't take a bunch of broken puppets and turn them back
into policemen just by waving a magic wand. Punch has come out on
top. And the little children clap, loud and hard as they can. But if
someone comes up and steals their lollipops after the show, it will
serve the brats right! You can't clap then complain. You can't sneer
then come begging. The knights take a certain snide pleasure in their
revenge. "Well, we can't keep you out," they answer, standing at the
doors of their secular sanctums, clouded in gloom, "but don't count
on us. You should have thought of that before!" Revenge is a tasty
dish, even served cold. The police lick their chops with a kind of gross
delight. A few of them spit at the poor, harried beggars. ("Sergeant,
let me lick your boots . . ." "And let me spit in your goddamn eye!"
Ah! Delightful exchange! . . .) But at midnight, intermission. Cops and
lambs, fleecers and fleeced, everyone is listening . . .

On the other hand, over at RTZ, it's one great big party. The main
studio is jammed. Boris Vilsberg is there, by his microphone, waiting,
people all around him. Maybe a few too many for comfort, judging
by the somewhat anxious look on his face. Rosemonde Réal has come
and gone. Fifteen minutes ago she showed up at the station, stuck

her head in the door, took one look at the squalor . . . ("Excuse me, may I get by?" Three hairy young creatures, lying sprawled over armchairs in the middle of the hall, and not budging an inch, sneering back a reply: "Go ahead. Crawl over." And the sweet things adding: "What's the matter? Afraid you'll catch our crabs?") Now, it's all well and good to spout the leftist line to "the people"—bless their hearts—but she really wasn't ready to face its results herself, and at such close range. "The American Embassy, please!" she tells her chauffeur. The ambassador is a friend of hers. And there, at least, the guards make sure not to let in the rabble. . . . (Strange, how every patrician-turned-prole has that critical threshold, where the old caste-consciousness comes to the fore. Right, Monsieur de La Fayette? . . .) Some hardier souls than Rosemonde Réal did manage to wade through the scruffy, stinking mob. First and foremost, Fra Muttone, still all aquiver from the Pope's brilliant message, having devoured it word by word, and dying to discuss it. Very elegant, as usual, with his slim, stately bearing, his silvery hair, curling slightly at the temples, his black alpaca suit (just right for a fancy première), his shirt with the ruffled front. No trouble for him to squeeze through. Slithering in and out, like an eel. And gently mopping his brow with a handkerchief, trimmed in lace. The heat, in fact, is unbearable. The studio, built for two hundred, must have five hundred packed in, at least. Though with so many camped on the floor, waiting for midnight, it seems more a mass of bodies than faces. As for the buffet, set up in back—a tradition at RTZ for special occasions —it's long since empty. Not a drop left, not a crumb. One great big black, dressed to the hilt, is standing there roughing up the helpless waiter, as if trying to shake loose a few hidden bottles . . . "Well, what do you make of it?" asks Fra Muttone, finally working his way up to Vilsberg. "Not too good, I'm afraid," Boris mutters. "After the President speaks, they'll grab the mike and we won't get a word in edgewise. The boss was thinking of going right off the air, but I begged him to change his mind. We'd never get out of this place in one piece!" And so, in today's mass media empire, the role of a Kerenski doesn't pay much anymore. A statement or two, and pffft!, that's that! . . .

Among the Africans who clean up the slop and swill of Paris, deep in the filthy cellars where the creatures of light have stowed them by the thousands, an unchanging dialogue takes place, for the tenth time at least, intoned, almost chanted, mechanical refrain or plan of action, we can't say for sure:

"If they manage to land in one piece, what then?" asks "the Chief,"
"will you all climb out of your rat holes too?"

"All depends. Will there be enough rats?" chants another.

"By daylight," the ragtag priest replies, "they'll be thick as the
trees in a giant forest, sprung up overnight in the darkness. Zimbawe!"

"Zimbawe!" blindly chant a thousand voices . . .

At the Arab bar, Café Oasis—lights dim, metal shutter pulled down
—Cadi One-Eye holds forth on the telephone, tirelessly repeating his
orders:

"Don't hoard. Don't be selfish. Share whatever you have, even
with the ones who've done you dirt. Treat them all like brothers.
Remember, the time for violence is over. Allah be praised, we're not
going to need it. They're already dead. Unless their President's
speech revives them. Patience, patience. It won't be long now . . ."

The President of the French Republic presides at this moment
over one hundred peoples. One hundred governments, around the
globe, in each of the twenty-four time zones. All glued to their radios.
In Rome, the Pope is kneeling before a cross, a Brazilian crucifix with
a figure of Christ that looks like Saint Che himself, while in Paris, the
Cardinal, apostle to the poor, wriggles and squirms on his hard
wooden stool. . . . Colonel Zackaroff looks at his watch, and tries to
rouse the general, asleep at his desk, head cradled in his arms between two bottles of vodka. . . . "How beautiful and green your eyes
are, darling!" whispers Norman Haller, through an alcoholic haze.
. . . Minister Jean Orelle sits fingering an antique revolver, a hand-
made 1937 Soviet model. He gazes in fascination. God knows how
often it must have jammed, back in that wonderful Spanish war!
. . . Josiane shakes her head and keeps repeating, as she counts her
furniture: "We'll never get our things in the Arabs' place upstairs.
They won't all fit . . ." Fugitive from justice, Luke Notaras roams the
edge of the Esterel range, along the coast, in search of the French
army. . . . But of all the actors lit up by our spotlights, piercing the
darkness of this historic Easter Sunday, the strangest of all, without
doubt, is Monsieur Hamadura, caught in the beam just as he's loading
his car to drive south. Steel glistens in the moonlight, as Monsieur
Hamadura, with the greatest of care, places four rifles into his trunk,
well padded with blankets. Magnificent rifles, with telescopic sights,
relics of his Indian hunting days, shooting elephant and tiger. As for
the long-awaited speech, Monsieur Hamadura couldn't care less.
He's not going to listen. Gleaming whiter than ever in his swarthy

face, his teeth open into a great, broad smile. Clearly Monsieur Hamadura is happy. He's about to leave on his final hunt . . .

Old Monsieur Calguès looked at his empty glass, thought a bit, then slowly and deliberately poured himself another. The Mozart concerto had stopped abruptly. Then a moment of silence. That instant of grace, that brief instant of perfection, like the flash of a shooting star: the soft, cool wind just beginning to bathe the terrace; the delightful landscape glimpsed in the moonlight shadows; the garden heavy with the fragrance of pine; the church tower plainly seen from the terrace, reaching high, as if to seal a timeless pact with Heaven; and, with it all, God, so terribly close, laying a comforting, loving hand on the old man's shoulder . . . The shooting star burned out as a voice announced:

"You will now hear an address by the President of the Republic."

Thirty-eight

"My friends and fellow countrymen . . ."

The voice was calm and self-assured, solemn but forceful. One could sense that these were no offhand remarks, that the President had labored long and hard, searching his soul, that he himself had weighed every word before writing it down. Many of the older people listening thought back to the grim, distant past, to the years between 1939 and 1945, when heads of state, speaking to their people, really had something to say, and the people, something to ponder. The younger ones had never heard anything like it, and many were suddenly struck by their hollow existence, that void they had taken for meaningful life, decked out in the trappings of historical dialectic. To their great regret, but too late to matter! (But maybe it won't have been in vain, if God, the resurrector, the dispenser of eternal life, restores the whites to their proper place when they rise from the dead at the crack of doom . . .)

". . . Five hours from now, as day dawns on this Easter Monday morning, we shall either have lost or preserved our integrity as a nation, so jealously guarded for a thousand years and more. At this juncture in time, a fearful and fearsome honor is ours: that of serving as a test, an example, a symbol. For other Western nations, too, are faced at this moment with a similar threat. And they too, like ourselves, are unwilling to confront it. Five hours from now, a million refugees will peacefully begin to set foot on our soil. Refugees whose race, religion, language, and culture are different from our own. For the most part they will be women and children, jobless and needy peasants, all fleeing from famine, and misery, and despair. Dramatic examples of that ever-growing store of surplus humanity, victims of the soaring birthrate that has long been the curse of our century's waning years. Their fate, indeed, is tragic. But our own, in turn, is no less so. If human nature were not as it is, if it truly could have been changed by the active, new ideas to which we've paid lip service in recent years, then perhaps, in fact, we might have been able to welcome the Third World here, to our shores; to open our arms and hearts to these first of their number, and proceed together to build ourselves a new society better fitted to face tomorrow's teeming world. As it is, we can't help but admit that our national reaction, at the crucial moment, has been one of repugnance: that kind of terror that the past has always seen produced by the confrontation between the races. Except for a few social dissidents and idealists—fanatics or misfits, for the most part—our people have fled from the south in droves. One of our nation's most prosperous regions has turned into a wasteland, simply because those who lived there preferred to leave it all behind, rather than share their lives in an effort at coexistence. The reaction is hardly new. History offers us many examples, though our conscience—perhaps to its credit—has chosen not to remember them all. But therein lies the difference: I have no choice. As your President, elected by the nation, I cannot fail to act. I know, of course, that most of our people consider it inhuman and unthinkable to throw armed might against a weary, starving, and defenseless opponent. Yes, I know how they feel. And yet, my friends, the fact is this: cowardice toward the weak is cowardice at its most subtle, and, indeed, its most deadly. And so, they all hoped that the army, with no such scruples, would come to the rescue. Though clearly they had little faith, I'm afraid, since they all turned and ran. At the first signs of flight, my duty demanded that I order the army to take up positions along the coast. The result is that now, should we only choose to do so, we are perfectly able to repulse the invasion and destroy the invader. Assuming, that is, that we are willing to murder —with or without regret—a million helpless wretches. Past wars have abounded in just such crimes, but conscience back then hadn't yet learned to waver. Survival was all, and it condoned the carnage. Besides, those were wars of rich against rich. Today it's the poor who are on the attack, with their ultimate weapon. And if we respond with the same kind of crime, not a soul will condone our action. Our integrity as a nation will have been preserved, but we surely will bear the mark of our deed forever. Certain forces abroad in the world today know this only too well: those dark forces bent on destroying our Western society, ready to plunge forward in the wake of the invader, behind the convenient shield that our guilty conscience provides them. My friends and fellow countrymen, I have, therefore, ordered the army to open fire, if need be, to prevent the refugees from effecting a landing. But if I have decided, after sober considera-tion, to deny the armada its one last chance, I do so only to save you yours. And so, I am asking every soldier . . ."

The voice stopped short. For at least thirty seconds the sentence hung suspended on the airwaves, and nothing was heard through that eternity of silence but the President's labored breathing. When he finally continued, it seemed he could hardly speak. His voice was so much weaker and slower, so unsure of itself, so choked with emotion. It was clear that he had put his prepared speech aside. (Some time later, in fact, historians found the typewritten text in the studio archives. Comparing it with his actual remarks, they all agreed that, just at the final moment, his will had apparently cracked, like a cliff long eaten away from beneath, and then suddenly crumbling.) Shocked by what he had written, tormented by the thought of the awesome results his words might engender, the President had changed his mind after thirty seconds of final reflection, and had let his heart and his conscience speak out. And for thirty seconds the world, too, heard only its own anxious breathing. Then each word, heavy with meaning, like handfuls of earth thrown into the grave and onto the coffin, words of farewell:

"... And so, I am asking every soldier and officer, every member of our police—asking them from the depths of my conscience and my soul—to weigh this monstrous mission for themselves, and to feel free either to accept or reject it. To kill is hard. Even harder to know why. Myself, I think I know. But I don't have my finger on the trigger, and my gun isn't aimed point blank at some poor soul's flesh. My friends, whatever happens, may God help us . . . or forgive us."

Thirty-nine

On that Easter Monday morning, the sun rose at 5:27. Between the last word of the President of the Republic (ten after midnight) and the first rosy glimmers of dawn on the water, five hours and seventeen minutes, exactly, hung over the West.

No "Marseillaise" had followed the address, contrary to custom—a custom continued throughout the years, for some bizarre reason, despite the droll anachronism of its stirring lyrics mouthed by the flabby new breed of *"enfants de la patrie."* Instead, in Rouget de Lisle's rightful place, more Mozart. Just like that. All of which prompted Colonel Dragasès to conclude that France, in her panic, was showing a little tact at last, and that maybe, for all her faintness of heart, would loathe herself less. When man finally conquers his false self-image—be it only a dim and time-worn reflection of an all-but-vanished shadow, left lingering faintly in the back of his mind—there's nothing much to do but play him his taps. There were two men, that night, who came to the same conclusion.

First, Monsieur Jean Orelle, in Paris, with a telephone call to the station to air the Mozart Requiem again. It was clear from the President's dramatic finale that his will was no longer his own. Well, if all was lost, why not face the fact squarely? During his long career, the minister had lived through too many disavowals, he had witnessed too many defeats, all touted as triumphs to the gullible public, or as noble self-sacrifice, or national redemption. He had heard them all followed by pompous hymns, whose flood of words succeeded in washing away their shame. May as well die a dignified death when you've lived too long, turned so many pages—intelligently, of course, but without the slightest notion that these were the last in a drawn-out tale—and suddenly stumble across the words "The End," words you thought were way off in the distance, haloed in justice, perfection, and universal love. Words ablaze, in fact, with nothing but hate, and looming up so quickly that they deal you a deathblow straight to the heart. Could humanity have lost its way somewhere inside the maze? Did you shut too many doors? Doors you should have kept open, whatever the cost, instead of digging pitfalls and traps to catch the blind? How many escapes did I help to block off? Myself, Jean

213

Orelle? The whole world read me, listened to what I said, discussed
me devoutly, turned me into a sage, heaped me with honors, bowed
and scraped, drank in my words and lived by my deeds, transformed
my life into a royal road, straight as an apostle's conscience and fair
as a prophet's holy vision, while Truth, with her bruised and bleeding
feet, wandered, lost and rejected, among the thorns and brambles of
a tortuous path. . . . How many gates did I help to fling open? Gates
to delusion! Ah, I should have been more careful. I knew, after all.
I knew that Truth always goes her way alone. If the masses join in,
if they fall in step behind her, it's a sign that she must have sold
herself out. But I let myself be fooled. Monsieur Jean Orelle . . .
Requiem! Yes, let everyone hear it! Maybe some will understand!
. . . The minister carefully examined the revolver. The 1937 Soviet
model. His hand fell once more into long-forgotten gestures: defense
of Madrid (Spain), liberation of Paris (France), capture of Chungking
(China), attack on Salisbury (Rhodesia), ghetto revolt in Atlanta
(U.S.A.) . . . This time the old revolver didn't jam. They found the
minister sitting slumped at his desk, his head in a pool of blood, as
if his mouth had spat it out and were trying to suck it back in. Just
before dying, he had scratched out this curious phrase: "Impure or
pure . . ." Since he always had reveled in obscure pronouncements
—and even more so late in life, when he took almost senile delight
in excessive abstruseness—people groped far afield in their search for
the meaning. His many biographers racked their brains on the posthumous puzzle. One hit it quite close, when he saw in the phrase a
reference to blood, and, more abstractly, to Orelle's pure—or impure
—motives at the moment of death. Strangely enough, to the best
of our knowledge, no one grasped the connection with the "*sang im-
pur*" of our old "Marseillaise," that vile enemy blood to be spilled in
the cause of freedom. (Of course, the national anthem was changed
not long after. And about time, too . . .)

As for Colonel Dragasès, he had little taste for Mozart. It was all
right in principle. But there had to be some more military way of
confronting oblivion. And so, he hounded his staff: "Get me some
bugles and drums, goddammit! If there are any left . . ." A call went
out the length of the front. (As a result of which, by the way, it was
learned that in the five minutes following the President's address,
five more units had slipped off into the night, or joined the ranks of
Panama Ranger.) The marine commandos saved the day. Four strapping specimens in camouflage suits, crosses dangling against their
hairy chests, went crawling on their bellies over beaches and rocks,

yelling "shit" at each verbal offensive from Panama Ranger's pacifist crew—invisible in the darkness, but the front was alive with them, you could feel them in the air, like insects burrowing under the skin, or some gangrenous rot—and, with drum or bugle, as the case might be, slung over their shoulders, they made their way to the headquarters in the villa.

"You know how to play taps?" the colonel snarled.

"Commando specialty, Colonel! That's what we use to go over the top. Works even better than the cavalry charge. Chad! Guiana! Djibouti! Madagascar! Pam-pa-paam, pam-pa-paam . . . Very impressive. Objective? Slaughter! . . . By the way, the captain sends his regards."

"Fine. Give me a round of taps, and try not to flub any notes!"

They stood by the five tanks of the Second Hussars, Chamborant Regiment, lined up in the garden outside the villa, under the pines. Two drummers, two buglers. Not much of a band. But there in the darkness they were loud as an army. Picture the scene. Moments after midnight, taps blaring out by the light of the moon. Pure theater! "Oh, that tugs at the heart!" moaned Undersecretary Perret, half in jest. The colonel was smiling too. A big, broad grin. Jubilation all around. The ones who truly love their traditions don't take them too seriously. They march to get their heads shot off with a joke on their lips. And the reason is that they know they're going to die for something intangible, something sprung from their fancy, half humor, half humbug. Or perhaps it's a little more subtle. Perhaps hidden away in their fancy is that pride of the blueblood, who refuses to look foolish by fighting for an idea, and so he cloaks it with bugle calls that tug at the heart, with empty mottoes and useless gold trim, and allows himself the supreme delight of giving his life for an utter masquerade. That's something the Left has never understood, and that's why its contempt is so heavy with hate. When it spits on the flag, or tries to piss out the eternal flame, when it hoots at the old farts loping by in their berets, or yells "Women's Lib!" outside the church, at an old-fashioned wedding (to cite just some basic examples), it does so in such a grim, serious manner—like such "pompous assholes," as the Left would put it, if only it could judge. The true Right is never so grim. That's why the Left hates its guts, the way a hangman must hate the victim who laughs and jokes on his way to the gallows. The Left is a conflagration. It devours and consumes in deadly dull earnest. (Even its revels, appearances notwithstanding, are as grisly an affair as one of those puppet parades out of Peking or Nuremberg.)

The Right is different. It's a flickering flame, a will-o'-the-wisp in the petrified forest, flitting through the darkness . . .

"That's fine!" said the colonel. "Good job! Now get back to your unit. And tell the captain thanks . . . Oh yes, on the way, you can check out the barbed wire and call in a report."

No sooner had he finished his sentence, than Panama Ranger sent back his reply to the bugles and drums. A studied cacophony, a jumble of everything more or less "in": *The Ballad of Man's Last Chance,* on guitar, voices spitting slogans, or singing songs—like *Khaki, Bye-Bye!,* or *Nini the Hooker,* or *The Case of the Motorized Crabs*—and all to a background of sputtering motors, of hoots and horns, of squeals of delight from girls being felt up and asking for more, even a neoliturgical hymn, some old spiritual changed for the occasion. It varied according to where the sounds came from, each one of the houses sharing in the racket.

"Pretty, huh?" mumbled the colonel. "It reminds me of all those New Year's Eves, when we were stationed in Tarbes. It used to drive my men up a wall. Me too, on boring nights like that. But I tried not to show how much it pissed me off to see the people having their fun. Just press a button, and boom! You see what you get!"

What they were getting just then, in fact, struck the general staff in the villa with its volume. The night wasn't even half over, and already the troop strength had shifted. How many did Panama Ranger have now? Twenty thousand? Twenty-five? And the army . . . ? They took another count, unit by unit: no more than six thousand, at the very outside. Not to mention, of course, group number three, the Third World contingent: almost a million refugees, biding their time, waiting for daylight on their grounded ships, and caught in the rhythmic sweep of a giant searchlight, mounted on the roof of the villa, like the culture the biologist checks in his microscope now and again, to make sure his microbes are still alive and kicking. (We can forget the fifty-five million Frenchmen, stunned by the noxious gases of modern thought, paralyzed where they stood, in grotesque positions, as if some director had frozen the background action on stage, to emphasize only the essentials.) The one common quality all three forces possessed was a consummate scorn. Could that be one explanation? . . .

"We're losing a thousand men every hour!" said Commander de Poudis. "And no one's even fired a shot."

"So what?" replied the colonel. "I see things from a different angle. The way I figure, if the hemorrhage keeps up like this, by five twenty-seven this morning I'll still have four hundred fifty men. More than I expected. With the undersecretary's permission . . ." (He was looking at Jean Perret. Both men seemed to enjoy still playing the roles of soldier and statesman.) ". . . I'm going to get rid of all those fancy toys you had them send me. I mean all those rubber bullets, fire hoses, tear-gas grenades, lead-weighted nets, and all the other fun and games we'd use on a mob of Latin Quarter kids. We'll load up with live ammunition, that's all."

"You do," Perret countered, "and you won't even have your four hundred fifty. You'll have fifty if you're lucky. Unless they decide to call it a day, and shoot you in the back."

"Well then, I'll die like an old-time sergeant, stuck away in our African battalion. That's not a bad death. A bullet in the back, and no one'll know who did it. What the hell's the difference? When you're dead, you're dead. . . . Well, are we ready? They've shot their mouths off long enough! What say we shut them up?"

"Good idea, Colonel!" Commander de Poudis agreed. "My ears can't take it! Let me volunteer . . ."

"But Colonel," Perret interrupted, "the real enemy is in front of you, out on those boats. It's not that gang of loudmouths behind you!"

"Oh, you think so, monsieur?" the colonel objected. "I can see you've never done much fighting. In war, the real enemy is always behind the lines. Never in front of you, never among you. Always at your back. That's something every soldier knows. In every army, since the world began. And plenty of times they've been tempted to turn their backs on the enemy—the so-called enemy, that is—and give it to the real one, once and for all. In the good old days you could even see two armies at each other's throats, in some stupid war or other, and all of a sudden they'd call it quits, and each one would pull a coup and take over at home. I'm sorry I wasn't around to see it! . . . No, my friend, in war the soldier's real enemy is seldom who you think."

"And when there are no more soldiers?"

"Then there's no more war. At least, not worthy of the name. Which is just what's going to happen this morning, by the way. When my last hussar runs out on me, you'll see. The country will be at peace. What kind of peace? I really can't say. I don't want to live through it, that much I know. Let the rest of them wallow in their peace! It's what they've been yelling for all these years, without the slightest idea what it was! If you ask me, they'll get what's coming to them, that's all. . . . Are you still volunteering, Captain?"

"Yes," Commander de Poudis answered. "You want me to shut them up?"

"Nothing would please me more!" replied the colonel. "They're not quite what I had in mind for the future of the nation. Take my tanks and get going! . . . The whole of our armor, in the hands of a sailor! Kind of funny, don't you think?"

Yes, of course! They both thought it was funny. The captain was laughing out loud. The colonel's eyes were alive with delight. They had understood each other. Every military man loves war. The ones who claim they don't are liars. Either that, or they should be chucked the hell out, sacked without pay, because they're really only civilians in disguise, like post office clerks. Both men had felt that the Ganges fleet was hardly the perfect enemy for their final fling at war. Now they had found themselves another, one that truly measured up, proper motive and all. And one that could even fight back. What more could you ask for?

And fight back they did . . . Since every young idiot's dream is to make like the Warsaw rebels—as long as there's no real risk that the grown-ups will mix in with more than a slap—five tanks, groping along in the dark, with no infantry support, are a windfall for ten thousand drunk and drugged heroes, sitting around all night making Molotov cocktails (first swilling the rotgut and wine, to be sure), in a wild hue and cry that made the madcap free-for-alls of the old Paris Commune clubs seem like pretty small potatoes. The girls in particular, vastly gifted in the ways of popular culture, took it into their heads to turn each occupied town into people's living theater. One big, live sex show, left and right, but only for the best of patriotic reasons. (Their brand, that is. Patriotic in reverse.) For making one Molotov cocktail: a blow job. For two: a first-rate lay, no holds barred. For digging one tank trap: a gang-bang for all the diggers . . . Since it had gone on like that for three days, bedding down each night in a different place after each of their highway "encounters," the troops of Panama Ranger had a hefty share of those clapped-up pissers that no revolutionary army worth its salt could possibly exist without. Now, if we think for a moment of the refugee fleet, and picture its even heftier share—complete with its assortment of pus, scab, and chancre—condemned for the last two months to a monumental daisy chain of sodomy and sex, then we have to admit that the union of these two races—not to mention the others—is bound to produce a result well worth watching. At long last, that famous and fundamental doubt ("Would you let your daughter marry a . . . ?") will burst like a bubble. Outside of that, we'll just have to wait and see what happens. After centuries of struggle with bacterial odds, the white race, finally, had cleansed its genes of the old-fashioned pox and its nasty results, zealously passed down over the years, but weaker and weaker with every generation. Now we'll have to start from scratch, that's all. Though, of course, we'll have plenty of time . . .

But let's get back to the front, and our heroes. And let's give credit where credit is due. Panama Ranger was anything but chicken. When four of the five tanks, submerged in a deluge of human flesh, like Gulliver in Lilliput, blew up in the joint attack of hundreds of Molotov cocktails, he stood up alone in the red-glowing darkness, and barked, "Leave the last one for me!" Behind him, his house was a pile of rubble. Buried inside, a few of his braves, caught napping where they lay. Commander de Poudis had launched the offensive, and Panama Ranger was playing the scene like a Western. Lit up by the fire, a bottle in each hand, he stalked forward, step by step, against his foe. The wild steel beast stopped dead in its tracks, as if cowed by his look. It's still far from clear what prompted the captain to open the turret and poke head and shoulders up out of his shell. Most likely to know who it was he was fighting. Or rather, to see. To take a good look. That physical need any real soldier feels, trapped in the push-button army, and faced once again with the timeless truth of man-to-man combat. What he saw there amazed him: a tall, slender young man in the middle of the road, standing calm and determined, feet spread wide. A smile on his face, eyes fixed in a blue, unblinking gaze. Alone—by choice—yet the picture of power. Strength and manly grace combined. "Are you having fun?" Commander de Poudis shouted. "A ball!" came back the reply. And it struck them both that they were laughing together. "I'm going to count to three!" the captain warned. "Me too!" was the answer. Which set the navy man musing on how much life had changed. "Time was," he thought, "man used twenty-year-olds like this conquering angel to build him his empires and amaze the world. Today we only use them to destroy —ourselves included—and for nobody else's amazement but our own." Then he thought of his son, Marc de Poudis, killed off the coast of Mauritania, with no smile on his lips, no chance to do battle. In the light of the thousand years soon ending, hadn't the poor boy chosen the wrong side somehow? . . . "Three!" shouted Panama Ranger, as he flung the two cocktails with deadly precision. One set the captain on fire, like a torch. The other exploded at the rim of the turret, and sent its flames shooting down inside the tank, blowing it sky high in no time at all. Panama Ranger gave a flick of the hand, like a friendly wave good-bye. . . . If we've gone into rather a lot of detail over this unique encounter, it's because in the dismal mass of firsthand documents for historians to ponder, this one alone leaves a different impression. Yes, there's loss of life, to be sure. But still, it stands out like a flourish of trumpets, sharp and clean. Finally! In the welter of actors and spectators caught in the whole tragic drama, now there's someone to be proud of. One man is dead, one man is still living, but that's not the point. The two were worth all the rest put together. Break up the pair, and the twin that's left serves no further purpose. Their clash, at long last, sparked the first heroic glimmer in the whole mucked-up mess. The historian turns the page and reads on. He'll feel little more than a twinge of nostalgia. But only the vaguest, since such timeworn feelings are really beyond his ken. At any rate, this encounter was the last one that night, and indeed the last one on that whole crumbling front . . .

"Well, it looks like I have no more armor," the colonel noted simply, as he heard the fifth explosion.

"I must say, you don't seem awfully concerned!" Jean Perret observed.

"And why should I be? They died a beautiful death. What more do you want? Death like that is a blessing! Why else do you think I sent them out there?"

"But a few hours from now, when the invasion begins, even five tanks could have helped you stop it!"

"Come now! You still think my men are going to shoot at that pack of miserable niggers? I'm not even sure I can do it myself."

"I just don't understand you, Dragasès! Why all the fuss then? Why that mad rush over the road to get here? Why all the trouble to stir up the army—or what little was left? Why even accept the assignment in the first place?"

"You'll understand soon enough, Monsieur Perret. As long as I manage to work things out to my own satisfaction. And I think I can."

"To *your* satisfaction?"

"Quite. Mine. And yours too, I imagine. And a few others like us. That's the main thing, isn't it? All the rest . . ." (He gave a casual toss of the hand.) "The important thing, really, is not to botch our exit, especially since it's for keeps. I'm sure it's going to work out fine."

It was just then that the radio crew in the villa received a message from the marine commandos: "Barbed wire cut all over, Colonel. Infiltration possible up and down the front."

"Well, what are you waiting for? Get out there and fix it."

The reply was concise. They had barely enough men on hand to keep up their patrols and maintain communications. But certainly not to go stringing barbed wire. That was for sure.

"Fine, fine!" said the colonel, and he gave the impression that he actually meant it.

A few more minutes, and it would be three in the morning . . .

Forty

At the selfsame hour, one hundred and forty-seven minutes ahead of
the refugees' actual landing, the myth of "redemption by the Ganges
armada" swept over the nation's industrial zones, in plant after plant.
Once again we should point out that this coincidental occurrence
was in no way due to any preconceived scheme on the part of the
principals, or to any concerted action by the usual phalanx of outside
agitators. If the Third World factory workers of France rose up in
spontaneous revolt that night—in places as far removed from one
another as Paris, Lille, Lyon, and Mulhouse—it's because for the last
three days the pent-up tension had built to such a pitch that the lid
finally blew, in a seething eruption of wild, expectant hopes. In ordinary times no one would have dared to take such risks. Every man
was intent on keeping his job and his hard-earned pay. (The unions,
of course, worked hard to recruit the swarthy rabble, and would
throw them into the fray from time to time, as the rules of the social
wargame demanded, though really with an eye to improving the
French workers' profits, perched up at the top of the salary scale.)
The best proof was the fact that at places like Rhodio-Chemical, for
example—and a few other highly politicized plants, where the great
emancipation revels had already begun on the day before Easter—
the Third World workers had resisted temptation, sticking grimly by
their machines, like a stray dog still clinging to a bone gnawed white.
But that didn't stop them from thinking. Perhaps they weren't willing for others to share in their fabled redemption, that symbol of a
million refugees, landing in France, to signal their deliverance. They
had lived their exile alone, despite the occasional hand of friendship
held out over the flood of false promises, and alone they would be
resurrected. When the factory loudspeakers had broadcast the final
words of the President's message, the unions lost all control. The
political cells exploded. And even Cadi One-Eye, in Paris, knew that
now he could never keep his people in check. (Any more than he'll
hold back his wife, Élise, speeding to the studios of Radio-East, a
razor hidden inside her stocking.) To be honest, we have to admit,
however, that the crimes committed that night, for the most part,
had no needless cruelty or malice about them, no excess of subtle

finesse, but seemed part of the natural order of things. One might have feared that this was to be the first wave of a fierce, brewing storm. Instead, it was the one last visible tremor in an underground upheaval. And it quickly subsided, since the country had drowned in its waters long since. Besides, one thing is sure. Even if Western-style law had survived, with its weighty decisions about justice as we knew it, the courts would have judged each one of these crimes as quite defensible on social grounds, going through the motions—for appearance's sake—and handing down suspended sentences, or light ones at most.

The first such crime was a model of the genre. It was staged in Bicêtre, in the slaughter room of a pork-packing plant, Charcuteries Olo by name. The three Africans who worked there—stunner, hoister, and slaughterer, respectively—could go through an average of a hundred ninety pigs an hour, in two or three cut and dried moves, each one repeated a hundred ninety times. A grisly and gory job, and one that the regular help would have no part of. Several hundred workers depended on these three men: the ones on the sausage line—stuffers, stringers, sorters—the ones on the tinned pâté line—packers and sealers—not to mention the various supervisory personnel, the wholesalers, the retailers, as well as an assortment of executives and stockholders. Let one of these three indispensable killers suddenly have to take himself a pee, and the whole production would slow to a crawl. Such breaks, therefore, were quickly forbidden, in return for which the three were rewarded with a few extra francs per day—what the front office jokingly referred to as "bladder compensation." Now it happened that, just that night, the management, sensing the troubles to come, and the shortages sure to follow in their wake, came to the conclusion that food would be trumps, and that the industry stood to make a killing if only huge stockpiles could be laid away in time. And so, the order went out through the plant to step everything up. It reached the slaughter room, moments after the end of the President's speech, on the lips of the assistant production manager himself, with the promise that the bladder bonus would even be doubled. "Sure 'nough boss," one red-spattered black assured him, "we can sure 'nough do one more at least . . ." The white man felt no more pain than any of the other pigs in the line. Stunned, hoisted, slaughtered . . . And hanging from his hook, between two blood-drenched hogs, he started into production. As he moved along through each successive phase, growing less and less like man and more like pork, he caused a certain amount of interest, but no special disgust. They had seen such things before, after all. At market, in the Congo. (Except, that is, for a few white women, who promptly took to their heels, or swooned dead away. As for the foremen, they just turned and ran. They had read the blank looks on the faces of their slaves, and had gotten the message.) The Third World workers went on with their jobs, conscientious as could be, even unto the final labeling of the tins where the white man's remains ended up as pâté. Perhaps we even ate some of him ourselves. As time went by and conditions grew worse, we tended to be a good deal less fussy. . . . Worth noting, in passing, was a certain worker-priest, sausage stringer by trade, who said a little prayer as he tied his last knot, and then murmured: "Forgive them, Lord, for they know not what they do." At which point, the production line stopped. Since all the police headquarters, that night, were deluged with complaints of much the same kind (which they found rather hard to believe), and since the commissioner, left to shift for himself with a pack of demoralized men, had decided to wait until morning to look into the matter, the officials of the plant were quick to agree that the whole affair must have been an accident. An explanation, in fact, that they likely put forth themselves. "Well now," the manager ventured, after a minute of silence, "shall we all get back to work?" "Sure 'nough, boss!" replied the trio of killers, turned labor leaders all of a sudden. "Like ninety pigs an hour, man. Right? So France'll just eat less. Tough shit!" And they added, with their calmest and pleasantest of smiles, "Of course, man, from now on we get half the take . . ." Five minutes later, having emptied out his safe and handed a few envelopes to his faithful watchdogs, the manager snatched his family on the run, and made a dash southward, heading for Switzerland, only to be swallowed in the great glut of cars and the shortage of gas. Once again, if the reader wants a few more details, just for the record, we might mention that the gentleman was spotted for the last time, on foot, not far from Saint-Favier, of all places (where the Arabs, not content to have the swimming pool to themselves, had co-opted their way onto the town council as members of the dominant minority, and had finally taken it over). The poor man would never be heard from again. . . . All of which explains how Charcuteries Olo, of Bicêtre, finally came to be run by the workers.

In the hellish hubbub of the Quai de Javel, in Paris, where Third World labor amounted to better than eighty percent, the revolt took on a liturgical form, like a mass or a ritual sacrifice. When you take into account the fact that the profit potential of the automobile industry relies on assembly lines, strictly timed and paced, it's no surprise that poor, uprooted, illiterate folk, subject to all the concentration-camp fancies of a wildly disparate retribalized existence, should have endowed the timers—those high priests of clock almighty—with all the coercive and sacred powers of a religion forcibly imposed by the masters. Their resistance to this new faith depended on a kind of secret intrigue, replete with a whole spate of catacomb rites. If they wanted to catch their breath on the line, or settle their nerves—or just stop for a moment and muse on their distant palm grove, or the big muddy river running its course between grasslands and dunes— they would rush the prescribed moves through, then loll over the conclusion, as if they hadn't finished, daydreaming without letting on, hand resting on the tool in question, pretending to work. And during those precious moments, they would cast quick glances among themselves, fraternal glances that bespoke the same loathing of the clockers' steady pace, as much a rejection of the new religion as a need to rest. But the clockers were always there watching. No room, after all, for two cults at once. And they would speed up the rhythm, or divide the jobs to make them simpler and quicker. When you're manufacturing cars, it's no good to dream of exotic palm groves, or of kneeling down nightly in prayer, facing Mecca. And so, when the redemptive myth of the Ganges burst onto the scene, it was toward those million messiahs that all hopes secretly turned. This became quite clear at about the time of the São Tomé affair, when the armada had reached the height of fashion, and the famous slogan "We're all from the Ganges now" was dished up for every political and philosophical cause. Huge demonstration, but rather short-lived. Some eighty thousand workers, massed by their motionless assembly lines, shouting two slogans that seemed, on the face of it, wholly unrelated: "Get-the-Clockers-Off-Our-Backs, We're-All-From-the-Ganges-Now!" Then things calmed down and returned to normal, though the unions, surprised by the spontaneous uprising, had tried to keep the movement going so that they could take it over. Failing that, they settled for adopting the strange Manichaean battle cry that pitted Ganges refugees and clockers against each other as symbols of the eternal struggle between Good and Evil; the cry that they shouted through this plant and that, just to show that they were still a force to be reckoned with, in spite of the social tranquillity decreed by the beast to lull world opinion to sleep. (The clockers, at least, were given a bonus for the risks they faced.) And days went by. Until that night, when one of the time gobblers, chosen among the most ruthless of the lot, was trussed up like a sausage and laid on a piece of sheet metal en route to the body assembly, with a sign in Arabic around his neck: "For now the thousand years are ended." When the massive drop hammer fell against the metal to stamp it into shape, the clocker was nothing but a puddle of blood, quickly dried in the heat. A great roar went up and the assembly line stopped, as thousands of Arabs, next to their machines, fell prostrate toward Mecca, and gave thanks to Allah. The "underdogs" had had their scapegoat, and that was that. There were no other crimes in Javel that night. They needed only one, and everyone understood it. If we want to pursue the historical facts a bit further, here too—again, just for the record—we might point out that cars are still coming off the lines at the Javel plant, though they're awfully expensive and terribly scarce. They're reserved, first choice, for the officials of the new regime. To buy one himself, a worker in one of those people-run plants would have to pay ten times what he makes in a year. A pleasure he can ill afford. (He can take consolation, however, in using our public conveyances, chaotic and decrepit, or in joining the rest of the ill-shod pedestrians thronging the streets.) When the author of these lines returned to Paris after a lengthy stay in Switzerland, his car was surrounded by breathless little urchins, as if it were some new kind of toy. Of course, when they saw the Swiss plate, they all jeered and sneered. There's no changing that! But we mustn't digress . . .

In other industrial towns—Billancourt, Vénissieux, Le Mans, and the like--the rhythm of Western life floundered and drowned in quite the same way. The fact that it owed its existence to Third World sweat doesn't change the picture. One can even claim, at the risk of prison or social extinction, that under the Western regime the Third World did work efficiently, at least. It would have been best to take pride in the fact, and establish a just master-servant relationship, instead of groaning with shame at the height of our prosperity. But why complain now? It wouldn't have made much difference. Not really. With millions of us and billions of them, we couldn't have held out much longer. Now we're swept up in the Third World tide, and it's clear that their instinctual drives have won out hands down. Everything has changed. The way people talk, the way they behave, the rhythm and rhythms of life, the play of emotions, the level of production. A whole new outlook. Even their way of not giving a damn. (Then too, with sexual appetites given free rein, it seems that the white has become Third World, though the Third World hasn't turned white in the bargain. Clearly, they've won.) For every old

Ahmed who moans in private that "things were better under the French"—though he hardly remembers if he's talking about his native Algeria or his adopted France—how many millions scrape by on their share of the monstrous welfare budget, telling themselves that the wheel has turned, and that equality, at last, is no empty word? Such, more or less, was the prophetic vision—unintentional, no doubt—of a young West Indian girl that night, at her job in a Croissy electronics plant, exclaiming simply, as she plunged a screwdriver into her supervisor's breast: "Plantation days are over!" A remark with a lot of history behind it . . .

Occupied too, that night, was the hallowed pavement of the Boulevard Saint-Germain, but this time for good. To comprehend fully the scope of the event, we have to go back a few years, to that scene of racial crisis, that Fashoda of black against white, the Café Odéon. Faced with the example of urban America, fallen little by little into total decay, certain observers had seen the confrontation as a sign of the inevitable, though they took care not to say so in print. That wasn't the kind of thing one wrote those days, nor will it ever be again. The pure of conscience, on the other hand, roared out a mighty chorus. Endless variations, in every key, on the famous theme: "No dogs, no niggers." (Hyperbole, to be sure. That wasn't it at all.) What the owner of the Café Odéon had said at the time was this:

"I've been running the Café Odéon for almost a year and a half. It's kind of a bar and ice cream parlor combined. Most of my trade are Africans and West Indians. Anyway, on December twenty-seventh, while I'm out of town, two tough guys go over to this other table and crush out their cigarettes. Right on the table, I mean. So the help kick them out. The next day a lady complains that some character is trying to give her a hard time. One of the waiters—the name doesn't matter—goes over and tries to straighten him out. He gets roughed up so bad, he winds up in the hospital. When I get back, a week later, I put my foot down. Don't serve any troublemakers, I tell them. Well, that's when they start giving me the business. Frankly, I can't take any more. It's a losing game. I'd rather close up . . ."

And he added, without thinking, leaving himself open to the usual epithets and insults: "How do you like that? Calling me a racist! Me, a Jew, who fought against the Nazis, tooth and nail!"

It was easy enough to understand what had happened. The blacks had decided to take over the Café Odéon, and had proceeded to make life miserable for the whites who frequented it. Now, it's a

known fact that racism comes in two forms: that practiced by whites
—heinous and inexcusable, whatever its motives—and that practiced
by blacks—quite justified, whatever its excesses, since it's merely the
expression of a righteous revenge, and it's up to the whites to be
patient and understanding. There was even that time, in Paris, when
an American "Black Power" leader came to the Cité Universitaire to
speak at a student rally, and began his speech by shouting: "Now
listen, I see we got some black brothers and sisters standing, and
some white folks sitting. Come on, white folks, let's give us those
seats!" And the most amazing part of it was that the ones he was
talking to got up, meek as lambs, while the others applauded. At the
Café Odéon things hadn't gone that far. The whites had held tight.
They weren't there to make trouble, just to sit and drink their coffee
in peace. Still, their very presence rankled, and struck the blacks as
a calculated slap. Hence, a string of those nasty harassments that the
Paris of the day found it tasteful to condone, at the risk of public
censure. The whites, as a result, began to keep their distance. And
the owner, seeing his business about to fall apart, thanks to a wholly
one-sided clientele, took steps to shore it up by refusing to serve
"certain" blacks (and not "any" black, as the papers of the time so
shamelessly reported). Poor man! From that point on, every black
student in Paris took turns in his café, spitting on the floor, breaking
glasses, glowering at the help, crushing out cigarette butts on the
walls, and the like. He closed up two days later, and his flight was
hailed as a noble victory for the universal conscience. The battleground, however, spread to the neighboring establishments, whose
owners—much more clever—hung on in different ways, with endless
"rap sessions" and much licking of boots, trying to keep their invest-
ments from sinking. The Café Odéon had been sold for half what it
was worth, and the value of the building whose ground floor it occupied was already taking a dramatic plunge. That was the way
matters stood, more or less, until that Easter Sunday night and Monday morning. The President of the Republic had no sooner finished
speaking, than the streets of the quarter, empty all night in anticipation of his address, suddenly came alive. Twenty thousand blacks—
students, mainly, and a smattering of young diplomats—streamed
over the hallowed pavement. Alsace-Lorraine had been retaken, and
this time they would never let it go! They came from every corner.
From their West Indian bars, their African dance halls, their rooms
at the Cité Universitaire, wherever they had been holed up, waiting,
expecting the impossible and hoping for the inevitable. At the Café

Odéon, one of them stood up behind the counter and declared, "A round for everybody, on the house!" The example was followed in the neighboring bars, but only in one did it threaten to cause trouble. The owner, not a man to be trifled with, grabbed his ever-ready pistol from the till, and brandished it at the crowd submerging his bar like a great spring tide. At which point, a hulking brute from Guadeloupe —head of some student activist group or other—went swaggering up, hands by his sides, and stuck his chest squarely in front of the barrel. He apparently had a first-rate memory and a talent for imitation, because, standing there eye to eye with the owner, he proceeded, quite simply, to recite. And it was as if the President himself were speaking:

"And so, I am asking every soldier and officer, every member of our police—asking them from the depths of my conscience and my soul—to weigh this monstrous mission for themselves, and to feel free either to accept or reject it. To kill is hard. Even harder to know why. Myself, I think I know. But I don't have my finger on the trigger, and my gun isn't aimed point blank at some poor soul's flesh. My friends, whatever happens, may God help us . . . or forgive us."

Having said his say, he burst out laughing, to his friends' applause. It was a curious moment, as hatred gave way to a subtler emotion, as if they were sorry to see the balance shift, and to lose that antagonism long advantageous to blacks of their position. Rising above the uproar, a voice cried out:

"Come on, boss! Have one on us! And tomorrow, if you're a good boy, maybe we'll even pay for our drinks! Cheer up, we all got to live, don't we?"

"Not at this price," the owner muttered, shrugging his shoulders.

Throwing down his gun, he pocketed the contents of the till. Then he walked out into the night, straight ahead, without looking back, as the crowd stepped aside and let him pass. A moment later, on the boulevard, he found himself forced into a doorway, as a solid mass of flesh came surging over the sidewalk, refusing to give an inch. The drudges of the depths had begun to swarm through Paris.

At this point a little-known event took place, one that historians, in their wisdom, prefer to pass over, since many a feather would doubtless be ruffled in today's high government circles were it to be discussed. We speak of the frenzied flight of all the coat-and-tie blacks before the army of African swill men, sweepers, troglodytes, and menials. They were led by their witch doctors, needless to say. Especially "the Chief"—that hero of the dismal cellar—and the rag-

tag priest—apostle to the slums, latter-day Cardinal Lavigerie himself, evangelist to the Africans and do-gooder of note. Ever since
some of their number had begun sweeping gutters—in those wee,
small hours, when their gentlemen brethren would pile into their
cars, parked all day on the hallowed pavement—the myth of a black
utopia had spread through their cellars and under the sheet-metal
roofs of their hovels. The tribal princes were the worst offenders.
What on earth did they have in common with the "poor nigger"
pushing his broom? Skin color? Come now! How maddening it was
for these upper-crust blacks, here in the heart of the capital, scene
of their social successes, to find themselves—on every sidewalk, by
every sewer, behind every rubbish truck—face to face with their
ragged doubles, cold and hungry, whose dark skin, peddled so
cheaply, offended that black pride of theirs that they valued so much.
We should pity them, really. That night they were caught in the
midst of a truly unbearable web of hate: abhorrence for the whites;
disgust and contempt for their gutter-dwelling brothers; and above
all, that loathing for the working-class black, who had tracked them
all the way to France, as they managed to escape the fate of the race
in the white man's wake. Yes, the redemptive myth of the Ganges
opened many a subtle rift. Nothing seemed clear anymore in those
murky waters of impending doom, waters that the beast had black-
ened by design, like an octopus spewing its ink. Could that be one
explanation? . . . Be that as it may, as soon as the shabby, swarthy
troops came trampling the pavement in front of the Café Odéon—
and other centers of the black utopia—the battalions of mannequins
took to their heels like a pack of scared rabbits. Still, we have to
admire their presence of mind. By daybreak they had pulled off an
amazing coup and saved their skins. Quite simply, they had made the
rounds of the neighborhood—a good one, as everyone knows—ringing all the bells, and saying something like this to each terrified
bourgeois couple at the door:
    "Monsieur . . . Madame . . . We've come to help you. Since mid-
night, you can see the handwriting on the wall. No more of those
special rights you've always enjoyed. Or, at least, you're going to
have to share them. First, with the Third World workers, and later,
with anyone else who decides to join their cause. The streets are full.
They've already taken over. Who knows? In a few minutes whole
families may show up at your door. And, like it or not, you'll have to
make room. They'll pitch camp in your parlor. Of course, we don't
begrudge our poor, desperate brothers. The ones who break their

backs working for you folks, the ones you couldn't live without. But the rest of us..." (students, princes, professors, diplomats, intellectuals, artists, trainees in this or that or nothing—take your pick) "... the rest of us are men of taste, steeped in your culture, your style, your way of life. Naturally, we want to preserve that elegance and refinement that we feel we owe so much." (Clever argument, that. It usually got them.) "Now, the best thing would be if we moved in here with you. Two or three of us, that's all. Better to share with us —thinking alike, the way we do—than to be invaded by a bunch of poor, ignorant beggars, who don't mean any harm, Heaven knows, but who just won't respect things, if you see what we mean. Madame ... Monsieur... It's getting late. When the others come and ring your bell, you'll really be much better off if they see a black face or two at the door. Come, let us take care of it. You go hide, and leave everything to us..."

They spoke so well and looked so neat—spotless shirt, plain dark tie, horn-rimmed glasses—that the bourgeois couple, backs to the wall, could only agree. The least of two evils. These look all right, after all. And they're clean, and they smell nice. Better a no-good fancy Dan snob than a plain, dirty nigger, no matter how honest. A gentleman, at least, won't touch my daughter . . . And so, with a simper: "Let us show you around. We could fix you a place. Maybe there, on the sofa . . . A bed, you say? Of course, that's the least we can do. We have two bathrooms, it won't be any trouble! And besides, it probably won't be for long . . ." Then the deathblow:

"Why yes, madame. For good . . ."

Quite so, for good! The rats won't give up that cheese called "The West" until they've devoured it to the very last crumb. Big and thick as it is, that will take them some time. They're at it even now. But the cleverest of the rats saved the best part for themselves. (Inevitable offshoot of any revolution.) Yes, privileges there are, born of that historic night, and hailed at the time as avant-garde triumphs. But everyone ignores them, or pretends not to notice. And anyway, on basic issues the new regime stands absolutely firm. Someone, for example, came up recently with a plan for discreet exchanges in the living arrangements. Half an apartment, occupied by blacks, for half of another, occupied by whites. No difference in the democratic use of the quarters, but only in their racial makeup. Certain whites who had managed to put aside some cash have been known to slip rather handsome bribes—sub rosa, of course—to their dark-skinned colleagues. It seems, in fact, that many such exchanges have been

worked out in the recent past, to everyone's satisfaction. But a stringent new law, intended to ensure a proper racial mix, has just put an
end to such relics of an age long past. Perfectly logical! No point in
abolishing the concept of race on a public level, just to turn right
around and restore it in private. That wouldn't make sense, now,
would it? . . . (As we write these lines, we can't help but recall an old
American law, dating back to 1970, forerunner of all antiracist legisla-
tion. The "School-Busing Law" it was called. In those days, in the
United States, the black and white races lived more or less apart,
secluded from each other. That being the case, it was decided, in the
name of integration, to transport a certain number of little white
children to black schools, and vice versa, in equal proportion. How
many tots traveled scores and scores of miles each day, while others
went the same route, exactly in reverse! Well, people protested. In
the name of useless fatigue, absurd expense, freedom of choice. In
the name of everything you please. But racism? Never! It was too late
for that. Why, the very word was distasteful. So busing won out, and
now they celebrate "Busing Day" in every school the whole world
over . . .)

In conclusion, a few words about the inevitable appearance, that
night, of the idiots, simpletons, madmen, and maniacs. When everything in society suddenly stops functioning rationally, that's when the
misfits crawl out of the woodwork. And with them their resentments,
their utopian visions, their neuroses and psychoses. Mad dogs on the
loose. A merry-go-round of feeble minds, free at last of all social
fetters. Historians faced with the mass of documents concerning that
night—some of which reveal quite incredible details—came to the
conclusion that society of that bygone era must have been oppressive
to the utmost, for its breakdown to unleash such a rash of psychic
aberrations. (Psychiatrists, by the way, exulted. They had long seen
society as fostering mental decay, and had gone so far as to turn the
insane back out on the streets, so as not to compound one oppression
with another.) None of which, however, takes into account the vital
role of the redemptive myth, self-inflicted and sublimated, like drugs
in the past . . . But let's go on. This isn't the time for academic debates.
Let's settle for a few simple facts, among thousands.

Sex crimes, small and large, were rampant on that night of nights.
From indecent exposure to all the rest. Never had so many organs
dangled from so many unzipped flies. While the normal people ran
off, or stayed in hiding, the public urinals (in Paris, especially, and in
all the big cities) had a sudden surge of traffic, the likes of which they

hadn't seen since the Liberation, in 1944. (It's no accident, clearly, that two myths of similar nature should produce the same results.) From satyrs to sadists was just one easy step. And so, the same young lady who felt she was being ogled and followed every day—a common enough symptom of the modern urban illness—was killed this time by some hideous sex-crazed slayer. (Even today, years later, they still dig up bodies of women and children from old abandoned building sites. Like those bombs from past wars, that surface in our cities every now and again . . .) The same outburst spawned a flurry of accusations and denunciations. So many, in fact, that the authorities, to this day, haven't managed to sift through them all. And when the post office finally came back to something resembling normal, they were amazed at the number of anonymous letters slipped into the boxes that night. Of course, that wasn't really so unusual. In times of exceptional stress, humanity plumbs its most gangrenous depths. One novel element this time, though: the loads and loads of letters from children, informing on Mommy and Daddy, if you please. Yet even there, no need for tears. In China, after all, during the Cultural Revolution, the youngsters had done much the same, with great abandon, and Heaven only knows how the West heaped praises on them for it! . . . As for old customs revived, let's mention just one: shaving the ladies' heads in revenge. Did such-and-such a secretary sleep with her boss, or this factory girl with her foreman? Next morning, they found themselves bald as a Buddhist monk. Not to mention the other forms of Gallic vendetta. Detestable, one and all! Tires slashed, house fronts spattered, windows broken, dogs poisoned, pastures plowed up, trees sawed in two . . . Of course, none of it tells us anything new about the consummate baseness of the folk of the time. At least their Third World confrères showed more dignity and style in settling their scores . . .

And lastly, under the "simpleton" heading, the droll case of three hundred villagers, living outside the Air France flight school at Deauville-Saint-Gatien, invading the airport at three in the morning. To protest in the name of their own jangled nerves? Not a bit! Led by the mayor, in official regalia, the bumpkin band—with pitchforks poised, and flanked by their tousled females, black claws set to pounce—went storming the control tower in the name of the peace and tranquillity of their cattle! (Indeed, revolutions have been fought over less. Who knows where man's noble ideals may be lurking?) The fact was that, with so many jets thundering overhead, the cows had quite simply begun to waste away. Now, in Normandy, if anything

is sacred, it's the cow! The poor peasants had demonstrated time and
time again, all to no avail, and their tempers were turning as sour as
their animals' milk. And so, no sooner had the President of the
Republic let down his guard on the mayor's TV screen, than His
Honor stood up, tossed off a shot of Calvados, and announced, "This
time, men, I think we've got them!" Traditionalist that he was, he
had the tocsin rung, and no one in the village doubted what it meant.
The Ganges fleet was none of their business! We don't worry about
politics here, we don't meddle in other folks' affairs! Just sweep up
in front of our own front door! But the airport, now, that's something
else! . . . Ah, what a delightful concept: a momentous, historic night,
and that single tocsin pealing loud and clear, to save a bunch of stupid
cows . . .

Forty-one

The stars had dimmed. The moon had set. At the foot of a tall pine sat Colonel Dragasès, warming his hands around a mug of steaming coffee. The searchlight on the roof of the villa was cutting its swath less sharply through the night. Not that the darkness had thickened around it, but rather because, as the outlines paled, they began to blend in with the moving white beam, pacing the beach like a sentry, glimpsed through the haze of the early-morning mists. Five o'clock. Everything was quiet on board the ships of the refugee fleet. Nothing was stirring. Only an occasional, barely noticeable tremor, rippling the surface of the bodies that lined the decks. Heads, most likely, rearing ever so slightly, as daybreak neared, to gaze toward shore for an inkling of impending destiny.

In Panama Ranger's camp, the noise had died down. Or, rather, it had changed, gaining in refinement what it gave up in volume. No sounds but guitars now, strumming to the dismal wail of those soulful ballads so very much in vogue. It was a time, indeed, when the popular song wallowed in melancholy, with its four-note laments intoned for oneself, one's fellows, all of mankind, and the rest. Whenever the pop tunes would lose their blaring charm, there was nothing left but to let oneself drown in the sticky-sweet syrup of human misery and despair, set to music of sorts, that one refuge of yearning and unfulfilled souls that had learned nothing else. It never occurred to any of them to measure that notion of misery against the past, or against their own well-being. For them it was a drug, and they needed to shoot up a good strong dose to keep themselves going, like addicts and their heroin. The fact that it was often hard to come by close to home made very little difference. Nothing stops an addict when he has to have his fix, and poisons like that are easy to import. There's never a lack of pushers. Besides, modern man has always had, tucked away in the back of his mind, that singular longing for total destruction, sole cure for the boredom and anguish that consume him. It's that hope that the beast had unleashed, exalting it in song.
. . . At that moment, in fact, a voice rose up over the rest. A young man's voice, pure and strong. And the others stopped to listen, then took up again in a chorus of responses, as they might have done at

vespers or the like, back in the days when such things were still sung.
(We should mention, in passing, that the slaughter of the ancient
liturgy, like the murder of everything else that was sacred, was no
random operation. The reader shouldn't think for one moment that,
when they choked it all dead with their own two hands, the priests
didn't know it would spring up again, in some other guise. They
knew perfectly well, and lots of them had reveled in giving the
enemy the best of their weapons. The sacred had no more need now
for God. The liturgy glorified mankind on earth. And the priests
themselves, freed of the burden of divinity at last, could be like all
the rest, and resume their status as everyday men . . .) What the voice
was singing was plainly obscene. But only the lyrics; and the young
man's inspired tone made up for them nicely, as he improvised his
chant:

"For the Arab kicked in the balls, lying bleeding on the sidewalk,
we'll tear this sick world down . . ."

"We'll tear this sick world down," the chorus echoed . . .

"For the working girl knocked up some Saturday night, with a
stupid damn baby in her belly, we'll tear this sick world down . . ."

"We'll tear this sick world down . . ."

"For the kid bawling his head off, who gets slugged by his old
man, dead tired from his noisy machines, we'll tear this sick world
down . . .

"For the poor, starving black who sweeps up the crap of the rich
people's dogs, we'll tear this sick world down . . ."

"We'll tear this sick world down," the chorus repeated. But as
things began to grow more tense, some made a few select additions:
". . . this goddamn, stinking, fucked-up world . . ." And over the
twang of strumming guitars, each voice drew out the refrain with its
own words of hate. (Someone, at a loss for adjectives, probably, even
tossed the phrase "human world" into the chorus, and never knew
how hard God tried to forgive him . . .)

"For the little old guy burping his gulp of wine at the charity
Christmas party, we'll tear this sick world down . . .

"For the check the big-hearted boss sends the priest at the charity
Christmas party, we'll tear this sick world down . . .

"For the black girl's naked flesh sold on millionaires' safaris . . .

"For the twenty-five wild boars the President bagged himself . . .

"For the millions of bodies shot full of holes by the gunrunners'
greed . . .

"For the caviar wolfed down in India, one night, when everyone else was starving . . .

"For the Indian dead of hunger at dawn on New Year's Day . . .

"For the Western murderers and the throats they slit, when people wouldn't bow down and believe their shit . . ."

The colonel finished his coffee, and observed, as he lit a cigarette:

"Now that one's more like it. Much more poetic. Even starting to rhyme. And that 'Western murderers' bit isn't far from the truth, by God! So sure of itself, that fine West of ours. So sure it could slap its blind culture on the world. So sure of the law that might makes right! Ah, the great things we did in the name of that law! And how nice it felt, for all those years, making everyone accept it!"

He turned to the officer and asked:

"Captain! How many murderers by last count, please?"

"As of five-fifteen, colonel, we had two hundred twenty. Officers, noncoms, and enlisted men. Not counting Monsieur Perret and his chauffeur . . . Wait, I take that back . . ." (He looked over and saw a figure fleeing through the darkness.) "Scratch the chauffeur. He just took off. That means two hundred twenty-one in all. Grand total. Which is two hundred down from ten minutes ago, by the way. With cards like that, we'll be out of the game in no time." (So saying, he stuck out his chin, froze his face in a rule-book stare, clicked his heels, and saluted.)

"What's with you?" asked the colonel.

"Model soldier!" the captain replied.

Then he started rattling off, all in a single breath, in his most ceremonial of tones:

"French officer extraordinaire! With incredible vigor and no thought for his safety, led his men past all known bounds of courage, and effected a first-rate retreat to the shores of the Mediterranean, submachine gun in hand! Decorated for services above and beyond the call of duty . . ."

"You wouldn't be pulling my leg, would you, Captain?"

"You guessed it, Colonel."

And they both burst out laughing. Then the captain went on:

"Frankly, I've never had so much fun. The ones who deserted had no sense of humor. That's their trouble. Like lots of people nowadays. A good sense of humor is pretty hard to find. So you're left with the cream, Colonel. The ones who think everything's a big goddamn joke, and especially all this bleeding-heart business."

"I'm afraid we're a little old-fashioned," Jean Perret broke in.

"Humor is out of style. Happiness is a crime. And ambition is just a dirty word. Everything that used to make life worth living, once upon a time. Why, when I was their age . . ."

"No comparisons, monsieur!" the colonel interrupted. "That's out too. Besides, what's the use? . . . Listen to those kids and their damnable prayers. Why, they're already old men and women at twenty. What kind of an inspiration is that for today's young people? All taking their cue from the poorest, filthiest, stupidest, laziest, scruffiest scum of the lot! And whatever you do, don't ever look up, or have any ideals. Never think for yourself. It's so much less sweat! Well, that's a hell of a way to try to build a world. Even one like theirs! Never let yourself climb up on anyone's shoulders and try to rise above the crowd. Just follow along in the gutter, down with everyone else . . ."

"Goodness, Colonel," the captain remarked, "you're getting awfully serious."

"You're right. It won't happen again."

Night was beginning to fade, and with it the sounds and voices so clear in the darkness. As Panama Ranger's litany grew dimmer, Colonel Dragasès took a megaphone and put it to his lips. And he stood there, feet spread, huge colossus of a man fairly bursting with health, facing north toward his attackers, and shouting:

"Screw you all, goddammit!"

Then he turned toward those around him, and added:

"Not very clever or original, but that's just the way I feel. Besides, they're not really the ones it's meant for, I don't suppose."

"Who then?" asked Jean Perret.

"The future, probably . . ."

From the occupied houses on all sides the answer was quick in coming:

"Pig! Prick! Asshole! Filthy bastard! . . ."

"See?" said the colonel. "They can't even say 'shit' with style anymore!"

"Cocksucker! Motherfucker! Murderer! Fascist!"

"Fascist," he echoed. "And imperialist. Capitalist. Racist. Militarist . . . When it comes to 'ists' I'll even insult myself . . . Hey, you guys on the roof! Thank those kids over there for me, will you?"

The machine gun on top of the villa spat out a few rounds. Day had begun to break, and the men could see what they were shooting at now. Then a volley of angry shouts, and the moans and groans of the wounded. Suddenly the squad leader threw down his binoculars:

"Good God, men, hold your fire!" he commanded.

"What's the matter?" the colonel snapped. "Don't tell me you're losing your sense of humor too!"

"No, Colonel. It's just that we damn near shot down a pack of padres!"

"So? Why should that bother you? . . . And anyway, how can you tell?"

"That's just it, Colonel. These are even dressed like padres. Like the kind I haven't seen in years and years! . . . They're coming down the path, thirty-two degrees east, at eight hundred meters . . . And they're singing! . . . The one in front has on a kind of pointy white hat, and he's walking under a parasol, or something, with this funny-looking gold thing in his hands . . ."

"No, no, no! That's a miter. And a canopy. And the monstrance for the Blessed Sacrament, you dummy!"

Forty-two

There were twelve of them. Twelve Benedictine monks from the abbey at Fontgembar. Eleven wizened, bent old men, faces soft and gentle as the Smiling Angel of the Reims cathedral, and one strapping man in his fifties, with dark, darting, deep-set eyes. And all of them dressed in their black sackcloth garb. At ten after midnight, in the abbey's great hall (where they had come to listen to the President's address), the abbot, Dom Melchior de Groix, had drawn himself up to his full, impressive height, and standing in his cloister stall, straight as an arrow for all the weight of his eighty-seven years, he had turned to his brethren with roughly these remarks:

"Three years ago, brothers, when we rebuilt the sacred and timeless walls of this deserted abbey, in spite of those floods of hate stirred up by our venture, we had no idea what purpose the Lord intended us for when He made us conceive our endeavor. Today, at this moment, the Christian West confronts its most perilous hour, and that purpose seems almost clear. We stand here alone, the last twelve monks to devote our lives to prayer and contemplation in an Order that has let itself lapse and decay into everyday concerns, into social action and misguided commitment; an Order that first denied, and soon forgot, that man is given his brief stay on earth only to earn his eternal salvation. Now if that sounds like vanity, may the good Lord forgive me . . ."

Off in the shadows, by the light of the flickering candles—there had been no electricity since the day before—a figure strode out of his stall, and knelt at the old abbot's feet. It was Dom Paul Pinet, youngest of the monks, and prior of Fontgembar. He gazed at the ground, and tried not to let his eyes show his feelings.

"But father," he said, "what you're proposing is nothing but vanity, I assure you. In the name of Our Lord Jesus Christ, who died for all mankind, I beg you for the last time. Please, don't go through with it."

"Brother Paul," replied the abbot, "if God, despite all expectations, has kept me alive to see this momentous day, He must have had a reason. Now, I know that you're going to frown on my decision. I know that you're going to consider my orders childish and futile. If

240

you wish, I'll release you from your vow of obedience. Temporarily, I mean . . ."

It wasn't really a very old story. Dom Melchior de Groix belonged to one of those wealthy families in which high birth and high finance had been bedfellows for better than a hundred years. When he took it into his head to rebuild Fontgembar, up in the Esterel range, along with a handful of recalcitrant old monks—die-hard traditionalists, one and all—he had no dearth of backers. The sugar tycoons, the textile kings, the banking giants all opened wide their coffers. The amount noised about was a billion old francs. Probably correct, though one did hear a figure as high as three billion. The bishops of France had no qualms whatever in pumping the sum up themselves, lending all the weight of their combined reverend voices to support their claims. "Where is all the money coming from?" they had asked in a pastoral letter of some notoriety. "Who are the financial powers behind Dom Melchior de Groix? And what right do they have to spend such amounts, when for months and months now other voices have cried out the misery and woe of the Ganges, of Brazil, and, indeed, of the whole Third World . . . ?" The press had jumped right in, of course, closely followed by public opinion en masse. On the air at Radio-East, Albert Durfort had come to the conclusion that "at that price the vow of poverty is a joke!" No sooner was it open and ready for its monks, than Fontgembar was swamped by reporters, photographers, and a battery of TV cameras, pointing like so many angry, accusing fingers. Beneath its towering walls camped thousands of young people, spray guns in hand, led on by their priestly legion, and splattering the buildings, newly restored, with their salvos of painted curses. In huge red letters. So big that one message could be read far and wide: "PEOPLE! THE SWEAT OF YOUR BROWS LINED THIS PLACE WITH GOLD!" Dom Melchior had made a courageous stand. But only one. He had opened the doors of the abbey's great hall to an onrushing tide—writer types, film types, and those plainclothes-padre types, crosses pinned to their fatigues —and had stated, very simply, "I believe this is one of the most meaningful endeavors in which the Lord has ever allowed me to take part . . ." ("Sure, sure! The Lord!" several voices shouted. "Blame it on the Lord! Come on, who put up the money?") The old abbot, seeming not to hear, had continued: "May this monastery, rebuilt and restored with so much love . . ." (More voices: "Love thy neighbor, right?" "Love my eye, it's prostitution! A sellout to big business!") ". . . do its share to foster the feeling for God in man." ("Better to foster the feeling for man in God," bleated Fra Muttone, obviously present, and itching to get in his clever two cents' worth.) "Brother," Dom Melchior replied this time, "you must know that man's heart is moved only by beauty. Our wish is to live, within these fair walls, a life of true poverty, and to offer a strong Benedictine community a place in which to lead a life of prayer and contemplation. Yes, our efforts have met with a certain resistance. But hasn't that always been true of God's work?" His remarks were greeted with much hooting and howling, and the old monk found himself loathing the crowd. When he knelt for a moment or two before them, they were rather impressed, although no one was aware that he had, in fact, just mortified himself for his momentary lack of Christian charity. It was then, in the midst of an opportune silence, that the cruelest blow of all was struck. A voice speaking out—calm, somber, and controlled —obviously holding back to heighten the effect: "But father, you're a total of eleven monks here at Fontgembar, and it's clear that you'll never be more. In time you're bound to begin dying off, and no one will come fill the gaps. The Abbot Primate will see to that, I assure you. So we're really quite a way from that 'strong Benedictine community' of yours, that you seem to be using as a pretext and excuse. Now then, let's do a little figuring. Let's take a billion francs as a reasonable minimum. For eleven monks, that makes more than ninety million per monk. Which strikes me as rather a high price to pay for a life of poverty! Believe me, father, that's no little venial sin you've got there!" (The quote made the cover of *La Pensée Nouvelle,* against the background of Fontgembar's gothic tower. Exactly the kind of punch Clément Dio liked so much.) The speaker was Dom Paul Pinet. A Benedictine himself, sort of a roving inspector for the Abbot Primate of the Order, he had just arrived, direct from Rome. His Holiness Pope Benedict XVI, deeply shocked at Dom Melchior's excesses, had insisted that stringent measures be taken. The community at Fontgembar, he had ordered, should be disbanded at once, and the abbot dismissed. The buildings themselves, and the vast surrounding lands, should be turned over to the people, perhaps as a kind of farming commune, open to the young of every background and persuasion. (That last idea had sprung from the fertile brain of Dom Pinet, fresh from his success in radicalizing the state of Bahía, in Brazil, by secularizing all the abbeys of the Order.) The day before, Dom Melchior had replied to these several demands with a simple "no" . . . Scarcely had Dom Pinet hurled his accusation, when the old monk fairly bellowed, in a voice that was hard to believe: "Out! All

of you! Get out!" And get out they did, meek as lambs, to a man,
wondering what had happened—as they stood there gazing at the
gates, shut tight and chained—when, after all, they had come for just
one purpose: to "liberate" Fontgembar. At that point, things took a
rather sudden turn. "Let them croak!" one peasant-priest had decided. But a little while later, the monks numbered twelve. What had
happened was this. A few months after his famous declaration
(". . . that's no little venial sin you've got there!"), Dom Paul Pinet
appeared at the abbey. It remains a mystery, even today, what two
men as different as himself and the abbot could say to each other
during their long discussion, or how they could come to some kind
of agreement. The one, a monk straight out of the Middle Ages,
utterly unbending, as sure of his God as he was of himself. The other,
a militant, eager to tear down in order to build, a stranger to anything
and everything supernatural, wearing the habit, but only on rare
occasions, like those labor-camp pajamas ex-prisoners put on to com-
memorate the Holocaust ("Never again!"), out-and-out heretic in the
eyes of Dom Melchior, for whom the Pope was the Antichrist incarnate. And yet, at chapter that evening, the ten old monks looked on
in stunned amazement as their abbot asked them to approve a
strange appointment. Namely, the choice of Dom Pinet as prior of
Fontgembar, next in line to succeed him. Dom Melchior, in effect,
would merely live out the rest of his tenure. No doubt he had buckled
under the immense moral pressure that had set him apart, but hoping in his heart of hearts that God would pass judgment when all was
said and done. Now today, it was clear that God was on his side: He
had kept him alive, with one foot in the grave, for the moment of
truth . . .

"No," the prior replied, "I don't want to be released from my vow.
Events will work things out, believe me. Or divine will, if that's what
you call it."

"Very well, brother," the abbot continued. "You may sit down."

Then he opened the massive New Testament to a page marked
with a long silk ribbon, and he said:

"Brothers, as this new day is born, I should like you to call to mind
Apocalypse, chapter twenty: 'Blessed and holy is he who has part in
the first resurrection! Over these the second death has no power; but
they will be priests of God and Christ, and will reign with him a
thousand years . . .' Such are the words of Saint John, as he speaks of
the grace that lights God's chosen people on the harsh road of life,
to life everlasting and the joys of perfect knowledge. But today,

brothers, the end of the thousand years is upon us . . ."

Bending over the great tome, he read on, slowly: " 'And when the thousand years are ended, Satan will be released from his prison, and will go forth and deceive the nations which are in the four corners of the earth, Gog and Magog, and will gather them together for the battle; the number of whom is as the sand of the sea. And they went up over the breadth of the earth and encompassed the camp of the saints, and the beloved city. And fire from God came down out of heaven and devoured them. And the devil who deceived them was cast into the pool of fire and brimstone, where are also the beast and the false prophet; and they will be tormented day and night forever and ever . . .' And from chapter twenty-one: 'And he who was sitting on the throne said, "Behold, I make all things new! . . . He who overcomes shall possess these things, and I will be his God, and he shall be my son. But as for the cowardly and unbelieving, and abominable and murderers, and fornicators and sorcerers, and idolaters and all liars, their portion shall be in the pool that burns with fire and brimstone, which is the second death." ' Brothers," the abbot concluded, "the days of Gog and Magog are at hand. The nations, like the sand of the sea, have invaded the City. But the just will rise up. They will march with the body of Christ right to the shattered ramparts. . . . Do you think you can walk to the sea, brothers?"

A long murmur of approval rippled through the group. Ten addled old men, all but dead. Ten pious little robots, worn out by an excess of genuflections, vigils, plainchants, and fasts, catching a sudden glimpse of a meaningful demise. Both a final deliverance and a justification of long years in the cloister. "Yes, yes! . . . Forward, march!" they squealed, all aquiver. A few, farther gone than the rest, no longer knew what century it was. Others, shivering at night on their hard wooden benches, dreamed of an all-compassionate God, ready to welcome them with arms outstretched. Yes, march on, march on, to the end, at long last! . . . A dumbfounded Dom Pinet shook his head, struggling to make them listen to reason:

"But it's madness!" he shouted. "It's senility! Vanity! You can't force God's hand. You haven't had a sign. He won't answer you, believe me. He never has. Not for madness like this. You're out of your minds to dream up such a harebrained scheme. All you'll do is lose faith. You'll see, God won't be what you all imagine. What on earth do you hope to accomplish? Do you think you can wave the Host in the air, and hold off a mob? Like back in the days of blind superstition, when the Black Plague would mow down the bishop in his cathedral, just as he prayed to God to protect him!"

He was mumbling, bogging down in his arguments, deeper and deeper, unable to believe he had stooped to such discussion. It almost made him blush with shame.

"Have you finished, brother?" the abbot asked him.

Dom Pinet hung his head in defeat. Yes, of course he had finished. What more could he add, to buck this wall of absolute folly?

"In that case," Dom Melchior went on, "since you are the youngest of our number, and the strongest, you may carry the Host. I'm afraid I haven't the strength, and the rest of our brothers will need all they can muster for the long, hard walk. Luck is with us. The moon is out tonight. It will light our way.... *Exaudi nos, Domine.* Hear our plea, O Lord, Father omnipotent, God of the ages, and in thy mercy send down thy holy Angel from Heaven, that he may guard, support, protect, and defend all these, thy children, here before thee. *Per Christum Dominum nostrum.* Amen."

Outside, a deathly calm gathered around them. Down in the valley below, the little town was plunged in darkness. No more street lamps burning all through the night. No more headlights snaking their usual endless path over the winding highway. None of the array of familiar sounds that, even in the still, small hours, show that life is merely resting. No signs of life at all . . . First they passed through deserted hamlets. Winegrowing villages, nestled against the mountain. Solid, fortresslike villages that had bristled with pikes and slings in days of yore, when the Barbary pirates would foray against the coast, while the tocsin rang, and the priest and women prayed, and the menfolk would fight until victory or death. Now their grandchildren's grandchildren had up and fled. And all that they left in their wake—sole relics of their stay on earth, besides the unyielding vines of the past—were a forest of TV antennas on their roofs, two pinball machines, three table-football games, and the traveling exhibition of satirical cartoons from the weekly *La Grenouille* on display at the Youth and Culture Center. The one building, by the way, whose doors and shutters they hadn't bothered to bolt up tight. Proof that they didn't think too much of the place and deserted it with pleasure, or perhaps that they fed it to the flames to save the rest. Strung out across the front was a streamer proclaiming: "WE'RE ALL FROM THE GANGES NOW!" (The things the children did those days to have their fun! Instead of kicking a ball around, or hunting for mushrooms, or dressing their dolls!) And right underneath, on another streamer: "FREE FONTGEMBAR! DOWN

WITH MILLIONAIRE MONKS!" Yes, sweet little kids . . . Their parents had stood by while the brats (and those who pulled their strings) dabbled with hate to their hearts' content, stepping in just in time to bundle their offspring into the car and beat a retreat.

Along the highway, the old monks trudged on, hardly able to put one foot before the other, voices quivering out a Gregorian chant to help them keep pace. No less silly a tune than the ones Boy Scouts march to, but more apropos, and one they knew by heart: the litany of the saints. Droning on and on. *Sancte Petre, ora pro nobis. Sancte Paule, ora pro nobis* . . . And the dozens and dozens expunged, long since, from Rome's official pantheon: Saint Nicholas (little children), Saint George (the dragon), Saint Anthony (lost belongings), Saint Pulcheria (fertility), Saint Melorius (calm waters) . . . Leading the procession, Dom Paul Pinet. Teeth clenched, fingers clutching at the monstrance, he suspected the abbot of adding to the list, and even of dreaming up a few new saints, the way he had dreamed up a God to his liking. ("Saint Baptitian!" the old monk would intone. *"Ora pro nobis!"* the doddering band would answer.) Which is just what Dom Melchior was doing, in fact, inventing as he went, and laughing up his sleeve, as if he were putting one over on Churchdom's priggish powers that be. Were they passing a fountain? A patron saint of fountains seemed in order, and Saint Baptitian was born. Was his foot getting sore? Well, who cures ingrown toenails? Saint Podiatron, who else! . . . It was really great sport. Saints no one had ever heard of. Very much in his style. (After all, hadn't he filled a whole hall in his abbey with tawdry horrors, those hideous statues that every church for miles around had dumped in the trash, votive offerings included? He had cherished and preserved them, paid them visits every night. And from time to time he would kneel down before one and pray, with a smile, while Dom Pinet would look on in silence, assessing the toll that senility had taken. Then one day, finally, the prior had asked him, "Just how long do you intend to keep those monstrosities?" And Dom Melchior had replied: "Until they're replaced. Yes, they're ugly, I admit. But our men of the cloth have no taste in art these days. They're too proletarian even to notice. That isn't the reason. It's the saints they were trying to kill, not their statues . . .") Next in the litany came the legion of Our-Ladys-of-this-and-of-that, drummed out of the corps as Marian deviationists, longtime foes of the party line. Then all the archangels of legend and myth, those wielders of sword and of flame, whose wings had been butchered to bits, ad lib, by the surgeons of the great ecumenical cause. Real or fictitious, they were all called up to serve ... As the band reached the outskirts of a town close by the coast, the abbot felt he could do with a moment to catch his breath. He gestured for a halt. But none of the old monks, feeble though they were, would sit on the ground in the presence of the Host. (Besides, if they had, they would never have gotten up.) Instead, they just stood there, agog and atremble, all slobber, spit and sputter. Like a scraggy clump of leafless black trees, swaying in the wind ...

Drained of its inhabitants, the town had managed to preserve their hatred. Everywhere you looked. Outside the parish hall: "MONEY = MORTAL SIN!" On the walls that ringed the villas where the bosses used to live: "KILL THE CAPITALIST BOURGEOIS PIGS!" Unlike the other less pretentious houses, with their doors and shutters all carefully closed, these villas had the look of a battleground about them. Broken windows, ripped off their hinges. Furniture hacked to pieces, strewn about the grass. Mattresses slashed, stuffing bulging from their guts, pathetically dangling from ornamental railings. Flowers trampled in the gardens. And this time the troops of Panama Ranger weren't the least bit to blame. The people. No one but the people. They had watched as the rich, first to pick up and run, crammed their autos (too big) with their baggage (too much), while they (too many) packed their own cars (too small) with belongings (too few). And their blood, in short, had begun to boil. So much so, that before skipping out themselves, they had eked out one hour to take their revenge. Grim revel, though. They were in rather a hurry, too. (No time to laugh and sing, or to dance the old Revolutionary rounds while the bonfires fed on the rich man's wealth, the way people did back when it all began, in the days of the Terror.) Hearts full of hate, bellies full of fear. And only time enough to go through the motions. No strength to clutch at the myth of the Ganges, turn it into a sword, or a battering ram, or a bulwark of faith. Just a sly parting kick, with no risk whatever, and off to the north, every man for himself, and the rich can go hang. ("Wait, who's gonna give us jobs, goddammit?") Heaven knows how much talk had gone on, those last weeks, in the plants where they earned their bread after a fashion, and not a bad fashion at that! The walls were still dripping with their fresh-spewed slogans: "WORKERS, GANGES REFUGEES, UNITED FOR FREEDOM!," "BOSSES OUT, PEOPLE IN!") And in the end, utter panic. Stampede. Empty streets ...

"I wonder," said the abbot, standing in the moonlight, gazing at the walls and their verbal barrage, "why they didn't make the most of their chance once they had it. When you make a great show of believing in something, you go all the way. That is, if you're really a man."

They had started up again, stumbling and staggering over the pavement. From time to time one aged brother would fall, palms scraping against the sidewalk, bleeding, and the abbot, apparently still going strong, would help him to his feet. Another's forehead was covered with blood. "Ah, martyrdom!" sighed Dom Melchior with a smile, as if it were some kind of blessing from Heaven. . . . The old monks were following blindly along now. They had stopped their chanting, saint after saint, and would ask now and then, whining like so many tired little children: "How much longer, father? Are we almost there?" Once past the factory just beyond the town, as they reached a grove of fragrant pines, Dom Paul Pinet, at the head of the procession, stopped abruptly in his tracks. He turned and faced Dom Melchior squarely. And there followed what must have been the strangest exchange in the annals of the Church, between an abbot, standing with his miter on his head, and one of his monks, Blessed Sacrament in hand, that holy white wafer in its sunburst of gold.

"No!" exclaimed the prior. "Enough is enough! How long will you keep up this silly charade? It's beneath you, father. And beneath me, too. Why, it's making a mockery of these poor old souls, dragging along like a bunch of tired sheep. And for something you've dreamed up out of whole cloth! Well, I see through it all. And I see through you. Tell me, father, when did you lose your faith?"

The abbot smiled. His reply was soft and calm:

"Please, Brother Paul, be careful what you say. Don't forget, you're carrying the body of Christ."

"Then here! You take it! It's your turn now. We're almost there. And besides, what's the difference?" (He was holding the monstrance out at arm's length.) "There's nothing in there anyway. Just a lot of foolish nonsense!"

Dom Melchior didn't budge. He stood with his eyes riveted to the Host. Finally he answered:

"Don't you think I've known that all along? No, I haven't lost my faith, Brother Paul. I really never had it. Like a lot of our finest priests these days. And even some of our finest popes. No question, Benedict XVI has faith. It's eating him up. Just look at the havoc he's wrought in its name. At least, what passes for faith in his mind. Because real faith, the kind that moves mountains, I mean, simply doesn't exist. It's all just a pose. All pretense and sham. That's why it's so strong.

Faith, you say? No, Brother Paul, I only wish I . . ."

His sentence hung in midair. All at once a man loomed out of the pines, from his resting place after a long trek on foot. A young man. Corduroy pants, suede jacket. Pretty curly blond hair. Winsome good looks, despite the fatigue that furrowed his classic features.

"If you want, father, I'll carry the Host the rest of the way. Or until you're ready to carry it yourself."

"Are you a priest?"

"Yes, I am."

"What's your name?"

"Pierre Chassal."

"Abbé Chassal?" exclaimed Dom Pinet, who hadn't taken his eyes off the young man. "Not you! You haven't come all this way to recant! Not today, of all days!"

A few years before, Abbé Chassal's name had been a household word. A young priest destined for a brilliant career, he had married a beautiful, chic young thing—at the archbishop's palace in Paris, no less—daughter of a prominent Parisian family, and in no time the couple's name was on everybody's lips. Toast of the new, progressive Church. As a spouse of the cloth, little Lydie had developed a style all her own. Photographers loved to take her picture, erotic as could be—long hair down the back, long skirts, black boots—and all the more, since everyone knew how she lusted after Pierre's priestly flesh. As for him, he reveled in his untoward role. "Lydie," he would say, "is my pathway to Christ." And what's more, he meant it. Enough to write it in papers and books. Enough to repeat it over television and radio. Standard-bearer of the updated Church, he had set out (with the archbishop's blessing, by the way) to rebuild the priesthood, revamp the Church, and refashion faith itself. Many followed his example and took themselves wives, though rarely with his flair. Cheap, ugly, vulgar types, for the most part, these padre chasers. And Pierre's Lydie reigned supreme. Then one fine day, silence. Our famous couple had dropped out of sight, and no more was heard about Abbé Chassal. Cleric turned cuckold, he had holed up in an obscure little parish on the wrong side of town, and promptly gone to seed . . .

"Yes, today," the young priest replied. "Today we're all recanting, more or less. Trying to find out where we really belong."

"But this . . . this charade!" Dom Pinet objected.

"I've played plenty of charades in my time. This one will make up for the rest. May as well go out in a blaze of glory."

"What are you doing here?" Dom Melchior asked.

"I came south like a lot of other priests, father, to hail what I thought would be mankind's redemption. To welcome the million Christs on board those ships, who would rise up, reborn, and signal the dawn of a just, new day. . . . We were five in my car. Not far up the road, we ran out of gas. So we started to walk. As we passed through the town, looking for something to eat, we saw you go by. I told the others: 'Look, you go on. I'll catch up later. I'm going to follow them. I want to watch the past gasp its last . . .' Well I did. I followed you. And what I saw touched me."

What he failed to mention was that, all along the way, he was touched no less by his own situation than he was by the doddering Benedictine band, staggering off to the last crusade. And he would moan as he walked: "My Lydie! My Lydie! Why hast thou forsaken me?" (Well, not quite, but almost . . .) But each time an old monk would stumble, each time the blood would trickle from a forehead, down a sunken gray cheek, his Lydie would fall further and further into the background, until she was all but forgotten, and Abbé Chassal was finally at peace.

"Did you hear what Dom Paul and I were saying just now?" the abbot asked him.

"Yes, I did."

"And you weren't put off?"

"No, it helped me understand myself better."

"You mean you've lost faith too?"

"I suppose so. That is, if I had it to begin with. Still, I've never felt happier than I do this morning. Or more content. I guess I chose the wrong pose before. All that pretense and sham . . ."

"Kneel down, brother, and I'll give you my blessing. Then our brother Paul will let you take his place. He'll be leaving us now. He still has his own brand of faith, but he seems to have stopped believing that the Host is the body of an omnipotent Christ. So we'll let him go off and welcome the Christs he believes in. And we'll keep the one we have. He suits us best. If, at the last minute, no sign from Heaven saves us, what does it really matter, after all? At least we won't have broken faith with ourselves. *Benedicat vos omnipotens Deus . . .*"

When the young man stood up, Dom Pinet thrust the monstrance into his hands, turned on his heels, and went striding off without a word.

"Brother Paul," the abbot called after him. "Aren't you going to embrace me before you leave?"

The prior froze in his tracks. He arched his back, as if bucking a gale.

"Let's not cut corners," Dom Melchior continued. "Let's act out the play just the way it was written. We're all that's left of the latter-day Church. No bigger than the handful when it all began. Since you made up your mind from the start to betray us, you may as well play out your role to the end. Come, give me the kiss of peace. Come, be my Judas . . ."

The latter-day Church stood whimpering about, with hardly a notion of what was going on. One was idly wiping his bruised and bleeding feet, raw from all the walking. Another was mumbling scraps of disjointed prayers that had managed to escape from the shipwreck of his mind. A third was smiling a beatific smile, while his neighbor—with no idea where he was or why—was crying his eyes out like a little lost babe. And one by one they would groan the same question: "How much longer, father? Are we almost there?"

Dom Pinet heard them, gave a shrug, and ran off down the road. Headlong flight. Clean break with the past. The old life ends, the new one begins. And he ran like a madman, as if the twenty centuries past, now over and done with, were hounding his tracks. As if he feared he might still be caught . . . The road led down to the sea. Panting, he reached the first cottages that lined the shore, and stopped to catch his breath. In no time he found himself surrounded by a crowd. A ragged young band, standing there leering, eyeing him up and down. (Some seemed to be grimacing, screwing up their noses, like a dog when he tries to place a new smell. They belonged to a group of people's theater, who had given up language for animal gestures, and whose whiffs and sniffs were their sign for confusion.) One especially dark young lady—hair down her back, huge deep-set eyes—took one look at Dom Pinet, and jibed: "What a nice little monk! Why, I bet you've got the prettiest string of big wooden beads!" He took out his rosary, hardly thinking, and held it up to show her. "Neat!" she exclaimed, and put it around her neck. A moment later, a smiling young giant had elbowed his way up front.

"See what we've got, Panama?" one of the men shouted. "A priest, of all things!"

"Good God! Just what we needed! Like we don't have enough already! And this one's not even in uniform . . . Say man, I bet you're some kind of real priest, aren't you? That kind that don't fuck between masses, I mean. What the hell are you doing here?"

"The same as you," Dom Pinet replied. "I'm here to watch the landing. There's a big deserted abbey not far up the road, back where I came from. With huge fields and gardens. And I'm going to take our poor starving brothers there, as soon as they land."

They let out a cheer, but their joy only seemed to sadden the monk.

"I know what you need, daddy," said the dark young lady, taking his hand. "You're not too old. And you're still good-looking, with those big black eyes. Besides, I have a real thing for rosaries. Wear them all the time. Even when I'm making love. That way, there's three of us. And my guy can give Jesus a nice big kiss between my tits. My name is Lydie. I'm nuts about priests. Come on, daddy, we don't have much time. Let's go make love. You've earned it."

The crowd parted to let them through, in a great smiling show of fraternal affection. "Maybe I'll have to," thought Dom Pinet. "The old life ends, the new one begins." Lydie gently squeezed his hand. Nothing nasty or ugly. All perfectly pleasant. But somehow he couldn't respond to their smiles. His lips froze, hard as he tried. The current of joy refused to flow. The sap wouldn't rise.

"What's the trouble, padre?" asked Panama Ranger. "Why so nervous? We're all your buddies. No one's trying to give you shit. And if you're still a virgin, man, no sweat. Lydie'll show you how. Or maybe your robe's in your way. Is that it? Well, rip it off, padre! Rip it off! When the sun comes up, that robe won't be worth a damn anyhow, believe me!"

Dom Pinet blushed.

"It's . . . It's not that," he stammered. "It's just that, in a couple of minutes . . . There are twelve old monks behind me, heading this way. A kind of procession. With the Blessed Sacrament, you know what I mean? And an abbot who looks like a bishop, with a miter . . ."

"What the fuck are they doing down here?"

"They say that the Host will stop the landing."

The troop let out a round of guffaws. The concept amused them.

"Shut up, you assholes," Panama Ranger ordered. "That's nothing to laugh at. It's kind of a nice idea. I like it. How about you, padre? Do you believe it too?"

"No."

"And them? Do they?"

"No, they don't either."

"Well, it's too damn deep for me. But look, man, as long as no one believes it, why not let them go hang, and take care of Lydie? Who cares what they do? It's no skin off your ass!"

"But we've got to stop them. They mustn't reach the water."

"Wait a minute," replied Panama Ranger. "I'm beginning to get the picture. It's like you haven't had your shots, right? I mean, like you still believe, is that it? You've tried your best, but it's kind of too late for you. So we're going to have to help you. You want me to block the road? You want me to head off your conscience for you? All right, don't worry. Your twelve old farts won't get by. Now scram! Come on, padre, into the sack! If you play your cards right, you and the Hindus can come off together. Them off their boats, and you here in bed. Believe me, man, this is your day to be born. I can see you now up in that abbey. You and Lydie, and a bunch from the Ganges. We'll send you a gang to help you . . ."

From the nearby shore a metallic voice boomed out over a megaphone:

"Screw you all, goddammit!"

"That's Dragasès," observed Panama Ranger. "Let the bastard have his fun! Soon he'll be all alone, and that'll be that."

The reply shot back from every house around. Like infants trying their lungs, the boys and girls bellowed:

"Pig! Prick! Asshole! Filthy bastard! Cocksucker! Motherfucker! Murderer! Fascist!"

From the roof of Dragasès's villa, a machine gun spat out a few quick rounds.

"The son of a bitch still has his teeth!" cried Panama Ranger.

From behind a garden wall he looked out onto the road, where they had all been standing a few minutes before. The first shots had scattered his faithful band, leaving ten or so lying wounded on the pavement. Whining, wailing, crying for their mothers. A few were crawling on their bellies—like snails trying to slither into the shade —and streaking a long trail of blood behind them. In the midst of all these sprawling figures, Dom Pinet stood erect, like a statue, hardly moving. He was clutching Lydie's hand in his, so tightly that nothing could have pulled her away. She was trembling. Then screaming.

"For God's sake, man," cried Panama Ranger, "what the fuck are you up to? Are you trying to get the both of you killed? Is that it, padre?"

The machine gun let loose with a final volley, and everyone realized that this was one padre who had managed, at long last, to square himself with his conscience. His body slumped as the bullets ripped through it, then went limp and crumpled to the ground. His fingers opened and released Lydie's hand.

"Lydie! Lydie! Get the hell down!" shouted Panama Ranger.

No need now. The shooting had stopped. Just up the road, coming right down the middle, marched the twelve old monks. They had spread out a canopy, and the abbot was walking beneath it, clutching at the monstrance. They were chanting. *Sancte Paule, Sancte Petre* ... But this time only authentic saints. For the few steps they still had left, the handful of saints not yet expunged would more than suffice. They were almost there. Podiatron and Baptitian couldn't help them much now, at the moment of truth. .... They filed between two lines of young people, some of whose faces even seemed to express a new kind of respect. The more sensitive of the lot. The ones who were beginning to doubt themselves, touched by the sight of a hopeless cause. A sight that brings out the best in a young man. Theirs too was a hopeless cause, after all, though only a pitiful few came to sense it. And those, too late. But perhaps it was just as well that way, since even Dom Melchior himself had stopped believing, and was nothing more now than a child's silly top, set spinning two thousand years ago, and wobbling, wobbling, about to fall ...

Then the silence was broken, and with it that hint of sympathetic feeling that many had started to find unhealthy. The abbot stopped a moment before the body of Paul Pinet. Only the closest ones heard him murmur, "It were better for that man if he had not been born . . ."

"Oh no!" someone cried out. "Not those words, thank you!"

Christ's words, just before the Last Supper, moments after he had told the Apostles that one of the twelve was going to betray him. Now, no one is quicker to recognize the Gospels than a defrocked priest, since they're always picking through them, Heaven only knows, to find some excuse for their own misbehavior. The speaker was a case in point. And he went on, shouting:

"Fontgembar monks! Hypocrite Christians! Pious frauds! Capitalist lackeys! No-good old bastards!"

The quality of insults declined in clear progression. The latter-day priests rejoined their age, much to their own relief, as hoots and shouts broke out from every direction. The respite from hate had been very short-lived. When it clings to the skin and gums up the heart, it's not easy to control it.

"Shut up!" cried Panama Ranger. "Let them by!"

Then he turned toward the villa, put his hands around his mouth, and called out:

"Dragasès, you asshole! Here's some reinforcements for you!"

Which sent his band into gales of laughter, as the twelve "reinforcements" stumbled off into the distance, like robots about to come unhinged. In the background, walking them along their way, the sarcastic twang of guitars, strumming out black tunes to a syncopated beat. And what fun it was to watch the old men stagger and reel, one after the other, slip, trip, almost fall, then catch themselves and push doggedly on, come hell or high water, like strange little antique music-box figures, all jerks and twitches. At the head of the procession walked Abbé Chassal. But he wasn't stumbling. Hands joined, he was praying. Every now and again he would turn and glance back over his shoulder, ready to spell Dom Melchior, if need be. (No need, the abbot was still going strong, still holding the monstrance out high before him.) It was only as he turned to take one last look—as Dragasès's sentries came into view—that he caught sight of Lydie. When the snide guitar escort had turned around at the border, bowing out with a mean little musical sneer, Lydie hadn't joined them. She had stayed behind, and was standing alone in the middle of the road, confused, as if somehow there were something she had missed. It was then that he saw her. Then, too, that he promptly proceeded to forget her. The long nights of love in this woman's arms, the masses intoned scant moments after, her image on the Host as he bowed at the altar for the consecration ... No, none of all that had ever existed. Abbé Chassal was praying. To whom, he couldn't say, or why. But one thing he knew. He had heard the call. It was finally clear that, if God exists, He had put Lydie here on this earth for one reason: to lead him astray. Lydie, the Ganges, his past transgressions, the illusion of man's redemption—it was all blending now into one huge temptation, and he turned his back, calmly spurning it forever. (Not unusual, really. Hopeless causes—even bad ones, or ones condemned, at least, by the mass of opinion—always attract their last-minute champions, bound and determined for no apparent reason. The ones you would least expect, whose sacrifice wipes clean what seemed to be the evils, and justifies everything one wanted to destroy. And we wonder, "what if they were right?" But by then it's too late. The wheel has turned ... History is strewn with the corpses of those heroes, with never a monument to call them to mind. No doubt, in the realm of the dead, they've built themselves a world quite different from our own, but one where we too would feel very much at home, if only we hadn't destroyed our moral fiber ...)

"Glad to have you, gentlemen!" cried a voice from a rooftop. "But just how far do you think you're going?"

Standing on his terrace, legs spread, arms akimbo—as if he were

master of the whole wide world—Colonel Dragasès stared at the
weary little band. Clearly they had no intention of stopping. They
hadn't even looked up. They seemed unaware that the soldiers were
there. He called out to warn them:

"Hey you! Father! You're less than fifty yards from the water. If
that mob lands all at once, you'll be trampled to death. We won't be
able to help you. Don't go any further. It's suicide, believe me!"

But they walked on, like ghosts. No more chanting. No more whining. Gliding noiselessly along, bare feet hardly scraping the gravel-
paved road. The sun had come up, and its sidelong rays, setting the
gold of the monstrance ablaze, turned the Sacred Host into a floating
ball of flame. Silence, heavy and complete, hung over the sea, the
shore, the houses. And over the whole of the landscape beyond.
Flights of seagulls flew by without so much as a peep; while down on
the ground, the moles, mice, and rats were deserting their burrows
and scampering off. All the fauna still left in this part of the coast
were scurrying north. The spontaneous migration just before the
disaster . . .

"My dear Colonel," asked Jean Perret, "what does the book say a
unit should do when the Blessed Sacrament goes by?"

"Time was, monsieur, you presented the colors and told the bugles
to sound a review. But today, who knows? No one has any feeling for
the tried and true theatrics. They want to be free to follow their
conscience. Especially soldiers. So I guess you can stick your finger
in your nose, or turn your back, or stop what you're doing and kneel.
Take your pick."

"Well then, I think I'll kneel."

"You're the government now, monsieur," said the colonel, eyes
twinkling. (They were both enjoying themselves to the fullest, living
their roles in absolute earnest.) "Whatever you say goes. I'll see that
the army obeys your orders."

And he barked:

"Everyone down on your knees over there! And let's not forget
how we cross ourselves either! Forehead, chest, left shoulder, right
shoulder. All right, men. Hop to it!"

Around the villa and under the trees, twenty hussars and a captain,
genuflecting. On the left flank, another captain and six marine commandos, reciting the Paratrooper's Prayer (". . . and give us, O Lord,
what no one else will touch . . ."). On the right flank, nothing. For
the simple reason that the right flank had vanished. Abandoned rifles
lay scattered on the path of its final desertion. One last lieutenant,

hidden by a thicket, hesitated a moment, crossed himself, and ran off behind a pack of gigantic rats, northward. The ghost of the army had paid its respects to the ghost of religion . . .

Standing on shore, with their feet in the water, the monks had finally stopped. Twenty yards lay between them and the grounded prow of the *India Star*. Twenty yards of shallow water, clear and blue, translucent in the morning light, symbol of all that was left to protect the past from the future. The chasm between two worlds would be filled. The sole defense of the Western World was this saltwater Rubicon, this expanse that even a child of five could cross on foot, so long as he kept his chin above the waves. But Rubicons have little but emotional value. Their banks widen or narrow, as the case may be, depending on the cowardice or courage of their dwellers. And this one was no exception. No need to look further for another explanation . . .

The colonel had come down from the terrace of his villa, and stood waiting in the garden, leaning against the railing that ran alongside the beach. Close by, the undersecretary and the army. And up on the roof, the last machine gun aimed out to sea.

"Almost six o'clock," he said. "The barbarians are late. You'll see. As the years go by, things are going to get later and later."

He turned around and pointed to a spot up the slope of the mountain behind them.

"You see that village? Well, when I order a withdrawal—which shouldn't be long now, I don't imagine—we'll regroup up there. Will you be with us, Monsieur Perret?"

"Of course. But why that village? Why not one of the others?"

"Probably because I like it. No other reason. I've taken a shine to it, all the way from here. See how nice its proportions are? How it clings to the land, how it looks like the kind of place you'd want to live in? We've got to finish our little drama somewhere. May as well pick a setting that's going to make us happy . . ."

Up in the village, his eye pressed to the spyglass, old Monsieur Calguès watched and smiled. He seemed to know just what the colonel was thinking. And why not? Partaking of the same communion of thought, it was no surprise that they should understand each other, even at such long range. That was part of the Western genius, too: a mannered mentality, a collusion of aesthetes, a conspiracy of caste, a good-natured indifference to the crass and the common. With so few left now to share in its virtues, the current passed all the more easily between them.

On the bridge of the *India Star*, the monster child in his fancy cap suddenly began to drool. And the deck came alive, a billow of concentric circles. A thickening mass of human flesh, as every body rose to its feet. Then the next ship, and the next, and the ones after that.

"The jig is up," said the colonel, simply.

Too well bred to indulge in a memorable mot! But that one said it all, and he tossed it off with a little mock salute.

Forty-three

The West had just been through its longest day. This was the shortest. In five minutes everything was settled. And although the shock left a score of cadavers lying on the beach, evenly divided between the two sides, still, it wouldn't be right to speak of a battle, or a skirmish, or even a scuffle in fact. It was, without question, by far the least deadly of all of mankind's total wars. What struck the Western observers the most—those few who would speak to historians later— was clearly the smell. They all described it in much the same terms: "It stunk to high heaven . . . It bowled you over, wouldn't let you breathe . . ." As the decks sprang to life with their myriad bodies— men, women, children, steeping in dung and debris since Calcutta —as the hatchways puked out into the sunlight the sweating, starving mass, stewing in urine and noxious gases deep in the bowels of the ships, the stench became so thick you could practically see it. At the same time, a strong, hot wind had gusted up from the south, the kind that always heralds a storm, and it smelled as if some vile, rotting monster, jaws agape, were blowing its lungs out in huge, fetid blasts. Not the least of the reasons for the rapid defection of the bulk of Panama Ranger's doughty band. Later, when the history of brotherhood's D Day was officially rewritten, their rout was explained as "the forward unit's march to the rear, to prepare appropriate welcoming procedures." (How's that for a laugh!) The plain, simple fact was that, half in shock and half in terror, the sweet little dears held their noses and ran. How could a good cause smell so bad? The thought had never crossed their minds. They were too immature. They should have known. It's the evil causes that smell the best. Like progress, prosperity, money, luxury, ethical conduct, and nonsense like that. Or maybe it suddenly struck them—too late—that they really had picked the wrong side after all. And although, in their anguish, they didn't cry for Mommy, the image that sprang up in many a mind was a little white fifth-floor kitchen—staircase K, building C, low-rent housing unit outside of town—and in it a nice, trim, middle-class mother, vision of happiness now lost and gone forever . . .

"What a goddamn mob!" said Dragasès. "Not going to give us

much breathing room, are they! Good God, what a stink!"

He tied his handkerchief around his face. Only two sardonic eyes shone under his helmet. And he watched as Jean Perret and the twenty hussars did likewise. Then he added:

"See? We're outlaws all of a sudden! It doesn't take much!"

"Well, Colonel old boy," the undersecretary interrupted. "I think our job is cut out for us now. That's something, at least. Why stand on ceremony? Let's see how you're going to get out of this one! Look, it's so thick with bodies, you can't see any water between the boats and the beach."

True. But for that matter you couldn't see the boats now, either. Their sides were alive, like an anthill slashed open. Using whatever they could lay their hands on—cords, cables, hawsers, worm-eaten rope ladders, loading nets lowered along the hulls—the horde was slipping down into the water. Endless cascade of human flesh. Every one of the boats, teeming, gushing with bodies, like a tub brimming over. Yes, the Third World had started to overflow its banks, and the West was its sewer. Perched on the shoulders of strapping young boys, first to land were the monsters, the grotesque little beggars from the streets of Calcutta. As they groveled through the wet sand like a pack of basset hounds, or a herd of clumsy seals exploring an unfamiliar shore, with their snorts and grunts of joy, they looked like an army of little green men from some remote planet. Behind them the bulk of the mob marked time: up on the bridge stood the dwarf, cap on head, staring blankly at the beach, as if waiting for a message from his hideous cohorts, some kind of report telepathically transmit-ted. And the monsters snuffled and sniffed at the sand, mouthed it by the handful, struck it with their fists to make sure it was real, and, convinced that it was, sprang somersaults over their horrid, twisted limbs. Yes, the country would suit them fine. No question . . . They jumped up all at once. Clearly that was the sign. A great hue and cry rose over the fleet. The human cascade began pouring again down the sides of the ships, swelling into huge wave upon wave of flesh, bodies upon bodies, pushing, shoving toward the shore, rolling in to the monsters and moving them along.

"They're too horrible to look at," said the colonel, coldly. "It's too much, damn it! We can't let something like that go on living. They don't have the right . . ." And he shouted out, "Captain!"

He was calling to the officer up˙on the roof, squatting next to his machine gun, ready to fire.

"Come now, you're not going to shoot into *that!*" exclaimed Jean Perret.

"Yes, precisely! That! I can't stand the sight of those miserable, ugly bastards leading the pack, like a goddamn flag. The least I can do is shoot down the flag!"

"But you won't make a dent!"

"Maybe not. Too bad. But we've got to put some order in that filthy mess somehow. Even if it won't make a damn bit of difference. We're a symbol. Those freaks are a symbol. So we'll spray them with a round of symbolic bullets, and if some of them croak, well, so much the better! At least yours truly will know the reason why." And he called out, "Let's go up there, Captain. If you've still got a conscience, now's the time to forget it. Sit on it, damn it! And for God's sake, fire!"

The machine gun loosed a long, crackling volley. Like target practice. Then silence . . . There's nothing more ghastly to watch than misshapen gnomes or mental misfits writhing in pain. Caricatures of suffering bodies. Blank, gaping stares, trying to comprehend. Blood flowing from monstrous, malformed flesh. Inhuman cries from the lips of the dying . . . Ten lay there on the sand, in the throes of death.

"Nice martyrs," the colonel observed. "A present to the new world, compliments of Constantine Dragasès! You'll see, it'll put them to damn good use!"

On the roof, the captain fired off his last shot. From his pistol, this time, stuck into his mouth. Ten helpless dwarfs, lying murdered on the beach. And a first-rate officer . . . Pffft! Just like that!

"He had no choice," said the colonel, very matter-of-fact. "I knew that would happen. Once the sun came up, it started him thinking. Plain as the nose on his face. Started him asking questions, but not about himself. About them, and how he fit into the picture. If he thought like a leader, it would have been different. Like a real man, I mean. But no, not a chance! You can bet your sweet ass, when he pulled that trigger, he felt like one of those grisly bastards! Tried his best, but just couldn't hold out. Got sucked in by all that brotherhood crap! Like a goddamn epidemic. Well, you see where it got him! . . . All right, let's beat it. No time to stand around and chat . . ."

"Then you practically killed him," Jean Perret interrupted. "Why? If you knew . . ."

"Look," Dragasès replied, "we may as well clean out all our traitors right now, even the ones who don't know that they are, who could screw us to the wall, good intentions notwithstanding. Last-minute traitors are the worst kind of all. Once we're up in The Village . . ." (He pronounced the words with a touch of solemnity that merits the use of capitals from now on.) ". . . we'll refuse to admit they exist. Take a look behind you. You'll see, they're on their way."

Jean Perret turned away from the water. In front of him, nothing but the flashing of boot heels, beating a quick retreat between the trees, and the backs of speckled uniforms disappearing in the distance ... The last of the hussars were turning and running. One of them shouted, as he dashed from the villa, with the long, silent strides of an old campaigner, "Good luck anyway, Colonel!" And the sound of his voice made it clear he wasn't joking. A sad farewell. A couple of words that said it all. Sorry, Colonel, we can't go along with you this time, this is how it's got to be, we're taking our conscience but we'll leave our hearts behind ...

"No regrets," said the colonel. "No, no regrets, really. Though I guess I should have let them all be killed, last night, like Commander de Poudis. And their officer with them. What kind of a world will it be for them now, dragging out their useless lives? ... Monsieur Perret ..." (He was smiling again.) "... let's be on our way! Forces of law and order, regroup!"

One truck was enough. Law and order didn't amount to much. No more than a handful. A sergeant and three hussars, the marine commando captain and five of his men, the colonel, and the undersecretary. Twelve in all.

"Nice number," remarked the colonel, as he jumped in next to the driver. "Now step on it!" he told him. "Turn right out the gate, then your second left. That'll take us to the highway. And if anyone tries to get in your way, run the bastards down ..."

"Wait," Jean Perret shouted, suddenly remembering. "What about the monks?"

Dragasès shrugged. The truck was already rolling, picking up speed down the sandy path outside the villa, shifting from first, to second, to third, sharp turn at the gate, motor rumbling and roaring. Submachine gun on his lap, the colonel pressed his nose against the window, peered out at the street, poised and ready to fire. But the street was empty.

"The monks?" he repeated, finally. "My dear Perret, in a righteous cause like ours, we've got to have our martyrs. Got to even the score, if you know what I mean. Our side and theirs. Their freaks, our monks. Without a few martyrs, it wouldn't be healthy. If it makes you feel better, we'll stick up a monument to them in The Village. In front of the church. How's that? With a nice little inscription: 'To the twelve monks of Fontgembar Abbey, massacred on Easter Monday, victims of the barbaric ...' Barbaric what, in fact?"

Like law and order, the monks had amounted to little or nothing.

Victims of their trade, in a manner of speaking. The moment the monsters had bitten the dust, splashing in their blood just a few yards away, the good monks had rushed to their side without thinking. Reflex action of sorts. Very fitting and proper, professionally speaking, at least if one stops to consider their age, which imposed certain rather outmoded ideals. At any rate, there they were, kneeling on the ground, each one beside his expiring little creature, all moving their lips and waving their hands in the sign of the cross. A scene hard to imagine. Even harder to believe, if you think what they were doing. Baptizing, no less! Perfectly correct and according to the rules, this slapdash rite for infants dead or dying. God's mercy allowed it in times gone by, before today's clerics got a notion to change things. "I baptize you Peter, or Paul, or whatever, in the name of the Father, and the Son, and the Holy Ghost . . ." As simple as that. Ten seconds, that's all. Which is just what the addled old monks were doing, caught up in a sudden flash of grace. (How else can we explain that return to the quintessential, to the source of it all, when everything around them, in fact, was about to end?) And so, ten ignorant, mindless Ganges monsters, misery incarnate, absolute zeros in the warp and woof of life, rose to Heaven that morning, no doubt to a blare of trumpets triumphant, as millions of the Blessed cooed a sweet, celestial welcome to their tardy and most unexpected brethren! If there really is a guard at the gates of paradise, he must have given a wry little smirk, with a roll of his eyes, pretending to be cross: "Who on earth sent me up such a bunch of crazy names? Baptitian? Podiatron? Never heard of them! . . . Hmm! Oh, all right, go ahead. You may as well go in . . ." In the heat of the moment, the monks had dredged up whatever they could find in their worn-out old brains. But if there are still any Roman Catholics left today, any priests who still believe in baptism's power and glory, they needn't have the slightest qualms. Yes, Podiatron and Baptitian! Good names to know, proper saints to pray to! Protection guaranteed! Grotesque little duo, wrenched from the womb, now grown handsome as gods and wise as the Holy Ghost, sitting at the left hand of the Father Almighty, who indulges their every silly, saintly whim. *Ora pro nobis* . . . The ten seconds were up. Then death passed through, whisking off monsters and monks together. And after the horde, there was nothing left of the mingled corpses but a hand sticking up from the blood-soaked beach, a naked foot, the tip of a chin or perhaps a nose, an occasional face, vaguely seen through the sand, like a mummy in its wrappings. The shock of the first wave streaming off the ships had taken the old monks completely by surprise, as they knelt, heads bent, over each upturned brow, as if to unite them in the last breath of life. Moments later, the mob had trampled them all to death. Surging blindly forward. Unthinking, unwitting. Already gazing at the seaside villas, reveling in the windblown trees and flowers, probing with countless hands the first elegant railings that lined the beach, clambering, climbing, swarming through parlors and out other doors, pouring into the streets, still the same dense tide; but for those twenty martyred corpses the stampede had barely begun, stretching back to the ships, where the boa-like mass of starving human flesh was winding about in ring upon ring, each one waiting its turn to uncoil and strike.

The strangest conclusion one can draw from these five crucial minutes of that shortest day—though it would have been perfectly clear, had one bothered to read the signs—is the fact that the refugee horde seemed so blithely unaware that this land it was about to make its own could possibly belong to others already. It had, indeed, been drained of its human substance, and offered no resistance. And yet, there were many and sundry on the beach, though all for very different reasons: the monks, Dragasès and his men, as well as a rather goodly number of die-hard idealists who had stayed behind with Panama Ranger when the rest of his troop had gone running. With only one exception—a deliberate, gratuitous murder that we'll go into later—the mob, as we said, was merely passing through. If it happened to trample a few bodies in the bargain, it had no idea, surely, whose they were, or why. It crushed them to pulp just because they were there. Ganges monsters, Western monks. It made no distinction. It saw itself now as the one and only race. All others, quite simply, had ceased to exist. The Fontgembar monks died, not because they were white, but only because they were standing in the way. Not at all like the victims of the Gata affair, white strangers, members of an alien race, foreign body summarily rejected from the flesh. In fact, from Gata on, the woebegone fleet had begun to lose its loathing of the stranger. The emotion no longer served any purpose. It had simply dissolved and melted away. Much the same as with the Africans massed at the Limpopo, the Chinese along the Amur, the swarthy millions roaming the streets of New York and London, or the myriad blacks and Arabs ready to spew from the cellars of Paris. For them, the Gata dead spelled the end of the white race in toto. And that was that. It would have had to rise, miraculously, from its ashes, before they would give it a second thought now; and obviously, there on the southern coast of France, nothing of the sort was about to happen.

Their attitude became even clearer when the horde, in its second bound over the beach—beyond the purée of blood and sand that covered the bodies of monks and monsters—came up against two men dressed in black robes, who seemed to be waiting for them, calm as could be. If we point out that one of them, an old man, was facing the mob with a golden monstrance held up at arm's length, and that the other, hands together, was praying intently, it's only to recall that the two were, in fact, Dom Melchior de Groix and Abbé Pierre Chassal. Because as far as the mob was concerned, it couldn't care less, but plowed on, utterly indifferent, without so much as a second's worth of wonder. It didn't even notice. Not the monstrance, ablaze in the sun, nor the curious clothes these men were wearing, nor the whiteness of their skin. Kneeling, they would have been crushed, like the monks. But since they were standing, and since they held fast before the first ragged ranks, they found themselves surrounded, enveloped, absorbed, sucked up in the welter of humanity, and digested. Whisked off, still standing, packed body to body like the rest of the herd. Ganges refugees now, for all practical purposes, anonymous flesh in the midst of that mass, unknown even to those pressing in at their sides. Precious little time for their philosophic musings. True faith? Mere pose? They would never know now: both pose and faith were swallowed up forever, and nothing was left but the great gaping void. If the chaos of their minds thought of anything at all, as they felt themselves swept up in the huge human flood, it was only how foolish their illusions had been. They had pictured themselves standing, holding high the Sacred Host in the face of the invaders, stopping them in their tracks, even if only for a second, one single second before they died their martyr's death, but one that would have made it all worthwhile. . . . But their cherished second never happened at all, not a billionth of a second, or a billionth of a billionth, and that much, at least, their minds seemed to grasp. Caught in the crush, unable to move, Dom Melchior let the monstrance slip out of his hands, and it rolled along the ground, kicked by thousands of feet, like a rugby ball in a gigantic scrum. And he barely even noticed that his tight-clenched fingers were clutching at nothing but the empty air. Then the torrent split at a fork in the road, and the two men were swept their separate ways, never to meet again. What became of them, no one knows. Most likely, the old abbot—miter and all—died very quickly of fear and fatigue, not far from the beach. Pierre

Chassal must have wandered and wandered, like a poor, lost soul, uprooted and aimless. To this day, in the dull, drab egalitarian mass, impoverished and mindless, one still sees occasional flotsam of the sort, relics of the past, oblivious to the new order, and untouched by it. Like political prisons after any revolution, their ranks number many of the former leading lights. Businessmen, generals, prefects, writers. And a smattering, too, of the everyday people that the privileged classes—aristocrats, first, and bourgeois, in time—have always dragged along to disaster on their coattails, in part to flatter their own need for retainers, and in part because a few poor wretches will forever yearn to stand out and be different. But the new order needs no political prisons. The brainwashing will last for a hundred years. A thousand. The powers that be put up with these rare exceptions, and treat them rather like harmless tramps. No danger. They have no convictions. The worst they do is to stand, in some minds, for a kind of vaguely conceived resistance. They don't reproduce, they don't band together. As soon as they find themselves more than four or five, gathered outside on the steps of a church, or under the plane trees of some village square, they steal away, without a word, as if by some tacit agreement, avoiding the slightest temptation to indulge in communal existence. Since all of them are filthy and more miserable than the rest, and since all of them are white, they serve to make the great mulatto mix—the universal mongrelization—seem all the more desirable, not to mention the spirit of sacred solidarity that they steadfastly ignore. One look at them, and everyone can judge for himself . . .

Very different, indeed, was the way in which Panama Ranger and his diehards melted into the refugee ranks. Let's go back a few seconds. The horde has just climbed the first railings along the beach. Dragasès and his truck are already hurtling over the winding highway that leads to the mountain and up to The Village. Now that the first surprise is past—the long-dreamed-of event hasn't come off quite as planned—all those determined to see it through to the end come pouring from the villas, and cottages, and gardens, down to the beach to greet the Ganges armada, to welcome the refugees and guide their first steps. They will. They must. For their own self-fulfillment. Life is good. Life is love, and all men are brothers. No, we don't speak their language, but we'll understand, and so will they, our looks will say it all. Hands will clasp hands, arms fling about necks, bodies lock in embrace. With some good hearty slaps on the back, no doubt . . . Panama Ranger throws down his weapons, begins waving a welcome. Back a few hundred yards, he's managed to scout out an abandoned supermarket, full to the brim and ready for action. He's staked out the path. His pals stand waiting on every corner, already making great joyous signals, like traffic policemen who, somehow, suddenly seem to love their job. In the houses, the girls are bustling about, getting things ready for the long-awaited guest. Some of them are heating up huge vats of coffee. Lydie has hung white sheets from the windows. White, the color of peace . . . The stench in the air is even worse than before, but the diehards don't notice. Today they're fulfilled, beyond their wildest hopes. And again, guitars. And more singing voices: ". . . I'll give you my kingdom, for now the thousand years are ended, yes, the thousand years are ended now . . ."

Yes, they're ended. Period. Panama Ranger scans the surging mob, almost close enough to touch him, trying to find a smiling face, a glance to grasp the friendship in his eyes. But he looks and looks. No smile meets his. No one even seems to see him. And he holds out his hand in helpless despair, toward that solid wall of flesh, as if hoping for another hand to reach out and take it, to tell him a kind of silent thank-you, which would really be enough, no matter how everything else turns out. But no, nothing happens. No gesture of the sort. And a few seconds later, he's swept up in turn, carried off by the horde. Struggling to breathe. All around him, the press of sweaty, clammy bodies, elbows nudging madly in a frantic push forward, every man for himself, in a scramble to reach the streams of milk and honey, the rivers thick with fish, the fields fairly bursting with crops, growing wild for the taking . . . Hemmed in on all sides, he feels himself slipping, almost falling to the ground in a tangled maze of flailing black legs. Not alone now, though. There beside him, drowning too, an old woman, still kicking and elbowing herself afloat. A kind of frenzy grips him. His fists begin flying, hacking out a passage above his head, like a chimney poking through the mass of bodies, and he crawls out, breathless, pulls the old woman up to the surface with him, as if he were lifting her out of the water, saves her without thinking, without knowing why. Only then does it strike him. She's his one last hope. His one last chance to find a friendly soul in that wild, milling mob. And he clings to her, clasps her under the arms, that bundle of fleshless skin and bone, his one remaining link with life, one remnant of his noble, altruistic vision. He's finally seen the light. "They don't need me," he murmurs. "They'll just take what they please. I can't give them a thing . . ." The human torrent has split in two, rushes headlong into several streets at once, branches off with each new fork in the road. Panama Ranger feels the pressure subsiding. He can use his legs now, more or less at will, still caught up in the swell, but at least he can move. And he sets his friend down, stands her gently on her feet. "There, how's that?" he asks her. "You see? We made it." His reward: a wan smile. From now on he won't let her out of his sight. In time, when the ignorant horde starts its plunder, running amok through house after house, through shop after shop, stripping the abandoned supermarket bare, blind to the value of the wealth laid out before it, Panama Ranger will follow the lead. While disorder reigns rampant, he'll be there with the rest. Pillaging, looting. Amassing his pile of unknown treasures, snatched up right and left. Then at night, bedding down wherever fate takes him—now parlor, now barn—he'll open his bundle, and his friend will watch as he spreads his booty before their dazzled gaze, and inspects it, counts it: packs of cookies, cans of ham, a six-bladed jackknife, cigarettes, silk stockings, chocolate bars, watches, hunting gear, a flashlight. Anything and everything. Whatever he could grab. The old woman fondles, and paws, and sniffs it, trying to guess what each item is used for. When she does, she laughs. And he laughs with her. Ecstatic, the two of them. In seventh heaven . . . "Now that the revolution's finally here," he had said just a few days before, when his troops were holding the tollbooth on highway A7, "the first thing to do is enjoy ourselves, right?" But his mind fails to grasp the distance he's tumbled, the dizzying debacle. His treasures, lined up in a nice, neat row? The crumbs of abundance! They've smashed the machine, the pretty machine, and this is all that's left. And they'll never get it back together again. Perhaps he senses it, in a vague kind of way. But really, what's the difference? Squatting on her haunches, the old woman chortles and cackles with delight, enjoying herself, and that's all that matters . . .

As for his pals, they disappeared too, absorbed and digested in much the same way, though with somewhat less unhappy results. Only a handful were adopted, as it were, yet lots of them did their damnedest to be helpful, scouting the occupied villages, finding the shops that might be of some use, breaking in when they had to, but not without an eye to protecting the essentials—like the pharmacy, the grain bins, the garages, for example. But they soon got discouraged. Though the horde often listened and took their good advice—especially as a semblance of order developed—they no sooner gave it than they felt themselves rejected. The brightest among them were quick to understand: the more helpful they were, indispensable

in fact, the more hateful they became. And so, they let themselves
melt into the mass, where little by little the whiteness of their skin
began to pass unnoticed. Which was all they could hope for. Clinging
to their logic to the bitter end, they simply resigned themselves to
their fate. Today, in that area of France predominantly Indian in
population, they form a new caste of untouchable pariahs, completely assimilated, yet wholly set apart. They have no influence.
Their political weight is nil. To be sure, in the two ethnic groups new
leaders have emerged who hold sway with glib talk about racial
integration, and brotherhood, and such. But nobody really listens. No
one wants to have to remember the masters and mentors from the
opulent past. They're just in the way. A curious detail, though: when
one of them dies, they bury him in style. Like all the forerunners of
important revolutions. Take Lydie, for example. She was one of the
first. When she died, they suddenly called to mind those white sheets
hanging from the windows in welcome. And the schoolchildren,
prodded and coaxed by their teachers, wept their eyes dry with
floods of ignoble tears. The fact is that Lydie's death was anything but
heroic. She died in Nice, in a whorehouse for Hindus, disgusted with
everything in general and herself in particular. At the time, each
refugee quarter had its stock of white women, all free for the taking.
And perfectly legal. (One of the new regime's first laws, in fact. In
order to "demythify" the white woman, as they put it.) By Easter
Monday Lydie had been raped—on her famous white sheets, we
might add—and proceeded, not unwillingly, in those first chaotic
days, to tag after a troop of energetic Hindus, who had taken her over
in a kind of joint ownership, since she was very pretty, and her skin
was very white. Later, when things (and people) began to settle, they
had clamped her away in a studio of sorts, in Nice, with a number
of other girls similarly treated. A guard fed them and opened the
door to all comers. The enterprise was even given a name: the
"White Female Practice and Experimentation Center." But in time
prostitution was outlawed. (No less legally, of course.) Historians tell
us that it no longer filled a need, since white women soon lost all
pride in their color, and with it, all resistance. Could that be ... Etc.,
etc.

Clément Dio, too, died the morning of the landing. But all by
himself. After the address by the President of the Republic, he had
left the Hotel Préjoly, in Saint-Vallier, and wandered off into the
night, like a man in a trance. Somehow his feet led him down to the
coast. But his eyes saw only one endless image, burned into his brain:

his wife, Iris Nan-Chan, and his fruitless attempts to wake her, lying there suddenly limp in his arms, very dead. Sitting on the beach close by Dragasès's villa, he had witnessed, in his daze, a whole series of scenes that, just the day before, would have thrilled him through and through. He had thrived, after all, on always being right, and had spent his whole life avenging one Ben Suad, alias Clément Dio. But today, as his vengeance was about to triumph, he felt nothing whatever. Even the French army's wholesale defection—that army he had loathed, and locked horns with, and slandered—left him utterly indifferent. He looked on, apathetic, as the last twelve remnants got into their truck and beat their retreat. And it didn't even seem to cross his mind that much of the handiwork, in fact, was his. As the Ganges refugees stormed ashore, he wavered for a moment, as if he were wondering why he was there, and what he was doing. Then he got up, and all at once something came back to him. Something important. Bits and snatches of things he had said once before: "Monsieur Orelle . . . Do you think they have a chance? . . . It's the Last Chance Armada . . ." He broke into a smile. "Damn good!" he thought. "I really told it straight! Now here they are, and they've got me to thank!" That realization set his blood atingle. "Look, it's me! It's me! Dio!" And he waved his arms wildly, called out to the horde: "Let's tear down this mess! Let's begin all over!" But being rather small and swarthy—with his elegant crop of kinky hair, and a shifty look in his baggy eyes—and wearing a much too elegant jacket, he looked for all the world like one of those doormen who hang outside nightclubs to huckster the tourists. Death came in the form of a gigantic black, carrying a monster child on his shoulders, with a huge throng following after him, singing. He stopped in front of Dio, grabbed him off the ground, lifted him bodily so the twisted dwarf could see him. The creature, cap on head, took one look and gave a cry. For the third time ever. Our friend Dio, or Ben Suad, knew that he was done for, though he had no time to comprehend the verdict. The turd eater's fingers tightened around his throat, and his body was flung out over the sand like a limp rag doll. In no time, the trampling feet of the mob made it look like one of those mangled, bloody goats, swatted hither and yon in a game of Afghan polo . . . If, indeed, we can speak of a verdict, we can look for the reasons behind it. Here are two men, each in his own way an instrument of fate. One crosses the oceans, finds the other, and kills him, in a flash of inspiration, as if he knew precisely who he was. The one deliberate act of murder that the horde was to commit. Utterly senseless, by all logical standards. But if we choose, rather, to swim in a sea of symbols, deep and profound, a kind of logic begins to take shape. Namely, the Third World's staunch refusal to admit any debts, to dilute the radical meaning of its triumph by sharing its glory with alien beings. To thank them, or even accept their existence, would merely prolong a form of subjection. The turd eater settled things once and for all. Take it for what it's worth. Or perhaps there's another, more natural, explanation, and one that, frankly, we find easier to accept. To wit, that the monster couldn't stand Dio's looks. No, he simply couldn't stand them! . . .

Forty-four

Then the wind let loose. It was clear since morning that a storm was in the making. No worse than what one would expect, given the vagaries of Mediterranean climate, but still, so confined in both time and space that it seemed all the more intense. Like a cyclone, whipping up just one corner of the sea, and lasting for barely an hour. ... As the last refugee, waist-deep in the water, had left the last ship and was setting foot on shore, the skies burst open and rained down a deluge over the fleet, reaching in from the coast for about half a mile, as far as the mob had managed to push in its foray through the town. Now the downpour, in fact, was to play a crucial role. Until that moment, the Ganges invaders had been an aimless, shapeless mass, driven on by curiosity and very little else. The fabled countryside spreading out before them—with its neat, shaded streets, and their rows of homes and buildings that staggered belief—was such a far cry from their own vile existence that it seemed to inspire them with a kind of awe, or at least with a healthy respect. Throughout their long voyage the half-starved creatures had never ceased to dream, imagining a land in keeping with the myth that was sweeping them onward. And now that they were there, in the flesh, and could touch it, many simply couldn't believe their eyes. They fingered the trees, ran their hands along the sidewalks, the garden walls, the doors. Carefully, gingerly, as if any second the mirage might vanish. But then came the rain, and all doubts were dispelled. The mirage became substance. All at once, a mad dash to take shelter. Homes, apartment buildings, warehouses, churches. Whatever they could find. Not a door was left standing if they had a mind to smash it. Yet for all the absolute chaos of it all, something like a system began to take shape, and with it a kind of hierarchical order. The first ones to loot a construction site for crowbars, or to turn wooden planks into battering rams, were the ones who quickly emerged as the leaders. With each new door that crumbled to bits, the crowd cheered them on. In less than an hour everyone was under cover. On top of each other, crowded together, but at least under cover. They had simply taken over, and that was that. If not for the rain, things would have dragged on longer. When it did stop, finally, and when the wind died down, blowing the last dark storm clouds before it, they all reap-peared. Everywhere you looked. In doorways, on terraces, on balconies, in windows, on the steps of the churches. All the way up to the roofs of the tallest buildings, with their great glassed-in bays. Nothing but a swarming mass of black. Calling back and forth, over treetops and streets, from one elegant barbecue patio to another. Wallowing in joy. On a single triumphant theme: "See? We made it! We're here!"

It's not our intention to describe the manner in which the people from the Ganges settled throughout France, nor those who came after them. Fully described in edifying detail, as a model of collective initiative and organizational genius, the event takes up its share of space in all the new histories. (Chapter One: "The World Reborn.") Though with never a word about the storm and the rain, or the critical part they played ... Just one thing more. As soon as the frenzy of delight was over, it soon became clear that even for poor wretches long used to living on top of each other, the occupied strip of coastline would never be enough. But those who had climbed to the tops of the buildings discovered the length and breadth of their domain. Stretching as far as the eye could see, a lush, rich land stood ready to greet them. The houses, packed thick, were no blemish on nature. Indeed, it seemed to enfold and embrace them, and their very number made the refugees feel at home. Clearly this was no desert! Farther on, at the foot of the wooded hills, the scouts on the rooftops were amazed to discover vast orchards of trees, some thick with flowers, others in all their greenery, heavy with fruit. They passed on the good news, sang it out like town criers, or like muezzins atop their minaret perches. In no time it spread through the horde, from mouth to mouth. And everywhere—the streets, the gardens, the squares—people came together, in small groups and large, to talk, and talk ... We really must emphasize, one last time, the role of the rain and the scramble that followed in the newfound surge of acquisitive instincts. Quite simply, the mob had developed a morale. A spirit of steel. A conquering spirit. The result was that more than three-quarters of the horde—the strongest and most adventurous—decided not to stop, but to push on still further. Later, historians would turn this spontaneous migration into an epic, dubbed "The Winning of the North," a term we agree with, but only by comparison. One can't help thinking of the first panel of the diptych: the flight to the north, the pathetic exodus of the country's rightful owners, their self-willed downfall, their odious surrender. In a word, the anti-epic! Putting the two mobs side by side in the balance, one gets a clear picture ...

Forty-five

The waves that the storm sent lashing against the shore were few in all, but strong beyond belief. The fleet reeled beneath the first vicious blow. The rest merely finished what the first had begun. Attacked from behind, the immense *Calcutta Star* was wrenched back afloat with one shuddering heave of her giant hull. And as she was, a man was jarred awake. A man dozing, alone, at the foot of a smokestack, wrapped in white rags, left to founder in the torpor of his utterly harmless folly. His Grace the Catholic bishop, prefect apostolic to the entire Ganges region, opened his eyes. He gazed in wonder at the rain-swept deck. For the first time he saw a patchwork of rusting metal, hidden all during the voyage by the thick-packed mass of sprawling bodies. The ship groaned out her hollow echoes, like an empty tomb. And the storm whipped about through her truncated stacks, like organ pipes blasting out a hellish din, to a counterpoint of croaking, creaking joints. Every one of her doors was opening and closing, slamming back and forth. For a moment the hatchway covers would stand erect, then smash shut against the deck, as if the wind were fingering the keys of a giant bassoon, in an infinite mélange of outlandish noises. All the spars, hawsers, ladders, nets, and gangways that the horde had clambered over as it poured off the ship were beating out a rhythm on the sides of her hull, caught up in a kind of frenzied fandango. It sounded like a troop of horsemen galloping full tilt over a metal bridge, or like hailstones bouncing off a sheet-iron roof, only a hundred times louder. The bishop put his hands to his temples, clapped his palms against his ears so tightly that they hurt. At the same time he called out: "Where are you? Where are you?" He was doubtless thinking of the little girls and boys who had brought him food and drink in the shadow of his smokestack, and whom he would reward with a pat on the cheek, or a sign of the cross traced out on the forehead, depending on the state of his reason at the moment. But the ship was empty. And empty, too, all the other ships around. Every ship in the armada . . . The rain streamed down his bewildered face, slapped it so sharply with each fresh gust that he could barely breathe. Panting, he called again: "Where are you? Where are you?" This time he was thinking of the little old ladies who had crawled to his side through the darkness, and whose hands had brought him a taste of heaven on earth. Then the bishop understood that everyone had left him, and that he was all alone. He began to weep like a baby, dropped his arms to his sides. And the uproar shattered his ears, knocked him senseless, like a boxer with a deadly double hook.

He wasn't out for long though, a few seconds at most. When he came to, he was down on all fours. The ship had given a sharp lurch, and was listing. The shock, no doubt, had jolted him back to a semblance of sanity. Though not that it really mattered anymore: the *Calcutta Star,* pulled free by the storm, was lying on her side. Her smokestacks split in two and were tumbling down into the sea. The great organ was silent, and with it, the clack of the galloping hoofs, the spars and hawsers dancing about the hull. No sound now but the swish of the water sweeping over the deck in great gushing cascades. He heard himself mutter, "We'll both be relics together, only on different sides, that's all." And he heard the Consul gasp, "In the name of the Lord, eat shit!" Or at least so he thought. The fact is, the torrent that had battered the deck, splintering what was left of the ship's superstructure, swept His Grace off as well, and all he could see in the great liquid muddle were shadow dogs licking at a pool of blood on a shadow dock off by the port, in Calcutta. He struggled against the flood, crashed into a winch that was somehow still in place. A bloodied hand passed before his eyes, and he knew that he was dying, that the blood, this time, was his. No Latin words now for him to decipher ... The bishop of the Ganges had turned quite sane, saying simply, "My Lord, thy will be done." Then his head went banging against the rails, and his body, hanging on for another split second, hurtled into the sea, growing calmer by the moment ... "Who are you?" a voice asked him, trying to sound gruff. "The bishop of the Ganges." "Hmm!" the voice responded, "that's nothing to be proud of! Well, at least did you repent for your sins before you died?" "I think so." "All right then, go on in! Everything's forgiven ... No, this way! Over here! ... Just follow Baptitian and Podiatron, there. They'll show you the way ..."

Nothing was left of the fleet but formless carcasses strewn along the shore. Today only one little torpedo boat still preserves a vaguely recognizable shape. Every Easter Monday the regime decks it out in appropriate white bunting, and offers it up for public veneration. The pilgrims come to the beach in droves, all day long, and file past in silence. Here, too, they've distorted historical fact, making a spuri-

ous comparison with Cortés. (Albeit a Cortés who smashed his ships
on landing, instead of one who burned them.) Given such substance,
the myth has acquired the stature of a well-conceived plan, a political
decision in which every actor supposedly took part by deliberate
design. No longer a ragtag refugee horde, but a conquering army.
And the schoolchildren gaze at the little torpedo boat, drooling with
pride. Some of us, though, aren't taken in. Myself, for one. I know
that a few more miserable minutes, and the storm would have sunk
every ship in the fleet, and sent their black passengers to the bottom
of the sea. And I know too that God failed to give us those minutes,
those moments of grace . . .

That brief lapse of time caused one final result. Just as the storm
was beginning to die down, two planes approached the airport, and
prepared for a visual landing. Visual for good reason. It didn't take
long for the pilots to realize that nothing and no one was left on the
ground. Not a sound from the tower, not a car in the lots, no approach
lights burning, no radio beacon. Still, in spite of the storm, there was
no turning back. Loaded with medicines and relief supplies, cram-
packed as well with commandos of the cloth—squeezed between
mountains of crates and cases—the two planes, undaunted, banked
around for their landing, outlined against the darkened sky. The first
one was white. The second one, gray. No doubt the reader knows
already who was in them: our militant musketeers of Christian charity, those all-out sword-rattling Third World do-gooders, the holy
heroes of São Tomé. Number one, the Pope's white Vatican plane!
Number two, the gray plane of the World Council of Churches! Not
a one of the flying padres had been able to resist the tortuous call of
justice. As ever, their cargoes were nothing but a pretext. What really
mattered was to get there first, and by their symbolic presence to
give up the keys to the West, to offer them up in joyous abnegation,
and let the new world come to life at last. But cyclones' tails can play
treacherous tricks. The storm, as it died, struck one last blow. A thick
black cloud swallowed up the mini-squadron, and sent its thunder-
bolts crackling around it. Every light went out, every instrument dial
took a sudden plunge to zero. What one does in such cases is to step
on the gas and head for open sky. Which is what the pilots tried to
do, as the blackness hemmed around them. But the eye of the cyclone was watching and waiting. Gigantic air pocket, shaped like a
chimney. At such a low altitude, rare as it is, it never spares its
victims. One after the other, almost docile to a fault, still respecting
their traditional order of arrival, the two planes went crashing down

onto the runway. Number one, the white! Number two, the gray! Explosion. Fire. And no witnesses to see it, except old Monsieur Calguès, that is, behind his spyglass, smiling. No survivors either. God had denied His people their few miserable minutes of grace, yet He claimed His due in lives all the same ..

Afterwards, certain historians—though only a few—put forth a startling theory. To wit, that Pope Benedict XVI was aboard the white plane, and had died in the crash. Since only charred bones were found in the wreckage—no clothing, no personal objects of any kind—the speculation remained just that. (Wholly unsupported, except for the fact that His Holiness, indeed, was never heard from again. It was as if he had vanished into thin air, somewhere in the maze of the Vatican's garrets. After that Good Friday message of his, dripping with brotherhood and universal love, he had simply and literally dropped out of sight. We were told at the time that he was closeted in prayer, in a self-imposed exile under the eaves.) In point of fact, a spur-of-the-moment trip wouldn't really have been out of character at all. Three times in the past, in an effort to restore the faith in his office lost by his less-than-adventurous predecessor, this pontiff had manned the white plane himself, and flown to some battlefield to land in the thick of the fighting. In Rhodesia, for example—where Jean Orelle, too, had distinguished himself, you may recall—his spectacular arrival had led to the fall of Salisbury. Striding alone through the no-man's-land on the outskirts of the city, he had blatantly turned his back on the besieged white handful and had blessed the horde of black attackers. (It should, in all fairness, be mentioned that his presence did keep the victors from hacking their foes to shreds.) On his last trip—to South Africa, at the time of the famous native rebellion and general strike—he had almost managed to pull it off again. He had found himself mobbed by an adoring crowd of animist Bantu tribesmen and leftist Boer students, who worshipped the ground he walked on. Suddenly a police corporal, probably none too bright, threw a wrench into the works, just in the nick of time. Grabbing the Pope by the shoulders and shielding himself behind him, he had dragged him bodily off to his car, then out to the airport, shouting all the while to the rioting crowd, "Try to stop me, and I'll drill him!" The whole world shuddered in righteous indignation. . . . All of which explains why the notion of His Holiness flying off to the Ganges armada, and burning alive in his plane, is one that I have no trouble accepting. In fact, I must say that, from many points of view, it's one that I even find rather delightful . . .

Forty-six

"What say we sing!" said the colonel.

He had taken off his mask and was breathing great lungfuls of fresh air through the window, mimicking the pleasure of a satisfied gourmet. The truck was climbing its merry way up the winding road, between the rows of vines. With every turn, the brown-hued Village, high on its perch, drew closer and closer.

"My God, that smells good!" the colonel went on. "We're back where we belong, and everything's fine. So what'll we sing?"

"How about the 'Marseillaise'?" Jean Perret suggested, grinning.

The army burst out in a spasm of assorted chuckles, coughs, and cackles. As if the hussars and marine commandos were trying to see which ones could laugh the loudest. Nothing forced or bitter, mind you. Only a good, hearty laugh. Freed of all their burdens, they were having themselves a time.

"Just thought I'd test the people's morale," the undersecretary quipped.

He looked at the colonel, and again they burst out laughing.

"All right! Back in the closet with the 'Marseillaise'!" Dragasès decided. "Any better ideas?" he asked, looking at the captain.

"How about the tune they sing in the Legion?" the officer replied. "The one when they charge. It's stupid as shit, but at least it's direct. Besides, we all know the words."

"That's a thought," mused the colonel. "After all, we're kind of a foreign legion ourselves now. As foreign as they come. To everyone and everything. So I guess we have the right . . . No, on second thought, we don't. It's a tune with tradition. When the Legion sings it, it's because they've earned it. But us? Today? I really don't think a celebration's in order! Maybe tomorrow, when we're up in The Village . . . Anyway, I've got a better idea."

He glanced around slyly to see if they were listening. Then he cleared his throat like a banquet artiste, took a deep breath, and bellowed:

> "No, no regrets,
> No, I have no regrets.

278

What's done is done,
Good or bad, I guess,
And I couldn't care less,
No, no regrets,
No, I have no regrets.
La-la-la, la-la-la . . .
And to hell with the past!"

"What do you think?" he asked, as he finished. "Not bad, eh? It goes back a way. I can't remember some of the words, but you get the gist. Don't you know it?"

"No," said the captain. "What is it?"

"It was popular back in the early sixties. A singer named Piaf. Then the paratroopers took it over. Sang it at Zéralda. Algeria, remember? The coup that failed? General Challe and his friends? . . . Decided you can't fight a war with creampuffs. Which is what the French army was those days. A bunch of creampuffs . . . I was nineteen back then. Enlisted in the Legion. First Paratroop Regiment . . . And we sang it in the trucks on our way out of camp, when the regiment broke up. What a damn racket! Dead and buried, but still, what a show! . . . The way we felt then, I never would have dreamt we'd be singing it again, and for keeps this time! I guess there are some things that just won't die. Sooner or later, they're bound to come out. After everything settles. Like a bottle of wine."

"Well," said Perret, "this is one wine that's damn well settled! Twelve voices left. Not much of a chorus!"

"Never mind," Dragasès answered. "How much do you want to bet the twelve of us can make one hell of a noise!"

"Oh, I'm ready, believe me. You can count on the voice of the government, Colonel. It'll sing out of tune, as usual. But this time, at least, it'll give it all it's got!"

Veins bulging on their foreheads, necks swollen, faces scarlet, they blared it out at the top of their lungs. And, indeed, they were louder than a triumphant Catholic army chanting the Te Deum in the nave of a great cathedral. At every turn the truck went lurching, then staggered straight ahead, gaily biting its double tires into the embankment. The hussar who was driving slapped the steering wheel in rhythm, waving his arms like a third-rate hack, singing his heart out in some idiotic song. The captain sat pounding the dashboard with his fists. At each "No, no regrets" every rifle butt smashed against the floor of the truck. . . . If we probe the innermost feelings of this brawling band, the first thing we find is a kind of drunken esprit de corps. The festive ecstasy of tribal togetherness, the feeling of belonging. Few as they are, so few you can count them, they still thumb their noses at the rest of the world. Yet there's something else too, something more like desperation. The child, whooping it up, at night, on the lonely road, to forget that he's alone. Or perhaps the poor devil, shipwrecked in his lifeboat, singing anything at all, just to keep himself alive. Yes, that was part of it, too . . . The young hussars had their eyes on the fields, scanning the trees. Not a bird to be seen. Even the scavengers—crows and magpies—had made their escape. Nailed up tight, the winegrowers' shutters seemed to seep out of a kind of cataclysmic fear. All that was missing were the black crosses that, in ages past, marked out the houses where the plague had struck. The sun was shining over the deserted landscape with the same hard light that Johnson and White must have seen on the moon a few years before, as they squatted on their heels, next to the wreckage of their space shuttle, waiting to die . . .

"Shit!" yelled the driver. "What's that? Some fucking guy! I damn near hit him!"

Suddenly, silence. Robinson Crusoe discovering Friday's footprints! People on the moon after all! Then six grinding brakes, a well-controlled skid, the screeching of gears, an expert reverse . . . Some fucking guy! They all stuck their heads out the same side to look. Enemy? Friend? Dragasès loaded his submachine gun.

Yes, indeed, there was someone there, peacefully sitting by the side of the road, sticking up his thumb in a gesture that, under the circumstances, couldn't have been more bizarre. No doubt he was enjoying the humor of the situation, smiling broadly from ear to ear. White skin, pleasant face, but dressed like a tramp. Everyone seemed to think he looked familiar.

"How about a lift, Colonel?" he asked, simply, as if there were only one possible reply.

"Where to, my good man, so early in the morning?" the colonel countered, playing right along.

"Oh really, I don't care. After all the time I spent trying to find you, I'm not too fussy. Wherever you're going is fine with me. You are Colonel Constantine Dragesès, aren't you? Army chief of staff and commander in chief of the forces of law and order for the whole southern region?"

He spoke with a kind of mock-solemn smirk that immediately won them over. Clearly he was already on their side, banter and all.

Besides, by now they had placed his face in spite of the whiskers that almost devoured it. It's not easy to forget a full-face picture splashed across page one, especially when you remember the string of vengeful epithets that went along with it. Dragasès went on in the same high-flown tone, businesslike as could be:

"Monsieur Perret, let me introduce Captain Luke Notaras. Greek national. Commanding officer of the freighter *Isle of Naxos*. Remember?"

"The man with the red hands?" Notaras added, with a modest little smile. "The bloody freighter? The Laccadive Island genocide? Et cetera, et cetera."

"Of course," said Perret, nodding. "That's quite a list of honors. Congratulations. I know my classic quotes: 'There's no Luke Notaras among us, my friends!' And so on and so forth. It seems like a hundred years ago. But weren't you in prison?"

"That's right, monsieur. In Aix. But suddenly, last Saturday, no more guards! Flew the coop! And left the gates wide open! So I took the hint and left. Ready to march to the sounds of battle, except that there were none. Pretty much what I expected. When I looked down from up there, I saw you and your truck. And I said to myself: 'Now that's a break. I'll hitch myself a ride.'"

"Well, hop right up!" said Jean Perret, amused by it all. "I'm not sure whether, as fascist puppet in charge of the south, I have the right to pardon prisoners. But given the situation, I don't see why not. There! You're pardoned. Now how would you like to be minister of the navy?"

"What navy, monsieur? You mean you have a navy?"

He pretended to look all around as if he had lost something.

"Of course not. But what's the difference? The colonel has no army. Or practically none. And I have no territory. So we can finally get down to business. Now's the time when it's all beginning to have some real meaning."

"I think I see your point," Notaras replied. "Mind if I play on your team, gentlemen?"

Adopted in a flurry of slaps on the back, making the rounds of each large outstretched hand, named honorary Chamborant Hussar on the spot, and marine commando, *honoris causa*, Notaras climbed up into the truck and joined the singing dozen. All of them, off on a hell of a lark. As simple as that . . .

When they reached The Village they all jumped down. Dragasès split his troop in two. One half was deployed around the truck, christened the "command post" just for the occasion—much to everyone's delight—with the captain in charge. He had set up his submachine gun on a little clump of earth. (Fate, it seems, in one of those fits of illogic, had ordained that the best firing angles should all come together at the foot of a sixteenth-century roadside shrine, complete with its niche, and its Virgin, and its cross.) The other half was dubbed the "mobile column." Along with Notaras, Jean Perret, and the colonel, it consisted of a double line—two "pincers," as they called them—each with three marksmen fanning out to explore the terrain, in keeping with the best rules of urban guerrilla warfare. Pressing forward in a series of short, quick spurts—I'll cover you, you make a break, you cover me, I'll make a break—they had pushed to a terrace, with five little steps leading up from the road, all of them quite convinced, by now, that there wasn't a living soul left in The Village. But just as they reached that definite conclusion, a voice called down, laughing:

"What on earth are you doing? Some kind of maneuvers? It's all very instructive to watch from up here. But really, there's no need. I'm the only one left."

Dragasès looked up and saw an old white-haired gentleman, with a linen jacket and red polka-dot tie, calmly leaning on his railing, as if taking the air on a peaceful spring morning.

"Who are you?" he asked.

"Calguès. Professor of French literature, retired."

"But what the hell are you doing here?"

The old professor was rather taken aback. Even offended. Indeed, what a question!

"This is my home, Colonel! Where else should I be?"

"Where else? Where . . . You mean to tell me you don't know what's going on?"

"Oh yes, I know. I've been watching it all."

He pointed to a spyglass, on a tripod, beside him.

"And it doesn't bother you? You aren't going to leave?"

"I like it here. Why should I leave? At my age it's hard to make a change, don't you know?"

All terribly tongue in cheek, like Notaras a few moments before, but with much more finesse. The colonel stood agape. This old man was like a breath of fresh air!

"It's really a very fine glass," Monsieur Calguès continued. "It magnifies better than seven times. At six o'clock this morning you were out in front of your villa. I saw you pointing up this way, and

I knew right off what you had in mind. Later on, when you got into your truck, I counted. There are twelve of you, right?"

"Thirteen since the last turn," the colonel corrected. "And now fourteen," he added, with a smile.

"Twelve, fourteen, no difference. There's plenty for everybody. You must be ready for a meal, I imagine."

"A meal?" cried the colonel. "You've got to be joking!"

The old gentleman gave a deep comic bow, as if sweeping the ground with a great plumed hat. He nodded to Perret and Dragasès:

"Monsieur . . . Colonel . . . Breakfast is served!"

Up the steps, a rush of feet. Kids out of school. Recess, forever! What they saw spread inside through the open terrace door stopped them dead in their tracks. Breakfast? Obviously the old gentleman was a master of understatement. There, on a long, massive table, draped with a checkered cloth, pyramids of fancy sandwiches, neatly piled; thin slices of red ham, coiled flowerlike and set out on trays; bowls of black olives, and pickles, and onions; plates of all kinds; slices of egg next to slices of tomato, artfully arranged, first one then the other; anchovies wound round in little rosettes; goat cheeses slivered with the utmost care, just enough, not too much; bouquets of sausages; pâtés in stoneware terrines; uncorked bottles everywhere in sight; a tray full of glasses; cigarettes, cigars, matches; and over in a corner, the fine old brandy, surrounded by its squat and bulbous snifters.

"Are you . . . Are you sure you're all alone?" stammered the colonel, the first one to find his tongue.

"I've always enjoyed setting a pretty table," Monsieur Calguès replied. "It's so pleasant to look at. At five past six, I saw you all down there getting ready to leave. So I got right to work. There are a few things missing, but I hope you'll excuse me. I wanted to whip up a crème Chantilly, but you got here sooner than I expected. We'll just have to do without the sweets, that's all . . ."

"Good God!" shouted Dragasès, all of a sudden. "What's that?"

He was pointing to a young man, all in a heap in the corner, legs spread, head hanging, half hidden by the tablecloth falling almost to the floor. Hair long and dirty, flowered tunic, Hindu collar, Afghan vest. And lying quite still. A red spot on his chest, with a neat little hole, left no doubt whatever as to his state of health.

"You?" asked the colonel.

"Me," Monsieur Calguès answered, nodding. "I couldn't stand the awful things he was saying. In a war, even a hopeless one, some people have to die, or it wouldn't be right. I did just what you did. Down there, I mean. My personal war, just for the fun of it. No illusions, I assure you. Strange," he added, looking at the corpse, "I'd forgotten all about him."

"When did it happen?"

"Last night sometime."

"Better get him out of here before he begins to stink the place up," said the colonel, very matter-of-fact. "We'll take care of it for you."

And that was that. The whole of the young man's funeral oration . . .

"All right, let's eat!" exclaimed Jean Perret. "A toast, Monsieur Calguès, to the health of The Village!"

And he added in the most sham-serious of tones:

"By the way, how would Minister of Culture suit you?"

"Let's not forget the command post," Dragasès reminded them. And he turned to one of the marine commandos. "You . . . Since you managed to save your bugle, blow us a mess call. That'll knock 'em on their ass!"

Given the words the French soldier thinks of when he hears those notes—"It ain't shit yet, but it will be soon!"—one imagines them bursting against the Western sky, and sounding an accent of prophetic doom . . .

Forty-seven

France has given in. The inevitable has happened. Now there's no turning back, despite a few isolated local accommodations worked out here and there, when the two opposing forces could find some common ground. The rest of the world, having long held its breath, will learn what has happened. Some will revel in our fall, some will suffer along with us, depending on where their sympathies lie. But it's not my intention to present a panorama of our seething planet on that Easter Monday morning. The facts are still fresh. Then too, it would take volumes. And besides, what possible good would it do? My heart is in The Village. If I muster the strength to add a few more pages to a tale that has cost me my fill of tears already (despite the hilarity—that's the right word, isn't it?—bursting through the mournful events at every turn), I'll devote them to The Village. The most I can do is to sketch in, roughly, the conclusion of certain essential scenes. . . . (My God! Have I made myself clear, I wonder? Have I made you see the process of inexorable decay?) . . . certain scenes I've left hanging, from chapter to chapter, like time bombs, waiting . . .

Bombs that went off all at once, the whole world over. On the banks of the Amur. On the banks of the Limpopo. In Paris, New York, London. The Amur has turned yellow. Floating on its surface, thousands of corpses, swept along by the current toward the Soviet bunkers, standing deserted. The Russians have withdrawn. Orders of the Kremlin. With France the Enlightened glad to grovel on her knees, no government now will dare sign its name to the genocidal deed. One bullet and one only. Shot into the belly of a little Chinese child, by a Soviet general loaded to the gills with vodka . . . At Central Park the black tide is rising. Twenty-three floors in a single hour. "Black is beautiful, and all the maggots are white." Not a sound, in the words of that Harlem poet, "but the blade sinking into the oppressor's marrow." On the twenty-sixth floor, Dr. Norman Haller measures the march of time. Only two floors now between the past and the future. Over the phone, the mayor of New York sounds calm, almost resigned: "I'm really pretty lucky, Norman. Mine are three families from Harlem. The kids are little dolls. They didn't even spit at me.

I've got one on my lap right now. He's playing with my gun. Un-loaded, of course . . . What else could I do, Norman? We had no choice . . ." At No. 10 Downing Street, negotiations are in progress. The Non-European Commonwealth Committee has taken over Lon-don, politely as you please. Simple question of statistics. They com-pare the figures and draw their conclusions. Really, how stupid! We never imagined there could be so many! The Queen receives the leaders of the "Paks," stands aghast at one of their non-negotiable demands. Namely, that her younger son marry a Pakistani. To de-stroy a symbol or to make it their own? We could argue forever . . . As for South Africa, nobody gave her a thought. Even the loathing she inspired on all sides served no further useful purpose. Like a beach submerged in the onrushing tide surging over the Limpopo, she vanished from the map as a sovereign white state. With just one consolation: the fact that all her colleagues, who had so long dis-owned her, fell apart at the seams at the very same moment . . . In the Philippines, in all the stifling Third World ports—Jakarta, Kara-chi, Conakry, and again in Calcutta—other huge armadas were ready to weigh anchor, bound for Australia, New Zealand, Europe. Carpet-like, the great migration was beginning to unroll. Not the first time, either, if we pore over history. Many a civilization, victim of the selfsame fate, sits tucked in our museums, under glass, neatly labeled. But man seldom profits from the lessons of his past . . .

One last time, for the record, a typical example. The giant steam-ship *Normandie*, sailing from Manila, her French crew, to a man, "tired of waiting hand and foot on the parasites of the leisure class" (as their endless union pronouncements put it), and anxious to wel-come with open arms five thousand ragged Filipino wretches. But alas! Their ecstatic fraternal bliss was to founder on the rocks their first night out. To bring off those great feasts to feed the needy requires all the skill of the Salvation Army, or the Brothers of the Poor. Essential, too, if the charity valve is to function safely, is a docile acceptance on the part of the have-nots, and a muted largesse on the part of the haves. The attempt was sheer disaster. Not that there weren't enough supplies to satisfy them all. (Let no one accuse our late lamented French Line of anything like that!) It's just that when the Filipinos, fresh from the Manila slums, discovered the orgy of food and drink, neatly laid out on tables, deck by deck, they swooped down all at once, like a wild, mad horde. Eating, drinking. Looting, more precisely. Which was just what they were after. Then they looted the galleys. And after the galleys, the pantries and the wine racks. And even the huge cold-storage lockers, forced open under threat to life and limb. The whole ship, in fact. A cyclone, or worse! Her passageways strewn with broken glass, her elegant cabins lying in rubble, the great lacquered paneling, pride of her public rooms, smeared and defaced. Later, some journalist, in a statement that took the prize—and God knows how the papers, those days, bled themselves dry in a flood of arrant nonsense—claimed that the destruction was a radical reply to contemporary bourgeois art! To hear the bartender in the first-class lounge, though, that wasn't it at all: "A bunch of drunken pigs, that's what they were! If you want my opinion, the rich weren't so bad. At least when they had to puke they ran into the toilet!" Perhaps we should all have thought of that sooner . . .

But let's get back to more serious matters. Strangely enough, despite the devastation that adjective masks, I still can't write it without a little smile. Serious? Good God! Did anyone guess how serious it was? Even just a little? The way the French radio announced to the world the news of the landing, and France's passive reaction to it, are a perfect illustration.

It will be remembered that at RTZ, on Easter Monday morning, Boris Vilsberg had finally sized up the madding mob. In the studio, crammed with human flesh, so fetid one could barely breathe, the last comprehensible words he uttered, and the last to be heard, were: "For God's sake, someone open the window, before we all drop like flies!" (The sentence, by the way, went out on the air, and immediately set the tone for the rest of the broadcast.) He was sitting at his microphone, at the big round table. Fra Muttone was beside him, but strictly for that shred of symbolic value that still clung to his person. And above all to make sure that he wouldn't be cut off. A hostage, nothing more . . . It was happening just as Vilsberg had expected. But he tried to keep cool, tried not to lose his head. And he gave the control booth the sign for his theme, and the trembling announcer's usual introduction: "And now, Boris Vilsberg and his nightly opinion . . ." At which point, explosion. All hell breaking loose. Wild rush for the microphones of the zealots of The Word. Voices everywhere, screaming: "Screw Vilsberg's opinion! He can keep his opinion! It's the people's opinion that counts from now on!" With no less than ten microphones spread around the table, and a half dozen voices yelling into each, one can picture the result. But since all of them were spouting pretty much the same line—a world reborn, one race, one religion, no more exploitation of man by man, death to Western imperialism, universal love and brotherhood, and a thousand other goodies of the same confection—and since the volume drowned out almost all of what they were saying, they soon came around to putting some order into their frenzy. It was voted, by a show of hands, to let everyone speak his piece to his heart's content. But one at a time, and each one in turn. So step right up for the merry-go-round! This way for the tickets! And off we go spinning . . . Before very long a junta had emerged. A triumvirate consisting of a black street sweeper, obviously inspired, a young Vietnamese at school in Paris, and a radical student-power type, probably French. Then they took another vote. First a name, a distinctive symbol: the P.P.R.C., or the Paris People's Radio Cooperative, ready to serve the provisional government of the Paris Multiracial Commune. Adopted, again by a show of hands. No one knows who unearthed that brilliant little gem, but in no time the idea had spread far and wide. Everywhere, committees of the same stamp and stripe. Even at Notre Dame, where the Archbishop, bless him, had ordered the doors flung wide, and all the candelabra lit. (No one bothered to notice that the Sacred Host had been stashed away first—that's the only word—by some superstitious little curate.) Even at the studios of the national chain, where the handsome and talented Léo Béon, still riding high from his role at São Tomé ("We'll have to bring the poor souls to their senses!"), had appointed himself people's provisional director. And all these committees were rushing to swear allegiance to the Paris Multiracial Commune, which didn't even exist yet, except in the people's mind. RTZ—that is, P.P.R.C.—was right in the limelight. With a certain flair, too, we have to admit. The great talk machine whirred out its words. And again, another vote. This time to decree that only the junta would handle the news, and that only the people would give an opinion.

And news there was aplenty. No need to go looking. It flowed in from every corner of Paris. Like a waterwheel pouring out bucketfuls on end, the motorcycle troop of spontaneous informants kept the studio deluged with an endless flood of words. Some true. Some false. Some a little bit of both. Most often filtered, interpreted, staged. What they liked to call "life." "Where've you been?" "Notre Dame." "What's it like?" "Like something else, man! Out of sight! Thousands and thousands of our brothers and sisters. All kinds. Africans, Arabs. And old Esther Bacouba, making up a song off the top of her head. Something like . . . Well, I don't remember exactly, but I know it was tremendous. Kind of like this: 'Jesus, my brother, come down off your cross, and come live with us. 'Cause today's the day, your suffering is through . . .' Anyhow, the Archbishop bawled like a baby. And he gave old Esther a hug and a kiss . . ." More opinion from the people: "Watch out! Don't let those establishment padres sucker us back into the old-style Church. Pretty clever, those guys! Kept the people in their pockets for the last two thousand years. Damn sure that their Christ stayed nailed to his cross, meek as a lamb. You can bet they'll try again. So watch out, be careful . . ." Etc., etc. And a chorus of concern. Variations on the same theme, all you want to hear, until the next cyclist bursts in with his contribution. "Where've you been?" "Café Oasis." "What's up?" "Real wild, man! Finally got those bastards. The ones that were in on the murder, I mean . . ." Suddenly the people pricks up its ears, ready to dish out more of its opinion. The Ben Jalli affair. Tragic business, of course. Everyone remembers. A concierge near the Café Oasis. Killed some young Algerian kid. A tough little punk, but even so! Life was no picnic for an Algerian kid stuck away in Paris. . . . "Were there lots of them?" "Fifty, I guess. But they got a fair trial, man. The head of the jury was even French, some gal named Élise. And the lawyer was an Arab, Mohammed something. They called him 'Cadi One-Eye.' Forty bastards, guilty. Sentenced to die, man. Only ten acquitted. And a priest all ready to give them the rites . . ." More opinion from the people: "So maybe they didn't all pull the trigger . . . The concierge was alone in his booth when he killed him . . . But they're just as much to blame. In a different way, that's all. Even worse. More deadly. They were morally guilty. They accepted a racist murder. And besides, they signed a petition that night to free him on bail. Well, that was their own death warrant they signed! We're better off without them. They'll never fit into our multiracial world . . ." And on, and on, and on . . .

At the same moment, off at the other end of town, Josiane and Marcel sit in front of the radio, looking at each other without a word. They've gotten the picture. Finally she tells him: "The sooner you do it, the better for us. Go on up . . ." Marcel drags himself out of his chair, looks over his nice little living-room furniture (cut-rate, twenty-four monthly installments), sighs, opens the door, and tells the dark child lurking on the landing, "Take me to your daddy." And up on the sixth floor, in the two-room flat where Monsieur Ali and his brood live huddled—eight in all, with five kids and an elderly mother —he'll hold out his hand, and with the other on his heart, he'll hear himself pronounce these incredible words, sincere as can be: "Look, Monsieur Ali, the wife and me . . . Well, like, we've been thinking.

It just isn't fair. All of you, I mean, cooped up like this in a tiny flat. So we kind of figured that the two of us . . . I mean, we could get along fine up here. And in our place you'd have lots more room. . . . No, don't mention it. What's right is right. Got to help each other out nowadays, know what I mean? . . . Cute little kids you got there, Monsieur Ali. Nice and polite . . ." And that's that! One, two, three! No pressure this time. No physical force, no legal persuasion. And some people still say this world is dog eat dog! . . .

Meanwhile, at the station, more of the same: "Hi! Where've you been this time?" "Police headquarters." "The cops?" (A general sneer runs through the crowd.) "Yeah, the cops! But listen, I got some great news. First of all, there's only like ten percent on duty. And they're keeping them all inside. Won't let them out on the streets! The chief read a statement." (The cyclist pulls a crumpled paper from his pocket.) "I'm no good at shorthand, guys!" (Hearty laughs all around.) ". . . but I think I got most of it down. He said something like this: 'Although, as commissioner of the Paris police, I am fully empowered to take all steps I deem necessary . . .' ("A fat lot of good that'll do him!" More laughs.) '. . . I am anxious, at all costs, to avoid armed confrontation.' ("Man, that's all we need!") 'So let me assure you, no repressive measures whatever are being planned.' ("Damn right! The bastard has no more men!") 'I hope we can count on the people's good sense, whatever their race and social class . . .' ("Cut that last part! That reactionary 'race and social class' crap!") '. . . so that order can be restored as quickly as possible. As soon as the essential public services are guaranteed, we can begin discussing, in an atmosphere of calm, an appropriate governmental reorganization, acceptable to all . . .'[1] (Victory shouts. Some cheers, some jeers. "Let's hear it for the chief!" "String him up by the balls!" "Power to the people!" "Workers unite!") 'Now I'd like to invite representatives of all those factions taking part in the movement,[2] as well as those heads of the various public services and administrative branches still present in the capital,[3] to come to the central union hall at three

---

[1] What else could he do? With no orders from above, with a President prostrate with grief, weighing over and over, for the thousandth time since the end of his address, the pros and cons of abject surrender . . . A different plan for Paris than the one for the south? Too late now, much too late. Already years and years too late . . . (Author's note.)

[2] Note the bureaucratic, euphemistic jargon. Just a "movement," that's all! (Author's note.)

[3] Here, too, note the chief's clever dodge. A subtle slap at those who had turned and

o'clock this afternoon . . .' Hold it, troops, there's more! Get this: '. . . in the hope that, out of this noble theater of human dignity might come a more happy world for all mankind . . .' "[4]

More opinion from the people. But first, a heavy, unprecedented silence. The child has thrown his tantrum in front of the toy-shop window, screaming that he'll smash it. Now he has what he wanted. No more window between him and the toy he was after. And he holds it in his hands. He looks it all over, fingers it, sniffs it, and realizes that he doesn't even know what it's for. Will he throw it down and break it? Will he leave it in a corner and go play with his bits of string? It wouldn't be the first time. Besides, he's suspicious. Just what are they up to? What will they make him do in return for his nice new toy? Work hard? Be good? "It's a trap!" someone shouted. (The same one who accused the Archbishop of trying to sucker them back to the Church.) "The people's multiracial revolutionary movement isn't just some fun and games, some mask for all the old privileges to hide behind and thumb their noses!" He rattled on and on, and was loudly applauded. (Important point: this rugged little redhead belonged to the white race, no question about it.) As soon as he was through, another voice rang out. A big, good-natured voice: "Man, you stupid! Mamadou say you don't know ass from elbow! I don't want no pigpen, man. Sure, I want country too. Like everybody wants. But it's gotta be country that don't go fall apart. I eat good, you eat good, I drive car, you drive car. Everybody happy. But if you gonna drive car and you gonna eat good, you gotta have bosses. And government, man. And cops. They know how. You? You don't know nothing. As long as you give orders, man, that's all the fuck you care!" And he sat down, grinning from ear to ear, since the crowd was applauding him as much as the redhead. "It's really a very simple question," said the Vietnamese student. "What it boils down to is this. Will we or won't we accept technical help from an enemy regime that we've finally defeated, to smooth our transition to a multiracial state?" Like every simple question, this one was debated

---

run, a timid reminder of those essential virtues that govern societies, like responsibility, administration, and public service. Curiously enough, when all is said and done, he'll manage to save his own position (though with a one-eyed Algerian lieutenant by his side). *(Author's note.)*

[4]Not so dumb, this notion of a happier lot for the worker. An age-old ideal, it had already come about little by little, so naturally that they never even knew it when they had it. Far from it. But to have it didn't matter. What mattered was to imagine it, off somewhere in the future. Poor gullible humanity, always the same . . . *(Author's note.)*

hotly back and forth, until the principals gave up from sheer exhaustion. On Mamadou's side, the Third World natives, and a few other types who could see beyond their noses. On the redhead's side, all those once referred to as extremists, anarchists, fanatics, and fools. In the end, fatigue brought the two sides together. It was almost three in the morning, and they hadn't picked a single delegate to attend the police chief's meeting. It was then they remembered that Boris Vilsberg was still there. Silent and forgotten, he had listened intently to all the proceedings, numbed into a kind of weird waking trance. As if confronted again and again, by his very own presence. As if an endless string of Vilsbergs—with his voice, his face—had approached the microphone, one by one. Saying all those things he had mouthed through the years, over the airwaves at RTZ, no better or worse than the nonsense they were spouting, and certainly no brighter. He could see that now. (Though, of course, as a newsman he was slightly more informed.) Good God! That's all his life had been. Just words, words, words! . . . And finally, when someone turned to him and asked if he had anything to add—with a semblance of the respect the disciple owes the master—he answered in a whisper: "No, nothing, thank you. Nothing . . ." No doubt the most meaningful opinion of his career. In his place they elected the tireless Fra Muttone (in a triumph of endurance, like a long-distance swimmer), and Mamadou with him, along with the members of the junta, in toto.

What became of Boris Vilsberg, nobody seems to know. They say he went off to a collective farm, somewhere in the mountains, where he keeps his mouth shut and works with his hands. Be that as it may, he wasn't alone in his social demise. Compare, for example, the editor of *La Grenouille*. He had just finished drawing a certain cartoon, showing two men about to play checkers. One was white and looked uneasy, one was black and wore a grin. The caption had the black man saying: "Here, you take the blacks and I'll take the whites. Same as our women!" But just as he was putting in the last few lines, it struck him that, were he to publish that cartoon, his paper would be banned. When regimes and ideologies change overnight, one can't go on poking fun, and jibing, and joking, except by becoming an out-and-out turncoat. That realization so depressed him, in fact, that his face—as his colleagues reported some time later—froze in the look of a suffering clown. And he went through the office, shaking hands with his staff, and muttering over and over: "Please, go on without me. Do your best. Do your best . . ."

I have in front of me the list of members of the People's Assembly of the Paris Multiracial Commune, which met in the central union hall on Easter Monday, at three in the afternoon. From white official-dom, hardly more than a handful. Just enough to give an aura of professional competence and make at least something of a show of good will. For example, the chief of police himself, two or three ministers and highly placed bureaucrats, and those whom the President of the Republic had told, only twenty-four hours earlier, that they were "ready to sell out, to come to terms." Those he had accused of "feathering their nests with this contact and that," and of forming "a provisional government of sorts, already in the making." Those he had branded with these prophetic words: "Who cares what kind of power it is, as long as you wield it!" Among the latter, one certain obscure general, Tanque by name, an utter unknown, except for the fact that, long years before, coming up through the ranks, he had earned his first stripe—and his nickname of "Septic"—by ordering his troops in the Algerian campaign to fire on their fellow Frenchmen at Oran. . . . After the whites, their "contacts" in question. Quite a few in all. Led by the reverend religious and moral powers, walking on the rubble like Hindu fakirs over live, burning coals. The Grand Mufti, first and foremost. Which was only right. Didn't he represent the more than six million Arabs and Moslem blacks who called Paris home? (Let's not forget to mention too that, later on, in the first provisional government, he was given the portfolio of Human Equality, a new cabinet post, rather like a Ministry of Human Environment, but intended to fight the evils of racist pollution.) Next, His ubiquitous Eminence, the Archbishop of Paris, with as touching a show of good will as one could hope for. Embracing the Mufti before the crowd assembled—as inscrutable as ever in his great white burnoose—he made him a present of some thirty churches, to be turned into mosques. (It was one of the day's most tender and moving moments.) Next, an assortment of charity types, heads of this group or that for the betterment of Man. (Except for the biggest loudmouth of the lot, who had left for Switzerland, as he explained it, "to consult with his other Western colleagues.") Even the Grand Rabbi, snared in the antiracist surge, in spite of the fact that Israel herself was doomed not to survive it. Also, a cohort of subcontinent ambassadors —from the Ganges, India, Bengal, Pakistan—surrounded by throngs of devoted admirers, like generals fresh from triumphant campaigns. And other Third World ambassadors too, all speaking very loudly, all riding the crest of the wave, as it were, terribly proud of their respective armadas, about to set sail at precisely that moment. And every tongue drooling the same fraternal slobber. The whites, apologetic for being such poor hosts; the blacks and browns, with the magnanimity of numbers, quick to reassure them in the name of "the world reborn." The eve of a new Revolution. This time to wipe out not class, but race. The lion and the lamb, vowing to share their lot forever. And pressing in with all its bulk, the Third Estate—if one can call it that—a good three-quarters of the milling mob.

Also present was a rather large number of white women, married —like Élise, for example—to gentlemen of color. Everyone listened to what they had to say, though a few whites were noticeably less than enthusiastic, seeing them as symbols of the death of the race. A number of years before, Ralph Ginzburg, the famous American publisher, had printed a series of photos in his magazine *Eros,* which had caused not a little ink to be spilled. They showed an interracial couple—white woman, black man—in various stages of nude embrace. With a caption that read as follows: "Tomorrow these couples will be recognized as the pioneers of an enlightened age, in which prejudice will be dead and the only race will be the human race." Yes, that's what it was all about. And everyone listened with an almost religious awe, because, in point of fact, they spoke in the name of death. Only a white woman can have a white baby. Let her choose not to conceive one, let her choose only nonwhite mates, and the genetic results aren't long in coming. (In the first provisional government, by the way, Élise was named Minister of Population . . .)

Present, too, a number of other picturesque types. In the midst of the general panic and the disintegration of law and order, they had staked out their safe little claim, and wanted to be sure that everyone knew it. The kind that surface during every "liberation." Ostentatious champions of the winning side, always eager to lend their superfluous support. Like the Léo Béons, the Fra Muttones, the Dom Vincent Laréoles, and others of their ilk. Breast-beating frauds of every persuasion. They made a lot of noise, but not one whit of difference.

The great nameless mass was quite another matter. The dismal fauna of the Third World battalions, from the slums of Paris. And I have to point out that, moments ago, when I questioned whether anyone guessed how serious all this was, these certainly weren't the ones I meant. They're all there, every one. "The Chief," with his troop of rat-hole blacks and his white advisers (from the ragtag priest to the militant tough); Cadi One-Eye himself, and his whole entourage; Mamadou, still grinning from ear to ear; and all the kinky-haired, swarthy-skinned, long-despised phantoms; all the teeming ants toiling for the white man's comfort; all the swill men and sweepers, the troglodytes, the stinking drudges, the swivel-hipped menials, the womanless wretches, the lung-spewing hackers; all the numberless, nameless, tortured, tormented, indispensable mass . . . They don't say much. But they know their strength, and they'll never forget it. If they have an objection, they simply growl, and it soon becomes clear that their growls run the show. After all, five billion growling human beings, rising over the length and breadth of the earth, can make a lot of noise!

Meanwhile, along with Josiane and Marcel, seven hundred million whites sit shutting their eyes and plugging their ears . . .

Forty-eight

Around The Village, for a half dozen miles, the landscape stood deserted, cleansed of all foreign intrusion. A half dozen miles. No distance for any good infantryman to cover, up and back, even weighed down with gear. And every morning, four patrols of two men each would do just that, slogging over the terrain, to the four points of the compass, with Dragasès, Notaras, and Jean Perret taking turns at the spyglass, following their maneuver. Before long, the natural frontiers of their domain were standing out sharply against the surrounding chaos. To the north, in the hills, the Fontgembar Abbey, where a raid by the commandos had cleaned out a contingent of refugee squatters. To the south, in the valley, a shallow, sandy stream, flanked to the east and west by two winegrowers' farms, blown up by the hussars on their first night in The Village. Within those borders, any Ganges invader or white fellow traveler was shot on sight, and their corpses were left where they fell, as an example. From that point on it was simplicity itself to take in the whole of the West in one glance. The boundaries were clear. One look at the vultures circling the cadavers, hovering in a curtain of black against the sky . . . "That should make them feel right at home!" said the colonel. In his mind they were hunting, not fighting a war. The Village was out to hunt down the black, the way you shoot rabbit in a game preserve. And they posted a tally sheet outside the town hall, to record each day's bag, in the space reserved for official proclamations. It replaced a notice on "the war against mildew," another announcing the annual firemen's gala (complete with a round-robin bowling fest in the square, and a dance in the hall), and a third one publishing the marriage banns of Monsieur Gardaillou (Pierre-Marie), vintner by trade, and Mademoiselle Maindive (Valentine). God only knows what became of those two, or if they're ever going to savor the joys of a wedding morning: the hairdresser giving that final touch, the bridegroom choking in his pearl-gray cravat, the bride's aching feet in her fancy white slippers, her father's car heaped high with flowers, her friends and cousins—already a little tipsy—reaching out to catch her bouquet . . . Old Monsieur Calguès had preserved those three announcements, carefully filing them away in a folder, as if he believed in his new official duties as "Minister of Culture." For what is culture, after all, but a reverent collection of the records of the past?

The first two days' hunt produced eloquent figures. And the sergeant of the hussars applied all his talent to keeping them in order —four vertical lines, neatly crossed by a fifth, drawn over and over —biting his tongue in rapt perseverance. A fine old tradition: the notches scratched into the butt of the rifle, the bombs painted on the rudders of the plane, the tank turrets covered with the silhouettes of tanks! Tally: Ganges, one hundred seventy-seven. Fellow travelers, sixteen.

"Just what do you mean by 'fellow travelers,' Sergeant?"

"Any white that's gone over to the black side, Colonel. When I served in Chad I knew a few that would shoot us in the back. We called them 'nigger-lovers.' "

"Nasty business!" the colonel replied. "But what's the difference between the two?"

"Very simple, Colonel. 'Nigger-lovers' are what they start out as. They wind up as 'fellow travelers' later, when there's no more white left in them at all. Sort of the final stage, I guess. So as long as we're going to kill them, I figure at least we should call them what they are. Anyhow, we picked off nine of them today, all with one round. Not to mention the forty-two Ganges bastards. The rest of them grabbed up the wounded and beat it."

"We've seen the last of them for a while," said the colonel. "At least, until the planes come around."

"Planes? What planes?" Jean Perret piped up.

"Our own, goddammit! With the pretty little markings. You know. Blue, white, red. Unless they take the time to change them. But why the hell bother? They know I have no planes. No chance of shooting up the wrong damn side. You'll see! I bet you the first one flies over by the end of the week . . ."

Hanging from the back of an old bench, in the square, where the "government" was lolling about beneath the trees, the colonel's walkie-talkie sputtered out a message:

"Reporting a group of people sighted at Fontgembar, Colonel," said the voice of the commando captain. "All whites. Maybe four or five. Hard to be sure. They're hiding."

"Well, get the hell in there and smoke the bastards out. They're probably scared shitless. There's two of you. What are you waiting for, damn it!"

"That's not the problem, Colonel. They haven't fired a shot. In fact, I think they want to surrender. They've got like a white cloth tied to some kind of stick, and they've been waving it through the slit in the door for the last ten minutes."

"Well then, yell to them to come out with their hands in the air. I'll be right over. Just watch out for a trap . . ."

And he turned to Perret:

"Do you want to come along?"

No, it was no trap. At the very first command, a voice shouted back from inside the walls:

"With pleasure! That's what we're here for!"

There were four all together. The first was an old man, ramrod straight, with deep-blue eyes. His close-cropped white hair seemed rather at odds with his drooping mustache. Under one arm, an antique of a shotgun—unloaded, barrel broken—a white handkerchief tied to the end. His other hand was waving in great gestures of friendship, and he shouted as the colonel and the others approached: "It's about time! Thank Heaven! We were beginning to worry. There's only one road, and with all of you shooting at anything that moves, we thought we'd better wait . . ." He introduced himself: "Jules Machefer, editor in chief of *La Pensée Nationale*, God rest its soul. Like everyone else, I decided to run. But at least I'm running in the right direction . . ." A statement that brought him a rousing ovation. (Unless such a high-sounding word is a little out of place for the crowd of four in question: Dragasès, Perret, the commando captain, and his one-man detachment.)

The second of the group was a sight to behold. Not only because he belonged to another age, but more so because of the bizarre way he was dressed. He too was an old man, not quite as erect as Jules Machefer. But still, he shook all the outstretched hands with a vigorous grip and a look to match. "Let me introduce the Duc d'Uras," Machefer interjected. One would think that the duke had dressed in a hurry, with anything he happened to find lying around. The weekend flannel pants and sturdy walking shoes were both practical enough. But then, the tight-fitting habit, straight from the hunt, with silver buttons struck with the d'Uras crest. And around his middle, a broad white leather belt. The riding cap perched on his head and the hunting knife dangling against his side completed the hybrid disguise. With one last detail to spice up the stew: a tricolor mayoral sash around his neck. Noticing the rather bemused expressions, he hastened to explain:

"When Monsieur Machefer came by rue de Varennes to pick me

up, he told me I had just five minutes to get ready. First I put on what I thought would be best for traveling. Then I said to myself, since this might well be quits, why not dress up in things that meant something to me? After all, I could have put on any number of things. It's 'Captain d'Uras,' you know. Retired. Minister plenipotentiary, first class. Officer of the Order of Malta. Gentleman of the Pope's Palace Guard—underground, of course, since Pius XII . . . Beautiful uniforms, each and every one. I hated to part with them. But the hunting outfit goes back farther than them all. And I did come here to hunt, you might say. Besides, I wore it a lot more than the others. It's something I'm at home in. As for the sash . . . Well, I'm just too fond of it to leave it behind. And it's not that I don't have the right. I really am a mayor, you know. All very legal. Uras, in the Vaucluse. Fifteen families. At least, there were . . ."

He closed his eyes, as if he were kneeling in prayer before a grave. Then he added, with no trace of maudlin emotion:

"And now, if you want to laugh, please feel free. Mayor without a town, minister without a country . . ." (He turned to Perret.) ". . . I'm not sure we're all that different, you know!"

"Ah, but that's where you're wrong, monsieur! We have more officials than you can shake a stick at. All we needed was a mayor. Now we've got one. You're elected!"

"Oh? And what are my duties?"

"None at all, of course!" replied Perret, laughing. "But the rule of law, monsieur, is a sacred institution!"

"And what about us?" shouted two voices, righteously indignant. "Don't forget us. Don't we get to do something, too?"

Two big strapping specimens, probably in their thirties, dressed in corduroy, with hairy black arms, each one with an old Springfield rifle in his hand, having themselves a wonderful time, like the happy-go-lucky types they were.

"Let me introduce Crillon and Romégas," said the duke. "My chauffeur and my valet. Natives of Uras. Been with my family for ten generations. I tried to give them their freedom when I left, but they wouldn't hear of it. Insisted on coming along. And it's a good thing they did. We'd never have made it without them, believe me. There's nothing they can't do. Fix a meal, fire a gun . . ."

"I have a great idea," Perret broke in. "We already have all the ministers we need, a commander in chief, a loyal army, a first-rate mayor. But we don't have the most important thing of all. The people!"

"Damn it, you're right!" exclaimed the colonel. "Shame on me!

How could I forget! All right. Crillon, Romégas . . . You can be the people, how's that?"

They gave each other a nudge, and Crillon answered:

"I guess the two of us can handle it all right. Just one thing. Can we strike when we want to?"

"Strike? Already?"

"And picket, and carry signs," Romégas added. "I mean, we've got to know. Are we the people, or aren't we?"

"The right to strike is a sacred institution, like the rule of law!" Perret declaimed, properly pontifical, as if he were delivering a speech in the Chamber. "Both of them are sacred to our Western way of life! I give you my solemn assurance that the government is perfectly prepared to negotiate, within reasonable limits, of course, and with all due consideration for the welfare of the state. It goes without saying that you'll have to form a union. Or better still, two rival unions, since there are two of you. You'll simply have to picket at different times and places. The mayor will take care of all the details . . ."

The sentence trailed off in a jumble of laughter, hard as Perret tried to keep a straight face. The colonel was laughing himself to tears. The duke, picture of dignity and decorum, was stifling his heaving guffaws and sputtering gasps. Machefer and the army stood there applauding, cheering Perret on with a round of bravos, waving their berets. And the duke's minions, meanwhile, gawking at it all, terribly pleased with their role in the charade. Supreme delight, this moment of grace. This interlude that made up for vulgarities rampant. But one had to be part of it, really, to understand it. If one thinks of them there, so alone, so desperate; if one thinks of their utterly tenuous reprieve, of their knowledge that this was the end of the road, one gets some sense of their dizzy, giddy humor. A bottomless well, spewing up bits of truth, and sucking them down again to drown beyond recall . . .

The colonel drove the truck back, all flags flying. They sang out their chorus of "No, no regrets," and Machefer dredged up a little ditty from his past. A tune about a duke, that met with great success. Especially when the Duc d'Uras took one of the Springfields and, aiming it out the window while the truck rolled on full tilt, mowed down a trio of Ganges bastards, scampering off by the side of the road. Shot dead, through the heart. Great rifle to take on an African safari . . .

That evening, to celebrate the new mayor's inauguration, they had a little party. Monsieur Calguès made a very nice speech. Among his noteworthy comments, the following:

"I've consulted a number of history books to refresh my memory. Because your names—Monsieur Crillon, Monsieur Romégas— seemed to ring a bell. And what I found, my friends, is indeed a coincidence, as in the case of our colonel, Constantine Dragasès. But a remarkable one, as I'm sure you'll admit. It just so happens that at the battle of Lepanto, against the Turks, Don Juan of Austria had two French captains. And their names were, precisely, Crillon and Romégas! I hasten to add that they died in their boots, and that history seems to have recorded no descendants . . ."

After which they ate, still outside on the terrace. Eighteen settings. Including the sentries, who took turns between courses.

Forty-nine

Eighteen. Next day, at lunch, Romégas added two more settings.
Then the source of the reinforcements dried up for good, and the
Western World numbered twenty, period.

The arrival of the last two stragglers hadn't been an easy or a quiet
affair. Especially not quiet. At the crack of dawn, The Village had
been startled awake by a bristling round of fire, coming from occupied territory across the shallow stream. Through the spyglass all
one saw was a flurry of half-starved blacks bounding through the
fields, like a herd of frightened zebra, with no hint at all of what was
causing the excitement. Clearly, though, the shots were approaching
the shore, like a sapper's trench inching toward a town under siege.
Someone was shooting a path to The Village, systematically hacking
through the refugee mass. Or maybe two or three, whoever they
were, judging by the uproar and their very deadly aim.

"Damn good guns!" observed the duke. "Pretty heavy, I'd say.
More for elephant or rhino . . ."

The heroes of the fireworks hadn't shown themselves as yet, but
their tracks weren't the least bit difficult to follow. Black dead and
wounded lined the path of the commotion, as far as the ruins of the
farmhouse to the west, where it seemed to settle, unable to advance.
The invaders must have already formed into militias, because bands
of new arrivals were taking up positions, surrounding the farm, this
time armed with shotguns. Among them, a number of white fellow
travelers, and even a number of national guardsmen, whose uniforms
made them easy to spot. (A disciplined guardsman obeys the established order. That's the ABC, the backbone of the guard. And often-
times its shame.) No doubt the provisional government in Paris had
given orders to stamp out all remnants of racist resistance . . .

"Good God!" the colonel shouted. "Not guardsmen! Already? That
means they'll be sending the planes even sooner than I thought . . ."

All at once the farm was dotted with little clouds. Moments later
a crackle of explosions reached The Village.

"Grenades! The bastards! . . . Well, I don't know who's holed up
inside there, but we're damn well going to go over and get them
out!" (He turned to the duke.) "Your Honor, you and your men hold

the fort! And you, Monsieur Calguès, pour us something to drink. We'll be back in twenty minutes . . ."

An attack to remember. First victory and last. Hussar style, to perfection . . . Some six hundred yards from the farmhouse, the truck opened fire, full speed ahead, like a gunboat spitting death. The machine gun, hastily mounted on the roof, swept the landscape back and forth, with cavalier abandon, strewing bodies in its wake. The truck plunged ahead, tore through the Ganges horde and the guardsmen, like a reaper run wild in a field of grain. The mission took a total of thirty seconds at most, like one of those helicopter rescues at the front. The army jumped over the sides, hit the ground. The whole army—eight men, a sergeant, and a captain—shooting all the while, covering a passage from the farm to the truck, like a kind of escape hatch.

"Come on, in there! Move your ass!" cried the colonel, shouting to whoever was trapped inside. "This is the last train! No more on the way! We pull out in ten seconds!"

Two men came running toward them. They were up to their ears in cartridge belts and such, each one with two rifles with telescopic sights, one in each hand, glistening in the sun.

"God in Heaven!" shrieked Dragasès, aiming his submachine gun. "You! Number two! Who the hell are you? Start talking, goddammit, or I'll fill you full of holes!"

The man in question was dressed Western style, but his skin was dark, and he looked like a Hindu.

"Don't shoot!" he cried. "My name is Hamadura. Ex-deputy from Pondicherry . . ."

They hoisted him into the truck on the fly. He fell in a heap at the feet of his companion, as the truck lurched around a corner and sent them all rolling. Another fifty yards, and Dragasès yelled out to stop. There, by the side of the road, a guardsman stood staring in blank amazement at his mangled and bloodied hand.

"Who's giving you your orders?" the colonel snapped. "Better talk, goddammit, before I let you have it!"

The guardsman shook himself out of his stupor. He looked up. His face was contorted with pain. He had to struggle to get out the words:

"Orders . . . Orders from Paris, Colonel . . . Minister of the . . . the Interior, and . . . and National Defense . . ."

"What's his name?"

"General . . . General Tanque . . ."

"Thanks!" Dragasès replied. "Just curious, that's all . ."

And the guardsman bent over in a little comic bow. With an automatic emptying a round into his belly. (A logical way for him to say good-bye for good.) Then he crumbled to the ground, eyes frozen in a stare, and promptly bit the dust, while the truck barreled back up the hill toward The Village . . .

Any lingering doubts about the two new arrivals were quickly dispelled when Machefer, smiling, raised his glass, on the terrace, in a gesture of welcome:

"I know perfectly well who you are, Monsieur Hamadura, and just why you're here. Though you realize, of course—no offense intended —that your color and your background might give a little pause in a group like ours, to those who didn't know you. I happened to hear you, a couple of weeks ago, on that asinine broadcast over RTZ, when Vilsberg and that Rosemonde Réal woman were going at it to see who could spit out the most up-to-date drivel. I have to admit, when I heard you laugh, I laughed myself sick. I'm afraid you and I were the only ones, though. I wish you could repeat what you told them that night."

"Indeed I can," the ex-deputy assured him. "I remember it perfectly. Word for word. 'You don't know my people,' I told those buffoons, 'the squalor, the superstitions, the fatalistic sloth they've wallowed in for generations. You don't know what you're in for if that fleet of brutes ever lands in your lap! Everything will change in this country of yours. My country now, too. They'll swallow you up . . .' Then they cut me off. And I wasn't even through."

"Not bad for a start," the colonel observed.

"What I wanted to tell them," Hamadura continued, "was that, to my way of thinking, being white isn't really a question of color. It's a whole mental outlook. Every white supremacist cause—no matter where or when—has had blacks on its side. And they didn't mind fighting for the enemy, either. Today, with so many whites turning black, why can't a few 'darkies' decide to be white? Like me. I decided, and here I am. With my four rifles, and my friend Sollacaro here. I came across him on the road this morning, and I'll tell you, he's got one hell of a trigger finger! Anyway, thank you for coming to our rescue . . ."

"Monsieur Hamadura," Perret broke in, "I've got an idea for you. See what you think. We still have one cabinet post to fill, and it strikes me that you would be just the man to fill it. Monsieur Calguès is our Minister of Culture. Captain Notaras has the Navy. Monsieur Machefer, Information. Colonel Dragasès, Defense. What do you say?

Would you like to be minister of something too?"

The ex-deputy from Pondicherry looked at the eighteen grinning faces, and felt himself caught up in the humor of it all. Which was just the reaction The Village was after. Comedy, pure and simple. A quick, carefree death. No tragedy for them. Let the others languish in their deep, heavy drama. Let them drag it out to their hearts' content, to the stupid, bitter end of their dull, drab, egalitarian existence.

"Monsieur, I accept," he declared with a laugh.

"Fine!" Perret replied. "I hereby appoint you Minister for the Overseas Territories."

"All right. But if it's all the same with you, I'd rather keep the old-fashioned title: Minister for the Colonies!"

He too had understood.

"Now then," Perret went on, "what can we find for you, Monsieur Sollacaro? The one thing we don't have yet is a chaplain. And the way things are, we really can't afford to turn our backs on religion! I seem to picture you dressed in black, my friend. You wouldn't just happen to be a man of the cloth?"

Sollacaro was a wiry, rakish-looking type, tall and thin as a rail. Clearly a man of meticulous taste, elegant to a fault, from the cuffs of his white silk shirt to his splendid deep-pile alpaca coat, impeccably tailored. Of course, rather the worse for the morning's encounter. Trousers torn, alligator pumps all scuffs and smudges. But anyone could see at the very first glance that Monsieur Sollacaro wasn't one to cut corners when it came to high fashion. Nothing but the best. And a huge diamond perched on his left-hand little finger confirmed the impression.

"Me? Be your chaplain?" Sollacaro answered. "Listen, that's fine with me. I'm a Corsican and a Catholic, and I haven't forgotten a one of my prayers. But ... There's something I think maybe I should tell you first. You see, until last Friday, I had a little business. A club ... A ... All right, a cathouse, if you want to know the truth. But the best one up and down the coast. The Club Chic-Select, in Nice. Twenty gorgeous girls ..."

"You can say that again," remarked the colonel. "I remember one named Cléo. ... You're right, monsieur. There was no place like it!"

"Me too," said the duke. "I remember a little black girl. Couldn't have been sixteen. Léa ... Béa ..."

"Béa," replied Sollacaro. "That was last year."

"Ah yes, Béa," Perret echoed. "Though, frankly, my favorites were

Lucky and Sylvie. What a pair they were! Absolutely fantastic! All those meetings in Nice. Party congresses, conventions. Then those two at night. What a way to unwind!"

Emotion was getting the better of them now. Their past had a face. Their happiness, lost and gone for good, had a being, a name. The kind of happiness that the West sells for money. Its chic little sins. All very select . . .

"And what's become of those dear ladies now?" asked the Duc d'Uras, brushing away a furtive tear.

"Good question," replied Sollacaro. "That's how come I'm here. I managed to get them all out of the place in a nice fancy bus, and we started up north. No problems, not a hitch. Until we got to Montélimar. Then the roof fell in. We ran across this regiment . . . I mean, what used to be a regiment, before they went wild. You wouldn't believe it. Like a great big pigpen. And all kinds of people. Trash. Nothing but trash. Arabs, criminals, tramps from the street . . . My girls had a time, believe me! Every one of them. And when I say they had a time . . . My girls, with those animals! My gorgeous girls, doing it in a place like that! And for free, God help us! I'm telling you, it turned my stomach. You wonder how low the human race can sink . . . Well, then and there I knew it was war. Between me and that madhouse. Believe me, I know how to get even when I have to. I stole myself a car, turned around, and here I am. So make me what you want. Minister, chaplain . . . Anything you like, as long as Monsieur Hamadura here lets me hold on to two of his beautiful rifles . . ."

The high-class pimp's profession of faith burst the group's nostalgia. First they smiled. Then they laughed. The likes of Sollacaro, damning that "madhouse" to the bestial depths in the name of his "cathouse"! One house for another! What a delightful thought! Though much deeper, in fact, than first met the eye. And they all seemed to feel it.

Then the sergeant proceeded to record the day's bag. More marks on the tally sheet. Ganges, two hundred forty-three. Fellow travelers, thirty-six. And they all stood around, outside, in the little square, discussing the score. Already a daily habit. But one they would tire of in no time at all if things dragged on much longer. "Those planes," mused the colonel, "better get her damn soon . . ."

"Point of order! Point of order!" Perret piped up. "I see two hundred forty-three dead here from the Ganges. But, actually, there's no law that gives us the right to kill them. Just the opposite, in fact! Now, if the ministers don't object, I'd like to propose the following decree, retroactive to Monday, and to take effect immediately. I've just written it up."

He took a slip of paper from his pocket and started to read:

" 'In view of the state of emergency proclaimed throughout the south, the government hereby suspends, until further notice, all provisions of the law of June 9, 1972, said law reading as follows: "All persons found guilty of inciting to discriminatory, prejudicial, or violent behavior toward any individual, or group of individuals, for reasons of that individual's, or that group of individuals' race, color, religion, or national origin, shall be subject to imprisonment for a term of not less than one, and not more than twelve months, and to a fine of not less than two thousand, and not more than three hundred thousand francs. Furthermore, all persons found guilty of directly inciting the perpetrator or perpetrators of such behavior, either by means of inflammatory speeches, spoken or written, or of verbal threat in places of public assembly, or by means of printed matter, including all manner of drawing, engraving, painting, emblem, and other such graphic representation, sold, distributed, offered for sale, or displayed in places of public assembly, shall be prosecuted to the full extent of the law as accessories before the fact of said crime." Adopted this day . . . Et cetera, et cetera . . .' I know it's a little late," Perret continued. "But until today, who would have dared? I did a little checking. When that law was passed, there wasn't a single dissenting vote. I suppose my colleagues in the Chamber back then didn't see where it would lead. Or, at least, if they had a suspicion, they weren't going to run the risk of admitting it. There are times when dissent can be a dangerous thing."

"Don't forget, though, monsieur," the colonel objected, "if this decree of yours absolves us of racist crimes, won't it do the same thing for those bastards out there, who are after our hides? That law of June 1972 was a two-edged sword. It didn't specify what race or what color."

"Oh, really?" quipped Perret. "Now fancy that! Until last Sunday I never would have guessed! Well, it doesn't matter now. We're the only ones who'll know. Isn't it always the way!"

And they sat down to lunch.

Fifty

The plane showed up at the same time, next day. That is, the Thursday after Easter. As it skimmed low over the bell tower, they could see that it still had its original markings. But no dip of the wings in a friendly salute. It flew toward the stream, followed it west as far as the farm, swooped in a low arc for a look at Fontgembar and the farmhouse to the east, then headed back straight for The Village, fast as its jets would take it. Along the borders, thousands of bodies rose up as it passed, as if blown to their feet by its gusting breath. Moments later, a chorus of deafening cheers, circling the territory with a wall of joyous sound.

"Hit the dirt!" blared the colonel.

The windows in the town hall were shattered to bits, and the stone façade crumbled in a shower of bullets. The plane strafed a path a few yards above the rooftops, then disappeared off to the north.

"Just wanted to give us a taste," said Dragasès. "So we won't be surprised when the rest of them show up. Who knows? He may have been one of our old buddies . . ."

From out of the north, a low, distant roar, growing louder by the second.

"Tanque's planes," said the colonel.

They could already count them. There were six waves of three.

"Eighteen! They found eighteen pilots to accept this mission!"

In point of fact, there were three times that many. Three squadrons of eighteen in the space of five minutes. But they didn't have time for a final count. Which made their last moments that much easier to bear.

They were all on the terrace. Dragasès was in the middle.

"We have two choices. We can make a break for it. Together, or every man for himself . . . But take a look out there!"

He was pointing toward the countryside all around The Village. Everywhere, nothing but the howling, swarming horde. Thousands of human ants, streaming down the zigzag path from Fontgembar, in an endless column, bristling with fists, and sticks, and scythes, and guns . . .

"To end up, with scum like that, hand to hand, in one big massacre . . . No, that wouldn't make much sense . . ."

"And the second choice?" asked Perret, though they all knew the answer.

"Stay right where we are. We only have a few minutes to wait. I'd rather be killed by our own. It's much cleaner that way. There's something more final. No regrets, and all that . . ."

"I remember what you told us: 'We've got to finish our little drama somewhere.' Is this what you meant by an appropriate setting?"

"Exactly."

"I knew it all the time," Perret answered. "I guess we all did. That's why we came along."

Then he straightened up and smiled, as if an amusing idea had just struck him.

"Monsieur Sollacaro, since your memory is so good, and since you're our chaplain, maybe it's time for you to say a few prayers . . ."

The last couple of words were drowned out by the bombs. Suddenly old Monsieur Calguès's villa, built in 1673 to last a thousand years, was a heap of rubble, like the rest of The Village.

When the guardsmen showed up to identify the bodies, they found in the wreckage a tally sheet of sorts, still strangely intact. Ganges, three hundred twelve. Fellow travelers, sixty-six.

The final score. Noon, on the Thursday after Easter.

To which the following names should be added: Colonel Constantine Dragasès, chief of staff; Jean Perret, undersecretary of state; Calguès, professor of French literature, retired; Jules Machefer, editor and publisher; Captain Luke Notaras, skipper of the freighter *Isle of Naxos*; Hamadura, ex-deputy from Pondicherry; the Duc d'Uras, officer of the Order of Malta; Sollacaro, owner of a whorehouse in Nice; the Second Chamborant Regiment, with a sergeant and three hussars; the First Marine Commando unit, with a captain and five men; and Crillon and Romégas, natives of Uras, village in the Vaucluse. Twenty in all.

In memoriam.

It's only right that someone should remember . . .

Fifty-one

And I do. I remember, as I write these last few lines. I've told my story more for myself than for any who might read it. The new regime has its own official version, and I have no hope whatever of seeing myself in print. The most I can expect is that, some day, my grandchildren may read my words without too much disgust that my blood runs through their veins. Besides, how much will they even understand? Will the word *racism* have any meaning for them at all? Even in my day the meaning has changed. What I always understood to be a simple expression of the races' inability to get along together has become for my contemporaries—or most of them, I daresay—a war cry, a call to arms, a crime against humanity and the dignity of man. Too bad. Let them understand the word as best they can.

Maybe, at least, it will help calm their anger and allay their confusion if they know that I've written this account in Switzerland. (I think I've made mention of that fact from time to time.) Curious, the reprieve we found here within her borders, myself and a handful of others. Not the cowards. No, not the ones who whooped and hollered the loudest, and then were the first to run. I'm talking about those of us who headed for Switzerland in an effort to hang on to something that we loved: a Western way of life, with our own kind of people. Strange little country! Laughed at for years, for going about her business, never eating herself up with guilt, never beating her breast with remorse for her down-to-earth pursuit of the everyday pleasures. To be Swiss was to wear a yellow badge of shame. And all the proper-minded folk would point her out to the gaping clowns, and wag their fingers in scorn, or condescension. To think! A country that dared boast such selfish, abnormal values!

Then Easter Monday, and it all turned to hate. She had called up her reserves. Like every other time when war threatened to surround her. She picked herself a general. She sealed off her borders. Even worse! She threw out all her black, and brown, and tan! Or at least she kept them under such close surveillance that a hue and cry went up accusing her of building concentration camps and ghettos. None of which was true. Not a word, I assure you. Though a dark skin was, in fact, viewed with some suspicion. (And I wonder, by the way, if that really was so new for this land that was always in the forefront of freedom.) The UN, of course, packed up and left, along with its futile and meaningless cortege of charitable institutions. All at once, in Geneva, the air seemed clearer. You could take a deep breath. But needless to say, it didn't last long. Just a few short months. Not even a year.

Because Switzerland's foundations, too, had been sapped from within. The beast had undermined her, but slowly and surely, and it merely took her that much longer to crumble. Then in time, chunk by chunk, she let herself go, forgot herself and began to think. Her collapse was really in the best of taste. The famous shield of perennial neutrality still made a vague impression. The beast put on gloves before yodeling for the kill. From inside and out, the pressures grew stronger. A Munich-style coup. No way to avoid it. Back to the wall. She had to give in. And today she signed.

At midnight tonight her borders will be opened. Already, for the last few days, they've been practically unguarded. And I'm sitting here now, slowly repeating, over and over, these melancholy words of an old prince Bibesco, trying to drum them into my head: "The fall of Constantinople is a personal misfortune that happened to all of us only last week."

Afterword

I wrote *The Camp of the Saints* ten years ago. I was not, I am not, a sociologist. Nor am I a futurologist. I am simply a novelist who, one morning in 1972, at home by the shore of the Mediterranean, had a vision:

They were there! A million poor wretches, armed only with their weakness and their numbers, overwhelmed by misery, encumbered with starving brown and black children, ready to disembark on our soil, the vanguard of the multitudes pressing hard against every part of the tired and overfed West. I literally saw *them*, saw the major problem they presented, a problem absolutely insoluble by our present moral standards. To let them in would destroy us. To reject them would destroy them.

During the ten months I spent writing this book, the vision never left me. That is why *The Camp of the Saints*, with all its imperfections, was a kind of emotional outpouring. I came out of it totally exhausted, almost unrecognizable even to myself. I have written other novels since, but this one, I must say, seemed to have been dictated by an otherworldly force, by an inspiration from on high I wouldn't dare name. Only after I had finished the last chapter and reached the point of no return in the final confrontation between *us* and *them*, did I wake from the horror and become myself again, that is to say, a somewhat degenerate and overly sensitive Westerner.

As some readers may guess, the ending of the book was not at all what I originally had in mind. My pen simply disobeyed my muse, who urged the use of force against these unhappy people, who wanted me to throw them back into the sea by every possible means and to massacre them to save ourselves. Instead, giving up all pretense of resistance, I disarmed the army that was opposing them, for I myself in such circumstances would not have had the courage to fire one shot when brought face to face with those hordes of living, breathing misery. And so it was, for lack of what might be called literary courage, I denied to the white Occident, at least in my novel, its last chance for salvation. Otherwise, I would never have been pardoned.

When the first edition of the book appeared, it was badly received. The surrender at the end had no effect on the critics. I was called a "racist," the ultimate anathema of our hypersensitive and totally blind West, a West which has not yet understood that whites, in a world become too small for its inhabitants, are now a minority and that the proliferation of other races dooms our race, my race, irretrievably to extinction in the century to come, if we hold fast to our present moral principles. What I was saying, of course, was terrible. I waited patiently to be burnt at the stake.

But as time went on a strange thing happened. Little by little I was forgiven for this novel which seemed to be developing a life of its own as news of it spread from reader to reader by word of mouth, in spite of the disapproving silence of outraged public opinion. It was helped along secretly by sociologists, writers and politicians. All those who count in France, from left to right, began to read *The Camp of the Saints,* including the President of the Republic—but without admitting it, as if they were committing some evil but vitally necessary act. Although I was at a loss to explain it, numerous foreign editions cropped up across the world, all more or less underground, except perhaps in the United States, where I was surprised to see my book commented upon favorably in several widely read magazines and newspapers.

And, when there appeared on the shores of Asia, the shores of Europe and the coasts of the United States, flotillas of boat people similar to those I had invented several years before—when it was proved by irrefutable statistics that our land frontiers had cracked open in the United States and Europe and that these people were entering our countries by the tens of millions in an irreversible stream—when the slow, cancerous progress of compassion, which is only a misleading and lethal form of charity, duly laid siege to the Western conscience—when it finally became apparent that in the future the denial of essential and basic human differences would work solely to the detriment of our own integrity—then, at last, people began to understand what I had tried to express. I, the accursed writer, was transformed into a prophetic writer.

I did not ask for this, I did not hope for it. *The Camp of the Saints* is, above all, a symbolic book that is both opaque and transparent. This is how I judge it ten years after having written it. It is primarily a novel, a sort of anti-epic, a crusade in reverse, a book charged with all the convoluted instincts and contradictions of the white man. If someone, somewhere up there, inspired me to write it, that someone, I imagine, was trying to force us into direct confrontation with ourselves and with our own special destiny here on earth.

Jean Raspail
1982

Near the 25th anniversary of its publication, author Jean Raspail wrote about The Camp of the Saints *in this article for the June 17, 2004 edition of* Le Figaro. *It is translated from the French by Peter Wakefield Sault and is reprinted from* American Renaissance, *www.Amren.com.*

Fatherland Betrayed by the Republic

by Jean Raspail

I circled around this topic like a dog handler in the presence of a parcel bomb. It is difficult to approach it directly without having it explode in one's face. There is danger of civilian death. It is, however, the main line of investigation. I hesitated. Especially as in 1973, by publishing *The Camp of the Saints*, I had already said it all. I do not have a great deal to add except to say that the deed is done.

Since I am convinced that the fate of France is sealed, because "My house is their house," (Mitterand) inside "Europe whose roots are as much Muslim as Christian," (Chirac) and because the situation is moving irreversibly towards the final swing in 2050 which will see French stock amounting to only half the population of the country, the remainder comprising Africans, Moors and Asians of all sorts from the inexhaustible reserve of the Third World, predominantly Islamic, understood to be fundamentalist Jihadists, this dance is only the beginning.

France is not the only concern. All of Europe marches to its death. The warnings are precise – the UN report (which delighted some), incontrovertible work by Jean-Claude Chesnais and Jaques Dupachier, in particular – yet they are systematically buried and the National Institute for Demographic Studies [INED] pushes disinformation.

The almost sepulchral silence of the media, governments and community institutions on the demographic crash of the European Union is one of the more striking phenomena of our time. When there is a birth in my family or in the homes of my friends, I cannot look at this baby of our house without reflecting upon that which prepares itself for him in the negligent governments and what he must confront in his manhood ...

Without taking into account that those of French stock, bludgeoned by the throbbing tom-tom of human rights, of "the welcome to the outsider," of the "sharing" dear to our bishops, etc., framed by a whole repressive arsenal of laws known as "anti-racist," conditioned from early childhood with cultural and behavioral "crossbreeding," with the requirements of "plural France" and with all the by-products of old Christian charity, will no longer have any other means but to lower their children and to merge without kids into the new mold French "citizen" of 2050.

All the same let us not despair. Without doubt, there will remain what is called in ethnology some isolates, some powerful minorities, perhaps about 15 million French – and not necessarily all of the white race – who will still speak our language more or less unbroken and will insist on remaining impregnated with our culture and our history such as was transmitted to us from generation to generation. It will not be easy for them.

Facing the various "communities" which one sees being formed today on the ruins of integration (or rather on its progressive reversal – it is us whom one integrates into "the other," now, and more the opposite) and which in 2050 will be permanently and without doubt institutionally installed, it will be to some extent – I seek a suitable term – a community of French continuity. This one will be based on its families, its birth-rate, its endogamy of survival, its schools, its parallel networks of solidarity, perhaps even its geographical areas, its portions of territory, its districts, even its places of safety, and, why not, its Christian and catholic faith with a small chance if this cement still holds. That will not please. The clash will take place some time or another – something like the elimination of the Kulaks by suitable legal means. And then?

Then France will no longer be peopled, all confused origins, except by hermit crabs who will live in shells left behind by the representatives of a species gone forever which was called the French species and unannounced, by one does not know which genetic metamorphosis, that which in the second half of this century will have been clothed with this name. This process has already started.

There is one second hypothesis that I could not formulate otherwise than privately and which would require that I consult my lawyer beforehand, it is that the last isolates resist until initiating a kind of reconquest undoubtedly different from the Spanish but taking as its starting point the same reasons. This will be a perilous story to write about. It is not me who will be charged with this, as I have already done my bit. Its author has probably not yet been born, but this book will see the light of day at the appointed time, I am sure...

What I cannot understand and which plunges me into an abyss of sorry perplexity, is why and how so many informed Frenchmen and so many French politicians contribute knowingly, methodically — I don't care to say cynically — with the certain immolation of France (let us avoid the qualifier of eternal which disgusts the beautiful consciences) on the altar of an aggravated utopian humanism.

I ask myself the same question in connection with all these omnipresent associations of rights to this, rights to that, and all these leagues, these think tanks, these subsidized headquarters, these networks of manipulators insinuated into all the wheels of State (political education, judiciary, parties, trade unions, etc.), these innumerable petitioners, these correctly consensual media and all these "clever" folks who day after day and with impunity inoculate their anesthetic substance into the still healthy body of the French nation.

Even if I can, at a pinch, credit them on the one hand with sincerity, it sometimes saddens me to admit that they are my countrymen. I feel the sting of the renegade word, but there is another explanation: they confuse France with the Republic. "Republican values" have deteriorated ad infinitum; one knows it fully, but never with reference to France. However, France is from

317

the outset a country of [common] blood. On the other hand, the Republic, which is only one shape of government, is synonymous for them with ideology, ideology with a capital "I," the major ideology. It seems to me, to some extent, that they betray the first for the second.

Among the flood of references which I accumulate in thick files in support of this assessment, here is one which under the [deceptive] appearance of a good child illuminates the extent of the damage well. It is drawn from a speech by Laurent Fabius to the socialist congress of Dijon, 17th May 2003: "When the Marianne [statue of Liberty] on our town halls takes the beautiful face of a young immigrant Frenchwoman, this day France will have crossed a line while bringing alive fully the values of the Republic ..."

Since we are [left] with quotations, here are two to conclude: "No amount of atomic bombs will be able to dam up the tidal wave comprising human beings in their millions which one day will leave the southernmost and poor part of the world, to erupt the relatively open spaces of the wealthy northern hemisphere, in search of survival." (President Boumediene, March 1974).

And this one, drawn from the 20th chapter of *Revelation*: "The thousand years is expired. Those are what departs the nations which are at the four corners of the Earth and which are equal in number to the sand of the sea. They will go forth in expedition across the surface of the Earth, they will surround the camp of the saints and the beloved city." ∎

*Katharine Betts is a senior lecturer in sociology at the
Swinburne University of Technology in Melbourne, Australia.
She is co-editor of the Australian quarterly,* People and Place,
*which focuses chiefly on immigration policy questions. This
article is reprinted from the Winter 1994-1995 issue of* The
Social Contract, *Volume 5, Number 2.*

An Interview with Jean Raspail

By Katharine Betts

Synopsis of *The Camp of the Saints*

First, we must go back twenty years. It is 1973. For some years
now the West has lost all sense of belief in itself and, because of
this, has lost the will to defend itself. Such a clever and inventive
civilization, this Western culture, but the things it creates are ugly.
They destroy the self-respect of those who make them and of those
who buy them. And the ideas it produces are worse. The biggest
idea that this West of 1973 has produced is "the beast," the idea of
"world conscience." This beast is made of two parts, one of guilt
and one of anti-racism. The guilt portrays Third World poverty as
a consequence of Western greed, while the anti-racism condemns
any attempt by the guilt-ridden to protect themselves against the
Third World retribution that is to come.

The ugly material goods, the objects that corrupt their makers
and consumers, are produced by capitalists. But the ideas come
from the critics of capitalism, from left-wing activists and
journalists, and from churchmen. And here is a nice paradox: the
left dominate the media, but the right have to tolerate them because,
without the audiences that left-wing broadcasters attract, the
capitalists would have no means of selling their tawdry goods. In
France, in particular, a proud tradition has deteriorated. A limping,
ramshackle culture, full of self-interested cant, shot through with
veins of self-hatred, is to be tested. A mere hundred unseaworthy
boats will bring a million uninvited immigrants from the other side
of the earth, and France will be found wanting. It will fail the test

and all of the West will fail with it.

Over the course of fifty days the armada from the Ganges creeps nearer to the coast of the Midi. The media rejoice, while politicians and the armed forces fumble for a policy. Leaders in each European country agonize over their nation's culpability, and offer sympathy and praise for the voyagers in public. In private, they hope desperately that the ships will land on someone else's shores. But fate is bringing them to France.

Albert Dufort, the trendy radio journalist, knows that when the armada arrives the people it brings will set off a chain of events that will destroy modern France. But he believes that this destruction will mean the rebirth of man. We in the West are to blame for the injustices poor countries suffer. We condemned our Third World brothers by setting up walls to keep them at a distance. Now they have broken out of their prison and they are coming, seeking justice.

For Dufort, the journey of the armada symbolizes the international redistribution of wealth. He is transported by the imagery, by the symbolism of the events that he reports. With growing excitement, he coins the slogan: "We're all from the Ganges now." School children write essays eulogizing the armada's approach. Any doubts that serious men and women may have about redemption by invasion are washed away in a flood of emotion and self-flagellating rhetoric.

In the last days before the ships lurch through the Straits of Gibraltar to the coast, the French begin to panic. At the eleventh hour, the President orders the military to defend the country, but it is too late. Most of the men desert. The inhabitants of the south flee north, police abandon their posts, jails are opened, prisoners rampage. Dufort flees in his car to Switzerland and is murdered *en route* in a random act of violence. At the same time student revolutionaries journey south to meet their foreign brothers. They do not know that the people from the Ganges are not coming as brothers. The immigrant invaders hate the West, the civilization that has robbed them of the earthly paradise that should be theirs. Rather than rejecting the small welcoming committee of students, they scarcely see them. They surge through the students, and over them, spreading out over a countryside that seems, to them, to be empty of people.

But this is not just the story of the sea trek of one million in search of a promised land. In all the poor, desperately over-populated countries around the world, hungry souls are poised to follow. They are monitoring the fortunes of the armada closely. When France puts up only a token, last minute resistance, and the people of the Ganges swarm over the Midi, the others move, too. The beast has done its work and the Third World, full of a sense of injury and entitlement, takes over the First. After 1973, we are indeed "all from the Ganges now."

Who Is Jean Raspail?

The Camp of the Saints is a terrifying book. It holds the reader tightly, even while blood, filth and violence spill from its pages. Few would read it for pleasure. But is it prophecy? Some parts bear the stamp of 1968, the student revolt in Paris, and the particular left-wing enthusiasms of the period. But, twenty years on, the "beast" still speaks with a disconcertingly contemporary voice. The same agonies of guilt, and the same uncertainties about the right of nations to maintain their borders distort immigration debates today, even as they did in this unhappy, fictitious world.

Who wrote this book and why? My husband Gavin and I went to visit the author, M. Jean Raspail, in Paris in October of 1993. We wanted to ask him about his novel and to inquire, on behalf of *The Social Contract Press*, whether he would agree to a new edition of Norman Shapiro's English translation.

M. Raspail has a large ground-floor apartment in a modern building in a quiet and exclusive inner suburb of Paris. There is a glass case full of model soldiers in the lobby. The study is long and narrow, looking out onto a green and private garden, something quite exceptional for this crowded city.

The French *Who's Who* lists M. Raspail as a traveler and explorer, as well as a writer. There are books in the study, of course, but also many engravings of Native Americans. In 1950-52, he led the Tierra del Fuego-Alaska car trek, and in 1954, the French research expedition to the land of the Incas. Possibly the engravings date from this period, and from his association with

Patagonia. (In 1981 his novel, *Moi, Antoine de Tounens, roi de Patagonie*, won the *Grand Prix de Roman* from the Academie Francaise — the major prize for novels in France.) There is a large model battleship on the floor of the study. The original art work for the cover of the first edition of *The Camp of the Saints* stands on a side table; it shows a motley collection of boats which have come to rest in the shallows, while strong, brown-skinned men stride ashore across the beach.

M. Raspail is a tall man of soldierly bearing. He is a traditionalist. While he is courtesy and gentleness itself in his manner towards us, he dislikes the incursions that Anglo-Americanisms have made into the French culture. Though he once knew some English, he no longer wishes to use it. Gavin and I make do with our limited French.

Our first question is the obvious one: Do you think that the vision portrayed in your book is coming true? The answer: Haven't you seen the preface to the third (1985) French edition of the book? No, indeed we hadn't.

We should read it (See page xiii). This preface explains that the book is symbolic, a parable. History is speeded up to happen over the course of days rather than a couple of decades or a generation. In real life things don't come about so quickly, but the principle remains the same. The Third World invasion of the West is unavoidable. If we don't see it, our children will.

How did people react when the book first came out? M. Raspail said that the response was very different in the United States compared to France. He wasn't very well known in France in 1973 and the immediate reaction to the book was silence. It only began to sell six or eight months after it first appeared. It sold by word of mouth. Some people bought large numbers of copies — 100 to 150 at a time. In contrast, in the U.S. there was a strong reaction in the press immediately, some against, many for. He still receives many letters from the States.

We mentioned Gary Freeman's recent article on comparative immigration policy, and his comment that more and more analysts were taking *The Camp of the Saints* seriously. Did he think that this was happening? It was possible. But he then went on to talk a little about how he had come to write the book. It was an idea that came to him then — he couldn't write the same book today. It requires nerve to do such a thing. (In the 1985 preface M. Raspail talks about how the book took 18 months to write, and of how it consumed and aged him.)

We knew of Shapiro's English translation but we asked him about others. It has now been translated into every major European language, Spanish, Portuguese, German, Italian, Dutch and so on. In France, it is constantly in print.

Why was it that he had portrayed the conflict in the book in terms of race, brown and black against white, rather than in terms of conflict between groups marked out by different cultures? M. Raspail replied that this was a big question. He said that it is race that gives culture its mark in the beginning. Yes, different races can indeed assimilate to different cultures. He reminded us of the book's M. Hamadura, the black ex-deputy of Pondicherry, the one who joins the small band of stalwarts who hold out for a few weeks defending one last little corner of Provence. Hamadura says that being white isn't really a question of color — it's a whole mental outlook, a state of mind. But, Raspail said, later the racial distinctions can come back.

It had struck me that the book was every bit as much about his disgust with French society as it was about the Third World population explosion. So we asked him if the events of May 1968 in France, the student uprising, the wave of strikes, had had much influence on him. Yes, they had. When he was writing the book he had been full of a sense of the degeneration of his society and of its lack of intelligence.

We asked him about his vision of the West, this West that had lost all confidence in itself as a worthwhile civilization. Where did he think this mentality ("the beast") had come from? He said this was a difficult question. It was a collection of things; one couldn't really say. In one sense the West is more than ever triumphant, but it has a conception of the rights of man. In its original form this was an excellent idea, but it has now been misapplied and it is being used against France, the very country that had first conceived it.

We also asked him about his opinion of recent actions that the

French government had taken to try to tighten the rules governing entry for family reunion and for people seeking political asylum. Did he think that these measures would amount to anything? No. It is impossible to do anything. It's too late. There have been mass movements of people already and there are now too many to send back. "These steps that Balladur (the Prime Minister) and Pasqua (Minister for the Interior) are taking are just to appease the electorate. They won't make any difference."

How did he see the future of the West? "*Je n'en sais rien.*" (Literally, "I know nothing about it," but "I have no idea" is probably a better translation.)

Further Reflections

After we left we went straight to the bookshop M. Raspail had recommended in order to seek out the 1985 edition. It was now 11:30 in the morning. The shop was small and intimate, set in a back street. It was presided over by two men who reminded me of the novel's M. Machefer, the elderly and eccentric proprietor of the newspaper, *La Pensée Nationale,* and one of his acolytes. (Machefer is one of the few to warn of the dangers the armada presents. A few youths, young conservatives who share his views, help with the paper. But their voice is small and easily suppressed.)

True to form, both were smoking cigars, and empty champagne flutes stood on the counter beside them. *Le Camp des Saints?* Yes, of course they had it. A wonderful book — a true masterpiece. We also bought M. Raspail's most recent novel, *Sept Cavaliers.* This included a brochure about the author, describing his aristocratic and traditional vision. It quotes his words, "*C'est toujours l'âme qui gagne les combats décisifs* — It's always the soul that wins the decisive battles." Readers of *The Camp* will recall the passage where the armada is headed off from entering the Red Sea by a tough Egyptian admiral. The Egyptian's stance is closer to the firm resolve of the Ganges' immigrant invaders than it is to that of France. Raspail comments, "Two opposing camps. One still believes. One doesn't. The one that still has faith will move mountains. That's the side that will win. Deadly doubt has destroyed all incentive in the other. That's the side that will lose."

Is M. Raspail's novel a prophecy fulfilled, complete with an explanation for why the disaster happened and why it is now too late? Are we losing our heritage because we have lost faith in our civilization, and is the story now well on the way to its denouement? Freeman's work is a careful analysis of the increasingly firm response of immigrant-receiving nations in the face of growing pressure for entry. It suggests that we are looking at a conditional prediction in this novel rather than a certain prophecy. If nations behave in the vacillating and foolish manner described in *The Camp of the Saints*, then the serious situation that North America, Europe and Australia now confront will indeed worsen, and the outcome will surely not maximize human happiness, either for hosts or immigrants. But, if sensible and well-coordinated policies are adopted, M. Raspail's grand epic can be read as one picture of a possible future, a future that we may have the wit to see and the courage to avert. ∎

Newsday columnist James Pinkerton writes:

We were warned. Three decades ago, Jean Raspail published a novel, *The Camp of the Saints*, which served as a worst-case-scenario warning about the consequences of unchecked immigration into his native France and, by extension, into all of Europe. Raspail's book was a big seller in his home country, but his message was not heeded. Now, of course, he is being vindicated. Today, after 9/11, Madrid, London, and the broad-daylight murder of Theo Van Gogh, Paris is burning.

How could this have been allowed to happen? What led to this influx of lions into countries full of lambs?

In *The Camp of the Saints*, Raspail provided his answer. Those who welcome large quantities of immigrants, he gibed, were "righteous in their loathing of anything and everything that smacked of present-day Western society, and boundless in their love of whatever might destroy it."

This should serve as a reminder to us all: while a few in the West have been sounding the alarm against foreign invasion for many years now, many in the East have been sounding a clarion call of their own — that they're coming to conquer us.

Recent Readers' Comments
As posted on Amazon.com

This book, published in 1973, fits into today's troubled world and is perfect for our time....Compelling, moving, thrilling...buy it, read it, love it.
—Vincent F. Mannella, August 22, 2007

Monsieur Raspail is quite correct in speaking out loudly and honestly about the threat to the West, a threat consisting of massive numbers of cultural aliens who simultaneously envy and loathe our civilization and are hell bent on its destruction. He is also right in pointing out that the West is exhausted, decadent, and degenerate, that it is deplete of courage, will, and genuine intellect; all replaced by cowardice, complacency, a pathological self-loathing, and the most extraordinary intellectual incoherence and moral bankruptcy. This book is a clarion call. We should hear and heed it. I am afraid we shall do neither.
—Athanasius, NYC, August 13, 2007

I first read *The Camp of the Saints* about ten years ago. I have read it three more times. It is "a joke without a punch line." Raspail is a literary genius. His description of the end of civilization reminds me of Kurt Vonnegut's *Galapagos*. There is a dark humor that resonates through both tales, a harbinger of doom that the reader knows she cannot escape from, but like a train wreck cannot turn away. You will not finish this book and feel good. As a matter of fact, you will feel the gloom for days....It is politically incorrect. It condemns the modern fools who preach brotherly love but suffer from a deadly form of NIMBY (not in my back yard)...This is a must read.
—Kimberly D. Ritz, Boise, Idaho, May 18, 2007

This book is amazing. We are living it here in the USA with the invasion of illegals from Mexico. They are destroying our economy, robbing our welfare system, raiding our hospitals, and leaving little future for American children. The president spends his time with Iraq while the invaders have already gotten into the country and will only leave with force which American don't have the willpower to pursue. While reading this book I was amazed at how boldly it applied to today, right NOW. This author has somehow captured the future and has warned us.

—Mike Brown, Ketchikan, Alaska, April 18, 2007

A look at what the doctrines of "equality," "Liberty" and "Democracy" and decades of media brainwashing have done to the fighting spirit of western civilization.

—J. Roberts, January 29, 2007

Mr. Raspail's book appears to have been prophetic, in light of the current situation in Europe. His suggestion that the ethnicity of the "immigrants" was used as a metaphor for "others" was due to concerns for his safety. I recommend this book....

—Jean H. Leprime, Boston, MA, January 3, 2007

Jean Raspail's parable and caricature of what is to come, once seemingly so surreal, now approaches the documentary. Routine events of our day: Hollywood celebrities clamor to adopt Third World babies as if they were puppies in the window; Four decades of mass legal and illegal immigration now swiftly transform America town-by-town; Countless Orwellian "celebrations," often compulsory, as in schools, trumpet ever more "multiculturalism" and "diversity;" Finally, as in Raspail's scenario, none of these bizarre developments can be effectively criticized without critics becoming socially censored or professionally tarred. Would any Third World nation be considered "racist" if it did not want a European majority? Of course not. Given that inhabitants of non-Western nations would not for one minute entertain policies bringing about their steady demographic diminishment, while enlightened Westerners from Scandinavia to Australia must applaud their own, or at the very least pronounce it "inevitable," you have to wonder if previous besieged callapsing civilizations were likewise first rendered intellectually defenseless. We have become our own Trojan horse.

—Tom Andres, California, September 22, 2006

Camp of the Saints is more a fable than a true novel. Raspail knew that if the Europe of his time kept to its downhill run of selfishness, cynicism and moral decadence then the scenes he describes can be its only fate. Only Raspail was wrong about the identity of those immigrant hordes. It's not the outcastes of India who are threatening the stability and future of Western Europe...nor is it the West Indians or East Indians. Rather it's the Muslims of North Africa and the Middle East, sitting right on the other side of the Mediterranean, steadily pouring into France, Spain, Holland and Italy for the last several decades, who truly are menacing Western Europe and who eventually may come to dominate it.

—Caesar M. Warrington, Lansdowne, PA, July 24, 2006

This controversial book is a must for anyone with doubts about "mass immigration" or the merits of international migration. It describes a situation in which France is selected as a final port of destination for a band of East Indian refugees (over one million strong) who find a means to leave their wretched conditions during a time of famine. These 'few' become the future basis for a full scale colonization of France.

Though somewhat futuristic for the time, it did capture in essence what the future of France was to become, even insomuch as getting the name of the current Pope Benedict correct....Without giving away the entire plot: the French national military loses in the final pages with few shots having actually been fired. At that point an Orwellian society emerges out of the ashes in some sort of multi-racial commune.

—A. Wexler, Orlando, FL, April 21, 2006

I believe that the most powerful attribute of this novel, 33 years after its first publication, is how prophetic and lucid this work is...Reading this novel is like reading a textbook on sociology, international and environmental politics combined. A must-read for any humanist, for anybody concerned with the future of mankind.

—Ary Malaver Copara, Athens, GA, March 7, 2006

Editor Wayne Lutton discusses how The Camp of the Saints *was received by reviewers when it first appeared in the United States in 1975, and illustrates this with excerpts from some of the many reviews that were published. This article is reprinted from the Winter 1994-1995 issue of* The Social Contract, *Volume 5, Number 2.*

The Emergence of a 'Classic'

By Wayne Lutton

> "Forget *Jaws* and *The Towering Inferno*.
> This is the ultimate disaster novel."
> —from an ad in the *New York Times*
> August 19, 1975

The Camp of the Saints first appeared in France in 1973. It soon became a best-seller and foreign rights were sold. By November 1973, the Trade Division of the respected New York firm of Charles Scribner's Sons contracted to publish an English-language edition. Scribner's secured the services of Norman Shapiro of Wesleyan University, Middletown, Connecticut, to translate the novel. *The Camp* was released in this country in the late Summer of 1975.

The book was immediately attacked by the guardians of liberal opinion. Paul Gray fired one of the first salvoes in the August 4, 1975, issue of *Time* magazine. Under the title of "Poor White Trash," Gray dismissed it as a "harangue" and a "bilious tirade" that read as if it had "come off a mimeograph machine in some dank cellar." He accused Raspail, and by clear implication his American publisher, of "exacerbating" racial enmity.

The editors of *The New York Times* found the book so offensive that they published two attacks on it, the first in their issue for Wednesday, August 13, 1975, where Richard Lingeman fumed that "reading Jean Raspail's novel *The Camp of the Saints* is like being trapped at a cocktail party with a normal-looking fellow who suddenly starts a perfervid racist diatribe." As far as Mr. Lingeman was concerned, "on the subject of race [Raspail] apparently becomes a bit loony." Dubbing him "the white man's Franz Fanon," Lingeman dismissed his assumptions as "preposterous" and the story as "grotesquely orchestrated." The novel is "bilge," he warned.

After this panning by America's "newspaper of record" failed to kill sales of the book, the Sunday *New York Times Book Review* launched a second attack on October 5, 1975. If readers and other book reviewers who take their "cue" from the editors of *The Times* didn't get the message the first time, Thomas Lask repeated the charge that the story line was "preposterous." Granting that "we may need the message," Lask chided the author for engaging in "windy rhetoric." *The Camp*'s "moral is overwhelmed by its flaws as a work of art: the narrative is sluggish, the symbolism banal, the scolding tone an affront to the readers."

The New York Times "line" was parroted by other reviewers, especially on the East Coast. Representative of these was the review written by short-story writer and critic Silvia Tennenbaum for *Long Island Newsday* of September 10, 1975. Ms. Tennenbaum called it a "Fascist fantasy...a disgusting book" purveying a theme that was "hideously corrupt." "Fascist rhetoric" marred what she emphasized was "the crudest kind of propaganda, the kind that works on our deepest fears and exploits our hidden disaffections. It is, as I said in the beginning of this review, a truly disgusting book."

To Bruce Allen, in *The Providence Journal*, September 28, 1975, *The Camp* was "a jerry-built nightmare," a "diatribe," and a "psychotic fantasy." Moreover, the story was "foolishly conceived" and "blindly over-written." Finally, his Rhode Island readers were advised that Raspail's novel was simply "a dull and stupid book." So there was certainly no need to go out and purchase a copy.

Further afield, one Virgil Miller Newton, Jr., writing for the *Tampa Tribune* of September 5, 1975, complained that his editor had forced him to review what amounted to "a flood of bilious exacerbation from France."

Conceding that Raspail was an award-winning author in France, the Florida critic noted that his work "hasn't raised a ripple in the more realistic American literary world." Newton the Younger came up with a new literary twist of the knife: he attributed much of Raspail's "vitriol" to the "fact" that Frenchmen were haunted by an apparently congenital inferiority complex." Today France is nothing more than a second-rate country and not a very good one in our industrial age. This, of course, has left the modern Frenchman in quite a quandary." As a consequence, Newton declared, Raspail was simply exhibiting the French sense of frustration when he created a scenario for the end of Western civilization.

Not to worry. From the comfort and relative security of Tampa Bay, Mr. Newton opined that "of course the world faces a great problem in feeding the population explosion during the next 25 years. But I personally don't think we're going to face a racial apocalypse....The brains who gave the world television, nuclear energy, the computer, and put a man on the moon can solve this problem, and without French leadership, too."

To the dismay of the Smart Set, *The Camp of the Saints* did not die a quick death and expire on the remainder tables. James J. Kilpatrick highlighted the novel in both his widely syndicated newspaper column and in the pages of *Nation's Business*. Dartmouth English Professor

Jeffrey Hart praised it in *National Review.* In addition, smaller-market newspapers and journals across the country praised the novel and encouraged their readers to buy it. Thanks to the efforts of independent-minded editors and reviewers, word of *The Camp*'s existence spread, and the book became a success.

No small part of *The Camp*'s initial success in the American market, and its enduring readability, was due to the English-language edition prepared by Professor Shapiro. The task of translating any work of literature is not an easy one, especially where the author makes allusions to places, people, and events that are not necessarily familiar to even educated foreign readers, as was true in several instances in Raspail's novel. Quite aside from its "message," the Shapiro translation of *The Camp of the Saints* remains a work of genuine literary merit.

Further, Professor Shapiro took to answering some of the most outrageous attacks on the book. For example, in response to Silvia Tennenbaum's review in *Newsday*, Dr. Shapiro observed that "it shouldn't take much literary acumen to realize that it was *intended* to shake up the complacent ostrich mentality to an awareness of the major problem of our time: overpopulation...." Elsewhere he pointed out that *The Camp of the Saints* is not "a propagandistic, racist tract, but an intentionally graphic warning of what may well happen to our world if we ignore the real villain of the piece: overpopulation."

Unfortunately, anyone consulting *Book Review Digest* or other literary indexes will not be apprised of the fact that *The Camp* received such wide acclaim in the United States, especially in smaller publications. We are pleased to be able to offer excerpts from a number of the favorable reviews.

John Barkham
Syndicated Book Reviewer
July 23, 1975

This book is a French entry in the fiction disaster stakes, and, as you might expect, it is more logical and less imminent than its American counterparts. But its scale is apocalyptic and its implications awesome. It leaves flaming skyscrapers, sinking liners, and even earthquakes as simple local problems. How can you top the racial clash of civilizations postulated in this vivid French novel?

To call it terrifying would be an exaggeration, but that is likely to be the impression it leaves on more thoughtful readers, for what Jean Raspail pictures is a global Golgotha...His novel is predicated on the supposition that the population time bomb ticking away in India and elsewhere in the Third World will reach explosive force around the beginning of the next century. Then, according to present projection, the human population of the planet will have reached seven billion, less than a tenth of whom will be white.

It is not a pleasant situation to contemplate. Raspail has done more than contemplate it: he has painted a fictional but depressingly convincing picture of the human catastrophe which conceivably would occur. The eruption is triggered by Belgium, which, as an act of benevolence, adopts some 40,000 starving Indians from the gutters of Calcutta. For them, life in Belgium's white society is the purest nirvana. Like wildfire the word spreads through India. Thousands, hundreds of thousands of Indian mendicants ask, demand to be "adopted" by Europeans.

But no European country wants to be overwhelmed by blacks, browns, and yellow people. The Third World comes anyway in an armada of ancient ships. Europe braces for invasion by almost a million starving, desperate people. France is the center of the crisis. What will the French do?

New York, Paris, Rome, London and other capitals become armed fortresses. The Third World has discovered that the white race is rich, and to be rich is better than to be poor. What began as an essay in Christian charity by the Belgians has turned into a race war with whites about to be engulfed by swarms of nonwhites. Raspail's imagination is totally unfettered....

No wonder this novel has created such a deep impression in Europe. It sounds a startling tocsin, and whether you accept Raspail's nightmare or not, his premises are sound. Nature has a way of dealing with over-population by any species, and if it doesn't happen to the human race as blueprinted here,

it could happen some other way. This is a story to read, mark, learn and inwardly digest, especially by those under 40.

Book Browsing
The Charlotte Observer
August 3, 1975

If you want to be in the international literary "with-it" group, grab *The Camp of the Saints* by Jean Raspail. Already acclaimed in Europe the novel struck me as a combination moral *Jaws* and *Brave New World*....It's macabre, chilling, overdone, but it makes a point. And the point is vital. The tide is pushing it ever closer to you and me.

Henry Orland
St. Louis Globe Democrat
August 9-10, 1975

At sore points of history mankind is often graced with genial thinkers, prophets, writers who are able to put their fingertips on wounds developing or festering in ' the *corpus humanus.* A generation ago Orwell and Huxley set ominous problems before us; and we still grapple with them. Now there is Jean Raspail. The Academie Francaise was farsighted enough to award him the Jean-Walther Prize (1970) before he had written this apocalyptic novel. After having read *The Camp* I rank him above most Academicians. The translation is a work of art.

Raspail's basic premises are irrefutable: in a very short time the Third World population will outnumber the inhabitants of the Developed World by almost eight to one; essential resources will become scarcer, and many familiar issues will be perceived in racial terms. Few people are willing to face these chilling facts. Raspail digs into them with existential relish....

The Camp is not a sociological treatise, nor a symbol-laden philosophical dissection of the erosion of Western Civilization. It is a gripping piece of fiction projected into a future practically upon us....

With a pinch of passion and ironic eloquence, the author uncovers the ineluctable truth: the greatest threat to our most cherished values — freedom, compassion — is the population bomb. He does it with great stylistic aplomb, through discomforting, infuriating detail, and with enervating verve. No reader can remain unaffected by the questions raised in this compelling novel. Raspail has succeeded in challenging the contemporary mind, and, hopefully, shocking it into healing action before it is too late.

Richard Langford
The Weekender
August 3, 1975

The Camp of the Saints attracted much attention in Europe and has been a best seller in France. By Jean Raspail, the novel describes the end of the white world and the beginning of the black.

The novel takes place in the near future, at a time when the poor, impoverished, starving nations suddenly decide to abandon their homes and descend in multitudes upon the West....

Simultaneously, in New York, London, Manila, and in Latin America and Australia, huge masses of "have nots" leave the ghettoes and begin the peaceful takeover of the wealthy, mostly independent portions of every city. Part of the power this novel asserts stems from the presentation of political, official discussion of how to handle the huge social changes taking place. The rationalizing, moralizing, confused mouthings of the more liberal "haves" ends in ironic self-defeat. Religious leaders, teachers, news editors, TV journalists, all see the upheaval in the light of their individual motives, and each is consumed in his own passion.

The Camp of the Saints is dramatic, satiric, strong medicine for liberals and "bleeding hearts." It offers an apocalyptic vision that is all too valid, given known population figures and the decision by most nations simply to ignore the future....

The Camp of the Saints ... will be attacked by liberals, and its chilling vision of the final submission of the western world to the eastern is a nightmare as frightening as it is probable. Jean Raspail's novel is a major contribution to the swirling discussion of human survival, and it may very well change some minds. If it does, then it could affect the outcome of the very situation it discusses, thus offering again evidence of the power of fiction. Suspenseful and compelling as this fiction is, it may very well become truth — or change the course of events in such a way that the novel's very existence prevents the apocalypse it predicts. That kind of fiction is, indeed, powerful, and *The Camp of the Saints* is just that kind of fiction.

Alfred Coppel
Peninsula Living
August 9, 1975

I cannot recall when, if ever, I have read a book of such stunning force and disturbing content as Jean Raspail's *The Camp of the Saints*. I am no stranger to the apocalyptic novel but this work has invaded my consciousness and disturbed my conventional wisdom in a remarkable way.

More remarkable still is the fact that it is being published here in the United States, for it raises questions of morality and survival that few liberals, or even moderates, have any intention of confronting.

As in all powerful works of fiction, the basic story — the premise — is both simple and plausible. At a time in the very near future, a time of famine and deprivation in the Third World, a great throng of hungry Indians take up upon themselves to commandeer a fleet of rusty steamers in Calcutta and embark on a voyage to Europe, the "promised land." These unfortunates are familiar to all of us. They are the skeletal shades of Biafrans, Bengalis, Bedouins and Mauritanians we see often on our television screens — the unwanted, the starving, the walking wounded of the Third World....

In Raspail's world — not too different from ours — the church has lost all traditions, all discipline. It has become an activist instrument for arbitrary social reform. The government of France (and, by implication, all governments) has lost touch with pragmatism. Inflamed by the communications media, permissiveness, and the guilt of affluence, Western populations face the prospect of invasion with mingled apprehension and enthusiasm. In a kind of humanitarian-egalitarian hashish dream, the West awaits the arrival of the pilgrims with no real notion of what is to come....

...The French president, slowly awakening to the incredible implications of an invasion by a near-million starving illiterate refugees from the Third World, tests the willingness of his defense forces to confront the invaders. The sailors rebel when asked to stop the fleet. Few men are willing to slaughter naked and starving multitudes. The Last Chance Armada is invulnerable: its greatest weapon is Western morality.

...The ordinary folk, confronted at last by the Third World, flee in horror. The army deserts. The hippies and radicals trooping into the south to welcome their "brothers" are overrun by a wave of dark humanity... Other armadas embark in Africa and Southern Asia. It is the end of the white world.

To call this novel frightening is an understatement... To call it the world of the future (if the developed world cannot come to terms with its own guilt) is certainly prophetic... This is a bitter, brilliant work. Read it and consider.

James J. Devaney
The Hartford Courant
August 25, 1975

This fascinating novel, if widely read in this country, is sure to raise both hackles and questions. The author has made it impossible to be neutral about his message.

Raspail's *bête noire* is the Third World, and those in Europe and America who, either through personal conviction or for reasons of their own, support the sharing of the developed world's resources.

...The emigrants are non-violent, but because of their numbers and utter degradation, are unthinkingly merciless to individuals who get in their way, either by accident or design.

The major part of the book concerns the reaction of the Western opinion-makers, who hail the migration as the hope of mankind, until they realize, too late, that the landing of the millions means the end of European civilization.

The characters are drawn in acid and the reader feels a sense of impending doom as Raspail uses the novelist's craft to pose questions which, sooner or later, must be answered.

James J. Kilpatrick
syndicated columnist
in *The Boston Globe*
August 29, 1975

Fifty years ago, T. S. Eliot told us how the world ends: Not with a bang but a whimper. In a brilliant novel just released by a courageous publisher, Jean Raspail says the same thing. *The Camp of the Saints* is one of the most chilling books of this generation.

...Not surprisingly, the novel has been viciously ridiculed by *Time* magazine and the *New York Times*....

...Raspail makes the point that horror is like beauty, which lies in the eye of the beholder. To the haves of the Western world, his vision is horrible indeed; to the have-nots of the Third World, the prospect is of paradise.

Who can blame the brown-skinned invaders for seeking at any risk to escape their misery? Yet who could absolve the pusillanimous western leaders for their failure to resist the swarming horde? Raspail absolves no one. The brainwashed West, in his nightmare, is incapable of identifying or defending its own values. Scarcely a shot is fired as the browns, the blacks, and the yellows swarm over the globe. And the curtain falls.

The work is much more than a novel. Two thousand years ago, according to the Population Institute, the world's population was perhaps 250 million. By the year 1000, the figure was only 350 million. In 1500, maybe 450 million. The one billion level was reached about 1800. A reasonably accurate census in 1900 put the estimate at 1.65 billion. Today the world's population is roughly four billion. Now take a breath: Between 1975 and 2000, the four billion is expected to double to eight billion and the growth will occur, overwhelmingly, among the

335

browns, the blacks and the yellows.

Those of us who dwell by God's mercy or by good luck in the "have" nations of this planet must think upon these things. What is to become of our political and cultural values? What of our shiny cities, our plump farms, our tidy little suburbs? Among the Third World peoples of Raspail's vision, the instinct to survive is fiercely developed. Do Western peoples have an equal determination?

Douglas J. Maloney
Pacific Sun Literary Quarterly
Fall 1975

If only the people of the Third World could seize power from the odious oligarchy of multi-nationals, corrupt statesmen, and the CIA, most of civilization's ills would vanish. We would live in harmonious propinquity, cheerfully sharing our resources as Nirvana is at long last achieved. Right?

Not according to Jean Raspail's powerful, almost stunning book. He is certain to be denounced as a racist, fascist, or whatever "ist" is popular these days, not only for commission of the most heinous sin against radicalism — disagreement — but for his eloquently blistering and sardonic attack on the hypocritical platitudes we liberals and conservatives alike use to insulate our over-fed hides from the guilty knowledge that people elsewhere are living in abject misery.

Everyone deplores the fact that more than a billion people are starving and suffering, but what would we do if millions of these unfortunates set sail for California to share in our bounty? Sink the ships? Machine gun them as they wade ashore? Welcome them in the name of kinship? Most liberals would not care to put their credo to such a test. But this is precisely what happens in *The Camp of the Saints*, when almost a million Indians depart for France from the shores of the Ganges in a "Last Chance Armada" of rusting, stinking hulks. As the fateful convoy wallows across the seas, France is torn by a moral crisis of unprecedented acuity.

Moreover, Third World people everywhere are ominously waiting for the outcome of the invasion. In fact, the Third World has launched a war against the West, armed with a weapon far more powerful than all of the arsenals of modern industry — helplessness. Unless the fleet is turned back, the first foray will be followed by one after another, totally engulfing and paralyzing the Western countries....

Raspail is a powerful and fluent writer. His use of simile and metaphor enhances the chilling realism that is maintained throughout the novel. He is often misanthropic, but his bitterness is laced with a Gallic elan that is infectious....

He has turned a lofty ideal into harsh reality, like turning a butterfly into a caterpillar. Those most quickly disillusioned are the radicals. They don't realize that to the Third World hordes, they also are pampered whites, indistinguishable from their hated brethren. As they rush to greet the

336

invaders they are trampled or swept away....

The Camp of the Saints was a best seller in France and is bound to become a source of controversy in the United States. Liberals will probably condemn it as a racist polemic because the author refuses to ignore some unpleasant truths and makes most leftists appear fatuous or sanctimonious. But much of his finest vituperation is saved for the acid bath with which he showers the unfeeling complacency of the world's privileged few.

Whatever your political orientation, it's an exciting, superbly written book....

Lin Williams
"World At Large" column
Maple Heights (Ohio) *Press*
November 13, 1975

The ingenuity and determination of those trying to rip off the world is astonishing. The newest gimmick in the arsenal of blackmail — mass invasion by unarmed civilians — is particularly frightening in its potential.

The first test of this technique was launched last week by King Hassan of Morocco who sent tens of thousands of his subjects into the Spanish Sahara on a "March of Conquest."

The column advanced some six miles toward the Sahara capital of El Aaiun, but drew up short before a 15-mile long mine field posted and marked by barbed wire. The Spanish lobbed over a few artillery rounds to emphasize their determination to resist with military force... After shouting a bit and running up a red flag ... the Moroccans began trekking home, claiming a "symbolic victory."

...The Spanish authorities demonstrated that nations with a will to resist despite maudlin public opinion can resist criminality.

This newest wrinkle in modern banditry is disturbing because it was taken straight out of a French novel just recently translated and published in the United States. The book is titled *The Camp of the Saints* and deals with a fictitious invasion of France by a million Ganges Indians.

...the novel describes the conflict between the pacifist nations which rush food and assistance to the oncoming ships and the tough nations which resist the invasion.

In the end, France gives in to "compassion" and allows the fleet of Indians to land. The first whites to be killed are those "liberal thinkers" who rush to the ports to welcome the invaders. Then all whites in Europe are overcome and wiped out systematically. The dark skinned races triumph.

The plot may seem far fetched in synopsis but Raspail's development of the themes is all too plausible....

Raspail takes to task all the institutions that lately have taken the lead in preaching a doctrine of white-guilt and Third World "rights" to the earned wealth of the Western nations.... Raspail's novel is controversial, but thought provoking.

Susan Bernhardt
Sunday Peninsula Herald
Monterey, California
September 21, 1975

"Chilling" is the word printed on this novel's jacket. It is an excellent description....

It's not for the squeamish or those of an "ostrich" bent. It is graphic (but matter of fact) in evoking the hordes of "invaders" who set sail in an antique armada from the banks of the Ganges on their crusade to reap their share of the world's land and goods....

There is never any doubt what the culmination of the invasion will be, and therein lies much of the book's devastating chill factor. So expertly is the novel built that the many changes of scenes and the philosophical discussions by the characters don't detract but only add to the irrevocable cataclysm.

Meantime, Raspail has made an eloquent statement about world conditions, the class society, modern politics and about the hearts and minds of people.

Rick Neumayer
Louisville (KY) *Courier-Journal*
September 28, 1975

This propaganda novel is at once a terrifying nightmare and sedulous polemic, the thesis of which is that the decadent West has lost its soul, no longer believes in itself and therefore lacks the will to survive. It links civilization inextricably with race: whites are the "chosen people," but being white "isn't really a question of color" but "a whole mental outlook."

Nevertheless, the reader must face up to the world's grotesque overpopulation and the unlikelihood that wealth will be redistributed voluntarily. Raspail argues that "even if the specific action, symbolic as it is, may seem farfetched, the fact remains that we are inevitably heading for something of the sort...."

Choice
November 1975

Raspail's Spenglerian premise, that Western civilization must decay from within while at the same time its outreaches are overwhelmed by masses of darker-skinned humanity, is given a new and frightening twist... Raspail's thesis, too persuasive to ignore, is that a racial apocalypse is at hand, one that signals the collapse of civilization as we know it. Although the author's argument is potentially racist, Raspail makes clear his belief that the Third World's vengeance upon its white oppressors will be total, a vast chaos without political organization and consequently without hope for conciliation... *The Camp of the Saints* seizes the imagination. Recommended.

Directions
September 1975

Translated from the French, Raspail relates the quite possible tale of hungry Third World masses embarking to the prolific, contented West... Understandable, but confused reactions arise in the Western countries; fear combines with armed protectiveness and impractical humanism.

A novel of ideas ... the grim

thesis keeps the reader turning pages and, in doing so, she or he realizes the enormity of trying to solve the world's problems; the haves and the have-nots remain tensed in confrontation. Translator Norman Shapiro (Wesleyan University) has done a good job with a difficult book.... Recommended, but get of copy of the French edition, too, for your modern language collection.

Jeffrey Hart
National Review
September 26, 1975

Earlier in the century, the avant-garde artists deliberately outraged bourgeois expectations. Fauves, cubists, dadaists, Joyce, Stravinsky: the riot outside concert hall or gallery, the novel confiscated by customs officer — these were the defining events. In a curious way Jean Raspail's novel *The Camp of the Saints* is reminiscent of that sort of thing. It, too, is an assault, a scandal... In freer and more intelligent circles in Europe, the book is a sensation and Raspail a prize-winner.

In this novel Raspail brings his reader to the surprising conclusion that killing a million or so starving refugees from India would be a supreme act of individual sanity and cultural health... His plot is both simple and brilliant....

A great fuss is currently being made over Jean Raspail's supposed racism, but some distinctions need to be made. For "racism" has without a doubt become the great taboo of our times, and like all taboos is routinely exempted from critical examination. But what is racism? Most people do not now and have not in the past subscribed to esoteric theories regarding the superiority of this or that race. Most people, however, are able to perceive that the "other group" looks rather different and lives rather differently from their own. Such "racist" or "ethnocentric" feelings are undoubtedly healthy, and involve merely a preference for one's own culture and kind. Indeed — and Raspail hammers away at this point throughout his novel — no group can long survive unless it does "prefer itself." One further point is implicit. The liberal rote anathema on "racism" is in effect a poisonous assault upon Western self-preference.

...Despite the huffing and puffing among the respectable types, Raspail is not really writing about race — he is writing about civilization, and in particular the civilization of the West. He is stating an obvious but outrageous truth. Civilization involves particular forms of being. It is not an amorphous mass. As Frederick Wilhelmsen put it over a decade ago in these pages: "In order to be, a society must defend itself against whatever and whoever might threaten its existence. The inability to defend oneself against the enemy has always been the sign of approaching death.... Men can live and act together only if they are bound together by code and custom, myth and legend, sculpture and song... Where such underlying orthodoxy is lacking we find ourselves in the midst of an aggregate of ghettos, not a society." ∎

Related Readings
Recommended by the Editors of THE SOCIAL CONTRACT

Robert Ardrey, *The Territorial Imperative*. New York: Atheneum, 1966.

Milica Zarkovic Bookman, *The Demographic Struggle for Power*. London & Portland, OR: Frank Cass, 1997.

Vernon M. Briggs, Jr., *Mass Immigration and the National Interest*. Armonk, NY: M. E. Sharpe, 2003.

Patrick J. Buchanan, *State of Emergency: The Third World Invasion of America*. New York: St. Martin's Griffin, 2007.

Garrett Hardin, *Living Within Limits: Ecology, Economics and Population Taboos*. New York: Oxford University Press, Inc., 1995.

Samuel P. Huntington, *Who Are We: The Challenges to America's National Identity*. New York: Simon & Schuster, 2005.

_____, *The Clash of Civilizations and the Remaking of the World Order*, New York: The Free Press, 2002.

Wayne Lutton and John Tanton, *The Immigration Invasion* Petoskey, MI: The Social Contract Press, 1994

Michelle Malkin, *Invasion: How America Still Welcomes Terrorists, Criminals, and Other Foreign Menaces to Our Shores*. Washington, DC: Regnery Publishing, Inc., 2002.

Frank K. Salter, *On Genetic Interests: Family, Ethnicity, and Humanity in an Age of Mass Migration*. Brunswick, NJ: Transaction Publishers, 2006.

In addition to these books, there is a noteworthy magazine article using the scenario of *The Camp of the Saints* as a springboard for discussion:

"Must It Be The Rest Against the West?" by Matthew Connelly and Paul Kennedy, *The Atlantic Monthly*, December 1994, p.61ff.

About the Social Contract Press

The Social Contract Press has grown out of the publication since 1990 of THE SOCIAL CONTRACT, a quarterly reader on public issues and public policy in the interrelated fields of the environment, human population, international migration, language and assimilation, and the balance of individual rights with civic responsibilities.

Both THE SOCIAL CONTRACT and The Social Contract Press function under a publicly supported 501(c)(3) umbrella foundation called simply "U.S."

The Social Contract Press also provides a website which includes complete archives of THE SOCIAL CONTRACT journal along with a book store featuring publications on these same topics.

Visit our website:

www.thesocialcontract.com

to peruse our online bookstore
and to search the archives of
over 1500 articles, essays,
and book reviews from past issues
of

THE SOCIAL CONTRACT